The
Bones
of the
Old Ones

Also by Howard Andrew Jones

The Desert of Souls
The Waters of Eternity

The
Bones
of the
Old Ones

HOWARD ANDREW JONES

Thomas Dunne Books ☙ New York
St. Martin's Press

THOMAS DUNNE BOOKS.
An imprint of St. Martin's Press.

THE BONES OF THE OLD ONES. Copyright © 2012 by Howard Andrew Jones. All rights reserved. Printed in the United States of America. For information, address St. Martin's Press, 175 Fifth Avenue, New York, N.Y. 10010.

www.thomasdunnebooks.com
www.stmartins.com

Design by Omar Chapa

Map by S. Jones and Omar Chapa

Library of Congress Cataloging-in-Publication Data

Jones, Howard A.
    The bones of the old ones / Howard Andrew Jones.—1st ed.
        p. cm.
    ISBN 978-0-312-64675-2 (hardcover)
    ISBN 978-1-250-01513-6 (e-book)
    1. Human remains (Archaeology)—Iran—Fiction.   I. Title.
    PS3610.O62535B66 2012
    813'.6—dc23

                                                                2012016318

First Edition: December 2012

10   9   8   7   6   5   4   3   2   1

For Shannon.

Best friend, muse, first reader, and the light of my life.

Acknowledgments

I'm indebted to kind and talented people who generously gave their time and advice to help me create this book. Pete Wolverton is the sort of editor most authors can only dream of working with, one who digs deep into the text and thinks carefully about the characters, pacing, and plot. I'm immensely grateful to him for insightful commentary and guidance. I'm likewise lucky to be working with Bob Mecoy, my agent and friend, whose brainstorming sessions with me were invaluable for smoothing rough spots in the final stages. John O'Neill read a late version of the text and asked a host of perceptive questions that helped streamline and tighten the story. Nathan Long, Anne Bensson, Beth Shope, and John C. Hocking weighed in during earlier drafts with excellent suggestions that helped steer me toward the novel you hold today. Dr. Amira K. Bennison graciously answered whatever strange questions I asked about eighth century social conventions. Last but not least, my brilliant wife, Shannon, devoted untold hours to reading and rereading the text. She patiently acted as my sounding board, ruthlessly called me out on weak spots, and offered countless fine tweaks that enhanced the prose.

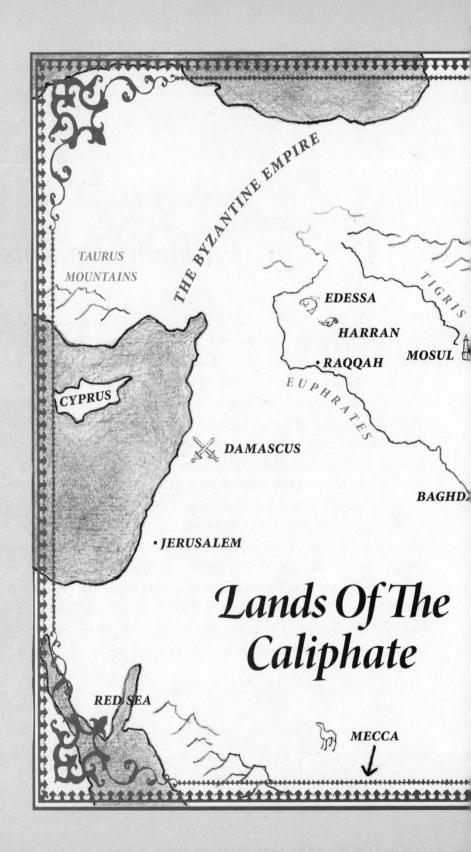

THE BYZANTINE EMPIRE

TAURUS MOUNTAINS

EDESSA

HARRAN

• RAQQAH

TIGRIS

MOSUL

CYPRUS

EUPHRATES

DAMASCUS

BAGHDA

• JERUSALEM

Lands Of The Caliphate

RED SEA

MECCA

The
Bones
of the
Old Ones

1

The snow banked knee-high against the walls of the narrow alley, and my boots sank into it as I pressed my back to the cold stone. I quieted my ragged breath and listened for the footfalls of my pursuers. They could not be far behind.

Thankfully the snow-clogged streets were already churned with footprints this morning; I was certain those who sought me lacked the expertise to identify my own.

Before long I heard the sound of snow mashed beneath swift, eager steps. I crouched to ready my weapons. Ambushes come down to timing, and I meant to judge my moment with care.

The footfalls stopped, then shuffled without advancing. My mind's eye had one of them turning a circle, just beyond my hiding place.

Their leader spoke in low, urgent tones. "The captain has to be close. Rami, you go that way. Sayid, you come with me."

One of his followers waxed confident: "We'll get him this time!"

I had dressed for the weather, with multiple robes, a cloak, and even gloves. As I was never a small man, I cut an imposing figure so bulkily garbed. When I leapt into the street, roaring defiantly, two of the three youths jumped back in alarm. The other dropped a snowball at the same moment I launched my own.

"Fly, dogs!" I cried, laughing. My first strike caught Imad, the deep-voiced thirteen-year-old, in the dead center of his chest. While he looked down in surprise I grabbed another missile from those cradled in my arm and flung again.

"Run!" Imad shouted, his voice breaking. He dashed away, little Sayid fleeing with him. I tagged his retreating back with another cast even as Rami ducked into the doorway to the jeweler's house.

"Ho, young one!" I advanced, one snowball brandished. "Prepare to meet your doom!"

Rami did not run; nay, the brave lad stood his ground and threw. His aim was near perfect, and caught me in the chest. At the same moment, I heard Imad and Sayid let out battle cries behind me, and I whirled. Their blows struck me in chest and shoulder even as I countered, laughing. It was then a frosty missile hit the back of my head. I felt my turban sliding toward my left ear.

"Ah!" I feigned sudden weakness and let my arm fall so that the snowballs rained about my boots. I clutched at my breast with both hands. "The lion falls!" So saying, I sank to one knee, then dropped into the snow. I lay rigid as a dying hero on a tapestry while my youthful companions cheered and cavorted with joy.

Their voices stilled at the same moment I heard the crunch of someone else approaching through the snow. I peered up to see my friend Dabir grinning at me, his blue eyes twinkling with amusement. He cradled a snowball in one hand. "Will you live?" he asked.

I sat up on the instant, adjusting my headgear. "What are you doing here?"

"This is the most direct route home from the palace."

His grin widened as he saw the expression on my face. The caliph himself had ordered me to ensure the scholar's safety by day and by night, but Dabir took a more casual approach to the arrangement. When last I'd seen him, he'd been sitting at a brazier in our receiving room, reading over some old Greek text. He had promised he would remain there.

Dabir dropped the snowball, and extended his hand. "No one was going to attack me, Asim. Captain Tarif came to get me."

That made me feel only a little better. He helped me to my feet.

"Where is he now?" I asked, suspecting already the answer I would receive.

"Oh, I walked back on my own. Tarif had more important things to do."

I sighed as I stepped back to brush snow from my robe.

Dabir smiled good-naturedly at the gathered children, but they could only stare back, shyly, even little Rami, our stable boy. They all regarded him with a certain amount of awe, for they knew him as a famous scholar and master of great secrets, someone to be treated with pronounced formality.

After a moment Rami worked up the courage to speak. "That was a good shot, Master."

Dabir chuckled. "Thank you, Rami."

"That was you?" I asked.

"You made too fine a target," Dabir explained. "What say you to a meal? Are you hungry yet?"

I was, in truth, for I had taken a long morning walk before joining the snowball fight. Thus I bade the children farewell. They were sad to lose me, and in truth I was somewhat reluctant to quit, but Dabir was clearly set on continuing alone if I did not go with him, and as usual he had not even bothered to buckle on a sword. And besides, the cook's fine pastries were now firmly in my mind. She was a harridan, but I could not dispute the excellence of her food.

So Dabir and I started for home.

Mosul was old . . . old almost as the Assyrian ruins that lay across the river, but not derelict, and sometimes showed a haggard beauty, for her stones had been set with care. Aye, her builders had been artisans as well as laborers, so that there were pleasing patterns in the brick and mortar. On that day, though, it was as if she had donned an enchanted cloak that restored her youth. Even plain features to which I normally paid no notice—the heights of buildings, the bricks of walls, twisted old tree limbs topping garden enclosures—were mantled in white and transformed into sparkling works of art. It brought a smile to my lips as we walked.

"What did the governor want?" I asked.

Dabir turned over a hand as we walked past the homes and shops that lined the streets.

"Ah, Shabouh has him worried. He keeps going on about the positions of the stars and bad omens."

I rather liked the pudgy court astrologer, but Dabir was skeptical of the man's auguries.

"He swears that this snowfall was foretold," he went on, "and that some old Persian star chart predicts even greater misfortune."

I frowned. That certainly sounded alarming to me. In truth, the blizzard that had struck Mosul three days before defied any experience in living memory, so a little concern was perfectly justified. "What did you tell the governor?"

"Well, I did not wish to dispute Shabouh, but it seemed unwarranted to worry the governor over isolated acts of nature. I told them I would take a look at the records in the university. By the time I've compiled a listing of all the unusual weather in the last hundred years, the snow will have melted and all this will be a charming memory."

"Do you think so?"

Dabir laughed. "Aye. When I was boy a great frost came to Mosul in early fall. It was so cold that ice formed over part of the Tigris. But it all melted by midday. Strange storms happen from time to time, and it is nothing to wring hands about."

In light of what befell in the coming days, you will not be surprised to learn that I reminded him of that pronouncement for years after, but I get ahead of myself. At that time I merely groaned a little at the thought of spending the day watching him read texts in the cramped university library.

"I did not say that I would look today," he added, clapping me on the back. "I plan instead to enjoy a nice game of shatranj near a warm brazier with my friend Asim."

Soon we reached home, and after a pleasant meal we sat down in the receiving room and set up the shatranj board. We had moved but a few pieces when Rami pushed through the door curtain. He was ruddy-faced from the chill and panting from exertion. "I have found a woman in the street," he gasped.

Rami's sudden arrival set smoke from our brazier dancing above the cherry-red coals and introduced a blast of cold air seasoned with the scent of horses and manure, for the smell of the stables clung to him.

Dabir paused with his hand over the checkered board between us, the emerald on his finger glinting. "A dead woman?" he asked.

"Nay, Master." Rami breathed heavily.

"You sound as if you have run a very long way," Dabir said patiently.

"She was being chased," Rami explained, "and begged me for help."

"Chased by whom?" I asked.

Rami shook his head. "She would not say. She was very frightened."

"Most like," I said, "you have found a thief."

"Oh, she is not a thief, Captain," Rami assured me. "She is dressed like a noblewoman. She talks like a noblewoman. And," he added, as though it were the most conclusive proof of all, "she is very pretty."

Dabir coolly arched an eyebrow at me before turning over another of my pawns. "And you have left her in the stables?"

Rami froze, then nodded, his wind-burned face reddening still further. He lowered his eyes.

Dabir must have recognized the boy's discomfiture, for his next question was very gentle. "What sort of help do you think she needs, Rami?"

The stable boy brightened. It was not every day he was invited to provide counsel for a great scholar. "There is something wrong with her, Master." His voice rang with conviction. "I think someone has placed a spell upon her."

"Do you?" Dabir managed to sound not the least bit condescending. "Very well, then, Rami, bring in your mystery lady. I will see her."

Rami grinned and backed out of the room, bowing formally. This sober exit might have been more impressive if we had not heard him immediately thereafter scamper down the hall at great speed.

Dabir turned back to me and grinned.

I shook my head. "That boy thinks wizards and efreet lurk behind every doorway."

"Who shall we blame for that?" Dabir asked. "I was not the one who told him about the ghuls, or the lion, or that thing formed all of eyeballs. The cook said Rami had nightmares for a week." He waved fingers at the board. "It is your move."

I grunted. Buthayna had told me the same thing, but likely with more venom. I studied the pieces with care, although I had lost focus upon the game—never wise when playing against Dabir. We were just beyond the opening array and he was already commanding or threatening most of the board's central squares. "This may all be some trick to ask alms from you," I said.

"You are so skeptical, Asim. You should try to keep an open mind. Besides, if this woman needs money, I shall give some to her."

He'd kept his eyes on the board and crinkled them only a little, but I knew he said this to bait me; for some reason my opinion of his financial practices amused him. In the ten months since our arrival in Mosul he had wasted cartloads of money upon an immense collection of old books and scrolls, and yet had not bothered to furnish all the rooms within the house.

I was still trying to decide whether to take Dabir's central pawn with my knight or to advance my left chariot when there came a muted screech from a nearby room. I raised my head in alarm before recognizing the cook's voice, and the lower answers of Rami.

"I should have guessed that," Dabir said. "Rami has brought her in through the kitchen."

I nodded.

"Likely," Dabir said, his head tilted to listen, "Buthayna questions the poor boy's wisdom in bringing an unattended woman into the house."

"She will blame me."

"Surely not."

"Watch," I said. "She will blame me, for she cannot blame you."

"Hmm. What shall we wager?"

The answer came quickly to me. "If I am right, you will take up sword practice again this week."

Dabir was a passable swordsman, but possessed the reflexes to be far better. He seemed always to find some other thing to do than join me for morning drills.

He nodded after a short moment of reflection. "Done. If you are wrong, you will try again with that text."

I stifled a groan. "The one where the Greeks are sulking at the siege? That's hardly fair. I'm trying to better you."

"I swear by the Ka'aba you would like it if you continued! You gave up before you reached the battle scenes."

"I suppose," I said, for I did not expect to lose.

Footfalls hurried toward us from the room adjacent even as I spoke, and within a moment the curtain was pushed smartly aside.

Buthayna entered, bowing her head to Dabir. Like Rami she brought cold air, but with her came more pleasant scents—onions, cabbage, bread. She was thin and stooped, with great gray wiry eyebrows. Many women her age dispensed with veils, but hers was thick. I think she meant the cloth to demonstrate her piety, although, as I had glimpsed her, once, veilless, it might be that she wore it as a favor.

"Master," she said, her voice deceptively sweet and creaking with age, "my nephew says that you have told him to bring a woman into the house to speak with you."

"This is true," Dabir answered.

Buthayna's eyes shifted to me with a hard look, then back to Dabir. "She has no attendants," she persisted.

"Does she look dangerous?" Dabir asked with great innocence.

"She does not, Master, but she is alone." She emphasized this last word as if he had somehow overlooked this crucial point. "Perhaps Rami did not convey all of this information to you?"

"It was clear," Dabir said. "But the woman may need our help. We will see her."

Again I received a look. I fully believe that Buthayna expected me to intercede to help her maintain proper decorum in the house. But I did not speak.

Dabir broke the silence: "Perhaps, Buthayana, it would be best if you accompany our guest."

The cook's yellowish eyes widened in surprise, then, apparently satisfied, she bowed her head. "As you wish, Honored One."

The moment she disappeared through the curtain Dabir smirked. "I will bring you *The Iliad* by midday prayers."

"Ah, ah," I countered. "You could see from her look that she found me at fault. And you intervened before she could fully speak her mind. You, friend, need to dust off your sword."

"But she—" Dabir fell silent as the curtains were pushed aside once more.

Buthayna poked her head through, then held the curtain open for another. "Master," she intoned formally, "this is Najya. She has not provided me with her last name," she finished, her voice laced with unspoken rebuke.

I had expected to be presented with a slattern in gaudy jewelry and bright fabrics, young enough to still be pretty. But our visitor was the very image of those aristocratic Persian beauties who walk with high-held heads through the court of the caliph. She not only looked the part, she had dressed it. I had been at pains to examine things more closely, as Dabir had taught me, thus I observed that the sleeves of her white gown were minutely frayed and the downward-pointing red flowers embroidered upon it somewhat faded. Likely they had been purchased from the castoffs of a real noblewoman, but they were certainly convincing enough to fool a boy. Even her movements were practiced, from her graceful entry to her dignified consideration of the room as she probably checked for our most expensive items. In those days, most of our mementos—displayed in niches Dabir had ordered built into our south wall—were peculiar rather than valuable, like the false efreet head and the mummified lion's paw, so it was not long before her gaze dropped to us.

Here I momentarily forgot my suspicions, and I would challenge any man who ever saw Najya's eyes to swear they were not arrested by them. Orange-brown ornaments, they were, that sparkled above her thin veil. Two perfect eyebrows arched above them, black like the long straight hair that crowned her more regally than jewels. She was no common thief.

We climbed to our feet. "Welcome," Dabir told our visitor. "Please be seated, and take your ease. Rami has told us that you need help. Buthayna, please join us." He gestured the cook to a nearby cushion.

Buthayna lowered herself slowly to the bare floor beyond the rug, as though determined to set an example of servile propriety.

I carefully pushed the shatranj board to one side and retreated to Dabir's left, standing against the far wall as the others took their seats. I did not put my hand to my hilt, but I was ready to do so at need.

Our visitor bowed her head to Dabir. She spoke, her voice formal and precise. "I thank you for your welcome." She paused, looking at the checkered board, seemingly to gather her thoughts. "And I apologize for interrupting your game. In truth, I hope only that you might be able to recommend a reputable caravan master."

I thought then that we must be dealing with an actress who also could imitate the sound of wealthy folk.

"I know several," Dabir answered. "Why do you need one?"

"I wish to return home."

"You are from Isfahan?" Dabir asked.

She looked sharply at him. "How did you know?"

"From your slight accent; then there is the imperial crown flower pattern woven on your clothing, and the decorative detail upon the toe of your boot. They're both popular among the aristocracy near the Zagros mountain range."

She stared at him now with wary appreciation. "Your boy said that you were an accomplished scholar, but I thought he exaggerated." Her head rose and she addressed Dabir formally. "You are correct. Isfahan is my home and I would very much like to return there as soon as possible. If there is anything you can do to assist me in finding safe passage, I would be grateful."

I thought then that she would ask for money. She did not, though, and I realized she meant Dabir to volunteer it, which he would surely do.

Dabir rubbed the band of his ring with his thumb, his habit when lost in thought. "You have no protection, and little money," my friend said after a time. "And unless you have some other belongings hidden in my stables, you have no traveling clothes. You are poorly prepared to venture cross country in this weather, especially as the men who kidnapped you are almost certainly still combing the city."

"How—" Her startled eyes swept over to me and meaningfully to my sword. She rose as if to leave, looking frightened and angry at the same time. "Do you know them?" she demanded of Dabir.

I was almost as disconcerted as she. If Dabir was right, as he usually was, I had completely misjudged her; it seemed she deserved my compassion rather than suspicion.

Dabir glanced up at me, then at the cushion at my feet, and I inferred that he meant me to appear less imposing.

Thus I took a seat beside him. Do not think I relaxed my guard entirely, though.

"I know nothing of your kidnappers," Dabir explained. "But, given your station, the condition of your raiment, and the markings upon your wrists, it seemed the most likely explanation for your presence in Mosul."

She eyed him doubtfully.

"Please be at ease." He motioned her to the cushion at her feet. "Why don't we start over. I am Dabir ibn Khalil and this is Captain Asim el Abbas."

Though I commanded no one there besides an adolescent stable boy, Dabir generally introduced me with the rank I held when we'd met.

She did not sit, nor retreat, though she seemed less likely to flee. Dabir carefully pulled at the fine gold chain about his neck and brought up the rectangular amulet normally hidden by his robes. He lifted it over his head and held it out to her.

"Dabir and I have sat at the right hand of the caliph," I offered. "We are no friends to kidnappers."

Hesitantly she took the thing and I saw her eyes rove over the gold lettering engraved there, commending all to respect its bearer, an honored citizen of the caliphate and friend to the caliph himself. Well did I know the wording, for I myself wore one, and it was a mark of esteem given to but a handful of men.

Her worry lines eased a little, and she looked up to consider Dabir in a new light.

"You have not told us your family name," Dabir said. "Is there someone we may contact for you?"

She lowered herself onto a cushion slowly, regaining some of her composure. "I am Najya binta Alimah, daughter of the general Delir al Khayr, may peace be upon him." Her head rose minutely, but proudly, and with good reason, for the general had been well-known in his day as a brave defender of the eastern border. "As to those who follow me . . ." Her lovely brow furrowed. "Their leader is Koury, and he commands powerful men."

"Is he, also, from Isfahan?"

Najya shook her head. "I do not think so. I had never seen him before, or the one he called Gazi. The speech and manner of both are strange."

"Gazi," Dabir repeated, and I knew from his more serious tone that the name meant something to him. "What do Gazi and Koury look like?"

Najya thought for a moment. "Koury is tall with light eyes. His hair is graying, and he has a noble manner. Gazi is . . ." Her lips pursed beneath her veil. "He is a dreadful man. He is short and broad but swift. He smiles often but it is not a pleasant sight." She, too, had deduced that Dabir recognized the names. "Have you heard of them?"

"They sound familiar," Dabir admitted. "Why did they take you from Isfahan?"

"I think they wanted me to find something, but I know not what. Or why."

"To find something?" Dabir asked, puzzled.

"That is what they were talking of when I came around. They thought I knew where something was." Here she paused, as if uncertain how to proceed.

Dabir glanced over to me before encouraging her to continue. "Perhaps it would be best if you tell us what you remember. Start with the kidnapping."

Najya breathed deeply. I sensed that she gathered not her memories, but her courage. "My husband and I were walking to the central square in the evening," she said tightly. "We heard footsteps behind us, and then a demand that I come."

"Who demanded?" Dabir asked.

"The man I learned later was Gazi. My husband drew his sword and fought them, but they . . ." Her voice trailed off and she did not speak for a time. When she spoke again her tone was low and dull. "He was killed."

It sounded as though there was more to be learned about the battle, but Dabir did not ask further. "I am sorry for your loss," he told her.

I usually remained silent when Dabir questioned folk for information, but a comment from me seemed appropriate this time. "As am I."

She glanced only briefly at me, then bowed her head slightly to us in acknowledgment. "Gazi fought as no warrior I have ever seen," she added.

This in itself was an unusual observation from a woman, and the look I traded with Dabir did not go unnoticed by her. "I have seen many bouts," she explained defensively. "My husband was an officer, my father a general."

Dabir nodded. "Go on."

"I tried to run, but Koury's men were too fast. Too strong. They covered my eyes and forced a drink upon me. A sour drink. I did not swallow but it burned my mouth and I grew weak. The world spun for a long while." She shook her head, troubled. "I really only have a few vague memories from then until I arrived here."

I could well believe that she was the daughter of a military man, owing to the clarity and precision of her account.

"What happened when you arrived in Mosul?" Dabir asked.

Her look was sharp. "You mistake me. I do not remember entering the city. Suddenly I was upright and conscious in the street. Koury was there, talking with me—as though he had been speaking for a while and I should know exactly what he meant."

"What was he saying?"

Again Najya shook her head. "There was some talk of finding a bone. I pretended I understood him, and when we neared the palace, I fled into the crowd."

"A bone?" Buthanyna repeated, incredulous.

No one acknowledged her; it was not her place to speak, and she seemed to realize her etiquette breach because she shrank lower, as if to disappear.

"And that was when you found Rami," Dabir prompted.

"Yes."

"How long ago was this?"

"No more than an hour. Less, I think. Your boy was very brave," she added. "He led me through a number of back streets. I do not think Koury could follow."

"Let us hope." Dabir looked as if he might say more, then asked, "How many pursue you?"

"In the square there was only Koury and two of his men. I did not see Gazi," she added. "But Koury's guards are incredibly strong. And there is something odd about them."

"How do you mean?"

"They dress all in black and their faces are hooded. They do not speak."

Dabir sat back and played with the band of his ring. And I studied Najya, mulling over her peculiar story. I could not fathom why someone would kidnap a Persian beauty, take her to a distant city, and command her to search for a skeleton, yet her very manner marked her as a speaker of truth.

"I think it best if you stay hidden for a while," Dabir decided. "Please consider this your home until we can arrange for safe escort to Isfahan."

She started to protest, but Dabir cut her off. "This is very important, Najya. Have your husband or family ever had dealings with magic, or its practitioners?"

I saw her lips part beneath her veil. After a moment, she shook her head. "No. I don't think so."

"Have you ever heard of the Sebitti?"

Again she shook her head. "No. Why?"

"It's an old group with warrior wizards named Gazi and Koury. But I do not think it can be them." Dabir said that last almost to himself. "Buthayna, see that she is given the guest suite, and please find a servant to attend her. One who can be trusted not to gossip, for our guest's location must be secret."

While the cook curtly acknowledged Dabir's directives, I groaned inwardly. There was little more in the suite than a mattress and an old chest. It was hardly fitting accommodation for a noblewoman.

"You have been very kind," Najya said, rising.

"It is nothing," Dabir assured her. "Give me leave to look into the matter. You will be safe here, this I swear."

"I would like to send word to my brother, in Isfahan," Najya told him.

"Certainly. Buthayna, see that she has what she needs, and have Rami ask after a caravan bound there. He can start at the Bright Moon."

"Yes, Honored One." Buthayna rose stiffly and led the way through the curtain.

Najya turned to look back at us once more, then bowed her head and followed Buthayna.

"Who are these Sebitti?" I asked quietly as their steps receded. "I have never heard you mention them."

"Why should I speak of fables?" Dabir frowned. "A mentor—a friend, really—was fascinated with them, and I recall only the broadest details." He shook his head. "I just don't understand why a ring of murderers and kidnappers would name two of their members after them. These aren't common names."

I felt a growing sense of unease. "You haven't answered my question."

Dabir's expression was still troubled. "You have heard of the Seven Wise Men?" he asked. "The Seven Sages?"

"Aye. Who has not?" They were famed for their knowledge of all matters, both arcane and mundane, and legend held that folk in need, if they be of pure intent, could find them to ask advice.

"They are the Sebitti."

"I've never heard them called by that name."

"It is from old Ashur. Their legend was born in that ancient time."

"So these kidnappers have taken the names of wise men?" Now I understood Dabir's confusion, and laughed. "If they meant to intimidate, wouldn't they assume a more frightening alias?"

"I think you're confusing wise with good. The people of Ashur, brutal as they were, dared speak of the Sebitti only in whispers."

I had learned a little of the folk of Ashur, who some call the Assyrians, and knew they had been a warrior people, ruled by blood-mad kings. Anyone who they feared must be dangerous indeed. Thus I began to feel a vague foreboding. "Why?" I asked.

Dabir's voice was grim. "They believed that when the lord of the underworld grew displeased, he sent forth the Sebitti to slay both beasts and men so that they might be more humble."

I tried to imagine the gentle, and sedentary, wise men of legend riding forth with swords and chuckled.

"So you understand my interest," Dabir finished.

"I do, but I don't understand your aim. If the lady has been kidnapped, we should turn her over to the governor or a judge, don't you think?"

He mulled this over, then shook his head. "Her story intrigues me . . ." His voice trailed off, and I thought for a moment he would explain further, but he did not.

Dabir's curiosity could lead him down dangerous paths. It was true that I felt badly for the woman, who would have to bear the shame of what had happened, and it was true that the circumstances were peculiar, but I did not see that our involvement was especially useful to her. And then another thought dawned upon me, one that I did not voice. Dabir mooned still for his lost love, Sabirah. He seldom spoke of her, but often stared at the emerald ring she had given him. It would surely be good for him to focus on another woman, and this Najya was a pretty one. Perhaps his interest had been piqued in more than one way.

I nodded as if his arguments made sense. "What do you mean to do?"

"I will make inquiries. Harith the innkeeper. Some of your friends in the guard. Captain Fakhir, or Captain Tarif. Surely one of them has heard of a kidnapping ring or strangers to the city matching these descriptions. Our guest strikes me as being quite memorable."

I had feared for a moment that he would be dragging me to one of Mosul's universities. "That does not sound nearly as bad as I had thought."

Dabir stopped in midstride, where I'd followed him into the hall. He turned with a knowing look. "You will stay here, and guard the woman."

Now that I did not care for. "The caliph charged me with guarding you," I reminded him. "You keep forgetting—"

"Asim, Najya is in far greater danger than I. If the kidnappers track her to the house, who will defend her? Buthayna? Rami? You must stay."

At the shake of my head, he added, "I will be careful, and I will return, or send word, by midday prayers."

There was clearly no moving him, and I couldn't argue that the woman needed no guard, so I merely frowned at his departing back and set to securing the house.

The caliph's largesse had afforded us a spacious building on a corner in a quiet neighborhood. There were three entrances: that off the main street, the stables that opened onto a side street, and the servant's entrance in the wall. This last I had insisted be boarded up when Dabir purchased the place, for with merely two servants we had no need of a special door. Most homes in Mosul lacked street-level windows, and ours was no different, though the second floor boasted several. I made sure that all of these shutters were barred and warned Buthayna to admit no one, then crossed the courtyard to inspect the stables.

The outer doors I locked from within, and all else seemed in order, so I returned in under a quarter hour, only to have the cook emerge from the shadows and press something toward me.

"One of your soldier friends brought this," she croaked. The object crackled in her hands as she shook it, and I recognized it for a sealed letter.

"Which friend . . . wait, how did you get this?"

"It was delivered."

I paused before speaking, lest I say something I might regret, while she returned to her cooking pot and began to stir. Though the rest of our home might be sparse, we had an exceptionally well-furnished kitchen, and one built inside the home, a luxury unavailable to most. Buthayna had gleefully claimed it as her own once she joined us from the governor's staff.

"I thought I had made clear," I said, once I regained my composure, "that the door was to remain closed and that only I was to answer it."

"So you did, but someone was at the door, and you were out in the stalls, so what was I to do?"

I felt my blood boil, yet did not curse. "Buthayna, you are not to open the door today unless it is Dabir, or this servant girl he wants to attend our guest. Do you understand?"

"As you wish." She turned back to her doings.

"If I am out in the stables, or up the stairs, you are to come and *find* me."

"As you wish," she repeated carelessly.

"Now who delivered this?"

"That big soldier from the palace."

"Abdul?"

"The polite one," she growled pointedly. "Yes."

"Thank you," I said as pleasantly as I could, and left her.

I returned to the sitting room and studied the brown paper in interest. The seal was familiar, for it had come from my former master in faraway Baghdad. Jaffar had sent letters addressed to the both of us in the last year, but this one was labeled solely for Dabir.

I am not a petty man, but I was rankled that Jaffar had not seen fit to put both our names on the letter so that I might straightaway read his news. Dabir and I had both, after all, been his servants, I for far longer. Likely it had merely been an oversight, but I would make no assumptions.

I was still frowning down at the thing when there came a rap at the door. I sighed, tucking the missive into my robe, rising quickly lest the cook decide to ignore me once more.

She shouted at me from her den. "There is someone at the door, Captain!"

I advanced to slide back the eyehole, thinking to find the servant girl she'd sent for.

Instead I saw a tall, silver-haired gentleman with light-green eyes. Behind him stood two men garbed all in black, with deep hoods.

The kidnappers had arrived.

2

"I have come for my daughter," the fellow told me in a deep, stern voice. I could not quite place his accent, although it sounded a little Persian. "I have been told that you have her."

I was rarely a quick thinker unless a weapon was in my hand, and I was momentarily troubled by his assertion. Might he have the truth of it, and Najya be the liar?

"Open the door and return her to me immediately," he continued, "or I shall call forth a judge."

If he meant to threaten me with mention of a judge, he surely had no idea with whom he spoke. Dabir and I were not only honored by the caliph, we were sometimes cup companions with the governor of Mosul. "Who are you?" I asked.

He glared, giving the impression he could see more than my shaded eye through the little opening, and I studied him in greater detail. I saw one unused to bending to any man. Indeed, he held his head as though he were accustomed to instant obedience. He was slim and straight-backed and as tall as myself. His beard and the hair that showed beneath his turban were gray, but here was no old man, rather one who had prematurely silvered. His thick robes, finely trimmed, must have warded him completely from the cold, for he looked not the least bit uncomfortable.

"I am Koury ibn Muhannad," the fellow said, his breath steaming.

"Do you intend to speak to me from behind the door?" The disdain all but dripped from his voice.

I slammed home the eye slot, then opened the door and stepped forward to fill the portal. My size did not seem to trouble this Koury.

"I am Asim el Abbas," I said.

"And do you have my daughter?"

I checked his men. Neither of them wore weapons or moved forward. Neither of them, in fact, moved at all. Both stood with their left arms raised to belt level at the same angle, their right hanging at their sides. I knew not what to make of this, unless they were especially disciplined soldiers whose master desired a uniform presentation.

Koury awaited reply.

My oldest brother, Tariq, may peace be upon him, once told me that each time you lie you foreswear a little of your own soul. As a boy I had accepted his words without question; as a man I better understood his meaning. Some lies are surely necessary, but I strove always to avoid them.

"It is true that a woman has come to ask help of my friend, the scholar Dabir," I said. "She may or may not be your daughter."

He nodded once, and his eyes were calculating. "The mystery can easily be solved. Bring her to me that we may see one another."

This was such a reasonable suggestion I was not sure what to do with it. I found myself stalling that I might gain more time to think. "What does your daughter look like?"

"She is well dressed, and very beautiful, with black hair and large brown eyes. Is this the woman who came to you?"

Instead of answering, I asked, "How did you lose her?"

Koury's mouth narrowed to a thin line, but he replied. "She is a girl of wild notions since her poor husband was murdered before her. She grew frightened in the marketplace and fled."

Surely the man looked wealthy enough to be Najya's father, and he even had an explanation ready for Najya's strange story—except, of course, that Najya had claimed to be the daughter of a famous, departed general.

"If I might see her," Koury pressed on, "we can quickly clear this matter up. I might even agree to reward a man who has given my daughter shelter. I am prepared to be very generous."

His words, sensible enough, were belied by a hardness of tone and manner that showed no fatherly warmth. Rather he sounded as if he viewed the woman solely as a commodity.

"Perhaps a judge would be useful after all," I concluded.

Koury's nostrils flared; one of his eyebrows twitched. Behind him both of the guards shifted their gloved left hands at the same moment.

"Sometimes," he said, his voice low, "men interfere in matters better left alone, through lack of understanding."

I merely nodded and held my place. "That is surely true." Then, by way of dismissal, I added, "Good day to you."

His lips drew up in a sneer; I stepped back and closed the door, immediately dropping the locking bar into place.

I stood a moment, listening for them. Koury said nothing more, and neither of his servants spoke to him, but I clearly heard them crunch away through the snow.

For some reason I discovered that my heart beat rapidly, as if I'd just sparred with a lethal foe. I put my right hand to my chest to feel its speed, wondering that I should be so affected. When Najya spoke behind me I nearly jumped.

"Are they gone?"

I turned. "Aye."

"They will return," she said darkly. "I must leave."

There were three doorways off the entry, and she was backing toward the one to the left.

I held up a hand to her. "You need not fear. Even if he finds a judge to hear him today, none will act without hearing first from Dabir."

She shook her head quickly. "You don't understand."

"You are safe here." I spoke slowly, for emphasis.

"No," she said more forcefully. "Were you not listening? Did he have his men with him?"

"Aye," I started to say more, but she cut me off.

Her eyes blazed. "My husband fought the both of them, striking them again and again, and doing them no harm. They would not fall. They cannot be hurt. And God help you if he also has Gazi with him, for that man fought circles around Bahir . . ." Here she paused, and her voice fell away. "My husband," she finished needlessly.

"Perhaps he did not strike deeply," I suggested, hoping it was true, "and Koury's guards wear armor beneath their robes."

"Captain!" She spoke now with great force, as though she meant to strike me with words until I took her seriously, "Bahir was skilled and daring, yet Gazi cut him to pieces." Moisture glistened in her eyes, though her voice did not falter in the slightest. "They cannot be stopped and everyone here will die!"

"Now there you are wrong." Something in my manner brought her eyes firmly to me, as if she saw me clearly for the first time. "I have faced stranger things than these and come out alive. I will not let Koury take you. This I swear upon my life."

Her answer showed more restraint. "I do not wish it to come to that."

"It shall be as Allah wills, but that does not mean I intend to wait for the sword stroke on my neck. Dabir will shortly return, and I can guess that he will wish us to ride straightaway for the governor. Let us make preparations."

She seemed calmer now, and unless I misjudged, she no longer saw me as an adversary. "You have great faith in your master. Is he, too, a warrior?"

"He is not my master, and his sword work is fair, though it is his wisdom we need most. Go to the upper floor and watch that corner." I pointed to the southwest. "A man positioned there might see both the front entrance and the stable door."

This must have seemed a good idea to her, for she started for the doorway to the dining room. "What are you going to do?"

I was unused to explaining my orders, but the question did not bother me overmuch. "I will have Rami saddle the horses. Then I will ready our gear. I'll get you a traveling cloak."

I was not sure what she meant by the searching look she bestowed upon me and there was no time to trouble myself over a woman's thoughts. I turned away.

Rami, anxious to please, set eagerly to work. As to winter wear for our guest, Buthayna's clothes would have been too small, and mine too large, so I raided Dabir's wardrobe and took the steps to the second floor.

The upstairs consisted mostly of empty rooms—they were intended for an army of servants we did not have. From a shuttered window Najya showed me one of the black-robed men standing statue-still down the street, outside the home of Achmed the jeweler.

"He watches, just as you said. Though I know not how he sees," she added.

His hood was deep and pulled low over his face, but it could be he sheltered his eyes from the glare of the empty white street and simply monitored with his ears. A thought occurred to me then concerning Najya's previous description of the guard's invulnerability. "Perhaps he is a kind of warrior ascetic. Some of them take drugs to render themselves insensitive to pain. It may be that your husband wounded them and they did not feel it, though they would have died later." This sounded more plausible as I spoke it, and I added: "That might also explain how they stand so still."

"They used some drug on me," she said slowly. "I suppose they could have other sorts. Look. Isn't that Dabir?"

I bent close beside her and could not help but breathe in a scent of jasmine from her hair. Sure enough, Dabir came swiftly down the road with that impatient, determined stride of his, heading straight to our door. I bethought then of how I had said Dabir's name to Koury, and I swear that my heart almost stilled when I realized there was no way I could reach him before the watcher should he choose to attack.

"Here is your cloak." I shoved it into her hands and leaped down the stairs.

I flung open the door, hand to my sword, eyes set on the motionless watcher. Dabir came on, his brows raised questioningly at me. They rose even higher as I beckoned him to hurry.

23

The watcher did not move, and once Dabir was in I closed the door and slammed home its guard. I explained quickly all that had transpired while standing in the entryway, then Dabir fell to asking questions. At about that time Najya crept down the stairs and stood listening, the cloak still cradled in her arms.

"Did you note any smell about the robed men?" Dabir asked me.

"If they smelled, they were not close enough to detect anything."

"What about you, Najya, when you met them?" Dabir faced her. "Was there any salty smell, or a strong herbal scent?"

"No. Why?"

"Just a thought. Asim, I think you have suggested a fine plan. If this fellow has gone to a judge, we shall go to a governor."

"What did you find?" I asked.

"An inn near the Tigris where Najya and Koury and two others checked in last night. They boarded no horses." Again he faced our guest. "Have you remembered anything further of arriving in Mosul yesterday?"

"No," Najya answered.

"The innkeeper said that you were alert and deep in conversation with Koury until late in the evening."

Her eyes widened. "I swear," she insisted, "upon my life and the holy Koran, that I remember nothing of this."

Dabir stared hard at her.

"I do not lie!"

Dabir nodded sharply, and I had the sense that he meant to question her more fully at a later time. "Let us go," he declared.

"There is one more thing," I said, and passed over the letter from Jaffar.

Dabir grew more concerned as he studied the wax seal. "What is this?"

"It was sent from the palace just before Koury arrived. It is from Jaffar, but addressed only to you, or I would have opened it."

He broke the seal. I could not see the writing, but watched his eyes search the paper. A shadow of gloom crossed his face.

"Is all well?" I asked.

"Aye," he said softly. "Sabirah has given birth to a baby girl, and both she and the child are healthy."

"Praise God," I said, heartily. "That is good news."

"That is surely good news," Najya added. "Is she your sister, or a cousin?"

"No." Dabir folded the letter and tucked it away. "She is merely a former student."

That was a minimal description, and I do not think it fooled Najya, but she did not press for further details. I tried to put a better face upon the matter. "It was kind of Jaffar to tell you," I pointed out.

Dabir stared at me pointedly for a moment, as if unsure as to my meaning. "Yes," he said slowly, without enthusiasm, then closed the discussion. "We must be going."

Only a short while later, Dabir and Najya and I rode out from the stables, the woman mounted on our old cart horse, for we had no other animals. Usually Dabir and I walked Mosul's streets, which are frequently crowded in better weather, but we wished to outpace pursuit if it came to that.

I caught sight of the black-robed guard as we left, but he did not follow, or even turn to acknowledge our passing. I watched carefully but saw no sign of further monitoring or pursuit.

We diverted around the few, well-wrapped folk in the street and passed walled homes and shops, our life breath rising in wispy clouds. Before long we had neared the great square that lay before the governor's palace, on the heights of the city at the end of a wide avenue that stretched the length of Mosul to the bank of the Tigris.

The governor at that time was Ahmed bin Hakim, a kind and generous man in middle age. He had been raised to office on a whim of the mad caliph, Haroun al-Rashid's immediate predecessor, Allah alone knows why, and had proved so popular with the folk of the north that he had retained his position even as most other appointments were handed over to the current caliph's adherents, which is to say allies of Jaffar's family.

Though quite pious—Ahmed had made the holy pilgrimage twice—he was not one of those religious men who seek always to point out the faults of others. He loved a good story, good food, and, as I had seen, the grape, though it be expressly forbidden. In all other ways was he devout, most especially in almsgiving and in good works, and I think it was due to his nature rather than a desire for praise. Two nights before, to aid the suffering of his people in the cold, he had decreed that a fire must be kept burning in the square in front of the old fortress, and so a great bonfire had been erected. As Najya and Dabir and I rode in, a flock of beggars and indigent folk huddled before it in relative ease, under the watch of a few bored soldiers. If the great cold continued, God help him to find more wood and to afford its cost, but the governor, like Dabir, had no head for money.

As you might expect, cloth and food vendors quickly set up stalls and carts near the fire to partake of the free source of heat, and to prey on those who wandered by to deliver alms to the poor or those en route to the governor's palace. With the merchants had come customers, and with them a few entertainers and game players, so that what had begun as an aid to the downtrodden had taken on new life as a street carnival complete with jugglers and stilt walkers, gamblers, and even wine merchants who lured in patrons with the promise that fruit of the vine inured one to the cold.

I did not care to ride into that shifting mass, where enemies might hide, but we had no choice if we wished to reach the palace. Scanning constantly for sign of ambush, I led the way, with Najya following and Dabir bringing up the rear. I fully expected to see danger before the others, thus I was startled to hear Najya call out in alarm just as we reached the far fringe of the throng. I turned on the instant to find one of Koury's hooded men at her side holding her mount's bridle. Koury himself was running up from a side street, his robe belled out behind him. The crowd turned to him as he called out in praise to Allah that his child had been found.

The cloak of Najya's hood had shaken loose and her face was obscured by a wave of midnight hair that slung back and forth as she struggled against the hand that gripped one of her ankles. Her patient old gelding shifted in consternation.

My mare, Noura, answered smoothly as I turned her. "Let the woman be!" I put hand to my sword hilt, and at that moment I saw the other black-robed man flanking me from the right.

Najya's captor did not reply, thus I drew my sword. A nearby man gasped, and I heard mutters about me. The crowd parted.

Koury pushed his way clear and strode up to us. His smile was thin, his voice loud so that it would be heard by the onlookers. "Ah, thank you." He raised his head sultan high. "You have found my wayward daughter."

"That remains to be seen," Dabir said shortly from my left. "Release the woman."

The other black-robed man had halted on my right.

Najya addressed the crowd in her clear, commanding voice. "This man is not my father! Do not believe him!"

The murmuring intensified even as the encircling wall of onlookers widened.

Koury laughed theatrically and looked to Dabir. "You see the sort of fancies that she takes. She is a willful, spoiled girl, and I have only myself to blame."

"This is a matter for the governor," Dabir declared. He looked only at Koury but pitched his voice loud enough to carry to the crowd.

Koury's expression hardened. "I am beholden to no man for her fate." He bared his teeth and lowered his voice. "She is *mine.*"

"Not at this time," Dabir responded sternly. "You'd best have your men leave off."

"You heard Dabir." I pointed my sword at the man on the left. "Release her."

This he did not do. He took one hand from the nag's headstall and effortlessly dragged Najya from her saddle as she shouted in protest and struggled in his clutches. The other charged my horse and struck out with a gloved fist. He connected, hard, and blood sprayed out from a gash near Noura's nostrils. She screamed in anger and pain even as the madman lunged at me.

"Dog born dog!" I cried, trying to steady my outraged mount. I did not know how a man might draw such blood striking only with his hand. Somehow he avoided Noura's dancing and grabbed hold of my boot with stiff fingers.

I leaned from my saddle to shroud the idiot by cleaving his skull.

My blade bit deep into his head, but the strike felt wrong. Those of you who have never brained a man with a sword—and may it please Allah that it be most of you, for there is altogether too much braining of men in this world—will not know that there is a distinct difference to the way a blade feels when wielded against a skull as opposed to most other objects. My blow caught in the fellow's head as if I'd sliced into a stump. He did not fall with splayed limbs and spraying blood. He did not even flinch. Even were I wearing a helmet I would have shown some reaction to having sharp metal bounced off my crown. Yet from him there was nothing. A cold dread certainty gripped me as I pulled my weapon free. This was no warrior ascetic. I faced dark sorcery.

Dabir shouted from up ahead and the crowd about us was calling out all sorts of nonsense, but I could spare no attention, for the enemy had hold of my boot with fingers of steel and snatched at my sword arm as well. Between its grip and Noura's dancing I had no good options. I dove at the thing, bearing down with my weight, my arm snaring it around the throat.

It twisted as I went down, throwing off my balance so that I did not land as I'd hoped. One of my knees bashed into its rock-hard thigh and I had to relinquish my grip on both its neck and my sword to catch myself. I scrambled through the mob-churned snow for my blade as I heard it rising behind me. I whirled, steel in hand, to face the impending attack.

It was then that Noura moved in, ears down. She landed hard on its back with both forehooves, and there was a cracking noise, as of wood being broken. The thing rose a little before Noura stomped it again, whinnying the while, yet again it tried to push itself up.

By the second time I had a plan. I sheathed my blade and while my adversary was half risen on creaking legs I charged into the monster and lifted it over my shoulder. Beneath that fabric I felt no flesh, only wood carved into limbs. It was a shock, but I did not break stride.

One arm smacked me hard in the back—it had aimed for my kidney, I think—and then I dumped it deep into the bonfire, where it hit with a satisfying crash, kicking up flames and a spray of sparks. Folk cried out in horror, not knowing, as I did, that it was a creature of wood.

It stood, clothing ablaze, and then folk screamed louder, for they saw the timber body beneath as the robes burned off. I snatched up a log and heaved blindly, taking the thing in the legs. It dropped, dislodging piled lumber to roll down across its body and partially bury itself.

I was worried for Dabir and Najya, so I did not stay to see if the wooden man was truly finished. I snatched an axe leaning against the pile of firewood and hurried on as a horn blared from the old fortress.

The crowd had spread out in a vast circle before Dabir, who warded the girl with a heavy pole probably snatched from a tent awning. Najya held Dabir's sword at guard, watching wild-eyed, her breath misting the air. One of the soldiers I'd seen earlier near the fire whimpered as he crawled across the snow, his blade discarded, his face covered in blood. Two others lay twisted nearby.

Koury's lackey strode for Dabir, swinging gloved fists. Gaps in the now tattered face fabric showed nothing but a hand-polished globe. Likewise formed of wood was his smooth neck and what I saw of his right shoulder. He resembled nothing so much as a life-sized, highly articulated child's toy somehow granted life.

All this I perceived in an instant; the cowering crowd, Dabir shielding Najya. Yet there was another oddity I have not yet mentioned, for Koury now sat astride a mount himself. Astonished as I was by the tableau, some small part of me questioned how he had managed to conceal such a beast without calling notice to himself. Unlike the face of the wooden men, the head of the horse he rode was marvelously carved, with a black mane delineated in exquisite detail. Its mouth was partly open, its nostrils wide and round. Where its eyes should have been were two large onyx stones. No reins did Koury need—he sat saddle like a general, watching intently, as though he commanded the figures merely by looking at them.

I called out to God and charged. Dabir saw me and advanced with the pole, striking hard at the legs of the wooden warrior, toppling it. I smashed the axe into the place where its spine should have been. A satisfying splintering sound resulted.

But the thing barely slowed. Bending joints as no human could, it regained its feet in an instant, the axe poking out from its back like an obscene handle. I brought out my steel, unsure how I might truly stop it.

I think that Koury might have kept on, but the arrival of horsemen, galloping from the fortress, decided the matter. Behind them ran a squad of soldiers.

Koury shouted something at us that sounded very much like a curse, then turned tail on his carven beast and galloped at great speed down the avenue. The wooden man with the axe ran after at an inhuman pace. Women screamed as it passed. In a moment they were lost to sight beyond the crowd, which rushed for a better look at the departing figures and chattered amongst themselves. The one I'd cast in the fire did not follow, but burned brightly amidst the logs.

I reached Dabir and he smiled at me, clapping me on the shoulder. "Well done. You are unharmed?"

"Mostly. You?" I saw for the first time that the knuckles of his left hand were stained with blood.

"The thing was faster than I thought," he said, seeing the track of my eyes.

We both turned to Najya then, and her eyes shone bright even as she panted. She lowered Dabir's sword slowly and it suddenly occurred to me that hers was a practiced stance. Either she had paid very close heed to the warriors she'd watched, or someone had trained her.

Before I could ask, my friend Tarif, the scarred captain of the palace guard, arrived on his horse. He reined in before me as his eyes swept the area in astonishment. "Asim—what has happened?"

"A wizard tried to kidnap this woman," I said, which might have sounded comical if men had not been lying motionless in the blood-drenched snow. "We were taking her to the governor."

Tarif seemed only to half listen. His mind was clearly occupied with the fate of his men. "A wizard?"

The guard who'd aided Dabir with the wooden man called to him, and Tarif nodded decisively. "Go on to His Excellency and report," he said to us both. "I will sort this out and join you as I can."

As Tarif advanced to speak with his subordinates, I whistled Noura to me.

My mount, a treasured gift from the caliph himself, trotted over at my summons but stamped and snorted, still agitated. I managed to calm her long enough that I might better inspect her wounds. I found that the left side of her face was swollen and deeply cut. I praised her for her bravery and despite her hurts I think she understood, for she lowered her head further and snorted softly. I led her by the reins toward the palace in the wake of Dabir and Najya, in the saddle once more.

Stablehands ran forward as we passed beneath the palace's entrance arch, and I demanded that a hakim come to look at my mare. Such was my demeanor that both groomsmen rushed away—to fetch the healer, I think—so I had to scare up a passing boy to bring me water and clean rags. I was reluctant to leave my horse in other hands, but the head stableman swiftly arrived, and owing to his assurances and Dabir's poorly concealed impatience I yielded the matter to him. I hurried off across the courtyard after Dabir, already nearing the entrance, and Najya, who had lingered a little to see if I would come.

The governor's chamberlain, Farbod, met us at one of the palace's two great sandalwood doors and, after introductions, escorted us through the entry halls. His staff struck the floor with every other step of his pointed slippers, producing a regular, steady thunk that put me in mind of a funeral drum. The high windows were shuttered against cold, so that darkness lay unusually thick in the hallway, and the flare of lanterns hung from the wall did little to push back the gloom. We came after him down the long, black passage, chafing behind the aged steward's slow, steady tread.

"This situation is even more troubling than it first appeared," Dabir said quietly to us.

Najya politely waited for him to continue, but I broke in. "You're 'troubled'?! Those men were made of wood! As was his horse—from where did it come?"

"He pulled something from his pouch," Dabir said, and his voice was halting. "And lo—it grew into the size you saw."

"Of course," I said, "he is a wizard." Why did it seem that we must forever contend with wizards to set things aright?

"He is worse," Dabir countered. "The Koury of ancient days was said to give life to creatures he fashioned from wood and clay. Just like this one."

"You think it is the same man? From thousands of years before?"

"We just fought men of wood," Dabir said fiercely. "I am willing to entertain the possibility. Najya, did you glimpse any other powers when you were with them?"

"I saw only that they were amazing fighters," she confessed.

"Did Gazi work any magic?" Dabir demanded.

The woman hesitated.

"What did he do?"

At the sound of Dabir's rising voice, Farbod glanced back over his shoulder. Almost we had reached the great doors.

Dabir's scrutiny seemed to wear down Najya's hesitation.

"He might have planned to work magic. He sliced my husband open and . . . I think he pulled forth his heart." Her eyes were lit doubly by horror and outrage.

Dabir looked as though he had been slapped. His whispered prayer was drowned out by the sound of the doors flung open from within by guardsmen. The right-hand one, Kharouf, with whom I sparred on occasion, nodded acknowledgment, then shifted to stand rigidly at attention, helm glinting under his turban cloth as Farbod led us past.

The cavernous hall was actually better lit than usual, owing to a row of smoking braziers beside each pillar that marched to the settee facing the door. Though the governor was not a warrior or huntsman, his walls were adorned with shields and crossed weapons from different lands and different times: lances, swords, pikes, spears, even axes, all in a variety of lengths and styles. Lovely woven banners hung at the heights of columns. I had studied those decorations on prior days and knew that each was threaded with the words of God from the Holy Koran. Most were concerned with justice and righteousness and the giving of alms, but also there were passages praising the glory of Allah, the most merciful. They had replaced the dusty standards of long-forgotten combatants, I had been told.

I but glanced at them as Farbod guided us on to the governor, who was warming his hands over a brazier just below the settee. A slight fellow with a thin brown beard shot through with gray, he was dressed in fine black and wore a green turban to memorialize his pilgrimage to Mecca. He stood looking over a weathered scroll beside the old astrologer Shabouh, whose jowly face was lined with worry.

Farbod stopped with a commanding thump of his staff and the governor waited for him to announce us, though he could see perfectly well who we were. Certain ceremonies had always to be observed, and he knew Farbod relished the roles of his office.

"Dabir ibn Khalil and Asim el Abbas are here to speak with you, Governor." Farbod bowed with grave dignity. "They have arrived with Najya binta Alimah, of Isfahan."

"Thank you, Farbod," the governor said, his thin voice low and formal. The governor inclined his narrow head, then addressed us in his more customary tone. "Peace be upon you," he said.

We returned his greeting, Najya replying more formally a moment later.

The governor nodded to her, then glanced at his chamberlain. "Farbod, you may go."

The elder bowed to the governor, backed past us, then turned his thick frame rather smartly and exited while his master beckoned us close.

"A soldier ran in to report unwelcome news," he said. "Is it true that you were attacked in the street before the palace?"

"Therein lies a tale, Excellency," Dabir replied.

"Speak, then."

Dabir proceeded to tell the governor that Najya had come to us because she was pursued by the same men who'd ambushed us in the square. He did not get far, for none of us could fail to note that the woman's attention was riveted by something on my left.

"What is the matter, young lady?" the governor asked.

"I would like to see that spear," she said flatly as she stepped past.

"Of course. Be my guest." The governor's hand waved belated permission; he turned back to Dabir with an expression of bemusement that transformed into mild irritation when the scholar, frowning, broke off his report to follow Najya. The governor wrinkled his brow at me instead. I offered empty palms and went after Dabir.

Najya was apparently fascinated by an ivory spear thrown in sharp relief before its shadow on the pale wall. It was long as a cavalry lance, and hung a few feet below a heavy, dark axe. The latter seemed the better weapon to me, but the woman had eyes only for the spear.

I wondered why I had never paid it heed before this moment, and I suppose it was because I had not expected to see anything strange upon the governor's walls, or that it was usually hidden in the shadows.

The old spear was carved all from a single piece, haft and blade, though I could scarcely imagine the size of the animal from which it had come. The tawny surface was exceptionally smooth save for strange carvings of sticklike men bearing spears against . . . the shapes were indeterminate. Blobs with fangs? The art was rudimentary. Upon the blade was a slightly larger and more detailed image of a manlike figure charging with a spear at another figure twice his size.

Najya advanced slowly toward it, her gaze unwavering.

Dabir had come up beside her. "Is this what you seek?"

The woman flinched almost as if physically assaulted, and stopped her forward progression. She turned her head to him and blinked as if clearing her vision.

"Yes." Breathing heavily, she looked again at the weapon, then at Dabir. The governor and Shabouh joined us, their expressions puzzled.

"It is like hearing a distant horn," Najya continued in a distracted way. "The closer I come to one, the better I hear the call."

"How many do you hear?" Dabir asked.

"Four." She was no longer looking at him. "This one is loudest because the others are so far away."

"How long have you felt this pull?" Dabir asked.

She stared at him for a long moment and something changed in her eyes.

"What is happening, Dabir?" the governor asked. "Is she afflicted with madness?"

Dabir faced him only briefly. "I beg your patience, Governor."

Najya blinked hard as a man will when trying to stave off sleep while standing sentry. "What is it you said?"

Dabir studied her for a moment before speaking: "You say that you are pulled toward the spear. How long have you felt that?"

She looked down and away, and when she replied her voice was very soft. "I do not wish you to think me foolish, so I did not speak of it. I'm afraid this is something that the wizard has done. I never . . . I just wish to return home." She raised her head and then, almost against her will, faced the wall and the spear once more. She took a half step toward it.

Dabir interposed his body between the wall and the woman. His voice was kind but firm. "I do not recommend coming any closer to that weapon."

She only stared at him.

"Why should she not?" the governor asked. "What is happening?"

My friend looked as though he were about to make some sobering pronouncement. Instead, he asked him a question. "Do you know from where this spear comes?"

"It was on the wall of the palace when I was appointed to my post," the governor answered. "So were most of these." He turned reluctantly to the astrologer. "Shabouh, you served the previous governor. Do you know anything of it?"

Shabouh bowed his gray head. "It has always hung here, Excellency, at least to my knowledge. I honestly paid it no heed until now. Farbod, perhaps, knows more."

It was then Najya lunged suddenly past Dabir and grabbed the weapon.

3

I darted after without thinking. Neither Dabir nor I were ones to touch women unasked, but we both lay hold of her arms.

Yet there was no moving her. Najya's whole body had gone rigid and she was fastened to the spear as surely as if she were bolted to the thing. She began to shake, as men will when they have the falling sickness, and she gripped the haft so tightly that her knuckles turned white.

"Pry free her thumbs!" Dabir shouted to me.

As I slid my hand beneath hers, my palm pressed against the surface of the spear, and a cold spread through me such as men must face when they die upon the mountaintops. I shuddered violently in the sudden chill and my mind flooded with jarring and disjointed images. I stood upon a plain sheathed everywhere in ice and snow. The sky was a slate-gray tombstone. A village of thatched round huts lay beneath a thick sheet of frost and snow. Strange beasts stomped across a frozen river, followed by giant manlike beings with long silvery hair and shining white skin. Fur-clad warriors charged with flint-tipped spears. Bodies lay strewn like leaves over the icy ground, stained red beneath them. A bearded man stared back at me through a slab of ice, his mouth open in a silent scream.

The visions vanished the moment I pulled Najya free with trembling hands. She collapsed senseless in my arms.

Dabir was there on my other side, demanding to know if she was all right, and what had happened to me. I lifted the woman in my arms and spoke with a trembling jaw. "The weapon is cursed," I told him. "Its touch froze me to the bone."

"Place her upon the settee," the governor ordered, and this I did, casting a blanket over her that I found upon the back of the furniture. By this time the guards had rushed forward, and the governor sent Kharouf running for the hakim.

"She lives," Dabir said, and he pulled fingers back from Najya's neck.

The woman's face was pale as the white marble inlays in the patterned floor. She shifted very slightly beneath the blanket, but did not open her eyes.

The governor frowned down at her, then turned to us, drawing himself up to his full height. Though we each topped him by at least half a head, we bowed in deference. "Explain," he commanded.

Dabir then relayed, in short, succinct sentences, all that we had experienced since Najya's arrival. I would have left to stand over a brazier, but I did not wish to appear disrespectful

The governor's expression grew more and more grave as he listened, but he asked no questions. My friend finished by pointing to the weapon on the column. "It seems, Your Excellency, that the wizard Koury captured Najya to aid him in finding this unusual spear."

"That thing?" the governor asked. "But why should anyone want it?"

Before Dabir could answer, the reception doors thumped open and Tarif of the palace guard walked in. He was trailed by four soldiers, each holding the corner of a canvas. Upon that canvas lay the blackened figure of the wooden man I had consigned to flames. One of the arm joints still smoldered. Tarif came to a halt six feet from the dais, and bowed.

The governor descended to speak with him. I glanced down at Najya; she was still pallid but breathing regularly. Dabir was scanning me with concern when I turned to him, but I waved him off, and we followed the governor down the steps. I managed at last to put hands over some hot coals, and breathed a quiet sigh, for the warmth was most pleasant.

"Set it down and return to your posts," Tarif directed his men.

Some called Tarif ugly, but that was not entirely fair, for when seen only from the right side he was a striking figure of a man. A Greek spear had smashed into his left cheek, ruining his lip and taking out a number of teeth in the bargain. He was better off than some with like injuries, for he could close his mouth and speak clearly, but his features were forever marred by lumpy flesh and a patchy beard. Despite all this, or perhaps even because of it, all of the governor's soldiers looked upon Tarif with favor.

As his men departed Tarif raised his deep voice to a more formal level. "Excellency, this is one of the wooden demons that the wizard set against folk in the square. Asim pitched it into the fire, where it died. The other one fled after killing two of my men and badly wounding another."

The governor stared down at the motionless form, saying nothing. The long-bearded court hakim came in through the open doorway, a female attendant trailing. They bowed to the governor, who pointed up to the settee, then moved off to obey.

"I set riders after the wizard who commanded these things," Tarif continued. "But he galloped away on a wooden horse, and vanished into the distance."

The governor prodded one of the wooden man's charred legs with his foot. "At great cost," he said reflectively, "I have set up a place for my people to find succor in the square of my city."

"You are a very shepherd to your people," Shabouh broke in, bowing his head.

You might think that Shabouh was one of those who sought praise from his superior by giving it, but you would be judging the poor old astrologer unfairly, for the comment was heartfelt and shared by anyone with sense in the whole of the city.

"This is not to be tolerated." The governor's head rose resolutely. "My people were endangered, and my soldiers murdered. Tarif, I wish you to find this wizard and bring him to me to answer for his crimes."

Tarif grinned fiercely. "Nothing would please me more."

"If I may, Excellency," Dabir said, "there is a man I know in Harran who is a great scholar, and knows much about the history of wizards, perhaps even the identity and powers of this one. I believe he could be of tremendous help to us."

This was the first I had heard of this matter, or of anyone important in Harran, and I eyed my friend curiously.

"I shall send for him," the governor announced.

"Better, I think," Dabir said, slowing his speech so as to be more respectful, "if I go to him. He is disinclined to travel and cannot bring his library with him. Together the two of us might find the clues we need to ascertain the true aims of this wizard."

The governor frowned. "What are we to do if the wizard comes for the woman while you are gone?"

"It was my thought that I might take the woman and the spear with me so that the scholar could examine them both."

The governor's expression had softened, but he did not speak for a long while. "I care not a whit for the spear," he said finally. "If I might rectify matters by hurling it into the Tigris, I would do so on the moment. But the young woman is afflicted with madness. Shouldn't she be left in the care of her relatives?"

Again Dabir bowed his head. "She has no relatives in Mosul, Excellency. And I do not think she is mad. Her reports match the strange things that we have seen. I suspect she is suffering from her treatment at the hands of the wizard. I hope that my friend—the learned Jibril ibn Jaras—may be able to help her."

The governor turned to Shabouh. "What do you think of all this?"

The astrologer patted his ample belly. This, I think, was the moment he had been waiting for. "Excellency, have I not been warning you of the dire signs? Merrikh and Mushtarie are both passing through Al-Jabbar."

"So you have said," the governor replied. "And things surely have grown worse. But what is to be done?"

A lesser man might have used that moment to further his own schemes at Dabir's expense, but Shabouh was no Baghdad courtier. "It is folly to hesitate," he said. "I think you should heed Dabir's plan."

"Let us go get this man of Dabir's straightaway," Tarif agreed, eager for action. "If Dabir knows about wizards, then let him come with us."

The governor considered this briefly, then nodded. "Let it be done. Make arrangements, Captain."

Tarif bowed. "We will see whether magic can stop a spear thrust." He bowed again and departed.

I smiled to myself, for I liked Tarif's sentiment well.

The hakim had been waiting at the edge of the conversation for a short while, and was staring down at the wooden soldier with great fascination.

"How is the woman, Ari?"

"She seems well enough." Ari sounded years younger than his white beard would have suggested. "She is weak, and sleepy. Rest would be good."

"What is wrong with her?" the governor asked.

"I cannot say, for certain. She is cold, and will not rouse from sleep. Your guard said she has suffered a fit. Is she prone to this?"

The governor looked to Dabir.

"We do not know her well," Dabir explained. "But she has undergone great trials, and may have experienced privation."

I thought to mention it wasn't privation, but a greater blast of whatever had almost frozen me, then realized that Dabir deliberately avoided further discussion of sorcerous doings, though I knew not why. Thus I stayed quiet.

"That might explain it." The hakim did not sound completely convinced. "If she is in your care, you must do better. She must be dressed more warmly in weather like this. She's chilled. I would see that she rests in a warm bed. When she wakes, give her a light meal. Broth. Tea. Durriyah will stay with her until she rises," he added with a look to his attendant.

"Thank you, Ari," the governor said.

The hakim bowed to the governor, nodded to his female assistant, kneeling beside Najya on the dais, and left the room. One of the guards closed the door behind them.

The governor turned to Dabir as the thunk of the door's closing echoed through the chamber. "I will house the woman in the palace this night, and tomorrow you may be on your way. I cannot say that I envy your travel through the snow."

"Sometimes one chooses the journey," Dabir said, "and sometimes the journey chooses him. If I may, Governor—I would like to study that spear in a room with better light."

"Of course."

As my friend moved to claim the weapon, I could hold comment no longer. "Dabir, that spear leveled the girl and set me to shivering. I don't know that anyone should touch it."

"Let us be sure, then," said Dabir.

He approached without hesitation and, over my objection, brushed fingers against the thing gently, once, twice, then grasped it solidly.

"Interesting," he said.

The governor waited for explanation, but I think it was my dumb-struck surprise that evoked Dabir's response.

"If the spear alone caused your reaction, some poor slave would have been frozen flat while hanging or cleaning the thing years ago. We would have heard of it."

The governor stepped forward to lay hand on the weapon himself. "Now that I look closely at this spear, there is something disquieting about it."

"I doubt it is dangerous unless Najya is touching it, or if someone is touching both Najya and the spear," Dabir went on.

"Why?" I asked.

"That," Dabir said, "is one of any number of questions for which I have no answer at present." He bowed his head to the governor. "With your leave, Excellency, there is much to do."

The governor asked us to sup with him that night before ordering one of the soldiers to remove the spear and carry it to a room in the east wing where Dabir would be working. Slaves arrived with a litter for Najya and I had a final glimpse of her being lifted carefully onto it before Dabir and I strode into the hallway. I bethought then of all that the lady had endured, and hoped for her sake that we might soon deliver her from her troubles.

Dabir set up in a first-floor room with two ample windows viewing the courtyard, which meant it was bright as well as cold. He questioned me at length about all I'd experienced when touching the spear, but seemed less satisfied the more he learned. Then he sent me back to our house to retrieve some old scrolls and a book. I did not ask why. Before I left I saw to it Kharouf was posted outside, for, while inexperienced, he was serious by nature and a capable soldier.

When I returned, I watched until late in the afternoon while Dabir turned the spear every which way and laboriously copied each mark he discovered on the old weapon, regardless if it seemed a carving or a scratch. Occasionally he'd pause to rifle through references. He grew completely absorbed in the work, as he was whenever presented with a compelling puzzle.

I did not interrupt him, even though I wondered why anyone would bother making a weapon from a bone. Perhaps its use was merely ornamental, for surely the edge would break under strain. I sat with my arms crossed near the brazier slaves had brought in, and my mind returned repeatedly to Najya. We were supposed to be informed when she recovered. I hoped the silence did not mean that her condition had worsened.

Dabir could not be parted from his studies for food, so I alone joined the governor, Shabouh, and several other court intimates. They pressed me for details about Dabir's discoveries but I could only shake my head. "Dabir never likes to speculate before he is more certain of an answer. He would not wish me to say." This was true, of course, though I could not have told them Dabir's theories even if I wished, for he had not shared them.

After evening prayers at the governor's side, a servant informed us that the woman had roused and asked for Dabir and me, so I excused myself and went to find my friend.

Kharouf still leaned against the wall outside. Inside, a partially eaten meal of stewed dates and lamb rested near at hand, but Dabir was otherwise as I had left him, studying a text and making notes. A densely packed ring of candles now burned off the encircling darkness.

"Najya is awake and asking for us," I told him.

"Ah. Good." He nodded, glancing up. "You should go talk to her."

"She asked for both of us," I said, though I was not entirely sure the servant had truly conveyed the lady's request.

"Yes, but I am busy."

If he was at all interested in her, he was doing a poor job of showing it. I began to think it was the problem, and not the woman, which held his attention. "What do you want me to say?"

Dabir looked blandly up from the scroll. "Convince her to come with us."

"Cannot the governor simply order her to do so?"

"Nay—she is not a criminal, and she is not of Mosul. The governor, being a just man, will not exercise authority over her he does not have. And she must accompany us, for her own safety." He looked back down. "Oh—ask if she, too, witnessed anything when she touched the spear."

Feeling somewhat useless to him otherwise, I had Kharouf point me in the right direction and then found a servant to lead me to the well-appointed room where Najya waited. There were braziers there, and a platter of breads and cheeses, and also a girl attendant who was brushing Najya's hair by candlelight as she sat on a couch. Najya had removed her veil and did not bother affixing it on sight of me. Without the fabric she proved even more lovely, with a clear complexion, a small, full mouth with bright lips, and a delicate, rounded chin.

I had a sudden misgiving about why I'd been thinking of her all day, and didn't realize I was staring until several uncomfortable moments passed while she waited for me to speak. I think she'd acknowledged me with "Captain Asim."

I brought myself back around with some effort. "It is good to see that you are well." I then noted that she wore a dark blue dress and decided to comment upon it, for women delight in such things. "Is that a new garment?"

"It is a gift from the governor," she said with disinterest. "Captain, the servants say I am to ready for a journey to Harran. But surely," she emphasized, "that cannot be right."

Here I'd been thinking I'd have to break the news to her, but naturally palace gossip had reached her ear already. I doubted that would make my mission simpler.

"So it is true?" she asked.

"There is a man in Harran who Dabir thinks can help you."

"Dabir promised he would help me return to Isfahan." Those stunning eyes pierced me like spear points. "That is two weeks the *other* direction from Harran."

When the matter was broached this way, I knew shame, for Najya was absolutely right—word had been given, and must be broken if Dabir had his way. Speech failed me, and as I struggled for a proper reply Najya's scrutiny intensified, which made concentrating on a response all the harder. I could not help wondering if Dabir had sent me in his stead because he'd anticipated some of this. "You are right," I admitted. "Dabir promised to return you to Isfahan. We fully intend to do so . . . but right now . . ."

Still she glared daggers.

The servant girl could not have been more than eight. She lowered her head while brushing, as if she expected us to begin hurling pottery at one another.

Truly, I had been more comfortable fighting strange monsters. "We didn't know the power of the men who had kidnapped you. Or that you suffered strange fits. Or that there was a peculiar spear involved. Did you, too, see strange visions when you touched it?"

At this last, she left off glowering; now her stare was more blank, which was equally disconcerting. It would have been nice if she made some reply. But she did not, so I was left to continue the conversation on my own.

"So. Eh. There is a man in Harran, and Dabir thinks he can set everything aright with you. Also, he is an expert on the kind of wizards that Dabir thinks are chasing you."

Najya pressed lips tightly together, then raised a hand to still the servant tending her hair. "Thank you. You may go."

"Madame?" The girl lowered the brush.

Najya turned her head, and her voice was firm, though not harsh. "I said to go."

The girl collected all the feminine beauty articles in a little basket beside her and exited hurriedly.

Najya waited until the girl had shut the door, then considered me with more care.

"I do apologize," I said. "But you were not conscious, and we . . . Dabir, I mean—"

"What did you see in the visions?" she asked.

I found it far easier to discuss the distressing images I had seen than to speak to her about Harran, so I welcomed the change of topic. I omitted nothing.

She did not listen like Dabir, with interruptions. Instead she waited pensively and allowed me to reach a natural conclusion. After, she sat looking troubled.

Once again I tried to prod her forward. "Did you see something similar?"

"Somewhat."

With that admission, it was easier to take the initiative. "You see, then, why we need to speak with someone better able to help you? Dabir would not have suggested going to Harran if he did not think it would aid you."

"I believe you," she said finally, and touched a hand to her face.

It was a relief to know my arguments were seeing me to victory, and I began to relax. Another fine point had just come to me, one I might have mentioned earlier if I'd been thinking more clearly. "If we return you to Isfahan, who is to say the sorcerers would not simply follow and take you away once more?"

She frowned, seemingly in acknowledgment. "Who is this man Dabir is taking me to see?"

"I do not know him," I confessed. "But he is a scholar who helped train Dabir. Dabir is one of the brightest men in the caliphate, and if he respects the fellow, he must be wise indeed. I am sure he will be able to cure you."

"Very well," She said resignedly. "I will go." She then addressed me with great dignity. "Your . . . friend is very kind to me. I will happily remuner-ate him for these expenses. My family is not without resources."

It took me a moment to decide how to respond. "That is thoughtful of you," I said at last. "But Dabir is not a hireling. He is a trusted servant of the caliph. He does not aid you for money or any other favor, but because it is the proper thing to do."

"You hold him in high regard."

"His wisdom has unraveled great mysteries." It occurred to me then that she still had told me little that Dabir had asked me to learn. "Your pardon, but one of the things he asked me to, eh, ask you was whether you yourself had seen visions. And what they were."

"The coals have dimmed," she said.

I had been looking at nothing but her for a long while now, and though I had noticed a fading light, it had not occurred to me to see if the coals in both braziers had left off steaming. I was not so foolish that I had missed her change of subjects, but I did not wish her to be uncomfortable, either. "Are you cold? Shall I call for more?"

"Nay. Though my skin is cool." She touched fingers to her face once more. "Are you warm?"

"I, too, am fine." Now that she mentioned it, I had been chilled ever since I had touched the spear beside her, but I did not mean to reveal it.

She adjusted herself into the cushions, then considered me seriously. "Tell me, Captain. Do you think I am a witch?"

"Nay."

"Do you think I am mad?"

"No, not at all. You have borne yourself through difficulties that would send some men quaking in fear."

She weighed me then with her eyes, and her shoulders sank a degree. She proceeded tentatively. "There is something I think I should tell you. Dabir should probably know. I did not say anything of it sooner because . . . well, I thought this would end quickly, and I did not wish to speak of it."

I could not imagine what she was about to admit, but she held my complete attention.

"Since I was a little girl, I have sometimes had dreams about things that had not yet happened, but that later came true. My grandmother used to call them visions."

I knew not what to make of this. "Did you dream about something that the wizards wanted?"

"I don't think so. My dreams were almost always . . ." Her voice trailed away. ". . . mundane."

"What do you mean?"

At last she seemed to relax. "Once I dreamed my grandfather would return home early with presents for me and my brother, and that he would bring my brother a toy sword. He did, the next day. I dreamt my cousin would find her kitten wandering in the field across the way when it went missing." She paused briefly, and her voice softened. "Once I dreamed my father was crying, and the next day we learned his uncle had died. Until now, that was the worst dream."

"And did you ever dream of these wizards?"

"No. But for the weeks before my . . . my attack, I had been dreaming of great fields of snow that covered rooftops. And—" She watched me for a moment, I think to gauge whether or not I would scoff or mock her.

"Speak on," I urged.

"There were strange beings all around me, and riders. Fierce warriors wrapped in furs, shouting and waving swords. Before us flew ghosts that chased down men. We were heading for a little hill in a valley, and I think you were there, fighting someone with a club."

I could not keep the skepticism from my voice. "Do your dreams always come true?"

"Only the true ones. But I can always tell."

As disquieting as her dreams were, I was no learned man, to guess their import. "This seems like the kind of thing wizards like. Did they ask you about your dreams?"

"I don't think so." Her lips twisted into a frown. "I scarcely remember my time among them. It is mostly hazy."

"Do you remember anything?"

She puzzled over my question for a moment. "After my capture, but before I came here, there is one moment . . ." Her voice grew more certain as she continued. "I lay in near darkness, in a stone room. There were a few candles." She pointed to left and right, as though placing memories. "I was groggy and light-headed, and it took me a moment to focus, but I grew alarmed when I smelled blood. I opened my eyes to see a woman was bent over me, and she, too, looked troubled. I thought she might be worried for me, and I asked if she had come to help." Najya's voice hardened. "But she had not. She pulled away as if I were a snake, and she spoke quickly with a man I realized must be standing behind me. I know only a little Greek, but I'm sure the man was worried that something had not worked, and that the lady hadn't done it properly. And that made her nervous."

"Do you remember anything else?" I asked.

"No, nothing," she said, and let out a long breath. For the first time that evening she wore her sorrow and weariness openly. I wished then that I was not a stranger, that I might comfort her. "I really thought the Greek woman was going to help me." I found that she was still looking at me. "I did see strange scenes, Captain," she confessed. "When I held the weapon on the wall. You said you wished to hear it."

Looking at her strained expression, I was no longer certain I wanted to know. "Is it worse than what I saw?"

"I saw everything that you did, but I was the one attacking. . . . And some part of me was glad for all that happened. I was fighting against those men, wielding a weapon, stomping through the snow, eager for blood. . . . And I cast great waves of cold from my fingertips."

I knew not what to say.

"I should not have told you that," she said, watching me.

"You should tell me—and Dabir—anything that you see. If he doesn't know all that you know, he cannot help you."

Still she stared, looking more lost and alone than ever, and I could no longer help myself. I stepped forward and sank to one knee before her. "You are not mad," I said. "I saw everything that you did. I faced the wooden men, and their keeper. I doubt nothing you have told me."

"But you did not . . . feel the vision the same way."

"The wizards have done something to you. And Dabir and I will set things right. This I promise."

She looked at me again in that way she had in the house, upon the stair, and I felt suddenly uncomfortable. I cleared my throat, and climbed to my feet, very conscious of her proximity. "Is there anything more you need? Do you desire female companionship upon the ride?"

"No," she said, which pleased me, for I had no stomach for shepherding a gaggle of women. "That will not be necessary. But I want a better horse."

I smiled at the thought of a woman's simple worries. "I shall find you one that rides most smoothly. I apologize for the cart horse's bony back—"

"That is not what I mean," she cut in. "I do not need some old woman's nag, but one that answers to my lead."

There was sense in this—if it came to a fight she might escape on a more responsive steed. "I shall see that it is done. Is there anything else you desire?"

"I should like a sword, Captain."

This startled me.

"I am a general's daughter," she reminded me.

I then recalled how competently she had held Dabir's blade. While it is true that women tire more swiftly than men, for they are weak, it can be prudent to show a woman how to handle a weapon, for it is a sad fact known by brothers, sons, and fathers that women sometimes must defend themselves when we are not at hand.

Najya took my silence as another challenge, and her chin rose imperiously. "I have one of my own, and I always wear it on my longer rides. As my blade is in Isfahan, I would prevail upon you to find me another."

"I will present you with the finest blade it is in my power to give," I promised, and the challenging look in her eyes melted away. A smile touched her lips. "Did you study sword craft with your father?" I asked.

"I did."

"Perhaps during our journey you can tell me more of him. I have heard great things about his skill."

"I would enjoy that."

She seemed in an easier state of mind, and it was a true pleasure to see her smile. I noticed too late that I had once again said nothing for a while. "I should go," I told her, though I did not move. "Is there anything else you desire?"

"Yes. I should write my brother another letter to let him know what has changed."

"A fine idea. I'm sure the governor will be happy to send a courier." I rose, then bowed my head to her. "Rest well. We shall depart in the morning."

"Go with God," she told me. I had the sense that she wished something else, but she did not speak of it, even as I lingered a moment in the threshold, thus I left her.

I found a slave in the hall and told him to bring parchment, ink, and pen, then returned straightaway to the room where I'd left Dabir, only to find him gone with the spear. Kharouf, lounging beside the room's brazier and picking through the dinner remains, told me my friend had hurried off just a few moments before, carrying the spear and a bundle of books and papers. "He said to tell you he was heading to the astronomer's tower."

Understand that I had always found Kharouf rather reliable, so his carelessness in leaving Dabir without guard thoroughly astounded me. "And you did not think to go with him?"

Kharouf answered quickly. "He thought you might be worried if you didn't know where he was. He asked me to stay."

"He could have written a note!"

"Oh," Kharouf said. "I suppose you're right."

I held off cursing him then and turned from the room.

"Should I go with you?" he called after.

"Stay and guard the brazier," I snapped.

So it was that I shortly found myself with a lantern, trotting up a flight of stone steps into the darkness. They marched up and around the inside of the old square tower. Narrow windows were cut into the wall every ten steps or so, casting silver moonlight across the stairs. I imagined portly Shabouh puffing up and down them every evening, and wondered how he was not slimmer.

I emerged at last into the cold night air, my breath clouding before me. Dabir sat on a wooden stool, a bundle of papers clipped to a table secured to the wall. A lantern dangled from a hook beside him, near the spear.

"Ah," he said, glancing up only briefly. "You got my message."

I snorted. "Did you deliberately trick poor Kharouf?"

"He kept asking questions." Dabir did not look up. He was tracing a finger over a manuscript. In a moment, he lifted a metal instrument to his eye and stared along it into the heavens. Near at hand was an inkwell and stylus, and I saw that he had been drawing a series of dots on a clean sheet of parchment. I could not imagine why he should be diagramming a star map.

"I left him there to guard you," I said.

"I am fine, as you see."

I sighed and stepped past him to place my hands on the scalloped crenellations, chest-high. The stone was heavy with cold that leached through my fingers.

Not even Mosul's largest mosque stood as tall as the tower. I gazed down upon the city, savoring the view. The bonfire blazed in the square, staining the diminished crowd in shifting reds and golds. Flickering light shown through many shuttered windows, and some folk had left their courtyard ovens smoking. Beyond the city's walls lay the long length of the Tigris, a deceptively placid ebon ribbon, and on its far side lay low mounds. These, too, were misleading, for under the blanket of snow were not hills, but the ruins of the ancient city of Nineveh, so vast that even after centuries of looting the stone, great swaths loomed intact.

My gaze was drawn past the ruins to the horizon, where the stars shone through crisp winter air in all their glory. The scattered fragments of the Milky Way glowed especially bright, and I lost myself in wonder for a time until Dabir laid down his tool and scribbled some notes.

I then considered the tower height. Roofless and open to the elements, it was empty of decoration or any furnishings apart from Shabouh's weathered desk, a stool, and a few hooks or metal loops for lanterns and banners. The space was no more than twelve paces from side to side, and on the north face, just a step or two from the battlement, was the square opening to the stairwell.

"So. What are you doing up here?" I asked him.

"Looking over Shabouh's calculations."

This pleased me, somewhat, though I tried not to gloat. "Didn't you tell me stars and planets could not map a man's fate?"

"They can't. But they surely hold many secrets we have not yet unraveled." He set down the pen and sighed. "Shabouh's right. The planets haven't been in this kind of configuration for almost a thousand years."

"And what happened a thousand years ago?"

To this he could only shake his head. "I can't recall reading of anything calamitous taking place around here then." He met my eyes. "But that is the problem with astrological predictions. Somewhere, something horrible is always happening to someone, and something pleasant to someone else. All under the same star sign."

"Well, was something especially bad happening somewhere else?"

"Not that I know of. I'll have to do some more research. Now. What did you find out?"

"Najya's agreed to accompany us."

"Did you ask her whether she had experienced any visions?"

"Aye." I then relayed what the woman had seen, and he plucked details up for examination like a jeweler eyeing diamonds. I went on to describe her "true dreams." He seemed merely curious until I mentioned what Najya remembered about lying on a table. At mention of the Greek woman Dabir's eyes widened and his mouth opened a little in surprise.

"What has you worried?" I asked.

He gathered up his composure and, after a moment, spoke calmly. "Did you think to ask Najya what the woman looked like?"

In point of fact, I had not. "No," I admitted. "But what does it matter if one of the Sebitti's attendants spoke Greek?"

"What if she's not an attendant, Asim?"

I was not sure what he meant by this, and could only stand in silence.

"Blood powers magic, Asim." He seemed unduly impatient. "Think. What magic worker do we know who is Greek, and a woman?"

That answer was simple, for we had met only one person with both qualifications. "Lydia?"

Dabir lifted his hands in exaggerated elation. "Yes! Lydia."

"You think it was Lydia?" I was surprised. Had he not warned me about galloping toward conclusions before saddling facts? "Surely there are other Greek women who practice sorcery."

He stared at me for a long moment. "You are, of course, correct that I should not automatically assume the worst."

I bowed my head in acknowledgment but, rather than calming, Dabir took to pacing as he thought aloud.

"Lydia is a sorceress of singular power. She called a spirit up from hell and placed it in a living man."

Her plan had been to do this to Jaffar, and not only had she almost succeeded, she had nearly entombed Dabir and me alive in the bargain. I needed no reminding. Dabir, though, went on.

"Even so great a necromancer as Diomedes could not conjure a complete soul. The bodies he animated were but husks, moving through a shadow of their former lives." He shook his head. "If the Sebitti were interested in working with any Greek sorceress, it would almost surely be her."

I realized then what he was driving at. "You think the Sebitti are in league with the Greeks?!"

"Behind them or merely involved, this cannot be good for the caliphate."

I grew conscious of the sound of footsteps. Dabir and I turned and saw the spill of lamplight on the steps, drawing closer as the scrape of boot sole on stone grew louder. I wondered if it might be Kharouf, or even Shabouh.

Instead, I saw that it was Tarif. His scar, lit from beneath, seemed especially grim that night. Perhaps because he was expecting the night air to be chill, he had thrown on a baggy robe, one that looked a size or two large for him.

"Shabouh," I joked, "you're looking thinner than I remember."

Tarif did not bother with an answering jest. His eyes scanned the tower with the practice of a trained soldier. I wondered if he had ever been up here before, and supposed that, like me, he'd had no call do so.

"Greetings," he said, and turned to contemplate the drop, stepping to the west face, across from us.

His manner seemed odd to me, and I was about to comment upon it when Dabir gripped my upper arm. I turned my head to face him, saw him mouth something to me.

"What?" I asked.

Tarif turned to face us and his eyes glittered strangely as he drew his sword.

"Sebitti!" Dabir cried. "That's not Tarif!"

A year before this, perhaps even six months before, I might have paused to question Dabir's reasoning, sense of humor, or sanity. Yet because I had grown used to his declarations, no matter how strange, I did not hesitate, and that is what saved me. That, and the fact that curved blades draw quickly, for Tarif was already swinging as I cleared the scabbard.

"Gazi's a master warrior!" Dabir shouted quickly.

I had not time for finesse. I caught Tarif's sword edge on mine, rather than my flat, and he bore down, grinning madly. He pushed in hard, seeking to shove me over an extended foot, but I dodged him, ducking a strike that sheared off the top of my turban. Tarif, or Gazi, giggled as the cloth fabric came down around my shoulders. Praise Allah, the wind whipped it back so that I was not blinded.

Dabir tried sweeping the fellow's legs with the ivory spear, but Gazi blocked the blow with his boot after only a negligent glance.

I took what I thought was an opening and drove in with a high cut. Gazi parried lightning-fast and swung for my chest. I just managed to block, but my grip and angle were poor. I turned as Gazi struck again and again, and we rotated about the limited space.

Dabir swung at Gazi's head.

The man ducked it, and I stumbled wildly backward as Dabir's spear blade passed a whisker before my nose. "Get down the stairs!" I shouted.

I fetched up against the wall. If Gazi had attacked me at that moment I would not be alive to write this, but he'd heard my warning and whirled to face Dabir. Probably he feared my friend would actually heed my advice to flee, which of course he had not done.

Dabir's stance was too narrow—he'd had no formal training with the spear—but he knew how to grip it, and he kept Gazi back with two swift jabs. The third, though, was just the same as the first two, and Gazi had learned the pattern. He stepped aside and grabbed the spear just past the blade, lunging forward for an overhead strike.

I might have killed Gazi then but Dabir would still have been slain by the Sebitti's downward blow. I managed to throw myself forward, sliding my blade under Gazi's. I blocked the strike at the hilt before it had full momentum, though I'd done it by defying any sort of proper sword technique.

Gazi's eyes brushed mine at the same moment his sword came clear. He sliced carelessly at my torso and I stepped back, remembering too late that I was near Shabouh's desk. I clattered into it. I felt sure then to feel the death stroke, but Gazi had retained hold of the spear with his off hand and used it to force Dabir to the stairwell while keeping his eyes locked on me.

Dabir struggled to control the back end of the spear haft, and suddenly found himself teetering on the edge of the stairs. Gazi grinned for only a moment, for he had been too clever. Dabir did not relinquish the spear as he tripped down the stairs, but held tight, which pulled Gazi's end along as well.

Finally the Sebitti was off balance; as he turned to wrest the weapon from Dabir, I swept in, hard.

Yet Gazi would not be so easily taken. He somehow anticipated my strike, and as his sword arm was not in position to parry, he released the spear and threw himself backward. My stroke missed, and I marveled as he tumbled in the air, touched down briefly on one palm, and somehow pushed from there up to the battlement, where he alighted on the balls of his feet.

I could never have managed that backflip, much less a safe landing on a merlon barely a hand's span wide. I think I probably goggled at him a bit, and as I did, his face writhed like a snake. In but two heartbeats he was another man entirely, an ebon giant who completely filled the clothing that had draped his guise as Tarif.

I knew then I had stared too long. I barely deflected a wicked cut at my jaw. He laughed as he leapt over my return slice at his legs, landing on a second merlon. I thrust again, but he jumped lightly to the battlement on my left.

As I swung to face him he sprang at me.

"Down!" Dabir shouted, and I dropped to one knee, spinning to face the rear as Gazi's redirected sword stroke brushed my beard. This time the scholar wielded no spear, but the lantern, which smashed and broke across Gazi in the midst of his leap. Flames raced over his clothing. The Sebitti stumbled slightly as he landed, but recovered fast, pivoting to face us. The fire ate at his robes, yet he stood ready with his weapon, looking more irritated than alarmed. I shot to my feet. He paused a moment with narrowed eyes, his mouth turning up in a disgusted smile. His form shifted, though his expression did not change. Now he was an older man, white as a Frank, tall as the black but leaner. He shook his head, once, his face now partially obscured behind the rising blaze, then turned his back to us and sprang for the balustrade opposite me. I ran after, but before I could reach him he had vaulted off into space.

Dabir and I reached the edge in time to see the fire failing as the wind from his descent whipped it away. And then he smashed through the snow-sheathed stable roof. There was a mighty crash of timber and sun-dried clay, and a spray of frost.

I stared down in silence for a short moment, slightly stunned, then turned my head to Dabir. "Was *that* something to wring hands about?"

He blinked at me, then burst into laughter. He stilled it after just a few moments, then fixed me with a warm but worried smile as he backed toward the stairs. "Come, Asim, I don't think Gazi's dead." He turned, spear in hand, and started down.

I came after. "Not dead?" I called to him. "He dropped eighty feet!"

"He jumped to put out the fire," Dabir said as he took the stairs two at a time, "and shifted to a form that he valued less." He turned the corner, winded already from the combat. "Probably he changed again the moment after impact, to an uninjured body."

"By God! How do you kill such a man?"

"Well, fire might have worked," Dabir offered.

"How did you know he was not Tarif?"

"His manner. His clothes. His sword."

"I wonder what Tarif will say when he learns of this," I said, picturing my friend's consternation.

We had reached the ground level, and the last window.

Dabir's expression was grave as he looked back at me. "Tarif is dead."

"How can you know?"

"Gazi must eat his victim's heart to assume the shape."

This cut me without warning. Tarif was my closest friend in Mosul, apart from Dabir, and one with whom I shared more common interests. Perhaps I should have guessed this already, but I'd hardly had time for deep reflection in the last few minutes. "Are you sure?" I asked, hoping Dabir had it wrong.

He made no reply, but pressed his lips into a doleful grimace.

As usual, Dabir was right. We raised an alarm and put the whole palace on alert. After an hour Tarif was found, dead and mutilated, stuffed behind some scrap wood outside the stable. As for a body mangled 'neath the torn stable roof, either that of Tarif's twin or an old Frank or a giant black warrior, there was no sign.

4

We left Mosul just after morning prayers and Tarif's funeral, presided over by a visibly mournful governor. He impressed upon us the importance he now gave this mission, specifically as regards to the wizards. They were to be executed on sight—this would have to serve for justice, he said, for he wanted no more of his people killed.

With Tarif dead, I was given command of the forces. I handpicked the twelve men I knew best, including Kharouf, who begged to be given a chance to redeem himself. The lieutenancy I awarded the stolid veteran, Abdul. He lacked Kharouf's wit and speed, but was efficient and experienced. He and I made a final check of equipment, animals, and men, then I gave the order to move out. Folk in Mosul waved at us in the streets as we left, which always lightens a man's spirits, but before long we were outside the walls and into the countryside, rendered stark and unfamiliar under the blanket of snow.

Owing to the weather we passed only two heavily bundled groups moving south that morning. Harran, the town where Dabir's scholar lived, lay upon the main western trade route, and so, while we knew that we would journey many miles in the cold each day, the road was well marked and we knew also that there would be shelter each evening. All manner of caravanserai dot the road up and down which merchants ride every day the greater part of the year.

In addition to all else he had supplied, the governor gifted Najya with a fine chestnut mount, and loaned me a mare so that Noura would have time to heal. The animal was more willful than mine, but responsive enough. I was most thankful, though, for my new hooded robe and gloves, along with the warmth of the horse's body against my loins, for the incessant wind was cutting and sent the vapor from our breath blowing westerly. Ice crystals soon collected in our beards and the scarves we wore over our mouths.

The wind rendered conversation a challenge, but come afternoon it had died down and Dabir called Najya up to ride beside him. I listened for a time to her answers. She was composed and formal, as I had come to realize was her natural inclination, and, moreover, sat her saddle with the ease of a cavalry officer. It was no wonder she'd wanted a better horse.

I left the two talking and took point from Ishaq, who had good eyes, for a while. Once we were through with afternoon prayers I put another soldier, Gamal, in the lead, and fell back beside Dabir. We rode in companionable silence for a long while.

"I see now," I said after a time, "that it is spear practice you need, not sword work."

Dabir had looked just as dour as I'd felt all that day, and it was a pleasure to see a smile cross his face, however briefly.

"I packed *The Iliad*, you know."

"Huh. That is strange, for I won the bet."

"I am not so sure. But I think more time spent on sword work may be in order in any case."

"Good enough. All joking aside, Dabir, can Gazi be killed?"

"He can be hurt," Dabir said, "that we know. Presumably if he can be hurt quickly enough to overwhelm his ability to preserve himself through changing form, he could be brought to an end."

"Good."

Dabir looked sidelong at me. "I am sorry," he said, "about the death of your friend."

I did not wish to dwell on that, though I had sworn to myself that I would see Tarif avenged. "I have another question. Koury can breathe life into wood, and Gazi can take any shape he wishes—"

"I'm not sure that's true," Dabir interjected.

I interrupted before he could distract me with a long exposition. "Regardless, these are powerful wizards. Why would they need Lydia? Or have you decided the Greek sorceress wasn't her after all?"

"Oh," Dabir said, "I'm more certain than ever that Lydia is involved. Najya tells me she remembers a short, dark-haired woman with large eyes, very pretty, well-dressed with an enameled necklace of some sort. Now while there are surely other Greek magic workers, some of whom are women, how many of them are powerful and beautiful? And do you recall her locket bearing the image of Saint Marina?"

I did not, but Dabir spoke on. "Jaffar remarked on it when he suggested it would pair well with a set of emerald earrings he'd been given by the jeweler Namad in payment for a market infraction."

"You still have not answered."

"Just as no warrior is good with every weapon, or no artist good with every medium, no wizard is master of every spell. Take a poet, for example. He's unlikely also to be a fine drummer or sculptor."

I grunted. "So she's better at something than they, who have had a thousand years to study their craft?"

"More years than that, probably," Dabir corrected. "But yes, and her expertise may be crucial to their aims in this instance."

"How do you reason that?"

Instead of answering, Dabir considered the frosty distance and reached down to brush something from his horse. He glanced behind us and I understood he looked to see where Najya was. She rode a full two horse lengths back, among the supply animals. Kharouf was immediately behind, but even he was some paces off.

When Dabir faced forward again, I assumed he meant to answer me in the instant, but he frowned instead, then demurred in hushed tones, "I do not like to speculate."

"Aye, instead you like to madden me. You must tell me what you are thinking."

His head tilted minutely from side to side as if he held an internal argument, then finally gave in, his voice low and intent. "We know Najya has been ensorcelled to compel her to track these bones. We know Lydia's expertise is with spirits, and we saw her put one in another person's body."

I did not like where he was going with this. "So?" I prompted.

The breath from his long sigh misted in the air before him. "I fear the spirit of the creature that once used these bones has been bound to Najya, and that is why she sometimes has lapses in memory and strange behavior."

"What! Are you saying that Greek witch deliberately infected Najya with some demon?" I made the sign against the evil eye and fought against the impulse to look back at the woman. The men riding before us didn't turn at my outburst, but I whispered back in any case. "Can she be saved?"

"It's my hope Jibril can safely 'break' the spear and cast out the spirit. That should render both woman and weapon useless to the Sebitti."

"If that is the solution, why can't we just break the spear now?" I asked.

"No." Dabir looked at me pointedly. "If it's some kind of magical tool, that is the last thing we must do."

"Why?"

"It would be like unblocking a canal while you were standing in its bottom. The water would rush in and surely drown you."

"I see," I said, though I didn't, entirely.

"I can't predict exactly what would happen," Dabir explained further, "but it wouldn't be good for whoever happens to be near the spear. And if something's locked inside, then . . . that something would be free."

"You mean like a ghost? Or a djinn?"

"Something other," Dabir said. "Something that we do not want to meet."

"Bismallah. Is this 'something' going to kill her? Will it drive her mad?"

"I don't know." Dabir measured me with his eyes before deciding how to continue. "Right now she seems to be in control. But I cannot say if that will last."

"Is your wizard friend powerful enough to fix her?"

"He is more a bookseller than a wizard, but he is well-read."

"A bookseller?" I felt a stab of worry. I hoped I had not oversold his prowess to Najya.

A smile played at the corners of Dabir's mouth. "If you expect him to have a long white beard and a turban with woven images of constellations, you will be sorely disappointed. Jibril makes his living as a bookseller, but he is one of the most educated men in the world. And he knows a great deal about magic."

"What is so great a scholar doing in Harran? You called it a heat-blasted hole."

"It *is* a heat-blasted hole, though it may seem less so this season. But fine schools have flourished there since ancient times. I studied at the largest one before being accepted at the House of Wisdom."

"With Jibril?"

"Jibril and I became friends because one of my teachers sent me to purchase titles."

"But he knows all about the Sebitti and their magics?"

"Yes."

I nodded, not entirely satisfied, "I know we're up against great wizards, but do you think that perhaps they just name themselves after the old Sebitti? Koury did not look thousands of years old."

"No, he didn't," Dabir admitted. "But part of their legend concerns immortality."

"I thought you said Gazi could be killed."

"I'm hoping 'immortal' merely means 'ageless.'"

"What is the legend?" I knew only what Dabir had mentioned in passing about the Sebitti that first day.

"Keep in mind the stories are very old." We stopped briefly as my horse paused to relieve herself. Once we were in motion again Dabir said: "Actually, there is not so much a coherent story as scattered pieces."

"Well, let's hear the pieces, then."

"Fair enough." Dabir cleared his throat and gathered his thoughts. "Well, there were seven sages whom the ancients thought had been sent by the gods to bring civilization to man. Their leader was Adapa. The Assyrians relate that he had broken the wing of the bird of the south wind, and was brought before the gods for punishment. Some of the gods spoke in Adapa's favor, reminding them of great services the Sebitti had performed already and swaying the decision of the others."

"How can any of this be true?" I interjected. "There are no gods but Allah."

"These stories come from a very long time ago," Dabir reminded me. "Details get garbled in the telling. It is like the story of the urchin and the gossip."

I looked at him blankly.

Dabir obliged with an explanation. "One gossip saw a boy stumble in the road, and the tale passed through her, to another, to another, all about the square and down the street, until the boy's mother came running out from her home, weeping, for she was told that her son was struck by a wagon and lay dying with his leg crushed."

"The story changed from mouth to mouth. Aye. Men lie and exaggerate, and forget details. So it was that Allah had to inspire so many prophets over the years, may peace be upon them all, for men could not properly remember his true word."

"Exactly. Perhaps what the old storytellers describe as gods were kings. The problem is learning which parts of any such story are true, and which parts are embellishment. I had always assumed that the Sebitti were a group of long-dead, especially capable warriors, but, well . . . here we are."

"You were going to tell me more about them."

Dabir frowned faintly. "Jibril is the real expert. I cannot remember all the specifics. I do know that Adapa was offered the food of immortality, and that he refused. The others, though, accepted. So that there were in truth only six immortals." He raised a gloved hand and folded down one thick beige thumb. "Gazi, the heart-taker, was said to steal the shape and physical prowess of any whose heart he devours, though not the mind, so that he grew in cunning but not in wisdom. There is one story about a clever widow who eluded him by feigning dismemberment." He folded down his first finger, and continued to curl the others as he worked through their names. "There is Erragal, master of the unseen, who was said to dwell in a deep cave beneath the tallest mountain. He used to enslave men to build great walls and palaces, but grew tired of that, and summoned dead men to work for him instead. There is the hideous Lamashtu, dark mother and mistress of the earth's hidden knowledge. She is said to be torpid and slow, but vicious when roused. When a child died in the night, or when a man was found with his throat slit, folk would whisper it was Lamashtu's doing. Enkidu was lord of beasts, roaming the woodlands and plains. In some stories he protected travelers from fierce beasts; in others he ran with the lions who hunted men." Dabir, having run out of digits, lowered his hand. "There is Koury, the master shaper and artificer, who brought a kind of life into clay and wood. It was said he used an army of stone men to build a fantastic bridge across the Tigris. Finally there is Anzu, the watcher of men, the spy and ferreter of secrets. He was the ear of the Sebitti, said to be the most generous of all, sometimes coming among men to bear gifts. One legend names him as a wise man who gave presents to the prophet Jesus, may peace be his."

"And you think we face all of these?"

"Allah preserve us if we do," Dabir said softly. "Two would be quite enough."

To that I could only agree.

We traveled until sunset that first day and went straight to bed after prayers. Late during the second day's travel Dabir pointed out a distant, white-capped peak where, he told me, Nuh's ark had come to rest after the flood. I had never realized it was so close to Mosul, and I fell to wondering if there might be anything left of it upon the mountainside. Dabir remarked the whole thing had likely long since rotted, but we agreed that in the summer it might be interesting to look for it.

Now those of you who are not travelers may wonder as to what a caravanserai looks like. There are all kinds, large and small, but the best are walled rectangles that can house large numbers of men, horses, and goods, and can be sealed off for the night with thick wooden doors. Many are built around wells, and the very best are manned with guards and staffed with merchants.

The caravanserai that night was of the better sort, and it had a little shop selling both chickens and eggs, which we put to good use, though the prices were high. The shopkeeper, a fat man with a lazy eye, actually sounded sincere when he apologized for the price, saying that his fowl were simply not laying as well in the cold, and he gossiped with anyone who would listen about the bad weather's effect on business.

Our meal was subdued until Kharouf spoke up from the fireside and asked for a story from me. Without too much reluctance I fell to describing my journey with Dabir through the Desert of Souls. The men all thought this a fine tale and praised me. Afterward, I portioned out the night's sentinels. There were enough of us that two could be spared for each of the three watches on one night, and sleep the next, so that none of us would suffer overmuch. Najya was excluded from this calculation, of course. You may think me overcautious setting sentinels inside a high-walled caravanserai sealed with thick doors and a great chain, but Dabir and I were uneasy as to the power of the enemies we faced, and there were at least a dozen strangers behind the walls with us.

Dabir was brooding and turned down my offer for a game of shatranj, so I checked over the arrangements while most of the men readied for sleep. They had erected a small tent between our three campfires for Najya, who sat quietly near Dabir. My friend remained close to our largest fire, looking over one of his scrolls. The spear, wrapped in a long dark package beside him, had not left his sight.

I took off my belt and set my sheathed sword close to hand before sinking down onto my bedroll to remove my boots. It was then I found Najya before me.

The cool wind set her veil rippling and her hair blowing. She pushed a strand from her fine-featured face. "Captain, I heard you say that you had brought your shatranj board."

"I have." I set my boots down side by side, in easy reach should I need to slip into them quickly.

"I had hoped we might play tonight. A quick game, before sleep."

I had never before played shatranj with a woman; indeed, it had never crossed my mind that a woman might know the rules. But then it was growing clear that Najya was a different sort of woman than those I had known before. I was not yet tired and the thought of spending time in her company did not displease me.

"I would welcome that," I told her.

I retrieved the board and the bag of pieces from my saddle gear, after slipping back into my boots. Najya and I unrolled our prayer rugs to sit upon, then placed pieces. I allowed her the black, so that she might move first, then asked how large a handicap she desired.

"A handicap?" Her eyebrows rose.

"I might give over my vizier," I explained, "or an elephant, or a knight, even one of my chariots, before the start of the game."

"Do you not think I can play you, Captain?" she asked.

The habits of women are confusing, for they take offense sometimes even when you mean only to be kind. "I did not say that," I said.

"I grew up playing shatranj across from my father, and my brother. And I bested them both."

I nodded once to her. "No handicap, then."

I could not quite read her look, but her voice was cool when next she spoke. "I have a thought, Captain. Let us make a wager."

Gambling for money is forbidden, as all right-minded know, but her manner gave me pause and I did not manage to frame a response before she continued.

"You look so sour. If you win this match, then you need not bother with my company in the evenings. I see that I make you uncomfortable."

I could not imagine how she had been left with that impression. She spoke on before I could protest.

"If, however, I win, you shall spar with me tomorrow evening."

The notion that I, the expedition leader, should trade blows with a woman under my protection struck me as comically absurd.

"Are you afraid I'm going to best you?" There was a challenge in those eyes now.

"No!" My response was louder than I planned. I managed to lower my voice, but not to frame more than a short expression of my bewilderment. "Why?"

"It is simple. I find myself in danger and since I . . . since my maturity, I have had no more training. My brother no longer would duel with me, and my husband always refused. I thought I would profit from renewed practice."

I found myself nodding slowly, unwilling to disappoint her but unsure how to proceed. "Well, I suppose that might be helpful," I said doubtfully. I thought then I might suggest someone else work with her—maybe Dabir would know how to teach her—but she did not give me the chance to speak on.

"Let us play, then, Captain."

So we did. I let her begin, and then, as is usual, we spent a long while taking turns maneuvering pieces into our battle arrays. She did not make the mistake of moving without watching me, as the young and inexperienced will do.

For a time our play took all our concentration. When she snatched my pawn with a knight one square from the far side of the board, I saw that she had the focus of a hawk and decided to better my chances by distracting her. "Tell me what your father was like," I suggested.

Her voice was soft, reflective, as she replied. "He was a good man, and brave. Gentle with his children and friends, but a lion when roused to anger."

I asked more about him, and anything she might know of his campaigns, and was surprised to hear that she knew far more about tactics and troop movements than many soldiers. She said it had pleased her father to speak of such things, and that she had first listened because she loved him. "And then I listened because I found such matters of interest. I used to beg him to tell me again of Iskander's battles at Gaugmella or Granicus, and he would set out stones and sticks to show me how the units moved."

Surely most fathers would not have discussed such matters with their daughters, nor allow them to spend so much time in the saddle. She had continued to ride, even after marriage, and she lovingly described journeys near the mountains outside her estate.

"I have been looking forward to the spring," she said, "and the bloom of the flowers as the grass turns a deep green upon the slopes. You should come and ride there then. You would enjoy it, I think."

"I'm sure I would. You sound as though you spend many hours in the saddle."

"I had little else to do once I married." Her eyes settled on her pieces. "The household was run by the servants. And we had no children," she added.

That she was barren struck me like a heavy blow and I could not think how to respond. Should I offer condolences?

She seemed not to notice my discomfiture as she brought out her right chariot. "Bahir was very handsome, and clever," she continued. "My father loved him, for he was a brave officer and a fine swordsman. But when he was not on duty, he seemed always to be out with his friends. He never had time for me."

She arched one slim eyebrow meaningfully. I understood then that she knew exactly what I had first assumed. Although I could not for the life of me imagine why any man would keep from Najya's bed, I had known soldiers who sought only the company of their fellows.

"That is unfortunate," I managed, lamely.

"I do not want you to think he was a bad man. I would not have wished that death for him." She then pushed forward her other chariot and her eyes flashed with impish glee. "You have become distracted, Asim. Check."

I was as startled by her use of my name as my sudden reversal. I could hear the smile in her voice as she addressed me. "I think that I shall triumph."

Most men know that to keep good grace with a woman you must not always strive to win, but I do not think I could have gotten myself out from the trap she had laid regardless. In a few more moves I was forced to concede. It being dark, I could not see through her veil, so the only sign I saw of her delight was the shift of her eyes.

"That was well done," I admitted. "I should like to watch you play Dabir sometime."

"I would rather play you," she said, and then froze for a moment, as if she regretted the words. "He is quite intense," she added. "I feel always as if he is watching me. Judging me."

"Surely not," I said, though I suspected she was right. "In any case, I underestimated you, and now must pay the price."

"I trust our wager is not too weighty for you?" she said thoughtfully.

"Nay," I said, "you beat me fairly."

"Very well." She sounded quite satisfied with herself. "Tomorrow evening, then. Good night, Captain." She bowed her head formally to me, and then withdrew.

After she retired I stowed away the board and pieces, thinking about the coming bout. The men would laugh at me, I thought, unless I was careful to make it a teaching exercise and not a contest, and they might tease me in any case. Yet I found that I did not care, and I was smiling when I crouched down beside Dabir, still sitting with a scroll by the fire.

"She is a fair player," I told him.

"That is good," Dabir replied without interest.

I decided not to tell him that she had beaten me. I glanced over to her tent, then lowered my voice. "I think she is feeling a little better."

"The gaps in her memory trouble her more than she is letting on," Dabir said, without pause from his reading.

"Eh. I think you may be making her uncomfortable."

Now he looked up, and the long, fire-cast shadows aged his face. "How so?"

"Well. You know how you are. Intense. That is the word she used."

Dabir toyed with the ring glinting on his finger. "I see. What do you suggest I do differently?"

"Perhaps you should not watch her as though she were an object of study."

Dabir deliberated before responding. "Asim, I think it is good of you to entertain her. The happier she is, the stronger she is likely to remain against the spirit. But you should not forget that there is something powerful within her that could take control at any moment. It's . . . unwise to . . ." He seemed to reconsider whatever he was about to advise. "I'm sure you are not suggesting that I relax my vigilance?"

"No," I answered reluctantly.

"But I will strive to be more cordial. I don't want to add to her burdens."

"That would be nice."

He nodded once and returned his attention to the scroll.

"What is it you are reading?"

"Passages from the Christian stories of the prophet Jesus, may peace be upon him. He cast demons and spirits out, but the writers do not say how."

I clapped Dabir on the shoulder. "If anyone can learn the answers, it will be you. But we should turn in, for it is already late. Sleep well, Dabir."

An amused smile stole over his features. "And you."

I strode back to my blankets, and burrowed in.

I did sleep well, as it happened, though I was roused before even the predawn call to prayer when those within the caravanserai began to bustle. There were only two small caravans that had taken shelter that night, but you would not have known it from the amount of peddlers who crept forth that morning. They hawked waterskins, wineskins, and the means to fill both. They called out about whetstones, kindling, horse feed, knives, cloaks, gloves, even perfumes, to take back to the ladies at home. Children scurried from campfire to campfire, bragging about the excellence of their mother's, aunt's, or grandmother's candied nuts.

There was altogether too much chaos to please me, so I posted Kharouf and another man to stand watch. I stood back to supervise the loading of animals and gathering of gear, and it was thus that I noticed a small boy passing through with a sack bulging with breads. He was turned away by Abdul, but ducked low, came around a horse, and made straight for Najya.

I might have done the same thing if I were ten or eleven, for young women were easier marks, and better to look at in any case. However, I didn't want any complications or delays. I stepped around Abdul, gruffly urging another peddler from our midst, and almost ran into Dabir, who stood watching Najya, the wrapped spear held still in one hand like a walking staff.

He met my eyes and I understood immediately that something about the situation had alarmed him. Najya was bent a little to talk with the boy, who was proffering her a sweet bread. She said something we could not hear, and then he giggled. It was not the sound of his voice so much as the quality of the giggle, its length, the way his shoulder shrugged. We had heard it from a grown man trying to slay us in the astronomer's tower.

"Ya Allah!" I dashed forward, hand to my hilt. "Najya, get back from him!"

The boy turned instantly. A normal youth would have been frightened to see a soldier bearing down, but this one grinned. His form blurred and shifted even as he pulled a blade from somewhere within the pack that slid from his shoulders. His robe ripped as he grew, his skin lightened, and before I reached him I faced a huge redheaded Frank with a thick beard.

"This time my sword is curved," he crowed in a surprisingly thin voice, and leapt at me, his eyes alight with joy. His clothes were all but shredded, and his feet were bare as he dashed through the churned and muddy snow. Yet, from his grin, you'd have thought he frolicked in the spring grass.

Najya shouted for me to be careful even as horses began to neigh wildly on every side, and men's voices rose in consternation and fear. I had no chance in that moment to learn what troubled them, for I was fighting for my life. I parried Gazi's strike at the upper end of his arc, before he built full strength, and even so he nearly overpowered me.

The Sebitti recovered fast and came with a sidewise slash at my head. I ducked, sidestepped, parried again. Around me soldiers drew sword against cloaked figures suddenly in our midst, but also against huge wooden serpents that had whipped up from the snow near Dabir. It was these, apparently, which frightened the horses.

I heard Najya's voice rise in a scream but was too busy to risk a backward glance. Gazi came on, his teeth exposed in a hateful smile. He feinted an overhead chop but I sidestepped and blocked the expected torso thrust. He rushed with a flurry of blows that included some strikes I never before had seen and barely kept off my flesh. His mouth slid into an arrogant sneer. Kharouf darted in to aid me and nearly had his head shorn off for his trouble; he threw himself to the side and still took a cut to the arm that sent blood flying.

I took the opening to slice mid-torso, but Gazi beat my strike aside. His grin widened, white teeth shining under his red mustache. "Too predictable," he told me. I think he meant to say more, but he glanced suddenly to his left and his eyes widened almost comically. He parried another of my blows dismissively, then, as a frightened horse dashed past, the madman vaulted onto the beast. Gazi's balance was obscenely perfect; not only did he land astride the mare, he somehow switched sword hands in the process to swing out at me. I dropped, and I heard his laughter as he galloped away. I shot to my feet and started after, but something frigid slid by and the sight of it stopped me short. It was a transparent woman all in white, radiating cold, her tattered garments and hair gliding out behind her as though she flew into a gusting wind. The ghostly form raced after him with outstretched arms even as Gazi fled through the open caravanserai doors.

I knew not what to make of that, but raised a hand warding off the evil eye and spun around to take in the scene.

Shouting soldiers strained at lead lines of curveting horses while strangers pointed and stared from a safe distance. Najya's tent lay trampled near Kharouf, who struggled upright holding one blood-soaked sleeve, his eyes glazed with shock. I shouted for Abdul to tend him. It was then that I saw the black wooden ram with its spiraling horns, straining against ice that encased it from the shoulder down. And beyond that, gliding over the surface of the snow toward Najya, was a second snow witch. Najya pointed at it in fear with a shaking hand, gasping long and loud, and stopped just short of another scream.

It was easy to see why. The ghost's face was her own, as if a sculptor had shaped it from snow and ice.

5

I stepped quickly between Najya and the ice ghost that mirrored her face, baring my teeth despite my own fear. But the thing did not attack. Instead it turned, gliding quickly for the stone wall of the caravanserai. The ghost struck it and passed through, leaving a spray of ice crystals and a dusting of frost upon the walls.

I turned, wrestling over all that I had witnessed. As an alarm bell rang I remembered that Najya had described a vision filled with ghosts that hunted men and understood with frightening clarity that her dreams did come true. Then I turned to Najya, who stood lance-stiff, her eyes wide and wild.

"Are you unharmed?" I asked her. "What happened? Where did the wooden snakes go?"

Dabir drew up beside me, the spear in hand. "She froze the snakes." He swept a hand to his right and I saw then two long humps of ice through which the wooden snakes were partly visible. A few paces past them was a robed man, frozen from the waist down, his hands moving spasmodically as Gamal stared in horror from a few paces off. I'm not sure if it was the ice or something else that troubled my soldier, namely that the robed man's hood had shaken free to reveal a smooth wooden oval in the place of a head.

"There were three man-shaped automatons," Dabir told me grimly, "two snakes, and the ram. Najya froze all of but two of the wooden men. They fled once it was clear they wouldn't win through."

"'Automaton'?" I asked.

"A Greek word—a device moving on its own."

I grew conscious then of a trio of our soldiers staring openmouthed at us. I pivoted and pointed them to their mounts. "See which way the assassin rode off!"

They fell over themselves to obey, dashing past a few others who were still calming horses.

Najya's breath steamed as her gaze shifted between Dabir and myself.

"This would have worked, Asim," Dabir pronounced, shaking his head. "They sent in snakes to frighten the horses. Wooden soldiers to fight ours. A ram to charge me and presumably grab the spear. And Gazi, of course, to take Najya. But she froze almost all of them. She just gestured with her hands, and ice formed around their bodies."

"I don't know how," she said, "and the women . . . when the men grabbed me I . . . those ghosts swirled up from the snow and attacked them . . . I was worried for you, Asim."

Though she paused, she sounded as if she were about to faint from lack of breath. Seeing her thus filled me with pity, and I sheathed my sword and stepped close to her. "They are gone," I said. "You are fine now."

"But how did I do it?" She sounded guilt-ridden, panicky.

"We shall talk about that later." Dabir offered her his waterskin, which she accepted numbly. "Sit at the fire for now and warm yourself. We'll need to leave as soon as we can sort this out."

She glanced desperately to me. "Dabir is right," I told her. "You may not know what you did, but you saved us, and for that we are grateful." I offered her a smile, and gestured to the embers of the fire. For the first time during any journey I wished that there were more women along, so that they could look after her properly.

It was then that the stewards of the caravanserai arrived, demanding explanation. Dabir did not like brandishing the caliph's amulet in public, for he said it reduced freeborn men to slaves, but his patience was thin.

The moment the owners raised their voices, he fished it from his robe via his neck chain. And soon the owners were bestowing salaams and such ridiculous apologies that Dabir was visibly embarrassed. They offered no more complaints, and insisted even upon reimbursing the money Dabir had paid for firewood and the rental of the space.

While Dabir dealt with them, I ordered Bishr and Ishaq to take axes to the ram—still quivering in its ice block—while Gamal and I handled the soldier; it was a little more challenging until we roped its arms to its sides. Before we were completely through, the soldiers I'd sent after Gazi returned. They reported him fleeing northwest, which was, naturally, our intended course.

We stopped hacking at Koury's monsters once we had them down to the ice, reckoning that they were ruined enough—the pieces stopped moving once separated from the main body. We enlisted help to set bonfires around the snakes and surrounded them with ax-wielding spotters. By then Abdul had patched up Kharouf and readied a status report. We'd been very lucky. A few of the men had been bruised by the wooden soldiers, and one had been kicked in the shoulder by a horse, but only Kharouf was seriously injured. His deep slash had been sewn and bandaged. He would be near useless as a warrior for a while, though he could still stand watches.

Dabir and I conferenced briefly while the men readied our gear. He speculated that Koury must have been somewhere nearby, but wondered if he might be able to control the wooden creatures from a greater distance. There was no way to know. When I pointed out that Najya seemed to be controlling the spirit's powers just fine, and to our benefit, he looked more troubled than pleased.

"For now," he said. "The sooner we get to Jibril, the better."

The journey of the next days was not so eventful, for there were no further encounters with any Sebitti. But we quickly learned that the snowfall was not an isolated storm, for it stretched on for miles, and miles. There was no end to it.

One good thing came of that fight. My men needed no warning to stay alert, and gave no trouble when I instructed them to wear their full armor from this point on, even though the metal was uncomfortable. I donned my own, an expensive linked shirt reinforced with stiff bands in key places, notably my shoulders. The armor was situated over my garments and under my cloak so that I did not feel its cold, but the thin metal coif dangling from the back and sides of my helm sometimes brushed my neck as we rode, like the icy breath of some djinn. Yet I'd had enough close head shots from Gazi that I tolerated the discomfort.

From then on, we looked, and probably felt, more martial. While I appreciated that the men took their duties even more seriously, I was troubled by the way they suspiciously eyed poor Najya. Homely Gamal especially was nervous in her presence, and I caught him making the sign against the evil eye whenever she looked his direction. Only steadfast Abdul had not changed his attitude.

It was not hard to understand their concern. The soldiers knew only that the governor had instructed them to safeguard us wherever we went, for the good of Mosul and the caliphate, and to kill the wizards—which we'd failed to do. They knew little of the bone spear, or the woman, but had now glimpsed potent magics from her and, at best, thought she had been cursed.

It is no good having the men in your command grumbling superstitiously, and when we stopped in a bare-bones caravanserai that night after our attack I gathered them to relate a little of the truth—that Najya had been imprisoned by the wizards we hunted and that the governor was sending us not only to stop them, but to free her of their spells. I thought to play to their vanity, for who would not want to aid a beautiful woman in overcoming villany? After I spoke, Abdul stood up and shamed them even better than I had done, mocking them first that they should be afraid of a woman and second that they should turn against someone in an hour of need. They promised then to be less wary of her.

Unfortunately the damage had been done, for Najya had seen their looks and overheard their muttering. She kept to herself and retired early to her tent. I thought at first she merely rested before taking up practice with me, but she did not emerge, so after prayers I went to stand beside the canvas.

"Najya," I said, "I am ready to help your sword work."

A long moment passed before her response, and I had to strain to hear her. "That will not be necessary," she said.

"Aye, it is," I answered. "I lost the wager."

Her response was sharp. "I release you from the obligation."

I sighed. "This is no time to sulk. You may well need to defend yourself. The dangers are greater even than we realized. Come out, and let me see your technique."

So long was the delay that I thought I had missed another soft reply. But just as I was readying to prod her once more, she answered.

"I will be out shortly."

Anyone who has waited on a woman knows they have a different understanding of time. I lingered for a while, listening to her rustle about, then warmed myself by performing a few sword forms.

The snow was gray under the light of the waxing moon, lacking only a fingernail from full. The crisp air caught in my lungs as I worked, and my breath misted as I changed my stances.

When Najya came forth I saw that she had left off her veil and that she wore only a light cloak over her dress. Her hair had been pulled back tightly, and she carried the sheathed sword I had found for her on the governor's wall, one a few inches shorter than standard length.

"You will be cold," I told her.

"I am fine," she insisted curtly.

Sensing that she was in a difficult mood, I decided against further argument. "Come, then."

I led her away from the circles of our men, who watched, curious, but did not speak.

We stopped twelve paces from where our horses were picketed, in the shadow of the caravanserai wall, the old stones of which stood a spear's length higher than my head.

"Let me see your stances and strikes."

Her chin rose defiantly. "You said that we would spar."

"Not until we cover our blades. And not until I see your technique. Show me what you know."

She stepped suddenly into a high guard, feet spread adequately, leading from her right. Najya showed me a strike, her hand level, then moved through middle and low stances, concluding finally with two overhead variations, one over her right shoulder, one over her left.

Clearly her father had drilled her many times, or her footwork would not be both instinctive and precise. "Why did you not lift directly over your head?" I asked.

"Father said I was not strong enough to make that strike worthwhile, and that I would be better to block over one shoulder or the other."

"What of a trailing stance?"

"I have not practiced it as much. Father said it, too, required more strength."

Her father had been correct. "What else did he tell you?"

"That most sword fights are over in the first strikes."

"Anything else?"

"That I was unlikely to hold my own against a stronger opponent, and that I must be swift and accurate instead."

Her father had the truth of it, and I reflected for a moment on the depth of his love, that he should so carefully work to give her these skills. "Most men rely on the power of their family to protect their women."

"Father was not like most men. Sometimes he was on campaign for most of a year." Pride rang in her voice now. "He used to tell my little brother I was more skilled than he."

"I doubt your brother liked that." I chuckled. "Forms are one thing. How well do you fight?"

"Shall I show you?" Once again her eyes flashed with amusement. She had cast off her dark mood like a cloak tossed down on a warm day.

"Shortly." I passed over a thick strip of leather. "Wrap that about your blade."

This she did, while I fastened one about my curved saber, then tied it carefully. I tucked it under one arm, then inspected the ties on her sword. Once more, I saw that she knew what she was about.

She grinned at me as I handed back her weapon. "Are you ready?"

"A moment. Let me first see your strikes."

"I have already shown you."

"I will call the blow, and you will attack. I will parry, and then call for another."

She bowed her head in understanding. Then did we begin a simplified sparring exercise. Najya was hesitant at first, but soon we fell into a comfortable pattern. Once I was sure she could increase speed and maintain control, I told her to block. At first I informed her where I would strike, and then I varied, encouraging her to return my attacks. This she did, with growing speed. She performed well, though she lacked stamina, and before long I saw her panting. She raised an arm to wipe her forehead.

I was readying to step back to chide her for resting in the midst of a battle, when she renewed the assault with what I thought was a high strike until she swung hard for my midsection. I barely caught the blow, but there was no satisfied grin from her. Aye, her mouth parted in a snarl and she came on with swift, vicious determination. Before, we had traded. Now she left me no room to counter.

"Good," I told her. "Good!" Her attacks were nimble enough to disable all but the most experienced swordsmen. Being that she was a woman, of course, opponents with skill could just fend her off and wait for her to tire. But she did not. She rained blows, and as I maneuvered away I bethought of the men who must be watching. I would hear about this, surely. Did she mean to humiliate me? Aye, I could parry, then thrust, but I did not wish to hit her so hard. Najya seemed to have forgotten entirely that we sparred. Somehow I had underestimated my ability to anger her.

It was as I blocked a cut to my head that the front end of her sword's leather came free. Fully three hand spans of the steel were revealed, the guard dangling like a shirtsleeve from the lower two-thirds of the weapon. I thought that would slow her, but she came on even more furiously.

"Najya," I shouted, deflecting a blow. "The cover's off!"

It was only as she drove at me with the point that I understood I was probably dueling something other than Najya.

The spirit had taken over.

Some of the soldiers had stepped up, bandaged Kharouf among them, and I sensed rather than saw their concern, for I had no sight to spare.

Najya shrieked and drove in with a fierce overhead blow, the same she'd said she lacked the strength to make. This I took on the side of my blade, and the power of it spread down through my arms and thence to my back and spine. Once more she shouted, but before she could land the blow I stepped in close and locked our hilts. I stared into her eyes. "Najya!" I cried, even as she strained against my blade. "Najya!"

All at once the fury faded and confusion bloomed across her face. Her strength ebbed and she slowly pulled back

"What's happened—" Her eyes fell to her blade, and the drooping leather sleeve, and she flushed. "Asim . . . Asim, I am sorry. Did I hurt you?"

Gamal chuckled, and then the laughter spread to the other watching soldiers. I ignored them, but Najya's flush deepened.

She lowered her eyes and spoke so softly that I almost did not hear her. "I am sorry." She dropped the sword in the snow, turned, and dashed back to her tent. I was too troubled even to heed the jests of the soldiers who asked if she was too much woman for me, or if I was too little man.

I took her sword back to her tent and stood outside it. "Najya."

A long moment passed before she answered. "I am here."

"I have brought your sword." I tried to put the best possible interpretation on what had happened. "It is not uncommon, in the heat of battle, to lose one's temper—"

"That is not what happened," she said bitterly. "You do not understand." And then the canvas was thrust aside and her eyes stared despondently up at me, as if daring me to disagree. "There is something else within me, Asim. It struggles to win free, and control me."

I licked my lips, wishing she hadn't deduced that. You can be sure, at this point, that others were listening, for our combat had drawn much attention.

"Nonsense," I said, feigning good cheer. I crouched low. "You have a warrior's spirit, but it is yours."

She looked on me with lips pressed tight. I raised a finger toward them. "We go to Harran, to help you," I said softly. "We must not frighten the men." I lay the sword in my hands, hilt toward her. "This talk of possession, in their hearing . . . Leave off it."

She bowed her head as though in defeat, which troubled me further.

"Feel no shame. Nothing that has befallen is your doing."

She said nothing, but she gently took the sword from me and lay it behind her.

"And your sword work is quite fine. The finest," I finished, "I have ever seen by a woman."

She gave me a last searching look, then withdrew without another word.

Dabir was furious, of course. I did not even have time to admit I knew I'd made a bad choice before he called me apart to ask how I could possibly have thought sparring with Najya was a good way to create a tranquil atmosphere. I could but turn up my hands.

Dabir repeated an admonition to keep her calm in at least two different ways, then, thankfully, fell silent on the matter, though I heard much about the fight from the men on our ride the next day, and, indeed, into the evening. No one but Kharouf, who grew more serious, seemed to take anything but amusement from the story, and, oddly enough, the combat seemed to have won over the men, who now spoke of her as their "little warrior." I could not be sure what Najya thought, for she kept her distance and would not return my looks. She politely refused my offer of shatranj the next evening, and I realized with a pang how much I had come to look forward to her company.

6

The next morning we reached Harran. It was an ancient place, passed back and forth between many hands, many times, which is likely why it is so well fortified. Dabir had described it as sitting in the midst of a sunscorched wasteland, but had neglected to mention a small river that winds along its eastern wall. In those strange times, ice rimmed the channel and dry, white snow blew across the horizon, but tracks of men and beast showed where the main trails lay. The wind had swept a few areas clean so that the flat earth shone brown and dark, and in other places piled the snow into high drifts reminiscent of the dunes I'd seen in the Empty Quarter.

As we hove into sight of the gate midmorning, we passed two long caravans moving toward us and saw another approaching the wall from the west. These we watched with care, but neither Sebitti nor their agents crept forth to challenge us.

"What are those?" I asked of Dabir, and pointed out strange structures clustered just outside the city—ribbed cylinders with small arched doorways half again the height of a man. They looked like no other dwellings I had ever seen, resembling nothing so much as immense overturned beehives. "Do people live in such things?"

"They do, and have," he answered. "For a very, very long time. Adam and Eve might very well have lived in one of those, for they fled here after their expulsion. Harran must have been a rude shock after Eden." Dabir smiled wryly. "To the south is a shrine to Sarah and Ibrahim, who dwelt and worshipped near a spring. As a result, there are many folk who go between the places on pilgrimage, and sight of ascetics and anchorites is common. Also," he added, "there are thieves and beggars who play at being holy men."

"That is no great surprise."

"Sadly."

Harran, I learned, prospered chiefly because it lay along a central trade route, so those portions of the city given over to merchants were well-designed. All the markets were roofed over with wood, forming long corridors filled with stalls. Even in that chill weather folk walked up and down them, looking over goods from many lands. There were rugs for sale, and spices, and weapons, and furniture, and food being served for hungry and thirsty passersby. The scent of cooked sheep set my stomach to grumbling. Dabir bought up a generous portion of lamb to give as a gift to his friend, and then we passed on. A brisk trade was running for robes and blankets in the markets, and folk shouted back and forth about prices that seemed high for such things—of course it is the way of merchants to raise the numbers when goods are in demand. Also there was talk of the strange cold weather. I overheard many wild theories about its cause—including the wrath of Allah, who is merciful—but not a one mentioned snow spirits or ancient bones.

The crowd was thick in places. I saw haughty Persians and garrulous Jews, stuffy Greeks with their guards, and shrewd-eyed Egyptians. There were even some Khazars, swaggering in their high boots, heads topped by furred hats. I watched carefully as we made our way through the city, alert always for men who monitored us too closely. Dabir led the way, the wrapped spear held upright in one hand like a staff, though he did not touch it to the ground. Najya walked behind me. This day she hid her face in a deep robe. Abdul led the escort behind.

Soon we fifteen had passed beyond the merchants' quarter and into an older section of the city. We stabled the horses and stowed some of our gear at an inn, then turned down a winding side street, where Dabir stopped beneath a weathered sign with the image of an open scroll. The shop doors must once have been painted red, but the color had faded almost completely to a dull brown.

Dabir opened one of the doors. While he paused on the threshold for his eyes to adjust, I took the lamb meat from Abdul and told him to post men about the building's exterior. Najya and I then followed Dabir through the doors, in time to hear a rough-edged voice call his name in pleased surprise.

I found myself in a rectangular room stuffed with papyrus and writing utensils and books of all sorts, organized on wall shelves and chests. Dim squares of sunlight shone high on the walls through small, screened windows.

A diminutive, potbellied man in his middle years was coming out from behind a counter, his face bright with a lopsided smile that showed small, well-tended teeth. He and Dabir embraced and exchanged warm greetings, and I thought then to observe him more closely, as Dabir might do. I could not quite guess his lineage. Azeri, perhaps, although he had something of the look of a Kurd as well. His robe was brown with frayed blue trim, worn thin in places, as was his carefully trimmed beard. The man resembled his store—both were somewhat shabby, but well-ordered.

"Why did you not send word of your coming?" Jibril said as they stepped apart.

"There was no time," Dabir replied. "And for that I am sorry. We need your help."

"It will be my pleasure." I think Jibril meant to address me next, but his eyes were drawn to Najya, where they remained. He looked as though he had suddenly found horse droppings in his stew pot.

Dabir introduced her as though untroubled by Jibril's reaction. "This is Najya binta Alimah, daughter of the famed general Delir al Khayr."

Najya pulled down her hood to greet him, and her fine, straight black hair shone as she bowed her head.

"By God and his angels," Jibril said breathlessly. "This is beyond me, Dabir."

I did not know how he could tell anything simply by looking at her, nor, obviously, could Najya, whose face fell.

"This matter is far beyond *me*," Dabir countered. "I need your help."

Jibril shook his head quickly. "There is a woman in Raqqa—"

"I need you, Jibril. We barely reached you alive, even with a full escort of soldiers. We have little time."

Jibril threw up his hands. "This is what you bring me, after all these years?"

"He brought a lamb, also," I said.

Both Jibril and Dabir fixed me with the same peculiar look, and I realized then how foolish I'd sounded.

Two men a little younger than me emerged from a curtained doorway behind the counter. They were taller than Jibril, and a little wider, but strongly resembled him. Gruffly he introduced his sons as they made glad cries to Dabir, who grinned more broadly than I'd seen in days.

I think the sight of his family embracing Dabir so fondly is what finally brought Jibril around, for his frown eased slowly into a wistful smile. "Yes, yes," he said. "We will have time for a visit. Ilias, Dabir has brought us a lamb. See that your wife gets to fixing it, then we can all feast together. But now Dabir and I must talk."

Ilias seemed almost as pleased to lay sight on the lamb as he had Dabir, and took it gratefully. The other brother, Muhsin, clapped Dabir once more upon the shoulders and said he wished his own sons to meet him.

Then Jibril chased them away and tried to look dourly at us. He turned at last to me.

"You must be Captain Asim." Something in the piercing way he considered me reminded me of my friend. "Dabir has told me much of you in his letters."

"I am honored to meet you," I replied.

"I don't know that you should be. Come, though, all of you. Let's see what you've gotten me involved with."

He barred the outer doors, then beckoned us to follow him deeper into the building. We passed through another room of the shop very similar to the first, and then we four were seated in an inner room upon worn but comfortable cushions. Jibril told us this was the chamber where he showed visitors his most valuable items. It smelled, like the rest of the place, of parchment and old stone.

While a young girl poured tea for us, I looked around and was struck by how much it resembled our receiving room in Mosul, complete to cubbyholes with odd sculptures and curiosities and a small, high window in one wall. I grinned over at Dabir. "There is something familiar here," I told him softly.

He nodded distractedly, watching Jibril, who waited impatiently for his granddaughter, or daughter—I was never sure—to depart. He bade her to close the lone door and, once she did so, arched an eyebrow at Dabir, which was somehow both a criticism and an invitation to speak.

Thus Dabir set to telling him all that we'd experienced since Najya had entered our lives. Jibril interrupted often with shrewd questions to improve his understanding. I had seen Dabir politely deferential many times, for a man who did not practice social niceties had no place in court, but with Jibril, he was uncharacteristically hesitant, as if he chose each word with great care. It made him seem younger somehow, and I could well imagine a beardless Dabir reporting other matters in this very room a decade earlier. As Jibril listened, his expressions drifted from curiosity to horror to astonishment and back again, though at no point did he offer suggestion or interpretation. Occasionally he asked a question of me, and he asked a number of Najya concerning her interactions with Koury and Gazi, though I learned nothing new from what she said.

Najya sat stiff-backed upon the cushion provided her, at my right hand, and strove mightily to look self-possessed. She did not entirely succeed, for she had pinned great hopes upon this man and eagerness was writ upon her manner. Dabir mentioned for the first time in front of her his worries that a spirit had been bonded to her and she stiffened further as her eyes narrowed above her veil.

When Dabir finished at last, Jibril reached up and stroked his beard.

There were two white lines in that field of black, and it was these through which he dragged his fingers.

"You do not look as surprised as I expected," Dabir told him.

"Oh, I am surprised," Jibril said. "I assure you. How could I not be?"

"I'd have thought you'd be as startled I'd met actual Sebitti as you would if I'd talked with an angel."

"Not as much," Jibril said cryptically.

"Can you help her?" I interrupted.

"I suppose I will have to try," Jibril said soberly. "But her farr troubles, me. I am not sure I have the strength to aid her. And I am a little out of practice."

"I would be very grateful," Najya emphasized.

Jibril favored her with a tight smile and bowed his head.

"What do you mean by 'farr'?" I asked.

"All living creatures have farr," Jibril said brusquely, but went on. "It is a kind of energy that extends around them. Only a few have the ability to see it. Most are holy men." He flashed a lopsided smile. "Others, like me, are simply cursed with the sight from birth."

"Do not say that," Dabir told him quietly.

Najya addressed him in a tense whisper. "What did you see? About me? In my farr?"

"I am no great seer." Jabril waved away the question.

"None of us see farr at all," Dabir reminded him soberly. "What is it you saw?"

Jibril shifted uncomfortably. "The way a farr looks varies, depending upon the emotions, physical health, even the sensitivity to the spirit world."

"And what of mine?" Najya asked, so forcefully it sounded more command than request.

"Yours is strong. Very strong." Jibril cleared his throat. "But with something dark fluttering at its edge. And there is something else. I am not sure how to explain the matter." He paused to gather his thoughts. "It is like a rip in the world that follows in your wake."

"A rip?" Najya repeated, incredulous.

"Yes," Jibril said quickly, "a tear, I think, between our world and that of some other realm. I've seen something like it, once, but it was fixed at the site of an old battlefield. Yours moves. It's a wonder to me none of you can sense it."

"I have sensed it," Najya confirmed bitterly. "But I did not know what to think. For a long while I have felt as though something else has been trying to seize hold of me, or that it watches from inside me. I was afraid I was going mad, on top of everything else."

"Perhaps we should have discussed the spirit's presence sooner," Dabir offered, sensing her consternation, "but I did not want to worry you unnecessarily and I could not be certain until Jibril's reaction confirmed my fears."

She nodded once, shortly. "That was . . . kind of you. However." Her eyes flicked briefly to touch my own, and they were steely. "I wish you to conceal nothing further. I wish to know everything, no matter how bad."

Dabir bowed his head to her.

"This may get much worse," Jibril warned.

Najya laughed shortly, without humor. "I have seen my husband's heart torn from his body, been taken by wizards, and played unwilling host to a vengeful spirit. I do not think it can get much worse."

"It could get worse," Jibril said, his look steady and ominous. He did not explain further, and no one asked for details, not even Najya.

She did have another question, though. "Why did they pick me?"

"Because your farr is very strong," Jibril answered. "You already have a close connection to the spirit world. It is even greater than my own," he admitted.

"But I cannot see farr."

"Nevertheless. I suppose that your strength and openness to certain energies make you suitable for the magics they performed. Now. Let me draw up a circle and I will see about severing the spirit's connection with you."

"What of the spear?" Dabir asked.

Jibril glanced over to where the weapon stood, still wrapped in its leathers, in a corner.

"First we will see to the woman. Now get up. I want you to move the cushions and roll up the carpets. This room will work as well as any. I shall be back shortly."

So saying, he departed, and Dabir and Najya and I set to work. The other two seemed uninclined to speech, and I was not sure what to say. For all the tension in the air, speaking of it felt like a trip cord to set off what would surely be a painful trap.

Thankfully, it was not long before the older scholar returned, bearing a wicker basket, from which he pulled forth a heavily weathered, leather-bound book. In a clipped, precise manner he commanded Dabir to draw out a circle four paces across, with an inner circle a foot from its edge. My friend stepped immediately over to the basket, withdrew some chalk, and set to work. Jibril joined Dabir, scribbling strange symbols and signs in the space between the circles, all the time consulting the old book.

Najya watched all, pensively, and I studied her, trying to decide if the guilt I felt was truly earned. I had held off from confirming her suspicions that night I'd dueled her both because Dabir seemed unwilling to discuss it, and because I had not wished to have her alarm the men. Surely it had been the proper course. Yet now I think she felt more alone than ever. I found myself sidling closer, and before I knew what I meant to say, I spoke to her. "I am sorry."

In a flash those brown eyes were upon my own, searching critically. I felt uncharacteristically small. Yet she did not speak, and once more I found myself floundering. "You were already upset that night, when you told me you were afraid something else was trying to control you. I did not want"—I cleared my throat—"I did not want you to feel worse."

"I understand," she said, and returned to watching Dabir and Jibril work with the chalk. Something in her posture loosened a little. "Do you think he can do it?" she asked quietly.

It took me a moment to follow the trail of her thought. "Jibril seems very wise," I told her. "And I have never known Dabir to fail where it really counts. He will not relent until he finds a solution."

She nodded but did not speak.

I knew not what else to say. I wondered about the soldiers outside, but reasoned that they needed no further instruction. Thus I remained with her.

Once Dabir was done drawing, he offered to hold the book Jibril kept peering at, but the older man told him everything within was coded. "Better that no one else knows its contents," he added. "I have peered a little further than a man should, and God and the angels may find me wanting."

Dabir withdrew to watch with folded arms as his mentor worked his way around the circle. It was another few minutes before he was complete, and then another longer while as Jibril meticulously inspected every inch. "It must be exact," he said, almost to himself. "Exact." He bent down and thickened a line beside a letter that resembled a snake swallowing a tree branch. Finally, after what was probably another quarter hour, he stepped back. "I think we are ready. Najya, I will need you to sit in this circle."

She inclined her head and moved to comply. I handed her a cushion to sit on as she stepped into the circle's midst. She set it down, then lowered herself with serene poise.

"Do not be frightened," Jibril instructed. "You may see magics, but you will not be harmed so long as you remain seated. Whatever you do, you must not cross the circle, or touch its edge."

"I understand." From her bold answer you might have thought that she had sat a hundred times in such circles, and was daily witness to the work of sorcerers.

Once more the door opened; this time it was Jibril's elder son, Muhsin, bearing a small, steaming bucket. The coppery tang of blood thickened the air. The young man's lips turned down disapprovingly as he placed the bucket beside his father.

"And you used the proper blade?" Jibril asked.

"Just as you said," Muhsin whispered.

"Good. Now leave the room. Do not enter until I emerge, regardless of what you hear."

The man bestowed a dark look upon us. "May Allah and all the angels shine down upon you," he said, then left. It was a blessing I had not heard before and I thought it peculiar.

"Let us be on with this," Jibril said. "The blood cannot cool."

"What manner of blood is it?" I asked, uneasy lest I receive the wrong answer.

"Goat's blood. Slain only moments ago with a special knife." Jibril paused only briefly to reach once more into the wicker basket. From it he produced an amulet on a silver chain, then hung it from his neck. Mostly it was black, as wide as a girl's fist and inscribed with a silver hexagon set with a small crystal in each of its five corners.

"You two," he said to us as he reached down for the bucket, "must stand back. If the spirit gets loose, it will likely come for the closest of us. And you don't have amulets."

I would have asked him what the amulet was for, but he was already cradling the bucket and carefully tilting its mouth forward with one hand as he bent toward the lines upon the stone. Blood spattered down upon the symbols etched between the circles as Jabril moved to each of them in turn.

Najya watched the grisly rain of liquid without seeming concern. When Jibril finished his circuit both circles and every symbol between them flared with ruby light, stretching upward half the length of a sword. Najya started but kept her seat and her fixed composure.

Jibril lowered his knees to the stone floor, his face upturned with closed eyes, and uttered strange syllables.

Dabir moved over to me. "Do not disrupt him," he said quietly, "in the midst of spell work. Even if there are more surprises."

"What sort of surprises?"

My curiosity was sated before he could answer, for Najya gasped and threw back her head, her back arching. Her face twitched and shook as though she were in pain.

I knew better than to cross the circle, but my desire to do so must have been communicated by my stance, for Dabir tightly grasped my arm. "Do nothing," he cautioned. "Entering the circle is liable to kill you and put all of us at risk."

"What is happening?" I asked.

"I believe the spirit is fighting to retain its hold."

Najya moaned, then let out a longer, higher sound that rose suddenly into a keening cry.

Jibril still chanted.

"It's working, isn't it?" I hoped aloud.

Najya's voice stilled and she raised her head, eyes glowing blue as the flame's center. Her teeth were gritted as she climbed shakily to her feet and put one foot toward the circle's edge. It was a small space—it took but one more step before she was beside it.

"Do not cross it!" I called out.

"That's not Najya," Dabir told me, which I had guessed.

Jibril's chanting intensified.

She raised one hand, then the other, and thrust them before her. The sorcerous circuit's light rose to meet her palms, a glowing, transparent wall. She pushed forward. The energy crackled about her fingers.

I turned to Dabir. "Is this supposed to happen? What should we do?"

Dabir's frown deepened and he cast a troubled look to his old mentor, rocking back and forth, still chanting. "We must trust Jibril."

As Najya—or, rather, the spirit within her—braced with more strength against the wall, the circle's lights brightened, until the whole room seemed aflame, from cubbyholes to furnishings to slatted windows. Her brow wrinkled with effort, and the cold light within her eyes blazed fiercely.

The barrier flared dazzlingly, flickered, and suddenly Najya staggered through, wrapped in red sorcerous energy, like lightning caught on the horns of cattle.

Jibril scrambled out of the way. Najya screamed, then sank to the floor with all the grace of an empty vegetable sack. The sorcerous energy around her vanished as suddenly as it had begun. She sat limply, head drooping, utterly spent.

I grew conscious then that Dabir had been gripping my arm for a long while—and that Jibril was covered in sweat.

"God and his angels!" Jibril breathed. His eyes were wide.

"Is she all right?" I asked.

Jibril did not answer.

So I hurried to Najya, who looked up at me with sad, tired eyes. Tentatively I smiled. "Najya? Did it work?"

"Work?" Jibril repeated from behind. "No, it didn't work! The spirit broke the barrier! A working barrier! It's beyond belief!"

"Then what is to be done?" I demanded.

"First we must get her someplace to rest," Dabir suggested. When I asked her if she wished aid to stand, Najya shook her head no, then tripped into me as she tried to rise. She was wobbly as a newborn colt, and I swept her into my arms with little complaint. Allah, but she was cold. I wanted then to brush her hair and reassure her that all would be well, which was a mad thing, and improper.

Dabir and I followed Jibril, who led us into the back rooms of his house, and Najya settled with her head against my chest. It was then that I felt a yearning ache within my breast, long absent, like unto hunger. Something changed then in the way that she looked up at me. I could not see through her veil in that dark hall, but her eyes gentled, and I knew that she returned my smile.

More than four years had passed since my first wife's death, may peace be hers, and a little more than three since I had divorced my second, the she devil. I was not unacquainted with the ways of women. Yet I was a stranger to the strength of passion that crept up to me on that moment, and it left me shaken. All unconsidered, Najya had lit embers in the darkened chambers of my heart, and of a sudden they blazed to a brilliance that blinded me.

7

With reluctance I set Najya down in a back room, attended by a sweet young woman with a prominent forehead mole. This was apparently one of Jibril's daughters-in-law, and she promised she would see to Najya's comforts.

I did not truly wish to depart, and I think by Najya's look that she did not desire to be left, yet I followed Dabir and Jibril, my head still spinning. It was as though a spell had been laid, for I could not stop thinking of her eyes and her long dark hair. I scarcely noticed even the scent of roasting lamb rising from somewhere nearby, despite that I had not eaten since morning.

"Jibril," Dabir said as we wound our way back toward the front of the house, "where is Afya?"

Jibril turned at the curtained entrance to the storefront, his mouth a grim line.

"Who is Afya?" I asked.

I came to a halt behind Dabir, whose hand tightened on the spear haft as he leaned up on it. "His wife. She would have come the moment she heard I was here. And she surely would have taken charge the moment she heard of Najya's distress."

Jibril paused with his hand upon the brown curtain fabric. Several times he opened his mouth to speak, but he seemed stricken.

"Oh." Dabir sounded as though he had been struck. "Jibril, I'm so sorry. Please tell me . . ."

"She is dead these three years," Jibril said in a tight voice, and pushed through the curtain.

Dabir's voice was strained as he followed his mentor into the room. "Why did you not mention this in your letters?"

"Your news was so good," Jibril answered gruffly. "And I could not bear . . ." He mastered himself and faced us. "That is not important now. We need to talk about the young lady."

Dabir's desire to learn more about Afya's death was a palpable force, writ not only in his face but in his carriage, yet he did not press for details. This was unlike him, and a sure measure of the high regard in which he held Jibril. I had grown curious myself to learn why she was so important to him. But then the older man said something that seized the whole of my attention.

"I do not think I can save Najya."

Ah, I have taken sword strokes that troubled me less.

"I don't know how she has kept the spirit at bay for so long. She must have tremendous strength."

"Or the spirit's strength is growing," Dabir ventured.

"Is there no way to get rid of it?" I asked. "No greater magic?"

"There may be." Jibril sounded doubtful. "I can give her this amulet." He touched the thing that he still wore about his neck. "I fashioned it to protect the wearer from the influence of spirits and it saved my life once. It may be enough to protect her from the thing's control, for a little while at least." He trailed off and led the way deeper into the rambling house, where we sat down, at last, to eat. Troubled as I was, I scarcely recall any details. Our host's family was kind and gracious, but Jibril, Dabir, and myself were hard put to speak, each for our own reasons. I believe Dabir modestly answered admiring inquiries and politely asked after each relative.

Once we were finished, Dabir and I joined the men of the family for afternoon prayers. Then Jibril rather curtly suggested it was time to look at the spear Dabir had brought with him from room to room, and so we carried it once more to the front of the house, where Dabir set it on the shop's counter.

He unwrapped the weapon, and Jibril ran his hands over the old, old bone and its figures, flinching a little as he did so. He confirmed that a symbol Dabir had seen was that for the Sebbiti known as Erragal. It looked like nothing but a squiggle to me until Dabir said it was a flame within a cave, at which point I recognized the pattern, as though I had been staring at the stars before being told by my father of the pictures they made.

Dabir pointed at the mark. "Does it mean Erragal made the spear, or that the makers revered him?"

"I cannot say." Jibril sounded tired. "But the weapon retains an immense amount of magical energy for something crafted an eon ago. It fairly vibrates with power."

"Can you siphon it off?" Dabir asked. "Or break it?"

Jibril considered this for a long moment before answering. "It is like looking at a well-locked door. Perhaps if I study it longer." He nodded. "It might be possible, although . . ." He looked glum. "I've never seen anything this strong. Never."

"Strong how?" Dabir prodded.

"Oh . . . I don't know. It's hard to explain." He sighed.

"Try."

"Say that you are on a ridge at night and see a campfire in the distance. That is what it is like to hold most items touched with magic. Now say you are on that ridge looking into the sun when it rises. That is this spear—but only when you touch it. Most of its magic is concealed somehow, probably by the same spell that locks off access to it."

"You say that it is powerful," I said, wanting more useful information. "Can we use it to force the wizards to undo Najya's curse?"

"Not exactly," Jibril said.

I frowned. "What is it good for, then?"

"What is it good for?" Jibril repeated. "Well. Magic might make this weapon very sharp, or accurate, if the right word is whispered. Or, it might be like a magical storehouse. The use of magic drains life, for magic creates, and you cannot create without destruction, lest you be God. Wizards sometimes store their power so that they can call upon it at need to cast their spells. It is like keeping a flame handy in case you need to set something on fire."

"A peculiar analogy," Dabir mused.

"You say that Najya senses other devices such as this?" Jibril asked.

"Three more," Dabir answered.

Jibril slowly rubbed his hand through his beard, then stared down at his fingers.

"Jibril," Dabir began, "you had me read the Persica of Heracleides. Do you remember?"

"Yes," Jibril said slowly. He still contemplated his fingertips.

"Heracleides mentioned some legends of early kings, but didn't discuss them in detail. He suggested both Staphylus and Ocnus as sources. You didn't have any Staphylus, and you said Ocnus was dreadful."

"Your memory's better than mine," Jibril said, "though you're right about Ocnus."

"Would that I had the memory of my best pupil, who forgets nothing once she has read it, down to the placement of words upon the page."

This, I knew, was Sabirah. Yet my friend was not long distracted by thoughts of her. He instead was like a leopard straining at the leash, a sentiment I shared. We needed answers, and we needed them now, so that we might act.

"Do you have the Ocnus texts?" Dabir asked.

"No one's ever bought them. Why do you want them?"

"I seek information about the time when Greeks said the Titans roamed the earth."

"What are Titans?" I asked.

Dabir briefly faced me. "Great manlike giants."

Jibril frowned speculatively. "Ocnus said the old Medes fought back strange monsters and spirits that had ruled the wastes since God fashioned the world. They chased men from their villages and hunted them in the snows, like beasts."

I brightened. "That sounds like the vision I had when I touched the spear!"

"We can look at him, but I don't know how much good he will be," Jibril warned. "He mentioned that in brief and then went on for a page or two with different spellings other historians had for the names of the monsters, and why his were best."

Jibril then beckoned us to follow. I knew firsthand how long it took scholars to find things, so I asked if I might bring groups of the men in to rest, warm themselves, and to eat, and Jibril distractedly said his home was ours. I then spoke to Abdul and arranged for him to allow the men inside in groups of three—we set three men watching from the second floor of the home, three from the alley, and three in front, with one from each group to come inside to relax in shifts. Also I spoke with Ilias and Muhsin about keeping their families inside while we were here. I did not tell them about a shape-changing assassin, but I did emphasize that we had enemies. Muhsin was none too pleased with this news and said little in response. By contrast, toothy Ilias seemed excited about the whole thing, pressing for details I could not provide. He arranged for food to be brought to the soldiers in the front room, and I made sure to hand over generous compensation for the humble fare.

Once everything was arranged, I went to look in on Najya, thoroughly unsure what I might say to her. I was so lost in thought I nearly ran into the woman I now knew for Muhsin's wife walking on tiptoes from the room. She told me the Persian woman was sleeping. Disappointed, but a little relieved, I decided not to intrude, and resigned myself to joining the scholars.

The whole place was like a library, stuffed with old things. Shelves were built into walls, and chests upon chests were stacked one upon another in hallways, each with labels denoting contents. Many of these labels were quite faded, so that I wondered if they had been written by Jibril's father, or grandfather, or some other more remote relative.

The layout was somewhat confused, so I had to ask directions from a young girl, who led me by the hand to a shelf. She did not speak, but pointed to an unused lantern set there. I took it, then she grasped my right hand once more and guided me to a narrow arched opening.

It was only when I beheld the steps beyond that I realized just how old the house must truly be. The stone centers were worn smooth and depressed from the passage of many feet over countless years. The little girl seemed uninclined to venture further, so I lit the lantern and waved farewell. Descending into that place felt much like venturing into a crypt until my light fell upon what lay beyond.

I had arrived in a cavernous space supported every few feet by rough pillars of earth and stone. Between each pillar were shelves, and each was stacked with mounds of scrolls. Upon a few of the shelves were paper labels in handwriting too faint for me to make out. If I had thought the scent of parchment and old stone was strong above, it was only because I had never known this place.

Two lanterns glowed dimly ahead of me, and as I walked forward I saw a scholar sitting near each one with a stack of scrolls and tablets.

I cleared my throat to announce myself, shifting uneasily, for the darkness could conceal too many things. "Is there any other way in?" I asked.

Both men looked up. Jibril answered. "There is an old, sealed exit, in the north wall."

"But it is secure?"

"It should be," Jibril said carelessly.

Clearly he was no more martial than Dabir. "I shall check it."

Finding that door was no easy matter. I passed case after case crossed by thick boards. Many of them held rows of clay tablets the size of platters. As the light from my lantern spilled over them I realized that they were covered with the peculiar symbols and scratches I had seen upon other old stones.

The door was almost completely hidden by a big pile of discarded wood and broken shelving, which did a fine job of barricading, but also rendered the backup exit nearly useless. The beam holding it closed felt secure to me, so I returned to find Dabir and Jibril sitting together on the stone floor, poring over a set of tablets. I passed over the lantern so that they might have better light to read by.

I sank down on the cold floor and my mind turned over many things while the two of them searched. I wondered first and foremost whether Najya could be freed from the spirit, but found that speculation profitless and frustrating, as there was so little I could do. So instead I turned to wondering what it would be like to have her in my home. I had fully expected to marry again someday, but had never really considered what that would be like in Mosul, where my duty was to guard Dabir. Would we have to maintain two households if I took a wife? If not, would we have to retain Buthayna, or might Najya do the cooking? She probably had servants to do such things for her. What sort of life could I offer?

Occasionally I heard voices from above, and thought each time that someone might come down to say Najya had requested us.

No one ever did. Closer at hand was only the occasional clatter of clay tablets as Dabir and Jibril shifted them, or sometimes a thoughtful or irritated grunt from one or the other as they read.

Time crawled in that place, and when a man has no answers to his worries, it is easy to brood. Some devil came to me and tortured me with fears; whether a Persian noblewoman would think a soldier beneath her, no matter how highly regarded I was by the caliph, and what her family might say to such a pairing even if I did not imagine the look in her eyes. Then I woke to the fact that these thoughts, too, were pointless, because none of us were likely to last the week. We had only survived the last Sebitti attack because the spirit had fought with us. If it turned against us, or if the Sebitti attacked in greater force, we were probably doomed, and the best I could hope for would be to go down fighting.

And then—and I knew later that it must have been an hour or more after I had descended—Dabir suddenly called Jibril to him. His voice was thick with concern.

Jibril rose and hurried over. Dabir handed a tablet up.

I came closer myself, though there was nothing I could learn even reading over the crouching scholar's shoulder, for the words they studied were wedges and squiggles and the like, all tightly jammed together.

I watched Jibril's gnarled finger trace over the antique symbols etched into the stone. I saw his mouth open in surprise and heard the breath catch in his throat.

"I have not misunderstood, have I?" Dabir's voice was taut as he asked the question.

"What is it?" I asked.

Dabir and Jibril chattered back and forth about the meaning of certain words on the tablet, and I grew impatient, for no one had explained a thing.

"What is it?" I demanded once I had lost almost all patience. "What does that old stone say?"

Dabir finally took pity upon me. "It is the account from an Assyrian scribe, foretelling that one day the ice will creep down from the mountains and the northlands."

"'And the trees will be brought low with snow,'" Jibril read slowly, sounding like an imam intoning words from the book-to-be-read, "'and the desert sands will once more know the touch of frost. Over them shall drift the women who chill the blood of men, and after them will come the mountain hordes and the beasts from beyond the gates . . .'" Jibril's voice faltered, and he glanced up at Dabir. "It may mean beyond the door, or the pass. It is hard to be sure."

I thought of the door to the spirit realm he said was attached to Najya, and the snow women she had already summoned. "Speak on," I said, my throat dry.

"This writer makes mention of the flood," Jibril said, "though he speaks not of Nuh, but of Utnapishtim, and God's promise that he would never again destroy the earth with water."

"Why does he speak of the flood?" I asked.

"Because he speaks of the world's end," Dabir explained. "The Khazars believe that the world will end not in fire, but—"

"—in ice," Dabir and Jibril finished as one.

"So . . ." I hesitated. "The Assyrian was talking about what had happened?"

"No," Dabir said. "He predicts what *will* happen. What is happening. Right now. I may," he added reluctantly, "owe Shabouh an apology. The scribe also writes about the positions of planets in the giant's constellation, Al-Jabbar."

That provided me no comfort, and I doubted Shabouh would be especially pleased either. While I struggled to absorb that, Dabir looked up at Jibril. "I have found nothing about the bones, though," he said.

"I have. Give me a moment." Jibril handed back the tablet and carried the lantern to the place he'd been sitting some fifteen paces distant. He returned with a worn piece of parchment wrapped about a dark wood rod. Both men knelt down again by the lantern as Jibril unrolled it. I peered over their shoulders and saw this time that the text was in Greek, which I recognized but could not understand.

"Ocnus," Jibril said. "And he's just as long-winded as I remember. But look here." He tapped a little picture drawn at the top of the page, a bearded head with a crown. A similar image appeared near each corner. "These are the five kings of men who fought the old ones. They discovered that fire and weapons fashioned from bones of their enemies worked best against these Titans." He paused, then read with flair: "'Most useful of all were the weapons carefully fashioned from the bones of their awful enemies, as you may remember that I described previously . . .'" Here Jibril paused. "I'm going to skip ahead," he told us, "because Ocnus goes on a bit about how important it is to cite you sources. Here we are. 'Their enemies were sorcerous enemies that would drink the blood of men if they wished, and they wished often to do so, which was very frightening, and many people were slain by them over many years, and much blood was spilled.'" Jibril glanced up briefly. "I told you he was bad," he said, then returned to reading the text aloud. "'When the monsters and spirits drank of the blood they took form, and awful magic gathered within, with which heroes could, after delivering death, thus fashion weapons to defeat their source and thereby to bring hurt to those without form.'"

Dabir read aloud from the manuscript. "'And thus did Bilgames turn the old ones back, and destroy them all.' Ocnus doesn't say how."

"By stabbing them with the spear?" I asked. "Does he say what the other weapons are?"

"No. He's long-winded on the most insignificant matters," Jibril said, "then glosses over the important points. But I have been reading Ocnus for the better part of two hours. The gist is that in a time of great snow and ice, strange beings that hunted men could take physical form when they took on matter from our plane of existence, and they liked blood. Five weapons were fashioned from the body of the most savage of all the spirits, and its life force was divided among them. They had planned for six, but not all of the spirit's energy could be trapped."

"Jibril." Dabir looked pensive. "The part that couldn't be trapped—would that survive?"

"It would depend upon the strength of the spirit," Jibril said. "Probably not, but . . . you're thinking that's what the Sebitti put in Najya?"

"I but speculate. Still, it would explain why she is sensitive to the bones, wouldn't it? Because they contained part of her own life force?"

Jibril looked stunned.

Dabir, though, was still thinking aloud. "The Sebitti surely knew of the prophecy the Assyrian mentions. They knew that the ice would come again, and that the weapons would be needed to fight the spirits."

Jibril assented with a quick nod. "Surely. Anzu and Koury are supposed to have worked with the Assyrians. They had to have known. They might even have been the ones who told the scribe who wrote this."

"What if," Dabir said slowly, "they're gathering these weapons to drive back the winter?"

Jibril's eyebrows rose in alarm.

"Wait a moment," I said. "You're saying the Sebitti are trying to *help* us? That they mean to find these bones to fight the spirits?" We had been ordered to locate and kill Tarif's murderers, not cooperate with them.

"I am just suggesting it."

"Please tell me," I said to Dabir, "you don't mean to turn Najya and this spear over to them."

"No, but we could ask them what they intend, if we could find a way to negotiate from a position of strength."

"That would be mad!" Jibril said sharply. "They cannot be trusted. Do not forget they were said to be the scythe to the grain, harvesters of men when the god of the underworld grew angry." His words were laced with venom. "The Sebitti cannot be reasoned with, cannot be negotiated with. They will lie, then take what they want!" Jibril swore then, rather foully.

Our discussion seemed to have unsettled the older man. By contrast, Dabir was strangely calm. He studied Jibril. His voice was very quiet. "You have spoken with them."

After a long, long moment, Jibril bobbed his head in assent.

"How long ago?"

"About three years."

"Jibril." Dabir now addressed him very slowly. "Did they have something to do with Afya's death?"

Jibril raised his head and shook it, as though he were in pain.

"What happened?" There was naked concern in Dabir's voice.

For a long moment, Jibril said nothing, and when he finally mustered the strength to speak, his voice was but a whisper. "There was nothing anyone could do for her. She was wasting away." He glanced up at me, then over to Dabir. "Always before I had used magic only to break things. To help people. I thought, this once, I might use it to help my family. Just this once."

Dabir would not relent. "And?"

"I . . . made bargains, and learned how to summon them. I called upon Lamashtu, mistress of life and death. And she came. Allah forgive me, but she came." He shook his head. "She swore she would save Afya."

"What did she do?"

But this question Jibril would not answer. He only shook his head. "And so she died, and I put away my books, and tools. I should have burned them."

"I am glad you have not," Dabir said.

Jibril's eyes gleamed wetly, and it seemed that he had aged a dozen years.

I felt for the fellow, but it was not my place to offer solace, and I did not think he desired it. "So what do we do?" I asked.

I think Dabir was grateful for the change in subject. He tapped his ring thrice, then cleared his throat. "Let us review what we know. A great winter has come, one predicted by the ancients. The Sebitti are working with a Greek sorceress to summon a spirit to find ancient weapons, which were fashioned to fight spirits that arrived with just such a winter. The weapons seem to be the only thing, apart from fire, that could turn them back, but they are also repositories of magical energy which might be tapped by any mage who knows how to unlock them. If I understand you correctly." Dabir looked to Jibril.

"You do." Jabril straightened a little. "And I'll tell you what must be done. We must track down the rest of these weapons and keep them from the Sebitti."

"You must be joking," I said.

"He may be right. If the spirit inside Najya is trying to claim its lost energy, we might free her by finding and banishing the magics in each of these bones. If it can't claim them in this world, it has no reason to remain in Najya's body."

This was the first hopeful news I'd heard. "But how will we find them?" I asked.

"Najya will lead us," Dabir answered. "She can sense their location, remember?"

"But what of her?" I asked. "What about this woman in Raqqa that Jibril mentioned? Shouldn't we go to her and see if she can remove the spirit?"

"This is beyond even her, I'm afraid," Jibril said. "And Dabir's reasoning is sound. If a spirit has no reason to remain, it is far easier to dispel. This may well bring a halt to the winter, and it will surely frustrate the Sebitti." His jaw set with determination. "I will go with you."

Dabir's eyes widened in surprise.

"You need me," he continued. "There is no one alive who knows more about the Sebitti."

"I cannot take you from your family. The odds against us are high. And you hate to travel! When's the last time you left Harran?"

"None of that matters now," Jibril said bluntly. "What good shall I be to my family if the world is frozen over? I will go with you. I am not so old, yet, that I am a burden. Besides, who else can unlock the power of the spear and the other weapons?"

I thought to hear Dabir remonstrate. But after a time he said only, "I shall be glad to have you."

8

When we left Harran the next morning Najya wore Jibril's trinket prominently. Dabir had spoken alone with her at length, after the evening meal with Jibril's family, and he told me that it had gone about as well as might be expected. I did not know what Najya thought, for she remained disinclined to answer any questions I put to her with more than a yes or no.

The wind shrilled and moaned as our horses plodded north across the plain toward the Taurus Mountains, where Najya said we must go to find the nearest bone. She said that it felt a little closer to Harran than Mosul had been from Isfahan, when she'd heard the call of the spear, and Dabir had calculated the rest. Najya insisted that she only sensed four weapons, including the spear, no matter that the accounts claimed five, and Dabir speculated that something had been destroyed in the intervening millennia.

"I suppose it is a wonder," he said, "that four survive after so long."

We two rode just behind Kharouf and far-eyed Ishaq, our vanguard that day. I glanced back to see Jibril riding at Najya's side, trying, in vain I think, to draw her out.

"At each stage," I said to my friend, "news grows worse for her."

"I worry there will not be good news for any of us for a long while," Dabir confessed. "I cannot help thinking the Sebitti are watching, or waiting."

"For what?"

"Perhaps they want us to find the weapons, then will move against us."

I grunted. "To let us do their work."

"Yes."

"We shall find out, in time."

I heard Jibril chuckle behind me and glanced back to see Najya gesturing to him, as if in midspeech.

"Jibril has her talking," I said.

"Good," he replied, then added quietly, "I am worried about him."

"Why?"

"Because he's not telling us everything."

"He does not wish to speak of his wife's death," I said. This, at least, was no great mystery.

"There is more to it than that." Dabir relented with a sigh. "But you are partly right. They were very close."

"I could tell that. My mother would screw up her face like that, sometimes, when she spoke of my father."

"Afya was very kind." He smiled wistfully. "Even when she scolded and he grumped, they were playful about it, and often I saw them holding hands, or touching a shoulder. His bitterness is new," he finished. "But I suppose losing the love of your life might make you bitter."

The way that his voice trailed off, it was easy to see where his own thoughts led, and I could not help rolling my eyes a bit. "Allah preserve me," I said. "You're not going to start brooding again, are you?"

He flashed a sad half smile. I thought I would point out the obvious, something that someone so intelligent should surely have noticed. "Sabirah is happy now, and has a child."

Dabir objected. "We know that she has a child. We do not know that she is happy." He fell silent for a moment, and then his words came sharp and swift. "I think I should have asked for her hand, Asim."

I could only stare.

He sounded defensive as he explained. "The caliph would have given me anything that day."

"Ai-ah! Jaffar would have been your enemy from that moment forward!"

"I am not sure that's very different now," he said quietly. "I was guilty, that day, of not thinking with my heart."

"And with good reason! Would not she have been shamed to have been pulled from her bridal bed? Would not you have ruined Jaffar's plan to marry her to that merchant family? And what would the merchant's family have said, to have the alliance with Jaffar's family dashed? Two of the caliphate's most powerful families would have been after your head!"

"I suppose," he said, "that you are right."

"No, you were right. I'm just reminding you."

He fell silent then, and perhaps because of the subject, my thoughts went to Najya, for it had occurred to me that she might be as lost to me as Sabirah was to my friend.

Something of my feelings must have shown on my face, for Dabir commented, "Here I am wearing a track into the same worthless ground while my friend is weighted with a heavy load." He added sadly, "I don't suppose it would have helped if I'd warned you not to grow attached to her."

Of course, he'd guessed it all. "I doubt it," I admitted. I stared into the distance, lest my longing be fully evident upon my face. "She is a woman such as I have never known, Dabir. I do not intend to fail her."

Dabir followed my gaze, beyond the dull white gray haze that was the horizon. "I shall do everything in my power to save her," he promised. I wished that he might tell me all would surely be well, but it was not Dabir's way to mislead his friends. I dared not ask him what he thought her chances were of surviving the whole of it, for I saw the truth in his eyes.

"Perhaps," Dabir said, "you've noticed the way Jibril and his family speak of angels."

He sought to distract me by changing the subject. It was none too subtle, but I was grateful anyway. "I had," I replied. "Why do they do that?"

"They are Sabians."

Now there were some Sabians living in Mosul, but most of them had fair hair. I knew little of them, other than that they were people of the book to whom prophets had come, like Jews and Christians. Yet I was still puzzled. "He prays five times each day, with us."

"Yes, that is the way of Sabians. They revere Allah and all his prophets, but they feel that there are other wise traditions to follow God. Many of them live in Harran, and are especially interested in angels. They think one dwells in each star, and that the truly virtuous may be reborn as angels when they die, to assist Allah's works."

"That is strange."

Dabir laughed shortly. "Yes. But so must many teachings seem to those who do not grow up among them."

I pondered that briefly, then strove unsuccessfully to think only of more hopeful matters.

Though we journeyed along another major caravan trail, we passed no living men in the hours after dawn, only three wandering horses. Disquietingly, they were saddled and trailing their reins. We gathered the animals and led them after us. The soldiers wondered whether the mounts had fled during a bandit attack, and I think they longed for action like me; they desired an opponent they could face and defeat and tired of the fruitless travel through the cold.

Just after midday prayers we saw a small village across the vast plain of white, and our horses picked up their pace, thinking that rest and food lay just before them.

Yet as we drew closer Dabir grew tense and shifted in his saddle. "Asim," he said, "do you see any smoke from that village?"

He was right. There should have been cooking fires, at the very least. Yet from the dozens of huts and outbuildings I saw nothing. "Nay," I told him. "Perhaps they conserve their fuel. It cannot be easily had in this place."

"Perhaps."

I knew better than to ignore a warning from Dabir, so I put the men on alert.

As we drew closer we saw that the village was oddly empty. No urchins threw snowballs. No children ran to the animal sheds for chores. No one was walking back and forth between the buildings. The wind alone moved in that place, moaning softly. Finally, though, we heard the whinny of horses calling to ours. I thought for just a moment all might be well, and then we discovered nine men and women lying in the road just beyond the last hut, as though they'd been overcome by cold during an attempt to flee. Each was covered separately in their own sheet of ice.

The soldiers muttered and made the sign against the evil eye, as you might expect, but I ordered them silent.

"What could have done this?" Kharouf asked me quietly. His left arm was still held before him in a sling, like a bird wing.

I could but shake my head. I doubted that there was some ordinary explanation.

We carefully picked our way around the bodies, peering alertly toward the shuttered windows and sealed doors, as if some earthly enemy lingered in wait. I raised my voice, calling out to any who might be in earshot.

After my second call I held up a hand, for I had heard the faint whisper of voices. "Hold," I ordered.

Over the snuffle of our own horses and the lonely wind I now perceived the low chant of a woman, though I could not make out her words. There was an answering mutter from male voices. I motioned Abdul to split our forces so that we might come to the square from three directions. This was swiftly accomplished, and as two groups of four trotted to approach from the flanks, I led the way forward, steel bared.

The narrow street broadened into a wide square centered about an old well. Its stones glistened with ice dusted over with snow, which would have looked almost charming had there not been three men frozen in upright slabs just to the right. Two were half turned, as if they had begun to run in the moment before death. The third had been caught flat-footed and stared out at us now through a dagger's length of ice, his eyes wide, his mouth gaping in terror.

To the left of these grisly monuments a half-dozen impatient horses were picketed—four saddled, two laden—and they whinnied again to our animals and pricked up their ears eagerly. More striking than all of this were the three living men kneeling on prayer rugs in front of a tableau of frozen corpses, and the woman before them chanting words in a language I did not know. The men echoed her. All were Khazars, the men in heavy furs and thick hats, armed with curved swords. The woman was small and thickly set. She was garbed in a bulky robe fashioned of gray furs, and her boots were adorned with bands hung with small iron animals.

As she fell silent, the Khazars looked up at us, and the rest of our force riding in from east and west. You would have thought to see fear in their eyes to behold so many tense, armed warriors, yet their expressions were blank.

"Have you come," the woman asked in heavily accented Arabic, "to witness the miracle?"

Dabir stared sternly at the gathered Khazars, and his voice was heavy with distaste. "What miracle?"

The soldiers behind us muttered darkly, and I heard Gamal asking permission to cast the Khazars naked in the snow. Abdul ordered him silent.

A bracelet that had been hidden by the woman's sleeve was revealed as she raised her hands. The animal images hung from it jangled together. "This is sign that the final days are come. Soon the savior shall walk the earth, and lead the just to paradise."

The wind keened then, as if it were a willful thing that had heard her words and approved them. Abdul had to snap again at the men to silence their outraged grumbling.

"How did you know where to find this miracle?" Dabir asked.

She raised her hands to the empty sky. "I followed the song heard in my heart."

Jibril drew rein beside Dabir and stared down at her. "Have there been other signs?"

"Are they not everywhere? Are you desert folk not brought low? If you do not turn from the false faith, you shall lie like these, forever within a frozen hell."

I heard the shift of hooves in the snow behind me and looked back to see a grim Abdul riding up on his gray mount. His eyes were narrowed, and his hand at his sword hilt. Yet the Khazars watched with seeming indifference, as though the warrior were no threat whatsoever.

"They insult God and his prophets," Abdul spat gruffly, "and mock these dead." Abdul was a quiet, amiable sort, and I was surprised to see him so furious. He would have attacked had I given him leave.

"Would you cut us down?" the woman asked, almost inviting destruction. "It will not stop the savior. Better to raise a sword against a snowstorm." Her throaty voice rose in a zealous quaver. "Slay us if you will—we shall go straightaway to paradise, martyrs who witnessed the hand of God."

"We will not kill you," Dabir stated firmly. "But you must depart. You profane those who perished here."

She stared at him, then chattered at her men, who climbed to their feet and walked to their horses. The woman smiled once more, her eyes lingering last on Najya. "We will go. We will tell others what we have seen."

I ordered Ishaq and Abdul to monitor the Khazars and told the others to search the village, mostly so they would be too busy to contemplate violence against the priestess and her followers, who were slow about departing.

Dabir, Jibril, and I joined the search, with Najya.

We looked for the better part of an hour, but found no creature alive in that frozen village. Men, women, and children were dead where they had dropped or where ice had propped them in place, their faces rigid in fear. Dogs, cats, even fowl, had died with them. Donkeys and horses were frozen upright in their stalls.

Najya spoke at last upon sight of a small family sitting around a cold brazier, their blue hands raised to the coals that had been extinguished at the moment of their death.

"What could have done this?" she asked, her voice low, her face hidden beneath hood and veil. And then she answered her own question. "It was the snow women I called, wasn't it?"

"How could those two have done all this?" Dabir asked. "It is something more powerful still." He did not say what that might be, and we did not ask. I don't think any of us wanted to hear the answer.

We knew not how to bury so many dead in frozen ground, so we prayed for them after we gathered fodder, and returned to the road.

We set double sentries that night, no matter that we took shelter in a large caravanserai with high walls. Jibril whispered to Dabir that whatever had slain the villagers would not be stopped with walls, and I knew he was right. But what more could we do?

A small caravan loaded down with textiles arrived from the south after us, and they quickly spread word of the grisly village to travelers from the north, who relayed that they'd heard of giant monsters roaming the wasteland, two-headed blood-drinking men, and other tales that sounded even less likely.

The soldiers were worried, for only fools are immune to fear, and we had seen much that would trouble any sane man. I shared with them the story of the ghul and the soldier's sister, thinking to reassure them that awful things could be overcome. I do not know that they were altogether heartened, even though they cheered in the proper places. The wind had come to seem like the enemy, and its moan had not relented since the afternoon, a reminder always that we were surrounded by an intangible antagonist of unknowable strength.

I had noticed Najya peering out from her tent, and called her out to play shatranj even though she had withdrawn by the time the men were bedding down around the fire. I honestly did not expect her to accept, but she said that she would, and I knew a fumbling, nervous joy as we set up beside the fire, which blazed on our right hand. Jibril and Dabir sat a little ways off, comparing the marks upon the spear with Dabir's record of them, and the two sometimes exchanged low-voiced comments. From their somber demeanor it did not seem like they made much progress deciphering all the symbols.

Najya spoke little until we were halfway through the game.

"Captain," she began quietly, her voice almost lost over the crackle of the burning logs, "I have noticed a theme in your tales."

Her renewed formality stabbed me. Still, I did not let the disappointment show in my voice. "What is that?"

"You meet a monster, and you kill it."

That was a drastic simplification. "That's one way to describe it, I suppose."

"Have you ever met something strange that you did not kill?"

"I have met evil things that I could not kill, though not for lack of trying."

"What of the spirit within me?"

How best to answer did not come quickly enough to me, and I found myself staring dumbly.

"What will you do if the spirit takes full control?"

"You are asking if I would kill you, and I swear upon all things that are holy that this I would never do."

My fervent reply gave her pause, and her next question was more subdued. "Suppose that the thing within me attacked you."

"I would find some other way to stop it. It is only your enemies who should fear me; against you I shall never lift a hand." Ah, that was too close. I wondered if my ardor was as obvious to her as it had been to Dabir.

She looked down at the board, and only after a long moment did she reach to take one of my pawns. I advanced a chariot to threaten one of hers, and she pounced upon it with a knight.

"Nicely played," I told her. "The amulet protects you now. You have no need to worry about such things." I put forth a pawn. Three squares more and it would reach the far side of the board. Yet I did not think she would let him pass.

"I dreamt again, last night," she confessed softly. "A true dream. You and Dabir and I walked in a dark cavern, surrounded by carven images. Like the ones on the spear."

That sounded both troubling and promising. "What more did you see? Did we find another of the weapons?"

"No. But I dreamed also that you stood within a fortress and recoiled from me when I asked your help."

That couldn't be right. "I will never fail to aid you," I promised.

She stared at me through her lashes. "How do you think this all shall end, Asim?"

Never before had I known such pleasure merely at the sound of my name. Yet my happiness was troubled. I forced cheer into my voice and relayed the best possible outcome. "We will find the bones and cast out the hateful spirit. Then I shall personally lead your escort back to Isfahan."

"And what of the Sebitti?"

"We shall likely have to fight them," I conceded. "Dabir and Jibril will concoct something clever."

"You have such faith in him."

"So should you."

It was many more moves before she spoke once more. "It is in you," she said, "that I place my faith."

I think I may have defeated her, that game, but in truth I was so pleased with her simple words that against that glow all else has dimmed.

Come morning the foothills of the Taurus Mountains filled the horizon. We passed through outlying villages as we drew nearer and nearer to the ancient city of Edessa. Najya informed us that she sensed one of the bones strongly now, and pointed northwest. "It is there." Her voice quavered with something between fear and excitement. "On the height of that hill."

Like Mosul, Edessa had overflowed its walls. My father, who had once been posted there, had told my brothers and me that it was older even than Mosul. From him I had learned Ibrahim had once been tormented by Edessan unbelievers who meant to burn him alive. Allah turned their fire to water, and transformed their firewood into carp, the descendants of which live on to this day in a pool of water. No man is allowed to slay them. Merchants sell special food to pilgrims who come to see the fish, and my father had told me the fish eat the food from your fingers. When I relayed this story to Abdul, he was as eager as me to see this, but it was not to be. We bypassed the city altogether, much to the disappointment of the men, who'd hoped for a warm meal at least.

By early afternoon we'd arrived at the small rounded slope Najya sought. There were tracks of beasts, but none of humans. Once we sat our mounts near the height of the place, I could look southeast beyond Edessa to the snow-white flatness from which we had come. To north and west mountains ringed the horizon. Here and there hawks soared, and below some wild asses rooted in the snow for grass.

Najya walked carelessly along the gentlest slope of the hill, near its crown. Dabir followed, and Jibril and I came after. The men began to unload our packs to set up camp at the base. I had no wish to advertise our presence against the skyline.

"Have you noticed," Jibril asked me softly, "that she does not mind the cold?"

Once he mentioned it, I realized Najya's outer robe was thinner even than mine, and, moreover, it had blown open in the chill wind. She had not bothered to draw it back. Thick, strong men like Abdul kept theirs tightly closed.

"She is too proud to show her frailty?" I offered.

Jibril cocked a thick eyebrow at me. "Too proud? Surely you do not believe that."

"No," I admitted. "But I do know that it was no spirit I spoke with last night, or this morning. That is Najya."

"So she seems," Jibril said. "But I see the spirit's dark farr more and more clearly."

I stopped with him, sensing he had some weighty matter to discuss.

He gave up waiting for whatever realization I had not reached. "There is something Dabir does not have the heart to say."

"What is it?" I knew then a mounting sense of dread.

"There may be a time when the woman can no longer keep back the spirit."

"But your amulet—"

He cut me off with a brusque chop of his hand. "The amulet will not work forever. The spirit is growing stronger. There may be no choice, in the end."

I scowled at him. "You need to spend less time worrying, and more learning how to break the spear."

"I am trying," he said, somewhat taken aback. "Do you think it is easy?"

He looked as though he meant to say more, but at that moment Najya reached a hump of snow near the summit of the hill and called out that it was here. I stepped away from Jibril and called down to the men to bring shovels.

Others have spread tales of the exploits I shared with Dabir, but I tell you that most of them get it wrong. They would have you think Dabir and I rode everywhere in ease, pausing only now and then to solve a riddle or slash our swords, then departing with baskets of jewels and the gratitude of beautiful maids. In truth we spent more time in the dark recesses of libraries, or riding through bad weather in forsaken countryside where there was neither good food nor drink, or shoveling. You would not believe how often finding secrets came down to manual labor.

Once the men and I scraped clear the snow, we found ourselves contending against cold winter ground. We were but a half hour into our effort when two of us at once, Abdul and I, struck bedrock. At Dabir's suggestion we cleared a larger swath of cold, dry dirt away, uncovering more stone, and he tapped it with the handle of a pick, listening carefully.

"Hollow," he told me. He stood and addressed the four of us who were digging, while the rest kept watch. "We must find the edges of this stone."

Other soldiers traded out, to spell each other, but Abdul and I did not relent, and soon stripped off our outer garments—no matter the chill wind, our labors warmed us.

By late afternoon we had exposed some eight feet, but never found an edge. Dabir said it was probably enough. He joined me as we set to the limestone with picks, which was hard going.

"Rock and more rock." Hot from the labor, Dabir had removed his gloves and now stroked his beard in thought, staring at the limestone slab, scored with our efforts.

"What now?" I asked.

"We need wine," Dabir said thoughtfully.

"Wine?" Ishaq perked up.

"Not for what you're thinking." Dabir smiled thinly. "Any sort of wine. Vinegar and dregs should be cheaper. I should say we need a dozen barrels of the stuff."

Ishaq looked crestfallen. The wiry Kurd was a fine fellow, but not so abstemious.

Dabir turned to Abdul, standing just to his left. "Ride to town and bring it as swiftly as you are able."

Abdul blinked at him. "Whatever for, Honored One?"

"To crack the stone," Dabir said impatiently; then, at the man's uncomprehending look, he added, "Go, take three men with you, and do not tarry."

Good soldier that he was, Abdul obeyed, though he looked as confused as I. He called the men with him and rode off at a good clip.

Dabir then ordered us to gather as much wood as we could find. "I want a mighty blaze, to heat all this limestone."

Najya passed me a waterskin, which I drank gratefully before passing back.

"What are you planning?" I asked Dabir.

Jibril exposed his teeth in an appreciative grin. "Dabir is thinking of Livy!"

"Exactly," Dabir said.

I did not know the meaning of the word; it sounded to me as though it were a tool or instrument of some kind. "What is a livy?"

"Livy is a who, not a what," Dabir explained.

"Livy was a Roman historian," Jibril told me. "He wrote in great detail about Rome's fight against Hannibal."

Now that name I knew, for some said Hannibal was as great as Iskander, one of the finest of all generals.

Young Kharouf had come up beside us, panting rather heavily, and I realized that he had been listening when he asked a question himself. "What country was Hannibal?"

"Hannibal was a general," Dabir said. "He fought against the Romans. You would probably enjoy reading of him, Asim."

"I am not completely unfamiliar with him," I said, and turned to Kharouf. "He took tens of thousands of men, and horses, and even some elephants, over tall mountains to battle the Romans, and he won many great victories." Saying this, I thought, would remind Dabir that I was not completely without scholarship.

"Correct," Jibril said. "While high in the range of mountains separating greater Frankistan from Italy, his way was blocked by gigantic boulders. Hannibal heated the boulders, and then poured sour wine onto them, and they cracked."

"Why?" Gamal asked. All of us workers had gathered round, and if Jibril had been a better storyteller he might have entertained us.

But he was not so fine. By the Ka'aba, the scholar loved to hear himself talk of learned things, and brought out the worst in Dabir. I forget the precise whys; either of them *might* merely have said that temperature changes are just as bad for rock as for metal, and that limestone is especially responsive to such things. That is how I best explain it.

"Let us hope that it works as well as the historian reported," Dabir finished.

Abdul and his men returned in the evening hauling a wagonload of bad wine.

"It was more expensive than you would suppose," he told Dabir and me when he'd guided the rig up the hillside and slipped down from his horse. "I made the mistake of sounding too interested in purchasing it."

Dabir waved off his concern. "It is good enough." He then commanded us to put out what remained of the fire and brush it from the slab. This we did, then four of us rolled bitter-smelling casks. Dabir positioned Abdul and me on opposite sides of the stone, one cask on its side beside us both.

"Open them," Dabir ordered.

Abdul and I stove in the casks with picks. Wine flowed free upon the stone in red streams like blood spilling across a pagan altar. The liquid sizzled the moment it struck, sending up a cloud of foul steam. The limestone groaned in anguish and a crack spread, widening and branching off through the ashes left from our fire. With another loud crack, the fissure in the stone widened.

"We need more wine!" Dabir called sharply.

Abdul and I broke open two more barrels. With the influx of more liquid, more popping and loud snapping sounded, and then the ground rumbled. The limestone fell away in two large halves. Dabir yelled to get back, and, too late, I remembered that the stone we'd broken did not begin and end directly at the hole we'd dug. The snowy ground gave way beneath me and I plunged into darkness.

9

The barrel dropped with me. I knew an instant of panic, and then my heels struck ground, for the hole proved only two spear lengths deep.

"Asim!" Dabir called.

I fell backward onto cold stone, though I did not strike my head, praise God. To add to my woe, the cask landed hard on my right, bounced over me, and rolled on, spraying sour wine the while. I reeked like a tavern after Ramadan.

I pushed quickly to my feet, gagging on the wine fumes, flexing and unflexing my left hand, which stung mightily. Fortunately neither the hand nor any other part of me seemed broken.

Dabir was backlit so harshly by the sun as he leaned in to check on me that he looked like a blackened paper cutout. Once more he called to me.

"I am all right!" I shouted up, though my voice was almost as unsteady as I felt. I could see nothing of my surroundings.

There was much shouting overhead about ropes and lanterns, and before too long Dabir was lowered down on the former while holding the latter. He advanced swiftly to my side. "Are you hurt?"

"More surprised than hurt. I stink."

"You do," Dabir concurred. A look of amused relief crossed his face, lit orange in the lantern glow.

Shortly thereafter Dabir called for the spear, and we were soon joined by Najya and Jibril, who carried torches, which we lit from the lantern wick. I ordered Ishaq and Gamal down to guard the entrance point and told the rest of the men to stand watch above, reminding them to look from the hill but to keep low.

The darkness covetously gobbled at our torchlight as we looked about so that we had only an impression of a wide space. The ceiling was fairly uniform at twice the height of a man, and the floor likewise was mostly level. The chamber was intermittently supported by thick earth columns, each smoothed over and painted with rounded black predatory creatures: scorpions, wolves, lions, and snakes.

Dabir tapped his fingers near a pictograph incised into the wall as we passed, glancing meaningfully at me. There were predators, yes, but there were also man shapes, with spears, and mountaintops, and low-lying clouds, or mist, or phantoms. It was hard to tell what exactly they were except that they had eyes and that they scattered fallen man figures in their wake. They were very similar to the carvings on the spear. You might think that I was pleased to know we were surely following the correct trail, but I felt on edge. Likely this place had been sealed since the time of Nuh or Moses. Who was to say what might dwell within? It would be a fine breeding ground for evil djinn.

"I dreamed this," Najya said quietly. "We will walk over there, to the left. That is where the bone lies."

"Did your vision show you anything more?" Dabir asked.

"Not of this room." Najya started forward past columns, which were spread irregularly through the dark interior. I took up a torch and followed, Dabir at my side. Jibril trailed, lingering to study the images, I think.

We proceeded only ten more paces before the space closed in to form a narrow opening. Najya hesitated, for rough chunks of stone and earth lay across her path, and the right-hand wall sagged inward. An old cave-in had wrought damage, and the straight way forward looked none too safe, thus Najya started to the left of a column.

"Hold," Dabir said quickly, and grabbed her arm.

She halted, eyes showing white with concern.

"There is something amiss." Dabir released her and bent to run a finger along the floor next to her feet.

"What is it?" I asked.

Dabir beckoned for my torch and with it examined the partially collapsed wall. He reached out, touched it, and peered closely. "This is deliberate," he said. "The wall has not collapsed; it has been carved to look as though there was a cave-in."

"Why?" I asked.

Dabir handed me the torch, searched through the stones beside the wall, then hefted a bucket-sized one, with a grunt, into the path before us. The moment it struck, an eight-foot span of floor dropped away mere inches from Najya's boot. She gasped. It was a long moment before we heard the sound of stone shattering against something in the gloom below.

"You should let Dabir lead," I told Najya. She did not dispute the advice.

Dabir took up the torch again and peered into the dark pit, the bottom of which we could not see.

We moved slowly but steadily from that point on. Less than two dozen steps farther, though, we arrived at a sealed door, of sorts. The torchlight flickered over a circular stone set into the wall and chiseled with the simplistic depiction of a snarling beast's head. I thought it might have been a boar, but the art was so rudimentary it was difficult to be certain. Four notches were carved about the grotesque face, clearly designed as handgrips.

Dabir pressed his palms gently to the stone, then stepped back to contemplate. "It can be rolled out of the way," he thought aloud. He pointed down at the curved bottom of the stone, at least half a foot thick.

"Perhaps," I said, "but it will not be an easy task."

He handed the spear to Jibril, stepped to the right of the stone, crouched, and ran his hand along it. Then he stepped to the side where I waited and repeated his actions.

"Think how long it has been since men stood here." Jibril's voice was almost reverent. "More than a thousand years."

"It feels like a tomb," I pointed out, for I felt no wonder, only the press of the blackness lurking on every side.

Najya stepped closer to Dabir, and I could not help noticing how she visibly struggled to take her eyes from the spear beside her. "What are you looking for?"

"Any kind of pulley or gear system would long since have rotted away," he said. "But there could be more weighted traps. They clearly valued this weapon, or they wouldn't have worked so hard to conceal it."

He stepped back and considered the door as a whole, then bent down beside it once more. I saw his expression clear. "Ah." He stood. "If we roll this stone along this useful track, it will strike these bumps." He patted a roughened patch of rock along the wall that looked little different to me than any other. "And then it will go off track and slam down to crush whoever's holding these convenient handholds. Ingenious," he added.

That wasn't the word I would have chosen to describe it. "How are we to move it, then?" I asked.

"Off the track," Jibril offered.

"Aye," Dabir agreed." He set to investigating the space to the right of the wheel, nodding as he did so. "Yes, if we roll it this way, the door will lean against the wall as it rests."

"You're sure?" I asked.

"Fairly sure," he said, emphasizing the first word.

"Fairly," I repeated.

"Just to be safe," he said, "don't use the handholds on the door. We must be wary."

"That had not occurred to me," I muttered, but I do not think anyone heard.

Dabir and I stepped to one side of the stone and pushed against it with all our strength. It was a challenge, but once under way, the heavy disc rolled aside and, as Dabir promised, leaned easily against the wall, showing no inclination to crush us.

A narrow passage stretched forward, one low enough that I would have to bow my head to proceed, though Jibril might have moved comfortably.

Dabir advanced slowly across the cave detritus lying over the uneven stone here, sidestepping a small whitish bug trundling across the trail. Once Dabir reached the tunnel's end his torchlight spilled into a small chamber with a rectangular niche carved into its wall a few feet off the floor, opposite us. There in the shifting glow I made out a gleam of ivory. Dabir was lifting his foot to cross into the chamber when he pulled suddenly back from the threshold, as if he had spied a scorpion nest.

"What is it?" I asked.

"Come here." Dabir bent to inspect the cave floor.

Jibril and I crowded forward. Once Dabir pointed to the ground, I perceived a line of bug husks and dust along the very edge of the doorway.

"Insects," Dabir said. "Hundreds and hundreds of dead insects. All on this side of the line. Whatever has been striking them dead has been doing so for a very long time."

"Step back," Jibril ordered gruffly. "Give me a moment." He passed me the spear.

We had to give him more than a moment, as it turned out. At Dabir's suggestion I hurried back to get a few more torches from the men above, making sure to retrace my steps exactly lest I trigger some other death trap. When I returned, Jibril had rubbed clean a patch of stone floor two steps from the doorway. Over the next quarter hour, while I held two torches, he labored over a small charcoal drawing I was becoming all too familiar with. A wizard's circle. He measured each symbol precisely, fussily rubbing out and redrawing portions several times, referring occasionally to his battered book. A half hour must have passed before he finally rose with a groan.

"We will see if there is a power there, and if so, the symbols I've drawn should break it."

Dabir had watched the entire process with great interest.

"Stand well back, Dabir," Jibril instructed. "All of you."

A troubled-looking Dabir gestured for Najya and me to depart, and we three left the tunnel to stand, looking in, beside the grinning creature on the canted stone door.

The older scholar raised his head and faced the ceiling. I realized after a moment he addressed heaven, for he was softly praying for Allah to watch over him.

Najya drew close to me, her expression taut. Her voice was a whisper. "The pull is very strong, Asim," she said. "With both the weapons close."

"You should stand further back," I suggested.

"That will do no good."

"Think of something pleasant. A ride, on your favorite horse, in the spring."

"Her name is Asilah," Najya told me, softly.

"Well, then," I said in a whisper, "think that you're at full gallop, and the wind in your hair is rich with the scent of spring flowers." I could picture the scene rather clearly myself, but found it distracting, so I focused on the tunnel instead.

Jibril raised a knife to his hand. I heard Dabir's breath catch in his throat. Before any of us could speak, Jibril cut his thumb deeply with the blade. He then squeezed the digit, dripping blood on the circle's rim.

The effect was immediate and overwhelming. The circle glowed with silvery light at the same moment a coruscating field of energy appeared across the entrance, a glittering window formed of lightning. It bowed toward us as if pushed on by a giant, invisible hand, then was drawn crackling into the circle's center. There was little sound, but the energy stiffened my face hairs and even those upon my arms and neck. It felt as though we were in the midst of a violent summer storm. I turned quickly and pushed Najya and Dabir to safety. "Back!"

So bright was the light it was as though we had opened a gateway to the sun. The bookseller scrambled back from the magic he had wrought. I grabbed his arm as he stumbled from the passage and pulled him safely to us. Then we four watched from a few paces beyond the tunnel mouth. Jibril's breath came in great gasps, and I heard him muttering in astonishment.

The energy flowed for long moments, brilliant but fluctuating in intensity. Its cessation was abrupt and final, and the little passage then seemed incredibly dim, even with the sorcerous circle still glowing.

"Amazing," Jibril breathed.

"That was well done," Dabir told him.

Jibril favored us with a lopsided grin, and for a moment I imagined him as a much younger man. "We shall see if it has worked." He slid carefully past the glowing ring. I felt Dabir tense beside me as his mentor thrust his hand across the threshold.

Nothing happened.

"I think that's done it," Jibril told us. "Stay clear of the circle," he added, as if the matter were not already obvious.

We followed with great care, conscious still that there might be more traps. Yet there was another reason for caution, beyond even the dangers we had already witnessed. As dark and foreboding as the cave had already been, the atmosphere in this smaller chamber was more oppressive still, and it took me a little while to see why. The walls were richly decorated with even greater detail, and in some places life-sized reliefs of men stalked unseen prey with uplifted spears. There were but two columns here, and all the vertical surfaces were smooth, apart from the shallowly carved figures. Even more time had been taken in the fashioning of this place.

My gaze shifted to the waist-high opening in the wall across from us, and thence to the long thick ivory piece I'd spotted from the entranceway. At that point, I understood why I was uneasy, for torchlight fell on a browned skeleton beside it. We had entered a crypt. I breathed out. This was no good deed. Surely any man revered so well deserved his rest.

I heard a swift breath beside me and found Najya staring fixedly at that niche.

"Easy," I told her. "Think of Asilah."

She managed a nod, but did not look away.

Dabir and Jibril had stopped at the doorway and now examined the wall at its left. Symbols were etched there, glowing intermittently with the same shimmering light that had flowed from the invisible barrier and into Jibril's circle. Three I did not recognize. A fourth, though, was that same squiggle of flame beneath an arch they had told me stood for Erragal.

"This puts matters in a new light." Dabir frowned at the mark with arms crossed.

"Do you mean the Sebbiti symbol or the fact that we're now grave robbing?" I asked.

Dabir absently answered while his eyes roved the images beyond the portal. "Erragal helped protect this weapon, so he surely knew where it lay. He seems to have made the spear. Likely he fashioned that club as well. Either the other Sebbiti work against him, or he is no more."

Jibril grunted in agreement.

Maybe this was interesting, but it had no bearing on our immediate situation. "If we must take that bone, let us do so and leave, Allah forgive us. I have no liking for this crypt."

"We must still be cautious." Dabir turned, and, picking his steps with care, led the way over to the niche. Finally he took to looking over the images painted all about the opening to the loculus. I stepped up beside him and stared down first at the gleaming ivory near the remains of the dead man's clawlike hand. The weapon was carved, as Dabir had noted, into a club shape as long as my leg and weathered with symmetrical brown stains at its smaller end, where dessicated, warped leather still hung—the remains of an ancient grip, and from the position of the dead man's hand, I thought it likely his people had interred him with his fingers wrapped about the weapon.

My eyes were drawn then to the empty eye sockets in the skull. Eternity stared back at me, and I looked away from the grinning visage. The body had been long in its tomb, for the bones were dry and brittle-seeming. Even still, they were of goodly size, straight and thick.

Dabir gasped beside me. "Jibril!"

I thought at first some harm had come to him, but Dabir's face was flushed with awe. "Do you see?" He tapped the stone beneath the niche, and an image there.

Dabir brushed grit from the decorations around the opening so he might see them better. The older scholar crowded forward, and I looked to

Najya, who stood with closed eyes just where I had left her. I checked also on the skeleton, for I was wary he would rise up and deal with those who had dared disturb him.

"God and his angels," Jibril said, and he and Dabir exchanged a stunned look.

I peered more closely at the images that drew them, and did not understand. These were more of the childlike drawings of stick men. Here one shot an arrow at a lion-like beast, there another figure with what might have been a cloak faced a monstrous serpent. All the figures but the first wore cloaks, no matter if they were grappling a giant-sized man or a boar, or confronting those drifting snow clouds with eyes.

"Do you think those men are fighting the sort of enemies we will face?" I asked.

Dabir spoke with barely suppressed excitement. "These aren't a bunch of men. These are the exploits from one man's life, the man who lies there."

"A mighty man, indeed," Jibril said.

I still did not see, and looked back and forth between them, tired of the games of scholars.

Dabir jabbed a finger toward the stone. "The carvings are crude, but they tell episodes from one man's life. The slaying of a lion. A battle with a serpent. The wrestling of a giant. The defeat of a great stag. Do you not see? And look, here—after he fights the lion he wears a cloak—"

It was then understanding came to me. "Herakles?"

"Aye!"

This truly was a wondrous thing. I could not have been more astonished if I had chanced upon a tomb of one of the prophets. I was to witness many marvels in my life, but that one still stands tall as one of the most thrilling. Here was a man from legend who had spent his life at great deeds, working always for his people, a hero so grand that his legends had passed on even to folk from different lands. I had no love for the thought of any kind of tomb robbery, but the thought of taking grave goods from such a man tormented me with shame.

"This is Anatolia," Jibril observed. "We are weeks from Greece. Weeks! It doesn't make sense."

Dabir answered. "It may be that his fame spread and the Greeks took up the story more eagerly than all others. Or it may be that he lived in Greece and ended his days here."

"There are no tales of Herakles fighting snow women," I pointed out.

Dabir accepted this truth with a tilt of his head. "Who knows what else has been forgotten, or changed in the telling?"

Behind us Najya finally moved, and we three eyed her as one as she stepped carefully closer. "It is still me," she said. "I but wish to see the pictures."

"That would be fine," Dabir told her. "But we'd best remove the club before you come any closer."

She stopped.

I put my hand into the niche, but did not yet set it to the old weapon. "I do not think we should disturb him," I confessed, and pulled back my fingers.

"We have no choice," Jibril said in his clipped way.

Dabir was a little more understanding. "If Herakles still lived, he would wield that weapon at our side. But he is gone. It is up to us to carry it."

Sometimes one hears words that are simply woven but rich with truth. Dabir had the gift of saying such things. I knew that he was right. I nodded once, solemnly, to the ancient skull. Be it Herakles or some other fellow, I meant no disrespect. I clasped the handle of the time-worn weapon, bending so that I might grip it in both hands. It was heavier than it looked.

I removed it carefully, watching both to see that I did not brush it against the top of the niche or rouse the wrath of the ancient. Herakles slept on, and the club came free. I then raised it in both hands.

There should have been no comparison between the holding of a simple club and a finely crafted blade. Yet I knew the exact same sensation brandishing that ancient weapon that I did when first practicing with my father's sword. It brought me joy, until I recalled that Najya had once predicted I would wield such a weapon in battle, and this unsettled me for some reason, moreso even than standing within the confines of the tomb.

After Najya came to look over the glyphs Dabir led us in a short prayer for Herakles, and we left, though not before stopping to once more seal the crypt with the round stone door.

The return trip felt much shorter, and the wan winter sunlight pouring in through the hole pleased us all, until we noticed that snow was drifting down.

Large white flakes decorated the turbans and shoulders of the soldiers as they stepped forward to greet us. Dusk lay at most an hour away, so I suggested we work fast to seal the tomb before we rode for Edessa.

"Seal the tomb?" Jibril repeated.

"We are hard pressed for time," Dabir reminded me.

"Surely," I said, "you do not think it right that we leave the way open so others can disturb the rest of a hero."

Jabril grumbled a little, but I'd made my point, and Dabir smiled in a resigned sort of way. He enlisted Jibril's aid, and between the two of them they reasoned that taking down the earthen pillar closest to the opening would probably collapse the roof. So long as I was to stand in the tomb's opening while I swung inward, they thought I would come to no harm. So it was that the first time I wielded the club of Herakles, it was to secure the man's resting place. It took but two swings of that great club, and then the pillar collapsed in a cloud of dust and a clatter of rock. The ceiling sagged immediately and Dabir shouted me to safety. As they pulled me up on the rope, the tomb's entryway was closed off in a rain of stone. For all I know, it remains sealed to this day, which is right and proper.

The men were eager to be away from that place, and to sleep at last in an inn, so they were quick about packing. Dabir and Jibril, naturally, took to studying the club, for its surface was also carved with figures, as well as another of Erragal's symbols. They were still talking about it as we rode out even though the weapon was tied to the side of my saddle.

Najya was on my left, and I caught her looking over at me. Or perhaps she caught me looking at her. She looked worried, though she denied it, and thanked me for my kind query.

"I hope," she said, a little gingerly, "that you can bring Noura and ride with me, in the hills, with Asilah."

My heart soared free for a moment. "I shall plan for that," I said.

Unfortunately, she fell silent from there and, with the thickening snow-fall and the darkening sky, I had to focus my attention on directing our course, for all beyond two horse lengths had become indistinguishable. We left the hill to traverse the white rolling plain.

After a half hour, with twilight upon us, Kharouf straightened in the saddle to my right and raised a hand to his brow to ward his eyes.

"What is it?" I asked him.

"I think there is someone in the snow ahead."

After a moment I perceived three figures on foot, walking confidently through the storm in a direct line for us. "The snow does not fall on them!" Kharouf's voice faltered in dread.

I saw that he was right. Though flakes tumbled everywhere, these three moved in a circle uncrossed by snow. My breath caught in my throat as they drew close, for I recognized one of them from his stately bearing. Koury.

The Sebitti had come at last.

10

Koury, with his silver hair, green eyes, and haughty manner, was, as previous, garbed in crimson, though this robe was far thicker than the first, and his hood was fur-lined. In marked contrast was the thickset, dark-haired woman beside him. The cloth of her robe was thin, and it flapped open to reveal a similarly thin, ebon dress decorated with red blossoms. Her skin was pale olive, as though she had been sick for a long while. Her eyes, though, were a vivid brown overlaid somehow with rose.

Their comrade was small and the shadow of his hood obscured his face so that I could see little more than a thin nose and cunning smile. He wore a tawny brown coat and thick gray breeches.

I sent Kharouf galloping back to form up the ranks. The Sebitti stopped a horse length before me, as if waiting. Dabir and Jibril came up on either side, with Najya close after; Abdul had arranged the men in an arc behind.

I knew not what more to do. We had orders to kill Koury and Gazi on sight, yet it seemed folly to try. If Gazi had been present, I might have felt differently, for it was he who had murdered Tarif, but something told me that neither of the others was him, and I was inclined to hear what they had to say in any case.

Dabir must have felt the same way, for he urged no action of yet.

Koury raised his palm to us. "Dabir and Asim." He spoke without emotion. "Again we meet." He indicated his companions with a nod. "My brother and sister are more forgiving than I."

The small one laughed. "Lamashtu? Forgiving?" His Arabic was spoken like a native. The woman glanced over at him, but it was Jibril whom she fixed upon with a sneer. He stiffened in his saddle.

"More patient, then," Koury continued with a humorless smile. He eyed us soberly. "We must speak with you."

"Talk." Dabir sounded remarkably nonchalant. As for myself, I looked to left and right, thinking to see other Sebitti allies at hand. Behind me my soldiers shifted in their saddles and a few horses pawed the frozen ground. I could see or hear nothing else. The snow fell, silent and blinding, in every direction.

"By this point you surely know whom you face," the small one said, steel edging into his voice. "A wise man would show respect."

"You cannot hope to stand against our combined forces," Koury told us sharply. "I do not threaten," he added, "I merely state fact. None of you need be hurt, so long as you are reasonable."

"I am a reasonable man," Dabir offered.

How strong were they, truly? Koury's confidence, I thought, might be feigned. Yet why meet here, unless they had us as they wanted us?

"We have watched you for a long while," Koury continued. "Your skills are not without merit, and, from time to time, we need men and women with skills, for we cannot be everywhere at once. I'm sure that you may not have quite the proper impression—"

"You belabor the point," interrupted the smaller man. "I am Anzu." He cast back his hood to reveal a lean, handsome face with well-tended beard and tousled brown hair. "And this is the Lady Lamashtu. You had better luck getting the spirit to help you than we did, so we let you go find the bones."

"I know that one," Lamashtu interrupted, her accent thick, her smile chilling. She had not left off staring at Jibril. "He once bargained with me for the life of his woman."

"And you killed her," Jibril said with gritted teeth.

"It was you who killed her," Lamashtu countered.

This accusation sent Jibril into a rage. "Liar!"

"That is unnecessary," Koury said sharply. "We must stay on topic."

"I am so sorry, brother." Lamashtu sounded not at all sorry, merely amused.

Dabir briefly considered his former mentor, who was clearly struggling to say silent, then turned his head to the Sebitti. "Why are you here?"

He sounded so casual. I hoped that he had some idea of what to do next. Najya, beside me, watched with wrathful eyes.

Anzu spread wide his arms, as if to indicate the blizzard. "Because we need the weapons you have obtained sooner than we planned. Look at this!" He laughed, and in contrast to the stiff, silent woman or the arrogant Koury, his manner was inviting. "It's not getting any warmer."

"Here is what we propose." Koury frowned in irritation. "From time to time we ally with mortals like yourselves—"

"Like the two of you," Anzu interjected smoothly, speaking, I supposed, to Dabir and myself.

"If you agree to do as we direct, we shall reward you," Koury went on. "Knowledge, power, wealth, whatever it is you desire."

"Life," Lamashtu offered in a low, whispery voice. She had not left off looking at Jibril. He scowled, and trembled, and mastered himself only with difficulty.

Dabir was still polite. "What is it you would have us do?"

"First turn over the bones you have found." Koury's voice was almost dull. "Then we would have you seek out the other two. You seem to have reached some kind of arrangement with the spirit; whatever you have promised her, then, we will fulfill."

Dabir did not correct this assumption about Najya. "That is not precisely what I meant," he said. "What is it you mean to do with the bones?"

Koury smiled. "I'm not sure you're fully capable of understanding that."

Jibril spoke then, steely-eyed. "They mean to blackmail the world's nations to follow them, or they will turn their lands into a frozen waste."

Something about Jibril's speculation amused Koury, who smiled broadly for the first time. "Your ideas are so small. It is enough that we allow you to live, and have a part of what we do. You should count yourselves fortunate. We shall be goodly shepherds. Wise. Firm, but tolerant."

"Once we have the bones," Anzu said genially, "all will be well."

"That," Najya declared beside me, "shall never happen."

She pulled something up over her head. At the same moment I recognized the amulet, she tossed it into the snow before her. It lay with its silver hexagon winking in the failing light

The cold, powerful voice that came then from Najya's throat was not that of the woman I had come to know, and blue ice seemed to gleam in her irises. "They made no agreement with me," she told Koury, her voice rising like the wind. "Only the woman whose body this was. You have opened the door, and have no hope of closing it!"

"Fight this, Najya!" I urged.

She did not respond to me. She tore off her veil and pushed back her hood. "These mortals gave me time to build my strength apart from you!"

The Sebitti looked on, though they seemed more appraising than alarmed, or even surprised.

"Asim!" Jibril shouted. "You must act!"

I drew my sword, not sure what I meant to do with it.

The spirit leapt off her horse. She did not fall, but was caressed by the whirling wind, which lifted her higher and higher—some six feet above the ground. She spread her arms, exultant, as if the wind were a lover and she thrilled to its embrace. Directly behind our line of men, materializing from curtains of falling snow, were rank after rank of women spun from ice and frost, and behind them lumbered larger shapes, indistinct within the blizzard.

"Ride!" Dabir shouted to me. He turned his head to the others "Ride for your lives!"

That we did, though something fragile within me had broken and I felt its ache. We kicked our horses into gallop. There was no time to think!

The Sebitti shouted. Some of their words I think were meant for us, but it was impossible to hear over the wind and the thunder of hooves and the cry of our men. As we charged around the ancient sorcerers, wooden soldiers and a great wooden snake rose up from the snow to shield their master Koury, at whom Gamal leaned out to swing. Anzu had somehow vanished. Lamashtu extended her hands and from them swept a pulse of intense heat that shredded seven of the snow women to raindrops.

Then we had ridden past. For a brief moment I thought we were clear, and then another line of drifting snow women emerged from the blizzard directly ahead of us. I slowed us to a halt, and my mare shifted restlessly beneath me. They meant to encircle us.

Dabir reined in beside, Jibril just behind. My friend tore free the ivory spear and cast its wrapping aside, where it fluttered in the buffeting wind. He looked up at me expectantly.

Never had I thought to make a cavalry charge with Dabir, much less while wielding a club against ghosts formed all of ice. I ripped the club from its lashings on my saddlebag. "Form behind us!" I shouted to Abdul, and he called the others into place.

"Couch the spear, like this," I told Dabir. I unlimbered the club and leaned down with it in my right hand to demonstrate. Dabir, on my left, rested the white spear against his saddle like a lance, then nodded to me.

We shall see, I thought, *how these do against the spirits.* "God is great!" I cried, and as the shout passed through to the men, I kicked my mount into gallop.

Our horses grunted their fear but sped on. I perceived then that the snow women formed more than a single line—they floated two or more deep.

Each of those ghostly women hung a handspan above the earth, and they reached toward us as we neared. All wore Najya's face.

Dabir struck first, piercing the creature before him and shattering her into a thousand white pieces. I leaned out and swung, wincing as my weapon plowed through a white face. It fell into icy fragments.

The moment she dropped, though, more were there to take her place, reaching with alabaster limbs, and beyond were dozens more. The temperature had plummeted around them and the air in my throat burned. Another Najya loomed, and another, and I struck and struck, crying out to God both to preserve and forgive me.

Suddenly we were through, and there was nothing beyond but the falling snow.

From somewhere far above came the screech of a hawk, multiplied in strength a thousandfold. Our mounts whinnied and scattered even as a cowled figure strode from the blizzard ahead on our left. It was Anzu, though I knew not how he outraced our horses. He whirled a silvery thread that he then cast toward us like a fishing line. It flew, borne on invisible wings, and pierced Dabir's horse in the foreleg with a spray of blood. The animal screamed, struggled to regain balance, then tumbled. Dabir threw himself clear just before he and the poor beast were obscured in the snow flung up by their fall.

"Give over the weapons, fools!" Anzu shouted.

I slowed my mount and swung around, searching frantically through the flying snow and press of bodies as I shouted for Dabir. Abdul and Kharouf, at the head of the column, had unsheathed their swords and rode even now for Anzu, who had pulled back the line and whirled it overhead once more. His movements were calm, unhurried, as if he were casting merely for fish. And I knew that he did not fear them, and that their challenge would only bring their death.

"Ride on!" I shouted. "Warn the caliph! Ride!"

They did not hear me, but I saw Abdul's round face turn toward me as the rest of the men thundered past. He reined in. Three of the twelve I expected were nowhere to be found, and I felt a sickening lurch of my stomach. The last time I had led men forth, none had returned alive. I did not mean to lose these fellows too. "Ride, Abdul!" I shouted. "Live to warn the governor!"

He raised his sword in salute, and I turned.

I arrived to find Dabir's horse struggling to stand and collapsing once more. My friend was on hands and knees some paces off, frantically searching the ground.

"The spear!" he yelled. "Help me find the spear!"

"There's no time! Climb on my horse!"

Dabir ignored me and continued his search. Jibril galloped up from somewhere, his mount stamping to a stop beside me. "Hurry!" he urged.

Anzu's needle emerged then through the meat of Jibril's shoulder. Dabir's mentor roared in pain, then was yanked backward off his saddle. He hit the ground with an agonizing groan. I whirled in time to see the Sebitti had somehow moved far to the left of where I'd last seen him. He held one end of the line that still pierced Jibril. Abdul's horse was galloping, riderless, away from Anzu's previous position, and Kharouf was shouting distantly for the men to charge. Allah, I feared they all would die.

I swung down from my saddle and hurried to Jibril. I meant to cut through the line the moment I reached him. The gleaming point of Anzu's weapon still stood out from Jibril's shoulder. Though the scholar's face was a mask of pain, and blood soaked his clothing, he was fumbling with something at his belt.

I tossed the club down beside him and pulled my sword free.

"No," Jibril said, then gasped, for the line grew taut. Anzu, it seemed, was trying to wrench his weapon from its target.

I stepped past and raised my blade.

"*No,*" Jibril insisted, and I paused. Was he stunned, or delirious? He had produced a book from his belt pouch and now ripped a page free with his right hand. Dabir came running up with the spear at the same moment Jibril pressed the paper to his shoulder, soaking it in blood. The parchment lit up with a flash and then Jibril touched it to the line. A heartbeat later Anzu stiffened in agony and he dropped to the ground.

"Hah!" Jibril spat victoriously. "I sent him my pain." He winced as he set up. "Blood is simpler to get today than usual," he told Dabir.

My friend bent to the scholar, telling him to hold still. It was then that our horses neighed and danced and cantered past us. A half dozen of the snow women sped toward us, glowing a bit in the dying light. Behind came what seemed, at first glance, a cloud of snow. Yet it was solid, and, like the women, moved with purpose. A frigid cold rose from them all, and I thought of the strange snowy blobs with eyes that the ancients had drawn on the spear. Was this what they had sought to depict?

I sheathed my sword and hefted up the club. "Get clear if you can," I said to Dabir.

"Asim!" Dabir called, but I was already charging toward the enemy, and calling out to God.

My first swing passed through the arm and shoulder of one of the frost women, destroying her in a shower of ice, then struck the second. She, too, dissolved. A third touched me with ice fingers so cold they burned, and the whole of my forearm numbed. I gritted my teeth as I pushed the weapon back through her, stepping forward into the next. Najya's icy face stared up at me and in the center of holes where its eyes should have been was a maelstrom of swirling blue and white. I closed my own eyes so I would not see as I jammed the pointed haft of the weapon into her forehead. I heard the fragments of her rattle together as she disintegrated. The other two had drifted on, but I could not chase them down until I confronted the cloud thing on my flank. It stretched a full man-height above me, and was easily the width of two wide stable doors. I saw no eyes or limbs within, but a wind rose up from it, of even greater cold than that radiated by the snow women. I gritted my teeth and stepped forward swinging, hoping Dabir could escape the two I'd missed.

My club tore a hole through the creature, yet it did not react. I was buffeted in a bone-numbing wind and I heard my teeth rattle. My arms shook as I swung again.

This attack tore another hole, and I might have rejoiced save that I saw my first strike already filling with more snow. I had to struggle hard against the instinct to curl in upon myself for warmth.

I swung, and swung again, staggering, and finally there came the sound of splintering ice.

I heard Dabir's voice. "Behind you!" And then he was at my side, and stabbing with the spear.

"Get back!" I told him.

He did not, though, and I glimpsed Jibril hurrying up as well, a paper pressed to his leaking wound.

I was numb now almost to the core of my being, and could no longer even feel the club I clasped, but I drove on. Dabir and I stabbed and slashed and bits of the monster fell away. Yet it always re-formed, seeming to draw sustenance from the storm and the wind. My breath came in gasps, and it felt as though I breathed in chunks of ice.

Jibril meanwhile had staggered directly into the cloud, raising his bloodstained parchment with shaking hands. He let out a full-throated cry and the paper dissolved in flame. It fell in ashes but for a spark that swept forth into a ring. I was warmed, instantly, to the core of my being, and the monster dissolved, a splatter of rain upon the snow. I dropped my arms in stunned awe at the sudden change in fortune.

Jibril sank to his knees. I helped him rise, but refrained from comment about the profusion of blood still leaking down over his clothes or his pasty complexion. His beard was white with frost.

Dabir thanked him, but did not look pleased. "What have you done, Jibril?"

"There was no choice," the scholar said wearily.

"There is no time for talk," I cried over the storm. "More of the monsters come." I pointed to two of the snow things barely visible against the darkness.

We turned and stumbled away as fast as we could, Dabir and I half-carrying the old bookseller. The vile clouds, at least, seemed a little slower than a man might run.

"Where's Anzu?"

"Vanished," Dabir said grimly. "I finished the other two frost women."

"Kharouf?"

"When last I saw, he was charging Anzu."

"The brave fool. I ordered them to flee. Their weapons would be useless against the ice spirits."

Dabir frowned in agreement.

I whistled in the faint hope our horses might return. They did not, of course. My Noura would have come running, but she was still in Mosul.

It was no easy going in that thick snow, but fear made us fleet. A look over my shoulder showed the cloud monsters trailing at the edge of sight, but with the storm and almost all daylight faded, there might be less visible spirits on any side.

Once more I whistled, and something black came sailing out ahead of us. For a brief moment I thought it might be Jibril's mare, but as it drew through the howling snow the image resolved into a person seated upon a carpet suspended a sword length above the earth.

"More Sebitti?" I wondered grimly how one of them might take to the club of Herakles across the forehead. I gripped the weapon tightly.

The carpet settled to the snow only ten paces off, and the person seated on the thing stood and called to us at the same moment. "Dabir! Asim! Hurry!"

It was a woman, and I did not place her voice no matter its Greek accent, until we had almost reached her. It was then that I knew her for the sorceress Lydia.

"Climb aboard," she urged.

Dabir's voice rose with incredulity. "You are the Sebitti's pawn!"

"No longer!" She spoke rapidly, her accent growing thicker as she did. "We have no time! Get aboard!"

The last time we had trusted Lydia it had nearly been our death. I fully meant to say something of this, but Lamashtu appeared then beside Dabir.

The Sebitti did not come striding slowly up, or drop out of the air, or even coalesce out of the mist. She just popped into being, and if I hadn't just then been turning to skeptically say something to my friend, I would not have noticed.

"Down!" I cried, and he acted without question. Mine was a powerful backhand swing, and it missed Dabir's head by inches. It seemed destined for Lamashtu's chest, but she sidestepped with inhuman speed.

She did not bother addressing me. "Thief," she spat to Lydia.

Again I swung; again the Sebitti dodged with stunning alacrity, the expression on her face not so much worried as annoyed.

"Give over the weapon, Arab," she ordered. She held out her hand as if she expected me to obey.

Dabir was up then with leveled spear. "What will you use it for?"

She grinned maliciously. "Something wonderful."

Dabir swung clumsily at Lamashtu. Only a moment did I wonder at his poor aim, for I saw then he'd deliberately driven her toward Jibril, who'd raised another bloody paper. He brushed against her robe, and the Sebitti was instantly consumed in a rain of fire.

Lamashtu shrieked as the blaze swept with alarming speed across her dress and into her hair, the sound cutting the air like the sharpest knife. She raised shaking hands, then vanished before I could land a blow.

Jibril sank to one knee, and I saw his eyes streamed with tears.

"By all that's holy," Lydia muttered. She sounded impressed.

"That . . . that's it," Jibril mumbled.

Dabir passed the spear off to me and bent quickly to his friend.

"Hurry!" Lydia urged.

I glanced back at the monsters, once again only a couple of dozen paces off.

Jibril was shaking his head, and sinking. And I realized that the white in his beard was not just snow. His face was deeply lined. He had aged decades in the last quarter hour.

"All that I have here . . . is yours," Jibril said, pressing the notebook into Dabir's hands.

Dabir took it without examining the thing, or caring that his hands were drenched with his friend's blood. "Jibril . . ."

"I hope I killed her. She tricked me, Dabir. She changed Afya, to save her." He choked. "I had to kill her. . . . I had to kill my Afya."

"Jibril . . ." Dabir's voice shook as he said his name.

Jibril gripped his hand tightly, and his eyes brightened with a last burst of strength. "Do not damn yourself, as I have done." His breath caught in his throat. "Look for angels."

"Allah," Dabir said, his voice failing, "shall send angels to greet you."

"That is not . . . ," Jibril said weakly. "I wish to see but one . . ."

"Hurry, fools!" Lydia shouted to us, and indeed, she was right, for the monsters were but a few paces off.

Jibril's eyes fixed on a point beyond Dabir's shoulder, and saw their last.

I pulled Dabir up and he choked out that we could not leave the body. Thus I grabbed the dead scholar and scrambled onto the carpet with Dabir, behind the Greek woman. Lydia spoke a phrase in a musical language and the carpet rose slowly, its edges fluttering. It did not hang loosely, but seemed flat, solid, as though it rested on a palace floor. At another command, we shot swiftly into the air and then away. From above I had a brief view of the battlefield—more of the snow women were knotted around a pair of figures that might have been Koury and Anzu, for dark men and beast shapes fought beside them. I thought also that I caught a glimpse of riders, my riders, galloping away at speed. I could not count their number. Of Najya there was no sign.

11

That carpet was very old, and a number of its threads hung out over the side, waving in the wind. I did not stare at them too long, for they threatened to shatter the already fragile illusion that I was in no danger while borne upon woven wool hundreds of feet above the earth.

Dabir was just behind me holding the body, his back against mine. Lydia sat in front, and she set hands to the carpet whenever she spoke a command. The rug itself was about ten hand spans wide and perhaps fifteen in length. And it was steady, no matter the speed or direction it took. The wind and snow pushed at us a little, yet my seating felt solid. That was good, for there was nothing whatsoever to hold on to, lest I wished to clasp Lydia. This, for many reasons, I was disinclined to do.

"Where are you taking us?" Dabir called up to Lydia. I could barely hear his voice, not just because of the wind, but because grief rendered him halting.

Her dark hair blew wildly as she glanced back over her shoulder. "Away!" And then she warily searched the darkening sky to right and left, and above. She put a hand to the carpet again and we shot upward. I felt my stomach rise, as though I had been thrown into the air by a horse.

Visibility here was just as poor as it was below, so there was not much to be seen, including, at that point, the ground itself.

Dabir forced more strength into his voice. "Lydia—can the carpet rise above the storm?"

"It could," she said with another brief glance, "but Gazi is here with his bird." Her accent again grew more obvious as she continued. "If he survived, he's probably circling on high."

I thought then of the huge creature that I'd heard flying through the center of the storm earlier, and I bethought myself of my duty to protect Dabir. In that, at least, I had not failed. But all else . . . "What sort of bird?"

Her head turned up. "Gazi killed the master of a roc many generations ago, and ate his heart. The bird has obeyed him ever since."

"Did she say a roc?" Dabir asked.

I was not sure she heard him over the wind, so I added: "Just how large a bird is it?"

"Large enough to bear two or three Sebitti. Large enough to lift a horse—or pluck you from the carpet." She seemed to savor the latter part of her explanation.

This I relayed back to Dabir, who in turn asked me to pass on our thanks.

"It is the bones I need," Lydia admitted. She raised her voice so that Dabir might hear her above the wind. "But I think you might prove useful. We will have to work together. To stop them."

At no point in this exchange did she look to me, and I realized I was merely along for the ride. It might be that if I weren't holding on to the club of Herakles, I would already have been rolled off to my death.

"Why," Dabir shouted up, "did you leave the Sebitti?"

"Because I could not trust them," she yelled. "We will talk when we land," she added.

Dabir nodded. Conversing upon the back of the carpet with the wind whipping into our faces and whirling snow bits besides was a little challenging.

It was easier for me, for I had only to lean toward her ear. I was hard put to bottle my rage, and the menacing snarl that came out surprised even me. "Are you the one who put the spirit inside Najya?"

She twisted at the waist so that we two looked face-to-face. But in that near darkness I could only be reminded of her appearance from the general

149

shape of her face and form. She was small and dangerous and beautiful, with a proud nose. Her hair was shorter than Najya's, reaching only the nape of her neck, and rich with curls. "If you push me from the carpet," she said coolly, "you and Dabir will plummet to your deaths."

"I am no murderer."

"You are the one who killed my father," she said sharply. "I have not forgotten."

She turned from me.

I could think of nothing further to say.

A hand closed upon my shoulder, and I started. For a brief moment I had forgotten Dabir was behind me.

"I am sorry about Najya."

At those words the rage dropped away from me, and I discovered that my face was wet. I brushed tears away and half turned to him. "I am sorry about your friend."

"His death gave us life," he said joylessly.

"And what does Najya's death bring?" I asked bitterly.

He squeezed my shoulder. "There may yet be hope, Asim."

That I did not believe, but I did not waste breath saying it to him. Instead I leaned back to warn him. "We cannot trust this Greek."

"We have little choice at the moment."

This was true.

I turned from him, and the time passed without words. The only sound was the plaintive whistle of the wind, which suited my mood.

Those who flew carpets in the old tales never rode them through snowstorms. I swiftly grew very cold, so that apart from dark thoughts about Najya and Jibril and the men, what chiefly occupied me on that trip was holding my jaw steady so that my teeth would not chatter. My feet grew numb despite my efforts to stretch and flex them within my boots. I had heard tales of men who had lost fingers and toes in the mountain heights, and I did not mean to be disfigured that way. I tucked my hands under my arms with the club still awkwardly gripped jutting behind. Just as my limbs were beginning to complain I felt us descend. The snow, at least, had stopped, and the moon was up. The ground lay hundreds of feet below, the rolling plain of snow a lambent blue in the moonlight. There were occasional trees, bent and skeletal.

I leaned forward. "Tell me where you take us."

"To my allies," Lydia said. I could see her profile against the sky as she half turned to me. "Will you try to kill me now?"

I had never killed in cold blood, and did not mean to do so then, as deserving as she might be. "No."

"Dabir I may need. You . . ." She twisted in her seat so she might fix me with a scornful look. "You had best say as little as possible."

Dark linear shadows resolved into the outlines of a small stone fort set atop a slight rise. There are many such on either side of the border, and most of them are abandoned and fallen into ruin, for the border itself has changed many times over many years, leaving the bones of men and their structures to litter the countryside.

Three of its four walls were completely intact, and stood three spear lengths high. The fourth, and nearest, sagged inward where it was not already crumbled away. Towers rose in two corners. Within the structure were the remains of three fair-sized outbuildings, one of which was covered by a new thatch roof. I knew a chill unrelated to the cold as lanterns showed me the now familiar pattern of a circle within a circle painted on the courtyard flagstones beside the north wall, half filled with characters. This one was far larger than that Jibril had drawn. It might easily have encompassed our Mosul stable. Soldiers were even now brushing snow from it.

A cloaked and helmeted warrior was posted on the height of one tower, and called down to the men posted in the fortress center as we descended past him to settle at its base.

The wind brought with it scents of cooked meat, and the smell of horses and sheep. Of more immediate import were the armed soldiers already stepping forward and forming into a line. I had counted several dozen on our descent. Fully ten of them were alert and ready to receive us, and their casually confident stances made it obvious these were no raw recruits or infantry levies. Each had cast back thick robes to clear the way to a sword, revealing chest mail known as jazerant, a kind of armored shirt made of small interlocked plates. Their coifed helms were decorated with horsehair plumes, dusted with snow and frost. And each wore a beard, black and thick as a patriarch's. A few were even lined with a little gray.

One, a little broader across than the others, stepped forward to salute Lydia, then quickly bent to assist her as she stood. She stretched her arms and back, for she, like us, was stiff from the long trip. It was impossible to ignore that she was a striking woman—though she was not so curvaceous as Najya—for the clothes hugged her wide hips and rounded breasts as she flexed. She was either oblivious or unconcerned, and was soon chattering at the Greek officer as the rest of the veterans regarded us dourly. I saw that if Lydia gave the order to kill us, it would be over quickly.

"I do not think we should move," Dabir said softly to me, "without invitation."

"Sound advice," I said from the side of my mouth.

Lydia was pointing at the thatched roof, and the officer was looking over at it, nodding as he made another comment. He was not as old as some of the men under his command, but his face was leathery, and one of his eyebrows puckered because of a scar.

I leaned back toward Dabir. "What are they saying?"

"She has conveyed that the scouting foray was more successful than she could possibly have dreamed, and tells him to keep the courtyard center clear. She said she will have to work quickly, and that the men should stand ready, in case the Sebitti follow."

"She must have a lot of faith in these fellows."

"As a matter of fact, I do," Lydia said as she turned to look down on me. She pulled a curling lock of hair from full lips. Behind her, the officer was ordering all but two of the soldiers off with him in short, barking phrases. "But I have other defenses, for even brave men like these will be insufficient against the Sebitti. I will have two of them dig a grave for your friend. But you two must come with me. Bring the bones."

"The body must be cared for," Dabir objected.

Lydia scowled. "The Sebitti and the spirits are looking for us now. Unless you want to end up just as dead as your friend, we must make plans to stop them. Now come!"

She turned with a whirl of dark hair and cloak and walked through the blowing snow for the tower base. Dabir and I climbed to our feet, slowly, like old men, cramped from the ride. Dabir glanced down at Jibril, then said something in Greek to the two waiting near the body. They exchanged a few words with him, then nodded assent. After that, we lifted the bone weapons and followed Lydia through the open tower door. Our guards came after. I couldn't decide whether to feel lucky or affronted they assigned us only two.

"What did you say to the Greeks?" I asked.

"To dig the grave, but to set Jibril's body aside until I had time for a proper ceremony. They said that there was an unused storeroom."

Soon we were before an ancient soot-stained fireplace filled with blazing logs. Lydia swept an arm toward the crackling hearth. "The fire is yours. Food is coming."

Gratefully, I stepped forward to feel the touch of warmth upon my cheeks.

"Your fortune has risen in the empire," Dabir said to Lydia. "Does that mean your opinion of the empress has changed?"

When last we'd met, Lydia had voiced clear contempt for the empress regent Irene, who she'd said was controlled by bearded fools.

The Greek lowered herself into the single wooden chair beside the fire. It was old and battered, but the small woman sat it with the dignity of a monarch on a golden throne. "The less we mention our last meeting," she said, "the better for all of us."

Dabir and I took the floor across from her. The Greeks apparently had no cushions. This meant we looked up at Lydia, even though she was two heads shorter than either of us.

Lydia raised a well-manicured finger toward Dabir. By that she apparently meant him to wait. "I know that you have many questions. But now is not the time. The Sebitti will be on our heels, and the ritual I must perform will take all the time we have."

"What sort of ritual?" Dabir asked.

"Did I not say to hold your questions?" Her slim arched eyebrows rose. "You are either my allies, or my prisoners. It is your choice. But"—she indicated me with a casual flick of the wrist—"if you choose to be prisoners, I have little use for your guard dog. I suffer him only as a gesture of goodwill. So"—she eyed Dabir—"what is your choice?"

"We are allies," Dabir said, "so long as we fight against the Sebitti."

"Of course. If you aid me, I shall let you both go free, alive. I will see you equipped with the appropriate supplies for return to your people. But I will keep the bones."

"For use against the caliphate?" he asked.

"You have other things to worry about, currently. But no, not for the immediate future, at least."

Even I could see the way her mind bent. She meant to place herself or some puppet upon the throne of Constantinople. These men with her were either members of her family guard, or the adherents of some powerful noble she worked for.

"So, we are allies." Lydia smiled thinly. "How nice. You will teach me to use the power in the bones, and I shall use them to control one of the great snow spirits to fight the Sebitti. I will presently begin its summoning."

Dabir made no attempt to hide his astonishment. "You're going to summon another one?"

"Who are you planning to put it in this time?" I growled.

She rolled her eyes at me. "I'm not binding the spirit to anyone, idiot. I mean to call one of the great spirits—like the ones I saw you fighting. Or more powerful still."

"What makes you think you can control one?" Dabir asked.

"Leave that to me," she said sharply. She tapped a fingernail against the underside of her lip, and her gaze fastened upon the club. "How is it done? Is there a certain phrase to access its magics?"

I looked over to Dabir, and he did not answer. How could he?

Lydia pursed her mouth, and her eyes narrowed.

Dabir wrestled with a reply as the woman's expression darkened. Finally my friend sighed with a slight inclination of his head. "Lydia, we have not yet unlocked the secrets in these devices." His hand drifted to the book in his satchel. "My friend Jibril and I made some progress, however—"

Her upper lip twitched as Dabir spoke; those delicate nostrils flared. When most women discolor because of sorrow or anger, they transform into ugly caricatures of themselves. By contrast, Lydia's beauty flared as her pale cheeks reddened. "You mean that you were just swinging the bones at those things?"

She saw the answer from our expressions, and she almost exploded with anger. A string of Greek words, some obviously profane, accompanied exasperated gesticulation before she pointed at Dabir. "The Sebitti thought you were some kind of mastermind!"

"Dabir is the brightest man I know," I shot back.

"Who else do you know?" she snapped.

"In our defense," Dabir said tightly, "we've had to learn on the run. We've had little time for research, and few sources to help us."

She composed herself and leaned forward. Her voice was low and tense. "Listen to me, wise man. The Sebitti didn't know I'd betrayed them until I plucked up the two of you. You can be sure they will shortly find their way to us, and it will not go well."

"I understand," Dabir told her.

"I'm not sure you do. With the right power, I can control the spirits as well as them. Better even. But I have a summoning circle to finish before I can even try."

Dabir eyed her speculatively. "You have been planning this for a long while."

"I have been prepared," Lydia countered, "to defend myself. That will be far easier to do with the bones than with ordinary blood magic. Now. You will put your lauded brain to working out how to tap those magics before we're surrounded by a band of power-mad wizards or we're hip-deep in an army of frost spirits." She rose, spat a few words in Greek to our guards, then strode from the tower, slamming the door behind her.

The guards then turned to us with grim expressions. I thought that they might demand our weapons, but they did not. Their bearing, however, indicated no illusion that our alliance was anything beyond a polite imprisonment.

"What did she tell *them*?" I asked.

"To make sure I worked." Dabir looked at me with a worried expression, then reached down for Jibril's notebook, which must have satisfied the Greeks because they exchanged a brief word, and settled into a wary watch.

A short time later, the door banged open, and a blast of air heralded the arrival of a soldier who carried a steaming pot of mutton broth and another with a tray of cheeses and breads and empty bowls. Also there were several jugs of what proved to be icy water. I had become greatly hungry and set to without waiting for invitation. Dabir but picked at the tough bread, his expression growing more and more clouded as he flipped through Jibril's book. I knew how he felt.

"We cannot dwell on what we have lost," I told him. "Eat. Gather your strength."

"That's not it," he said. "I mean, it is, but . . . Jibril's book is in code. It's a substitution cypher."

"What does that mean?"

"It means," he said wearily, "that I'm looking at gibberish until I can crack the code."

"Shouldn't you be examining the bones anyway?"

"I have looked at the spear a hundred times."

This was quite true.

"The club is little different," he went on. "I had hoped Jibril's notes might inspire me, but . . ." He lifted a hand, helplessly, and the book slid from his knees. He managed to snatch it before it fell, then sat it at his side and resumed gnawing on his hunk of bread.

"You should dip it in the broth," I suggested, "to soften it."

His look was withering.

At that moment one of our guards rose and demanded a question of Dabir, who answered in fluent Greek, then bent to retrieve the book.

"I thought you said it was gibberish," I asked.

"Why don't you look at the bones for a while?" he replied, irritated.

I did not think that would do anyone much good, so I kept eating. Dabir turned away to pace the room a time or two before sitting again to open the first page. He sighed, staring at a faint image there, then froze in place. I watched him, and I swear that he did not move for a full five heartbeats. Finally I heard him whisper, "By the Holy Ka'aba." His finger traced slowly across the page, and I saw him smile.

I leaned closer. "What is it?"

"Angel." Dabir looked up. "His last words, as Jibril passed off the book, were 'Look for angels.' Do you remember?"

"And?"

He spoke excitedly. "A substitution cypher has the same number of letters in a word, just different letters. So if I assume this word"—he pointed at the paper, on which I could only make out some dark squiggles from where I sat—"is angel, I can deduce other words that employ some of the same letters, and from there find the meanings of the rest. Do you see?"

I thought that I did. "How do you know that word is 'angel'?"

Dabir lifted the book up to me, and on the front page was a little faded sketch of a pretty young woman with high cheekbones and a slight overbite. Underneath the image was a smattering of unfamiliar symbols. "This is a young Afya," he told me. "His angel."

He then rifled swiftly through his own supply pack, produced his notebook, pen, and ink, and dropped to the filthy floor to draw up a chain of letters and what they stood for in Jibril's text. In a few moments more, Dabir took to studying the final pages of Jibril's book, sometimes referencing his sheet of letters. He must have understood what he was reading, for he looked absorbed, though troubled. The guards could not see what, exactly, he did, but seemed satisfied that he was busy.

Once I ate my fill, I thought of wandering to the door to learn how far Lydia was with her circle, but knew I would not be able to explain my action to the guards. I tried, and failed, not to think about Najya, and the future now lost to us. It was too painful to contemplate.

I knew that if I was to sit I would simply brood longer about smiles I could never see, so I decided to look at the bones. The club, at least, I had barely observed. Yet I found nothing that I had not already seen: dozens of stick figures facing beasts or striking poses. The only thing that even slightly resembled a letter was the emblem Dabir had identified as Erragal's sigil.

I had little gauge of time, but I thought it likely a half hour or more had passed. Dabir was now frowning into Jibril's book, which did not fill me with hope. "Do you have anything?" I asked.

He looked up and blinked distractedly. "Oh, yes," he said, though he sounded dejected. "But nothing we can use right now."

That wasn't much comfort. It was as I glanced back down at the weapon that I finally noticed something new. I grew more and more certain as I searched among the carvings, then positive as I rotated the club in my lap. I fought down a rising sense of excitement, set it down, then sank down beside the spear. As I turned it slowly, I understood what neither of the scholars had perceived, and I grinned.

"What have you found?" Dabir asked me. He might have missed the markings, but he had not failed to notice my sudden engagement.

I could not hold back a brief laugh.

"What is it?"

"Look!" I put my finger to the figure holding a spear beside Erragal's sigil. "Everything else besides this stick man fights someone else, or is a monster or squiggle."

"Yes," Dabir agreed slowly.

"But rotate the spear. What do you see?"

Dabir glanced at me, speculative, then gingerly took the weapon from me and did as I bade, slowly turning the thing.

I glanced over at the Greeks, who watched with interest.

"Again and again there is a figure standing alone," Dabir said. "But he is in a different position each time."

"It is a weapon form, Dabir! There is another one on the club."

He blinked at me.

"If you had ever actually bothered to train, maybe you wouldn't be so unfamiliar with practice stances!"

"By God! You are right!" He stared down at the weapon.

Those of you who are not warriors may not know that one of the tried and tested means of mastering a weapon is to practice proper stances and movements until they become automatic. Since antiquity, weapons instructors have devised patterns of these strikes and parries to aid in memorization, and these are sometimes conveyed in pictures. I had seen a number of them over the years, beginning with those carved on an old Persian chest my father had given me, may peace be his. But Dabir had never seen them drawn out like this.

I did not hear his sigh of relief, but I saw his shoulders ease, and he turned gratefully to me. "Asim, what would I do without you?"

Before I could voice a response, he spoke on. "They are wrong, all of them. Jaffar, the caliph, the governor. Lydia. They think I am the hero and you are only a shield."

"But I am your shield," I reminded him.

His look was grave. "Nay, you are more akin to my right arm. And you are always there to shake sense into me when I despair."

These words touched me, and even years later, despite all else, they bring a smile to my lips when I recall that day.

"What do you think will happen if we hold the weapons and move through the forms?" he asked me.

"Hah! You suddenly think I have the answers? Maybe it will unlock the magic. But maybe it's just advice on using the weapons."

He chuckled and smacked my shoulder. "There's one sure way to find out," he went on. "I'm just wondering if we should do so here."

I glanced up at our observers, watching with keen interest from their post by the stairs. "You think it might concern them if we start waving weapons around?"

"There is that. But I'm more troubled by what Lydia will do once she learns how to wield them."

"I think she is right about the immediate dangers."

"Yes," he said reluctantly. He then handed the spear back to me, shoved Jibril's notebook into his own shoulder satchel, and rose to approach the Greeks.

They stood on the instant.

In those days I knew little Greek apart from curse words, so I could only guess what they said. One of the two soldiers had a broken nose, and he did most of the talking. There were several exchanges, and Dabir turned to indicate the club and the spear, and possibly me. The two Greek soldiers then spoke to each other, and Broken Nose seemed to give assent, for he nodded as he answered.

I learned from Dabir that the Greeks would allow us our experiment so long as it met with Lydia's approval, and so long as it took place outside, presumably where we could not launch a surprise attack against them as we worked with the weapons. Thus we threw on our cloaks, gathered our gear, and headed out the door.

The biting chill in the outside air was a rude shock even though we'd been inside only a small part of this day. So fierce were the gusts that I thought for a minute the snow was falling once more.

The Greeks, no strangers to frigid temperature, were well mantled in thick garments. Some stood watch. Some were at work stuffing the gap in the wall with shattered clumps of stone mortared with snow and cold water, an ingenious strategy in this weather.

Those dozen selected to aid Lydia had been busy sweeping snow clear from the courtyard flagstones and running errands to and from where Lydia was painting symbols between the two circles. She used black on the light gray stones, as you might expect for the working of dark magic.

Broken Nose left us and advanced to speak with Lydia. He leaned forward over the ring of snow brushed from the circle rather than risk approaching closer, which amused me. Both Lydia and her second in command, the broad scarred one, looked up at his words, then over to us.

Lydia climbed to her feet. "Dabir. Come here."

Dabir traded a glance with me, then went off to speak with the woman. The other guard remained with me, looking alert and cold.

"Asim."

I thought at first I dreamed, for I had heard Najya's voice, faint, behind me. I blinked and turned, only to see a shape emerging through a gust of wind near the tower.

"Asim." As the figure spoke my name and extended snow-white hands I heard the strange, hollow quality to her voice and saw that she did not walk, but drifted.

I had been called by one of the life-draining frost women.

My Greek warden called out in alarm, but I advanced, the club at hand.

The tower door was just visible through Najya's outline. Her face was not a mask of frost like the others I had seen; it was more expressive and twisted in sadness as I drew close. "Why did you leave me?" she asked.

I hesitated even as I brought up the club.

"You said you would protect me."

I had never heard any of the other witches speak, and this one seemed inclined to talk, rather than attack. And then I remembered Najya's vision that she would come to me in a fortress tower and I would spurn her. Could this be what she had seen?

Yet this was not the woman I knew, just a thing in her image. "You are not Najya. Look at your hands, if you can see, for you have no eyes."

Dabir called to me; Lydia was shouting in Greek. But the wind was whipping up, and the thing with Najya's face stared at shaking hands before her voice rose in a wail of agony. "What has happened to me?"

Misgiving wrenched at me. I began to think that I did not witness a trick, but a tragedy. "Najya?" I took a tentative step closer. "Are you . . . is this your spirit, not hers?"

There were footsteps behind me, and I glanced back to find Dabir running forward with the spear. Lydia, the Greek officer, and half-a-dozen soldiers followed.

"Back!" I called to them, and held up a hand.

"Am I dead?" she asked me softly, and my heart ached.

Suddenly I realized what must have happened, and horror threatened to engulf me. "Is this your soul? Has she cast it out?"

Dabir joined me and stood with leveled spear, his eyes locked upon the snow ghost.

Again Najya eyed her hands, and her face twisted in grief. "Kill me," she said then, her voice a whisper of wind.

"Nay, that I will not—"

"Kill me. Do not let her have my body. I—"

She fell silent, and her face took on a placid expression.

"Najya?" I asked.

Lydia was chattering something in Greek to Dabir, who snapped back an answer.

A light like shining crystal bloomed in the sockets of those eyes and the creature flung herself at me like a youth eager to embrace.

12

Dimly I knew that strength ebbed from my body, but I found myself unable to act.

Dabir's battle cry was almost in my ear, and then, suddenly, the spirit broke into shards of frost and flakes that I stumbled through.

"Asim!" I felt Dabir's hand on my shoulder, slowing my fall so I could catch myself. He somehow spun to face me. "Are you all right?"

I was shivering, yes, but it was the shock of the moment that had wounded me more. "That was Najya," I said, looking to him for some reflection of the horror I felt.

"That was just a spell the spirit casts," Lydia said dismissively. "She sends forth her image to collect life energies for her sorceries." She then turned and spoke to the officer with the scar, who adjusted his horsehair helm and shouted men into their positions.

Her words were no salve to my torment. "It was Najya. She spoke with me," I insisted to Dabir. "Did you kill her?"

Lydia walked toward her circle. "If Usarshra found us, her forces cannot be far behind. I have work. Dabir, you'd best test your theory."

I glared her direction. "This is all Lydia's fault. There will be a reckoning." Also, the weapons forms were my idea, but I did not say this.

Dabir then took me by both shoulders. "Asim." He sought my eyes. "I do not think she is dead." He said this very seriously, very slowly.

Even so, I scarce believed him. "What do you mean?"

"You truly spoke with her?"

"Aye," I said. "She was confused, and did not know how she had gotten here. When she realized she was but a spirit, she despaired, and asked me to slay her. But then the spirit took back control . . ." I shook my head, trying to push the moment from my memory. "Do you think she was still there when you . . . when you saved me?"

"Najya and the spirit may be more closely linked than either realize," Dabir said. He released my shoulders. "Do you recall? When Gazi attacked in the caravanserai, Najya conjured frost women to defend you. Not the spirit—Najya. She was in control."

This was true.

"And now the spirit sent forth some part of herself to scout. But she accidentally included some part of Najya with her, before the spirit took control again. I think it likely that Najya's soul is still trapped within her body."

I caught sight of hope then, where I had only known despair, and I clutched desperately for it.

Dabir saw my look. "I cannot say for certain, Asim, but . . . there is still a chance. I have Jibril's notes—I could duplicate the spell he tried using to banish the spirit."

"But the spirit broke his circle."

"We," Dabir lifted the spear from the flagstone, "should be able to power a far greater one."

I smiled. Oh, certainly, there were immense challenges yet—avoiding the Sebitti, escaping from Lydia, somehow bringing the spirit into a circle once more—but Najya at least was alive.

"Come," Dabir said.

I nodded once, suppressing a shiver. "Very well. But I will try the form first, in case something goes wrong. And besides," I added, "your stances are too narrow."

Dabir smirked.

I had dropped the club while the spirit attacked. I knelt to rotate the weapon in my hands and considered the steps again. The form had seven movements, and began with the club pointed with heavy end toward the earth, to the right. From there it moved to what seemed a strike position from the high right, then up from low left. Then there were two block positions, one vertical, one horizontal, and finally an upper strike from the left. The pattern was designed so that the user would finish in the same stance he started with, a symmetry that I admired.

"Do you have it?" Dabir asked.

"It is not so simple as it looks," I explained. "I must choose how to move between stances." I scratched at my beard. "Will anything bad happen if I don't move properly?"

"Probably not."

"Probably?"

Dabir offered a lopsided grin.

So it was that I found myself practicing fighting stances under the stars and a full moon in a snow-topped ruin with an old club formed all of bone, watched by enemy warriors. After the first run-through I halted in the final position, waiting to see lightning bolts or rainbows or some other magical thing.

Nothing happened.

"Do you feel any different?" Dabir asked me urgently.

I shook my head, feeling a bit self-conscious. "No. Let me try again."

There proved to be many variations, because the more I considered the pictures, the more ways I thought possible to move between each stance. Each time an attempt ended in failure Dabir offered speculation that was mostly useless, for he was finally outside an area of his expertise.

After close to a quarter hour, I tried shifting the horizontal parry a little higher and adding a flourish to move lower into the next strike position. That proved the last necessary adjustment, although nothing felt different until I returned to the beginning stance. At that moment, my conception of the world around me changed completely.

The club, now light as a stick, glowed without blinding me, pulsing with a mighty heartbeat. I then understood what farr was, for I witnessed it myself on every hand. While I still saw the Greeks, I also saw the very force of their lives, even the beat of their hearts and the thread of blood through their veins. Too, I understood that the colors radiating from them were tied to choices they had made and deeds they had done. You would think that, being warriors, and therefore shedders of blood, they would be black as pitch, but most of them were touched only by a shadow of darkness.

Dabir, closer at hand, was brightly lit, tinged with a wedge of silver and black. The spear glowed in his hand, almost incandescent, but veiled, as if under a cover.

Dabir was talking to me, asking if I was well, but I did not answer, for I was gazing at Lydia.

I knew that she had sensed the release of the energy in the club, for she rose, stared, and immediately crossed toward me. She was darkest of all that I saw, with strings of brown and orange. Yet even she was crossed by patches of pure light, and silver. Hers was one of the strongest life forces present, and this strength was somehow like a beautiful musical note in harmony with that of the club, marred only by the discordant wail of tiny, black wraiths writhing within a packet at her waist.

"Asim?" Dabir's voice had grown more agitated. "Answer me! Are you all right?"

"He has gotten it working!" Lydia said, breathlessly.

"I am . . . fine, I think," I said to Dabir at last. I held my hand up so that I might see my own aura, and was not displeased with what I saw.

"What is it like?" she asked me. "What can you sense, and do?" She turned then on Dabir. "Why did you have him try it first?"

"He deciphered it, not I," he said. At her look of disbelief Dabir said, simply, "Asim is far more valuable than you realize."

This pleased me, but I did not comment, for I was enraptured by the magics. I sensed the lives of the animals in the barn, bleating sheep and patient horses, and knew their numbers. I reached a little further, testing the limits of my senses, and felt the life of rats nesting in the southeast corner of the stables, and a snake sleeping deep under a hidden stone in the north of the fortress. But I grew conscious of another force. It was powerful, and as I sensed it, even at a distance, I knew suddenly that it heard and desired the power of the club, and that it had grown excited by the awakened magics I wielded.

"Najya's coming," I said, and I realized then I did not know how to stop doing what I was doing.

"The spirit is named Usarshra," Lydia corrected. "Can you also sense the Sebitti?"

I thought to say no, but there were other sources. They could not sense me, but stalked us, like blind lions who crept forward ahead of Najya, readying to spring.

"They are almost here," I said. And then my awareness stretched further, and I knew that there was another tool, like the one I held, but weaker, somewhere further north, and one just as powerful south and east of us. Before I could give much more thought to that, I felt the awareness of the thing that was Najya reaching out not just for the club, but for me, and I knew no way to disengage. In a moment of panic I dropped the weapon.

It thumped to the ground, the narrow end missing my boot by only a fingerspan. Its power faded after a moment, and I shook my head. The real world now was dull.

"What did you do that for?" Lydia demanded.

"The spirit could sense me," I said. "It is very close, but the Sebitti are closer."

"Then there is no time to waste." She reached down for the club herself, clasped the end, then cursed as she tried to lift it. I thought her angry that it was so heavy, but her look had another cause. "It has stopped working!"

Dabir spoke quickly. "It must only be active if held by the person who—"

Lydia cut him off. "Obviously! Have him do it again and get over to the circle. Alexis!"

The officer with the scar turned quickly and saluted her. She gave him orders in Greek, and then he dashed away, barking at his soldiers, who scurried like squirrels. Those building the walls scrambled to find helmets and armor and I stopped to lift my own helm back to my head.

"She's told him to ready firepots," Dabir said.

I had heard of, but never seen, the secret weapon of Constantinople, and was thankful it would not be directed against us. That, though, was not my immediate concern. Quickly I told Dabir of the other bones I had grown aware of. "How far south?" he asked of the bigger one.

"It seemed near a great cluster of lives—maybe a city."

Dabir frowned thoughtfully, then motioned me ahead of him, scanning the walls as we strode ahead. "Our allies don't have a great deal of strength."

He was right. In all there were perhaps fifty Greeks, which was not enough to make the four crumbling walls look particularly well-defended, especially since ten remained below assisting Lydia. Many were equipped with bows, and some had javelins. The gap in the wall near us had been partly repaired, though I doubted a combination of ice and broken stone would hold out snow spirits, or, for that matter, wizards, for very long.

The courtyard was of decent size, some seventy-five paces across, with Lydia's circle taking up twelve of those. It was too large an area to defend with these few men.

"If she can't command this spirit, I do not like the odds," I said.

"I don't like the odds in any case," Dabir said as we neared Lydia's circle. "It's not what I would have done. Though firepots against snow spirits is not a bad idea. Did you have any sense that magic enhanced the club as a weapon?"

"Not really. It seemed lighter. That would make swinging it easier, but . . ." I let my voice trail off. I was embarrassed to say I had hoped for something more, like searing holy light.

Lydia had set up two small cauldrons just outside her circle. Steam wafted up from them into the chill air, and I knew from the disquieting smell exactly what was within. I shook my head. Jibril had worked the name of God into his incantations. Somehow I doubted Lydia had done the same, especially after I had seen the dark specters borne at her waist. I had meant to mention those to Dabir, but there had not been time. But then I glumly surmised he already knew Lydia's magic was black.

Dabir stopped beside Lydia. "Why do you need blood?" His tone was polite, betraying only a hint of challenge.

"I know blood magics," she answered. "This is my fallback, if I have trouble wielding the sorcery in the bone." She put gloved hands to her waist and turned to me. "What are you waiting for, Captain?"

It troubled me that I should be performing the movements under close watch of her and Alexis, who had just arrived to make a short report.

I decided not to ask where she'd gotten the blood.

She scowled at my hesitation. "Be on with it! Work the sorcery!"

Surely the scarred Greek would see what I did and be able to duplicate it after a few tries. But Dabir suggested no solution and I had none, thus I gathered my breath and moved through the form. In a little while the world glowed once more, and I tried not to stare overlong at the trapped spirits at Lydia's side. What *were* they?

There were more pressing worries, though, for with aid of the club's sorcery I felt the approach of other forces, like the onrush of a monster storm.

"Put it to the circle," Lydia instructed, and I swallowed my worries and sat the club's fat end to the circle rim.

She fished a pendant out from under her collar, kissed it quickly, replaced it, then came to my side. She gasped the moment she touched the club. Her eyes lit with innocent, childlike wonder. And then a blizzard of disjointed images hit me: Lydia's bearded father, face apoplectically red in anger, raising a clenched fist. A sudden plunge into dark, cold water. A smiling young man brushing his mustache and leaning forward with love in his eyes.

I released my hold on the club, for I had no wish to see more of her memories, and less for her to see anything of mine. She retained her own hold on the weapon, blinked at me, then raised her free hand to the sky and began to chant.

Instantly energy spun out from the club and filled in the circle rim and the characters as if they were lit by a fire beneath. The hairs on my neck and arms stood as they do when the air is alive with lightning. All about me the men shifted uncomfortably.

Lydia's clear voice rose in a long wailing note that turned swiftly to a rain of syllables in a language unknown to me. I have no love for singing to start with, and this grim melody flowed in unsettling ways. Her eyes gleamed, and her head was high. There, in her moment of power, she was like a savage creature of the elements, beautiful and terrible.

Dabir clung to the spear as Lydia's song reached crescendo.

A white mass was born high in the circle's midst and spilled out into a cascading wave of whirling snow, like a white sand devil, then spread out to the circle's edges, defining for all who watched the walls of the invisible cylinder that encased it.

The thing spun violently and twisted in upon itself and after a moment it was a lean wolf shape larger than an elephant, formed all of snow and frost. Its front limbs and part of its torso were transparent. It stood glaring down at us through sockets empty of all but a brilliant blue gleam.

"It worked! Praise the saints and the holy virgin!" Lydia laughed a little madly. She leaned against the club—still pressed to the circle—and shouted an incantation.

The wolf opened its mouth, and though its lips did not move, words streamed out in a torrent, like the wind given voice.

"Needwantblood! Give! Give!"

I am not sure it spoke Arabic, or Greek, or that it truly spoke at all, but I understood its craving.

Lydia shouted in Greek. Dabir was kind enough to translate for me, under his breath.

"She says that it must do as she commands."

The wolf sat back on its haunches and howled, a haunting sound so loud that I flinched.

Lydia lifted her free hand and began to shout another spell. She seemed agitated.

"Is it working?" I asked Dabir.

He looked troubled. "It does not seem to be."

Lydia finished this new spell with an exultant shout.

Yet the wolf only howled.

From behind on the wall came a cry of alarm. Dabir and the nearest soldiers turned with me.

A piercing call erupted so close that it might as well have been into my ear, and then a large object passed overhead at great speed. I looked up to find a gigantic amber hawk sweeping over the fort walls clutching a screaming Greek soldier in its talon. Its huge feathered wings beat the air above us, and the unfortunate Greek was dropped into a rank of his fellows. The wolf went berserk, growling and snapping, and, though it did not cross that invisible ring that kept it trapped, I swear that the air about us grew even colder.

13

Dozens of black-garbed men were racing through a postern gate that had no business being open, and wasn't the last time I had looked. I could only assume the Sebitti had worked some trick. The Greeks on the walls formed in ranks to launch arrows and javelins. At least twenty intruders dropped with the first volley, but then they were close enough to attack the defenders within the fort, and the archers ceased their work lest they hit their comrades.

I drew my sword.

"Spare the scholar and the woman," called a voice from amongst the black-garbed soldiers. "Slay the rest!"

The nearest Greeks shouted to God and St. Michael and unlimbered swords. Behind me Lydia was still exorting the wolf to do something, but it merely howled. On the north wall, a short swift man was sending Greek warriors tumbling with a blur of sword strikes and a hook propelled from the end of a shining silver line. Anzu was garbed much the same as the warriors he must have brought with him.

A huge black with a tremendous sword was behind the front rank of the intruders. He called out to me. "Do you remember me, Arab?"

Surely I did. Twice before I had barely escaped Gazi with my life. I slung my shield from my back and hurriedly dressed it.

"Do you think you can keep him busy for a few moments?" Dabir asked. "I have an idea."

Now I had no strong desire to face Gazi alone, for he was the greater warrior. But suddenly the Greek officer, Alexis, was beside me with his own sword, pointing at the enemy.

"We will entertain him," I said. "But hurry!"

I stepped forward with the Greek veteran. Gazi giggled at us, though he could not move yet to attack, for there were troops in front of him.

Black robe flapping like a cape, one of the invaders charged me with a high cut. I caught it on my shield, slashed down and tore out his unprotected throat. He fountained blood and dropped, frantically scrabbling at the wound.

Beside me Alexis bellowed a challenge and swung into our foes. I blocked a low strike from a tall man. My opponent grunted as his chest armor absorbed my blow, then tried to punch at me with his small shield. I leapt back. Gazi, moving up, was flanking me. I repositioned to keep him in sight.

Most men fight with straight blades, and unless they have seen action against Khazars or Indians, they think a curved sword cannot thrust. It is a common misconception. When my opponent's weapon passed from left to right, I back stepped so he missed me by a fingerspan, then smashed my shield rim against his sword. This left him off balance and open, and I drove my point under his right arm. He fell with a scream.

Alexis dropped another foe, and then Gazi was there before us, grinning. He looked us over, unhurriedly, then he giggled a little.

On every side were the battle cries of fighting men, and somewhere overhead the bird keened. Behind us the wolf howled. I had known many battlefields, but this was by far the strangest.

"He's very dangerous," I warned Alexis as we moved in. I did not know if the Greek understood me, and there was no time to say more.

Gazi charged, slashing suddenly at Alexis, who dropped to save himself from beheading.

I heard the cry of the great bird shred the very air. Gazi's eyes twinkled. The cursed roc was diving. If I threw myself flat, Gazi would drive a blade through my body, and if I retreated, the thing would likely crush me in its claws. So I drove forward.

I felt a brief moment of satisfaction when Gazi's eyebrows arched in surprise, but then he was all business, deflecting my onslaught with blocks that came with expressionless ease. Still, he retreated. I felt a rush of air behind me, but no talon pierced my armor. There was, though, a great wolf howl that distracted even Gazi, who winced in pain at the sound. I thrust in, but the Sebitti parried and grinned more broadly.

"Let me know," he said smoothly in a deep voice, "when you want me to kill you."

Again and again he deflected or sidestepped my blows and I wondered at his aim until Alexis rejoined me. I think Gazi waited until we both were fighting to attack so that he would not be entirely bored by the kill. The moment the Greek was with me Gazi launched into us, wielding that two-handed blade not like a butcher with a cleaver, as you might expect from the size of the thing, but like a dancer with a staff. Within the first few moments of the assault he had smashed twice into my armor with such strength it drove the breath from me. Alexis fared a little worse, for the blade took him in one leg. The Greek grunted and stumbled, but came on, limping and leaking blood down his boot.

Just as I was wondering how much longer the pair of us could continue amusing the Sebitti, I saw Dabir advancing from behind him. Flames burned along cloth tips that poked from the two jars he carried. He had brought the Greek fire. I shouted a battle cry and intensified my attack to keep attention on me.

The wolf howled once more. Gazi, meanwhile, laughed and caught my blow on his own sword, spun out, and struck hard. I lifted my shield in time, but the blow numbed my arm from fingers to bicep and split the metal. He pressed me back, and I am embarrassed to say that I lost my footing and spun in the snow. Down I went, landing heavily on my shield. My arm was so numb I felt the impact more surely in my shoulder. Worse, my back was exposed. I scrambled to face what I was sure would be a deathblow.

Alexis drove aggressively into the madman, buying me time. Say what you will about most Greeks, but I shall never suffer you to slander that fellow.

As I pushed back up to my knees I saw the bird sweep through again, claws outstretched. Dabir flung one of the pots and the projectile shattered against its immense feathered abdomen. Fire blossomed there and the bird screeched, flapping frantically as it climbed, one claw passing so close to Lydia that its passage cast back her hair and robe as though she walked into a mighty wind. The Greek woman was still stationed at the circle, holding the club and shouting spells. I had only a brief moment to look, but it seemed the wolf had grown even larger, and more substantial.

I would never admire the doings of such a man as Gazi, but I shall ever respect his ability. Somehow he *knew* that Dabir lobbed a pot despite the fact he was not looking at him. Gazi stepped to the side, sucking in his chest so that Alexis missed, then swung his sword out behind him and caught the firebomb in midair, shattering it. Little blobs of flaming oil spattered in the snow and a few hit my shield, but most of them caught upon Gazi's steel. He advanced, laughing with delight, the sword now flaming before him.

I staggered to my feet and stumbled forward to help the Greek. By the light of Gazi's blade I saw my sleeve stained with blood, though I could not tell if it was mine, for my shield arm was still mostly numb. I was surely not at my best, but I did not mean to abandon Alexis.

My ally ducked under that flaming blade. Gazi's return swing was briefly hampered as an icy ball thrown by Dabir smashed into his right shoulder, and at that precise moment the Greek's blade jabbed him along the upper thigh. The Sebitti hissed in rage and brought the flaming weapon down against the Greek's armored shoulder. Alexis sagged, falling with exposed neck, and Gazi's sword whipped back to strike.

I did not give him the chance. Any normal man would then have been overwhelmed as I rushed, but Gazi twisted and lashed out at me with his sword, scoring my armored shirt. The flames on his weapon had almost completely failed, although ghostly blue fire still danced along its edge, casting the madman's face in skeletal relief as he brought it back to guard.

I could feel that I neared the barrier holding back the wolf; not only did I sense the weird, shifting brightness behind me, the very hairs upon my body stood at attention.

"Drop back, Asim!"

This was Dabir's advice, but there was nowhere to go. I was winded and wounded, and Gazi seemed fresh. His laugh slid into a giggle as he feinted at my neck. I threw my blade up to block, but with a snakelike shift he brought the sword down at my thighs. I sank to one knee, hoping to catch it with both armor and blade. This I did, and I think the sword deflected part of his strength, but the blow still numbed my weapon hand and the strike cut into my armor.

Dabir shouted once more. "Asim, down!" So, suppressing my instinct to rise, I crouched lower and pivoted to intercept the next anticipated blow.

But Gazi at last gave Dabir full attention. I saw then that my friend had picked up a bucket from somewhere. The Sebitti paused to gaze quizzically as Dabir slung the thing back, like a boy hurling water from a well. Gazi leapt aside, but his leg injury hindered his spring, and blood arced out from the pail, coating the Sebitti's side.

Perhaps Gazi had not quite reasoned what was happening, for I saw a confused expression on his face as I threw myself flat. Behind me, the barrier dropped. The wolf stepped over me and leaned in toward Gazi, who screamed as the wolf's great jaws snapped down on him.

"Get out!" Dabir shouted. The cold from the monster stabbed through my fatigue and I scrambled away as the wolf's belly swayed above me. Gazi writhed in the monster's teeth, his form shifting to a swarthy thick man, then to a small woman, then to a slim youth, his body only partly visible through the creature's translucent maw.

As the muzzle grew more and more substantial Gazi's screams grew louder and did not leave off, even as the voice that shouted changed. Less and less of the wizard's body was visible through the beast. I was close enough to see individual hairs of its fur, close enough to see the blood streaming down Gazi's body, close enough to hear the crunch of his bones when the screaming stopped.

Tarif was avenged, and so, too, were all those who Gazi had murdered through the eons.

I joined Dabir, spear clasped in one hand, helping Alexis to safety near a wild-eyed Lydia. For someone who had finally gotten what she wished, she seemed none too pleased.

The wolf turned from the mangled thing that had been Gazi to slurp one of the blood-filled cauldrons. Everywhere knots of Greeks and Sebitti followers struggled, though far more on both sides now lay dead or wounded than remained standing.

"Turn the wolf on them," I said when I reached Lydia.

"It didn't work!" she cried.

"What are you talking about? You sent it against—"

Dabir explained quickly. "I had her drop the barrier after I drenched Gazi."

The shriek of the returning bird rent the night air.

I am not certain why it came back. I had thought it under Gazi's magical command, as the wooden men were controlled by Koury. Yet it may be that there was nothing magical about the beast but its size. Whatever the case, the singed roc dropped on the wolf with its claws outstretched. It may not have known that its master no longer cared what it did, or could ever care again; maybe it acted as it had been told, fighting until being signaled away.

The frost wolf spun to snap at the enormous bird.

"Move!" Lydia thrust her hand toward my shoulder and I withdrew from her, nimble as a drunkard. Black-shrouded figures flew from the pouch at her waist, ghostly, hooded, their rotting limbs transparent. I gaped in dread, almost too tired to raise my blade. A full half dozen soared out toward a familiar figure by the stables even now readying a silvery hooked line. I had the satisfaction of seeing Anzu's face go ashen before he dashed for cover behind a shed.

For only a moment I thought we might yet have a chance, for the surviving Greeks were regrouping. The Sebitti onslaught seemed spent. Then the vaporous snow spirits drifted down from the south wall and the ice barrier crashed in under the onslaught of a gargantuan white bear shaped from mist and vapor. Snow women poured in behind it. With them came a shrilling wind clutching at us with icy fingers.

Lydia, teeth gnashing, shouted something about the carpet, hoisted up the club and bore it in two arms as she dashed for the nearest tower. I put an arm about the sagging Alexis. Dabir and I ran after, the Greek warrior half supported by me. He was shouting to his men, but those few left alive were dying or fleeing, and I heard the torment in his voice that I knew too well, of a commander seeing his men fall.

Lydia threw open the door and raced inside. Behind us, so close that my ears rang, came a great roar and a blast of icy wind.

Dabir whirled and thrust the spear past my chest. I let go of the Greek and turned, raising up my blood-drenched sword.

The bear had followed, and stood fully a man's height over Dabir, advancing with a growl. As the wolf had been before it drank blood, it was ghostlike—the battlefield and drifting snow women were visible through its body. Its empty sockets blazed a brilliant blue.

Dabir drove it back with another jab and shouted for us to run. I pushed Alexis after Lydia, then grabbed Dabir's arm and pulled him with me through the doorway. The bear hesitated before stomping forward on its hind legs, then I slammed the door. I hoped it could not simply pass through the shelter like the snow women.

There was no sign of Lydia within the gloom, but there were stairs along the wall, and we heard her footsteps racing upward. Alexis had made it to the stair bottom, but his face was pale even in the feeble red light cast from the dying hearth.

"Keep moving, soldier!" I told him. I think he understood my tone more than my words, for his back stiffened and he took a step. I tore off my mangled shield and grabbed his elbow as Dabir ran up.

I was a third of the way up the stairs with the Greek when the cursed bear walked straight through the wooden door in a spray of frost. It let out something midway between roar and wind blast. I think Alexis was protesting, but I got him up to the next floor, and then I had no recourse but to ram home my bloody sword into the sheath uncleaned so I could push him up the rickety ladder.

We arrived at last at the tower height, where Lydia had laid out the carpet and now sat on it. Dabir stood behind her, frantically waving us forward.

In the courtyard below, the wolf had finally won. It was fully solid now, though it still seemed less a mortal creature than a being fashioned from snow in its shape. It was bent over the splayed, motionless corpse of the giant bird, greedily devouring it, uncaring that dozens of other spirits crowded around the carcass with him. Others were bent down over the Greek and Sebitti warriors: women, bears, smaller wolves, and stranger things I had no time to observe in detail.

"What took so long?" Lydia snapped.

Alexis slumped onto the carpet and I stepped aboard. I'd only managed to sink to one knee near him before she spoke her words and the fabric shot into the air and away from that terrible place. If I'd tumbled backward instead of forward into Alexis I would have fallen to my death.

Once I righted myself Dabir turned to converse with Lydia in urgent, low tones ahead of me. The fortress was already half a league away, praise God, distant almost as a dream. Or nightmare. From here I could almost pretend it was only a snowcapped ruin, except that I knew what looked like a large mound of snow visible over the wall was really the back of the giant wolf.

I turned attention to Alexis, feebly cutting away the cloth on his leg so he might see his wound. I told him I would help him with the bandage, but I saw then just how blood-soaked his garment had become. Our eyes met, and I understood that he knew he was but a walking dead man, and that he had suspected for a long while.

The carpet soared on, high over the landscape below, a pale blue in the moonlight. Above us loomed a wispy sheet of clouds, and I wondered if he might reach heaven faster, for being so close to it. For all that their ways are strange, Christians are people of the book, and the virtuous go to paradise.

Alexis twisted awkwardly so that he might look over his shoulder. Dabir was leaning forward, still in deep conversation with Lydia.

The Greek officer weaved a little as he turned back to me. "You must guard her now."

"Lydia?" I asked. Though my voice could barely be heard above the chill wind whistling past us, I think my skepticism was easy to read.

"The lady Doukas," the dying man corrected. His voice was failing. Slowly he blinked. "You must protect her."

I thought of all the reasons I should not—that she had cursed Najya, that she had tried to murder Jaffar, that she consorted with dark powers. I frowned.

"Swear, Arab," he said. He lifted up a bloody hand, looked at it as though seeing it for the first time, then made the cross over his heart, as Christians sometimes do. "Swear it."

"I will guard her," I promised, "so long as she is our ally, though her soul is mostly black. But I do it for you, not her, because you were a brave man and noble warrior."

He seemed to have trouble focusing, and I thought then that the color was draining even from his eyes, so white had he become. "We made a fine team," he told me.

"Aye," I said. "You were a good man in a fight."

"The better man." His lips shaped what was probably meant as a smile. It looked ghastly. "I'm the one who got through his guard."

I knew a brief stab of irritation, but saw that he still smiled, and I chuckled. He managed what might have been a laugh himself, but then he was silent forever after, and I had to lay him beside me, holding on to his shoulder.

I have never forgotten him. I hope that when I am called to paradise I, too, shall meet it with a jest upon my lips.

14

I shall not detail the shouted conversation that immediately followed on that sad flight; I shall merely say that Lydia was distraught to learn her man had died. She did not seem sad so much as angry, and at me, as if I had not taken proper care of a prized possession.

Once she had calmed down sufficiently, Dabir inquired as to my injuries—none of which seemed life-threatening, although my arm was quite sore. He then told me we were on our way to Mosul.

This seemed a remarkably bad idea to me. "Won't that just lead the spirits and the Sebitti to our home?"

"We won't stay long," Dabir said. "But we need rest. And you said the other bone was south."

"Do you mean to go after it?"

He leaned back, opened his mouth as if to explain, and then the wind swept hard from the left and tore his turban away. Dabir grabbed at the fabric, but it unrolled as it spiraled off into the sky like a living thing. He then pressed a hand to the spear lying half pressed under his thigh, to ensure its safety, and I glanced beyond him to where Lydia sat with the club across her lap. Alexis did not shift in the slightest from where I had put him, on his side next to me, his legs curled so that they would not hang over the edge of the carpet.

"I have an idea," Dabir said finally. "I'll need to get some answers from

Lydia before I can be sure it works. Do you think you can get the spear working?"

I had figured out the club; I saw no reason that I could not work out the spear as well. "Yes. What are you planning?"

He shook his head. "We will talk when we land."

We were on that carpet a very long time indeed, for it was a long way to Mosul even when soaring like a bird. Also, it was cold, and after the first hour we were forced to huddle together under Alexis' outer robe, which we spread like a blanket.

I was dismayed that we had once again missed our prayers. It always seemed to me that in those times when they might do us the most good we had no opportunity for them. Also, there was the presence of Alexis to darken my mood. It seemed that all our journeys upon the carpet would be in the company of a corpse, surely an ill omen. I bethought then of Jibril's body, still unburied, and I knew great sorrow, just as I knew that was likely nothing to what Dabir must be feeling.

Below us all was blue-gray where the snow threw back moonlight and black where it did not, outlining trees, rocks, or occasional buildings. One long winding patch of ink was a river and it silvered as we passed. After traveling a long while in silence, we began to drop lower and I could see flickers of light from dwellings glinting off objects outside. The carpet soon carried us a bowshot above Mosul's walls, close enough for me to see two warriors talking over brazier coals. They did not see us, praise God, for they would surely have raised an alarm. Dabir advised Lydia so that our course changed now and again. We flew low enough over a block of buildings that I might well have stepped safely onto a roof.

Finally the carpet arrived above the dark rectangle of our courtyard and settled gently into it.

I realized how tense I'd been only when I began to relax in the familiar surroundings. I climbed slowly to my feet, discovering a few new pains, then helped Dabir bear the body of Alexis into one of our empty rooms. Dabir had promised Lydia he would be buried in the Christian cemetery south of the wall, and I would see that it was done personally. Our tread wakened a visibly startled Buthayna, who volunteered with surprisingly few words to stoke the fire and warm something for us.

Lydia waited to the side of the oven, eager for the warmth. I couldn't suppress a grin when a bleary-eyed Rami stumbled into the kitchen to stare at us in shocked wonder. Dabir directed the lad and they both helped me to remove my armor. I was startled to catch Buthayna looking over at me with concern. I recalled then the multitude of red splashes staining my tunic and armor.

"It is not my blood," I said.

A savage laugh then fell from her lips, and she kept on chuckling from time to time over the next quarter hour. Even Lydia traded a curious glance with me at this.

I was famished, so hungry that I hardly savored the rice and stewed vegetables Buthayna set before me. The Greek woman ate nearby, forced into proximity because we both desired to be near to the oven.

Dabir went to the adjoining room to pen a quick note to the governor and I heard him bid Rami take it to the palace straightaway. He returned after having changed, replaced his turban, and washed, then reluctantly agreed that we speak in the kitchen rather than the receiving room. He chased out Buthayna, pulled out a chest she kept her larger pots in, and sat down upon it with his back to the stone oven. "It is time for answers," he told Lydia. "Clearly the ancients were right about the spirits: when they absorb enough life force, they become corporeal—at least temporarily."

"Yes," Lydia agreed.

"And somehow Erragal stored magic in the bones from one of these slain spirits?"

"Not just any slain spirits." Lydia set her plate aside. "The most dangerous and bloodthirsty. He captured its life energy as it lay dying."

"Why couldn't the Sebitti find the bones on their own?"

"Erragal hid their power." Lydia pointed over to the spear leaning in the corner by the club. "Unless you're holding one, even the greatest mage can't gauge the true extent of its power." She briefly faced me to ask, with a slight frown, "How far south do you think the other one is?"

"It is hard to say," I answered gruffly. I hadn't realized that Dabir had said anything of the matter to her, and I wondered, for once, at his wisdom.

"We can discuss that later." Dabir rested his hands on his knees. He was backlit by the firewood in the oven so that his beard hairs and a few stray turban fibers were sharply delineated. "What are these spirits, exactly?"

"I know only a little more than what the Sebitti told me. They may have lied. I'm sure now they lied about what they wanted the bones for."

"What do you know about the spirits?"

Lydia shrugged. "In the days after the fall, we shared the earth with many strange beings. My people call them chionzoe, though yours would call them djinn," she said with a hint of derision, "as though there were only one type of spirit. My ancestors thought them a kind of Titan, escaped from their prison when the gods were distracted. But the Sebitti say they were something else. Spirits from another realm that craved form and sustenance. They wandered down into the warm, soft places of the earth and they sucked the life force clean from everything in their path. They brought the cold with them when they came.

"People weren't very clever then. They all lived in dirty villages, and they didn't even have swords. They were no match for the ice that the snow spirits brought with them. They had to flee as cold spread across the land. And then, within a few years of each other, in the same tribe, the first Sebitti were born, Adapa and Erragal. A mage like that is born once in perhaps a thousand years, but here were two in the same region who could shape sorcery as easily as this ox beside me eats."

I scowled but refrained from comment.

"They marshaled their people to fight the frost spirits with fire and magic, and discovered bones from slain spirits could be used to hit them when other objects couldn't. As you deduced, when they consume life, they absorb its traits. Gazi's magic worked a similar trick," she added.

"Why didn't that one you summoned turn into a giant lamb then?" I asked. "It was drinking sheeps' blood, wasn't it?" I could have mentioned that it didn't become a bird or a replica of the slain wizard either.

She never answered my question. "Clearly the spirit killed a wolf or two in its time. They know what humans fear."

"Let us stay focused," Dabir said. "What happened next?"

"I was told Erragal used the bones to drive them back." Her voice rose in admiration. "He captured the most dangerous of the spirits and divided its power among five weapons. Some part of it escaped his hold, though, and returned to the spirit realms."

"The part you called back?"

"Yes. I suppose hate had kept the thing from dissipating, after all these years. It was challenging to find, but I did it," she said with pride. "I just don't understand why I couldn't bend the will of that one I called."

"You didn't control the will of the first one," Dabir pointed out, then shook his head as if regretting the observation. "Enough. What can you tell me about the Sebitti?"

She turned up her hands. "What do you want to know?"

"Let's start with their abilities, and their weaknesses."

She nodded at this. "Lamashtu may be the most powerful. She and Gazi certainly frightened me the most. She is smarter. She uses blood to power her sorcery, including her immortality. You saw what blood magic did to the old man? Well, she can throw spell after spell without much ceremony or effort. So long as she can get away to absorb more blood, she cannot be destroyed."

"His name was Jibril," Dabir corrected quietly. "What of the others?"

Lydia paused momentarily, out of politeness or a reasonable attempt at it, then continued. "I had seen little of Anzu's ability until this evening. He seemed harmless . . . good-humored." She paused. "None of the Sebitti really think of themselves as human anymore. I think Lamashtu looks on people as livestock, and Anzu views societies as grand experiments he likes to monitor. He's the one who contacted me."

"I see."

"He told me once that he had visited my grandmother to provide her with the sorcerous secrets passed on to my father. I'm not sure if he meant to instill gratitude or claim authority. Apparently he'd been hoping one of my family would grow into the gifted sorcerer they were after."

"So they had been grooming you?" Dabir prompted.

"He watches families or individuals who he thinks might have potential. He's the one who found the woman, Najya."

At that I let out a low oath.

She turned her head toward me. "You should blame him, not me, for what happened. It was my idea to leave the Persian's soul in her body so she could help control the spirit. The Sebitti thought I should cast her out."

"How kind of you," Dabir said dryly. I am glad he spoke, for a cold rage had seized me, and I do not think I would have managed a controlled comment. "Her soul is still trapped in her body with the spirit's. How long can it remain?"

"As long as she's alive," Lydia conceded. "But I don't know how you can hope to save her. You'd have to subdue the spirit and force it into a banishing circle. How are you going to do that?"

"You got her into this situation," I broke in. "You must get her out."

"I don't know how."

This angered me further. "You give up too easily. You have destroyed her life. You must find a way."

"That is easier said than done."

"We shall not give up," Dabir promised. "And I may know how we can get her into that circle."

At that, my interest and hope surged as one. But Dabir made clear that now was not the time by holding up a hand. "Right now I need more answers. Lydia, Najya's spirit seems to be strengthening all the time. Is that because of the snow women the spirit sends out? Do they gather life force for her?"

"I think so."

Dabir frowned. "Well. Let us get back to our discussion of the Sebitti. What of Koury?"

"His powers I think you know. He can shape wood, and clay to a lesser extent, then command it to do as he wishes. He has a few other tricks, but if he is separated from the container that houses his figurines, he does not seem so dangerous. He is their current leader, but he might be the weakest. Perhaps he is the best planner."

Someone who commanded such unstoppable beasts did not strike me as weak.

Dabir pressed ahead. "And what of Anzu's weaknesses?"

"He's adept at sneaking in or out of places unseen, but I had no idea he was so deadly until I saw him in combat. He may be more formidable than I first thought."

"Could Lamashtu have survived Jibril's attack?"

"Probably. She can vanish almost instantly, and heal herself with blood magic. Anzu once told me he was fairly sure she didn't need most of her organs anymore."

"Are any other Sebitti working with them?"

"Isn't that enough?" she joked. She saw neither of us smiling, and she sighed. "Erragal's had nothing to do with any of them for generations, though he was once mentor to Anzu and Koury. And he might have long ago been Lamashtu's lover. Gazi joked about that. It was hard to know what he meant, though. He was the maddest of them all."

I would have liked to hear more about Gazi, but Dabir changed the subject. "How about Enkidu? Or Adapa?"

"Adapa's been dead for millennia, and Enkidu wanders in the wilderness. They really weren't a united group," Lydia went on. "Ever. There have been larger and smaller numbers of them at various times, and only occasionally have they joined forces. And all have found different paths to sorcery and immortality."

"And how many others work with them?"

"Each has a few dozen followers and servants. All of them are normal humans except for Lamashtu's." Lydia licked her lips. "I saw one of hers, once. She passes on part of her blood magic to her followers. Their only vulnerabilities are extremes of temperature. They are preternaturally strong and fast, so long as they have regular access to blood."

Dabir fell silent and rubbed the side of Sabirah's ring with his thumb.

Light from the oven struck the stone so that for a brief moment it seemed alive with emerald fire. "You knew all this," he continued finally, "and their powers, and yet you turned against them. Do you wish for death?"

"My powers measure up to theirs," Lydia said haughtily. "With these bones, and the spirits at my command, I could stand against any or all of them. Or, I thought I could," she finished with a bitter twist of her mouth.

"But why challenge them?"

"They told me they would give me power to do what I wished with the empire. But the longer I was among them, the more I doubted. They had agreed too readily. And," she added, puckering her lips in disgust, "I tired of being treated like a lackey. I saw they meant to cast me aside as soon as I was no longer useful."

This seemed to satisfy Dabir. "And how is it you came to us?"

"I knew the Sebitti were on the move, in force, and followed secretly to see where they went. They thought I had moved off to ready my numbers to assist them."

"How did you know they were on the move?"

"I am not without resources of my own." She sounded pleased with herself.

"Resources? Explain."

"A woman has to keep some secrets." She flashed a sly smile.

Dabir might as well have been made from stone, so little impact did her charm have upon him. "Lydia, if we are to work together, I have to know what you can do. If you have some other tools or talents that can be useful, you must tell me."

Her playful lilt had faded. "You will not like it."

"I haven't liked any of this," Dabir said. His voice was clipped. "My mentor is dead. He was the closest thing to a father I have known. Dozens, perhaps hundreds, have perished, including the entire population of at least one village. Men, women, and children. None of them would be dead but for you, and Najya and her husband would still live peacefully in Isfahan."

She smiled without mirth. "Now we are down to it, aren't we? You blame me. If the Sebitti had not found me, they would have found someone else for their work. And if they had not found Najya, it would have been some other."

"Truly?" Dabir asked bitterly. "I thought you were the most gifted sorceress of your age."

"I did not say that."

"You certainly implied it. And it may even be true. You said on the carpet ride here that they did not have the skills to work with these spirits. It seems to me that you might simply have refused to cooperate."

"When offered such power, you think I would say no? Would you?"

"Yes."

She laughed. "How noble. But then you have fame, wealth, comfort . . . you have everything you want."

"No," Dabir said quietly, "I do not."

"Do you mean power? I can find no way into a court ruled by that idiot Irene and her bearded fools. They will not heed me—"

"I do not mean power," Dabir cut in, "and we have veered from the subject."

Lydia was not inclined to return to it. "Tell me, Dabir. What do you intend for me? Jaffar banished me from these lands on pain of death." She pointed a thumb at me without looking my direction. "You could have this killer lop my head from my shoulders at any time."

"That's not going to happen," Dabir said.

"Really? Why should I trust you?"

"We need each other," he told her slowly. Dabir shifted on the chest and spoke formally, and it was only as he went on that I realized he was fighting hard to restrain his anger. "I have no desire to see you executed or imprisoned. I have immense respect for your abilities, and your intellect. But I *do* hold you accountable for your part in all that has transpired, and wonder what you shall say when there comes a final judgment."

"Your opinion is irrelevant to me," she said stiffly.

Dabir took a deep breath and held it a moment before replying. "These resources of yours. What are they?"

Lydia weighed him with her eyes, then sounded weary as she answered.

"I work with the spirits of the dead, Dabir. Do not ask which ones, or how. But I can set them to watch, and know what they see."

"Are those the things you keep in the pouch at your waist?" I interrupted.

"No. Those are more special. And you don't really want to know what those are."

While some curiosity lingered, I concluded that she was right.

"I knew that the Sebitti were closing upon us at nearly the same time Asim sensed them with the club. One of my spirits was following them."

"Is it still?" Dabir asked.

She shook her head. "We have journeyed too far, and my control has lapsed. If you ever finish interrogating me, I'll summon a few to watch outside Mosul. Certain spirits are highly sensitive to otherworldly energies, so I'll call ones that should be able to detect the approach of the chionzoe. Now I have a question for you, Dabir. You say that you need me. Why? What is your plan?"

Dabir's eyes fell to me. "It will depend in part on whether Asim can get the spear working in the same way."

"I can do that," I reassured him.

"And," Dabir continued, "that we can find the other weapon and get it working as well. Can you fashion a banishing circle, Lydia?"

"Of course. The symbols are not fundamentally different from those of a summoning circle. But designing one may be a little more challenging," she added, "without my notes."

"I have Jibril's notes," Dabir offered.

"That may or may not be helpful. But, again, if you're planning on Usarshra standing obediently while we banish her, let alone cooperating to enter—"

Dabir interrupted her. "I'm planning on luring her in, and trapping her."

"Luring her in?" Lydia asked. "With what?"

"The bones." Dabir's gaze was intent. "She came for them once. She'll come for them again. Sooner than we want, probably."

"And she'll come with a whole army of spirits," Lydia decried.

"Then we'll need a very large circle."

"Powered by what?" Lydia's expression cleared. "The bones. Of course! But . . . then they are likely to become completely drained."

"Good," Dabir said fiercely.

She blinked at him. "I was going to suggest that we each take one when we are done."

"They must be destroyed," Dabir said in a tone that brooked no argument, "along with the spirits."

"Destroyed?" She leaned forward. "Then all of this will have been for nothing!"

Dabir actually snarled. I do not believe I had ever seen him so angry. "We shall be lucky, Lydia, to survive at all, or to save our people. That is what we 'get' from this. Now. Are you going to help me make this circle?"

Lydia blinked in surprise, for while she did not know him even half as well as I, she surely knew Dabir's measure and understood that this was completely out of character. "Are you sure it will even be powerful enough to stop Usarshra?"

"I can't be sure of anything," Dabir admitted. "All we can do is try."

"Why did you call her 'Usarshra'?" I asked.

"That is what the spirit calls itself; I know not why." Lydia shrugged, then addressed Dabir. "It's just gotten stronger since it left the Sebitti. And I think it will continue to do so."

"That's why we're going to try to find the third bone, tonight. If the circle's going to work, it has to be more powerful than she is."

Lydia nodded. "I suppose so."

He studied her quietly for a long moment. "I'll give you a better offer than the one you gave us, Lydia. If you do not want to work with us, I will give you one of our horses, and you will be free to go."

"You will fail without me."

"Surely we will have a better chance if you aid us," Dabir agreed.

"If I help you," she said slowly, "if I give up my claim on any of the bones, what will I receive?"

Dabir but stared at her.

I could not stay silent. "After all you've done, you want a reward?"

"You are not the only ones to lose friends and allies," she said.

"This is all your fault!"

Dabir interrupted before I could say more. "Peace, Asim. Lydia, I have moneys at my disposal, though I do not think this is what you want. I think I have enough influence to have you pardoned by Jaffar, for the caliphate will surely owe you its thanks, if this turns out well. A post might be obtained for you, though . . . you are a Greek—"

"And a woman," she finished caustically. "So best suited for knitting and rearing children, right?"

"By God," I interjected, "if you had stayed home making children, we would not be in the midst of this."

Dabir spoke quickly. "Asim, you are not helping. Lydia, treasures I can certainly promise you. I think a pardon likely, and I will do what I can to see that you receive a post. Mosul is ruled by a just man, and I do not think he would object to counsel from a woman, though I cannot guarantee anything."

She studied him. "It is not so different here than in Constantinople."

Dabir could only offer empty hands.

"There's no better option at present," she said. "I shall work with you."

"Good," Dabir said grimly. I think he meant to speak on, but Lydia did not give him time.

"Your plan has merit, but it will require some modification. Normally a person must stand outside a circle, with all the power sources, to activate it. And you certainly don't want to be inside one when you banish something."

That made sense even to me.

Lydia spoke on. "Usarshra may come for the bones, but we really can't expect her to pass over the boundary lines unless the bones are within the ring, and if they're inside, we can't very well use them to power the circle, because we'd be trapped inside the banishing sphere with the spirits."

"You sound as though you have a solution," Dabir said.

"I think I might be able to fashion a safe space in the circle," she said. "Like a hole through a pearl that you string on a necklace. It would be a protective circle inside the banishing circle. For us."

"Can that work?"

The Greek woman shrugged. "I've never heard of it being done before, but if I can't do it, nobody can. I will have to plan it out very carefully. If you're wanting to fit in all the spirits we saw this evening, it must be very large. Larger than the hippodrome."

Dabir nodded, looking almost relieved. "We'll draw it out in the countryside. Better not to bring the spirits close to here." He looked to us both. "Well, it is already late, and we have much to do. We'd best get your sentries in place, then see about this circle. Asim, can you master the spear's magic?"

I was bone-weary, and sore to boot, but I nodded my assent. "Aye."

"Keep in mind," Lydia said, not quite facing me, "that the moment you activate the spear it is like lighting a bonfire. You should release it the instant you confirm it's working."

This sounded like good advice, though from an unwelcome source. "I will do that," I agreed.

They headed off, then, taking the bones with them, for I wished to wash and change clothes. Also I prayed, answering the muezzin's call alone, and I apologized to God both for neglecting my prayers and for allowing black magic to be done in the household, for I was sure Lydia's sentries were no angels.

When I had finished cleaning up I took the spear, studied it, and no matter my fatigue, stepped outside to practice its pattern in the snow of the courtyard, now lit with the flame of dawn.

I rediscovered aches, though I think the exercises aided in stretching my tired muscles. Despite feeling weary and dull, learning the spear's pattern took a third the time it did for me to master the club, for I better knew how to read the pattern. After only a few tries I stood with the glowing spear in my hands. I did as Lydia recommended, and released the thing into the snow.

Once it dimmed, I took it inside and reported my success to Dabir. He wished immediately to learn the weapon form himself.

"But if I show it to you," I objected, "won't you activate it again?" I thought one "flash from the hilltop" bad enough.

"I can practice everything but the final move. Which you can show me out of order."

This was altogether reasonable.

Having had no training with spear fighting, Dabir took far longer to master the form. He thought the moves out rather than felt them, which true mastery would require. Still, in a half hour it seemed to me that he had everything, so he thanked me, wiped sweat from his brow, and returned to the receiving room.

He and Lydia had created a scholar's nest there, meaning that there were two cushioned areas and everywhere else were books, scrolls, papers, and writing implements. There were few places even to set one's feet.

Lydia was scribbling furiously on some thick rolls of paper.

Dabir walked carefully back to settle down near her, and put a finger to Jibril's book. I leaned the spear in the corner.

"How long is this going to take?" I asked.

Lydia paused to scowl up at me.

"It might take a little while," Dabir said. "You should try to grab some rest. You look awful."

"No worse than you," I pointed out.

"No, you look worse," Lydia said without looking up.

At this I grunted.

"I will be fine," Dabir assured me.

Now I trusted Lydia but little. I felt certain she would turn on us given a better opportunity. Yet I did not think one was ready to present itself immediately, so I retreated to my rooms. I thoroughly cleaned off my sword and then took a whetstone to its edge for some time—for only a fool is too tired to care for his weapons—then cleaned out the scabbard. Finally I bowed to the wisdom of resting for just a short while; there would be many more trials before us yet, and I'd be more useful in facing them with a little sleep. When I flopped down on my mattress and draped a blanket over myself, I did not remove my boots. I tossed my armor over my father's arms chest so donning it might be faster. I knew I should have cleaned the armor, too, and contemplated repairing its links, but that would have kept me up through the day.

Sleep fell swift and passed bereft of dreams. I cannot say what woke me, but of a sudden I came awake in the pitch-black of night and knew in a flash of dread I'd let the entire day pass unmarked. As I came to, all that we'd experienced fell suddenly upon me. Tarif's murder. Najya's disappearance. The flight of my men. Jibril's death. The fight with the wolf, and the sorceress in the house.

I sat up instantly and regretted it. Stiff muscles protested throughout my body, most especially in my chest and arm. I had expected no less, but just because you know a visitor will be an irritant it does not lessen the annoyance when he arrives.

I put feet to the floor, stifled a groan, stretched, then buckled on my sword belt, lit a candle, and set forth. I put aside a growing awareness of my hunger until I was sure about Dabir's safety.

Dabir was still in the receiving room, but he was snoring softly upon a cushion near the display shelf, head resting on his arm. I stopped with the curtain only partly open until I saw Lydia creeping up behind him.

Instantly I stepped into the room, hand to hilt. My movement betrayed me and she looked up. It was then I saw that she held a blanket in her hands. She froze for a time, then pulled her eyes from mine and draped the cloth over Dabir's shoulders, tucking it with care about him.

I walked further inside, treading lightly over manuscripts scattered like soldiers on a battlefield. Most of the candles had dimmed, and the brazier was cold and dark.

Lydia's tone was softly mocking. "Did you think I planned to smother him?"

"No."

I had instead thought she meant to stab him, but I did not say this. I moved closer and peered down at my friend, snoring peacefully. "Are your ghosts in place?"

"Ghosts?"

"Your sentries."

"Yes," she said with an amused smile. "My ghosts. They keep watch."

"Have you finished your studies?"

"I think so. It requires a little guesswork, but . . . it really is our best hope. I like what you have done with your hair, incidentally."

I had not bothered yet with a turban, nor had I brushed, and I was certain from her smile that I must look ridiculous. At my frown, she smiled the wider.

"The Sebitti or the frost spirits might be here at any moment. We must be moving."

"He needs some rest. The sentries will alert us, and the carpet can be ready on the instant."

I grunted.

She licked her lips. She opened her mouth, then closed it. I do not think I had ever seen her hesitate before, and I recognized that she was working herself up to speak.

"What is it?"

"Tell me about the ring he wears," she said suddenly.

I did not immediately answer, for I found myself wondering why she asked this.

From the bashful way her eyes dropped, she either felt awkward, or had practiced the look well. "The one he always taps," she said haltingly. "He said only that a friend had given it to him, though he said it was not you."

"The ring is not magic."

Her look was withering. "I am curious, not covetous. He did not wear it, when first I met him."

"Your memory is as fine as his."

"But not as fine as hers. Who was she?"

I considered the lovely Greek woman carefully. "How did you know a woman gave it to him?"

"I only guessed, until just now. He referred to a student of great memory. So he was tutor to a woman?"

"Little more than a girl," I admitted. "But she was very brave. And she could be as sharp-tongued as you, though she was gentle." I thought then of Sabirah sitting together with Dabir, chattering with him, and I remembered once more her simple wish that could never be granted, that she might wake each day and look upon Dabir. And I was filled then with great sorrow for my friend, and the girl. I thought, too, of Najya, and admitted to myself that, like Sabirah and Dabir, the chances were high that we should forever be apart.

Lydia misread my expression. "You were fond of her," she said slowly.

"She talked too much," I said, "but I like her well enough. My friend loved her with all his heart, and she with hers, and I think that they would have been very happy together. But she is married to another man, and he has only the emerald now to remember her by. I wish he would cease thinking of her."

She looked back at him, lying there. "Do you know, when I first learned that you two lived together and that neither of you were married, I thought . . ." Her voice faltered.

I did not follow her meaning.

Dabir stirred, and we two turned to stare at him. He snorted once and fell back asleep.

"I'm sorry," she said, and I blinked, for I had never thought to hear those words from her. About anything. I was still not sure how to respond, so she spoke on. "I see now that you are not just his guard, but his brother."

"Yes," I agreed, irritated. "What is it that you want, Lydia?"

She searched my face for sign of ridicule. "What do you mean?"

"You know what sort of man he is. And you know what sort of woman you are. You can see farr. Just as I saw it, when holding the club." I indicated the weapon lying near Dabir's hand.

Her brow furrowed. "It is not my fault if I have had to make harder choices than either of you."

"You think we have faced no trials?"

"I think that they have not troubled you overmuch," she said, her tone sharp. "Your farr is uncolored by doubt."

"My farr is unstained by dark deeds," I said, "though it has surely grown blacker in *your* company."

Her cheeks reddened and her chin rose defiantly. Dabir turned in the blanket, almost as though he sensed the coming torrent as surely as myself.

But Lydia did not speak. Instead she stilled, her eyes fixed upon the distance. They widened in alarm, then sought my own. "Something is coming," she said. She whirled, bent to Dabir, and shook his shoulder.

"What is it?" I asked. My friend stirred and blinked groggily.

"One of my sentries just vanished," she told Dabir.

He sat up.

"Only another necromancer could have sensed it," Lydia continued, "much less destroyed it in one blow."

I stepped over a book to lay hand upon the haft of the club.

The curtain into the room parted suddenly and Lydia and I both looked over to find a small, neatly dressed man in an off-white robe with the hood turned down. He stared at us from the threshold. In one hand he carried a thick white staff.

The fellow did not advance. He took in the room critically, pausing to consider the three of us.

His accent was so pronounced that it took me a moment to comprehend him. "I am Erragal," he said. "I am here for my tools."

15

Erragal did not have the presence of Koury or Anzu, and did not radiate Lamashtu's eerie sense of dread. Indeed, he barely reached even Lydia's height. His hair was dark and receding, flecked with gray. He wore no turban. His off-white robe was well-tailored, it was true, belted with a purple wrap, but it was hardly sewn with demonic symbols—indeed, I had seen slaves of the caliph wearing more decorative cloth. His beard was short, and almost completely gray.

I could not even be sure that he was not some other Sebitti given to changing shape, but Lydia had no doubt, for she sank to one knee and bowed her head.

Dabir climbed to his feet. From his composure, you would think he was often woken from sleep to greet ancient wizards. "I bid you welcome to our home," he said.

"I am not interested in your welcome," Erragal replied, his voice thin and measured. "You are the one who hunted up my tools? Are you the ones who called forth the spirits?"

"The other Sebitti sought them first," Dabir said. "We meant to keep the weapons from their hands."

This gave him pause. I sensed this was not the answer he anticipated, for there was intensity to his next question. "Why?"

Lydia rose and backed up a step. One hand drifted toward the pouch still belted to her side, then slid away as Erragal's gaze tracked there.

"Because they have lied, kidnapped, and murdered to obtain them," Dabir answered. "Because they have caused an army of winter spirits to sheathe the land in ice and slay everything they come upon. We kept the bones," Dabir continued, "so that we can use them against the spirits."

There was no mistaking Erragal's displeasure, for his frown deepened. Yet I had the sense Dabir's answer had given him more to think about. A long moment passed.

"I shall talk further with you," Erragal decided, then faced me. "Look across the river in a half hour's time, and you shall see a signal." He looked to Dabir. "What is your name?"

Dabir bowed. "I am Dabir Hashim ibn Khalil."

"You are known as Dabir?"

"I am."

"Let me see the tools."

I glanced meaningfully at my friend as he bent to retrieve the spear. I came behind him, the club carried in two hands. I was not at all certain what Dabir thought of this development, and could not read his intentions, so I simply followed his lead.

Erragal reached out for my weapon first, and as his fingers brushed its surface his expression softened. He turned it almost in wonder, as though he were coming upon a favored toy of youth. I let him take it from me and he did so, in but one hand, despite his seeming frailty. A wistful smile crossed his face, and then he motioned Dabir closer. My friend stepped up to his side.

Erragal's eyes met mine and his expression hardened again. "Meet me as I have said. I shall talk to your leader alone."

I thought then that he meant to step outside the room, or even that he meant Lydia and me to leave, for I could never have guessed that the floor at their feet would suddenly flare with a red circle of energy, complete with mystic symbols. Even as I cried out and reached for my friend, he and the sorcerer winked away.

"Dabir!"

"They are gone," Lydia said, as though I were an idiot.

"I know that! Get your carpet ready!"

"I will," she said. "But, Asim—we must prepare. We may be walking into a trap."

"A trap? For what? He has Dabir! He has the bones! Gather your notes, and your robes! Take Jibril's book," I added, then grabbed up my candle and raced for my chambers.

I took a brief moment to look again at my armor and see how stained and bent it truly was; the blood splattered over it looked like rust. Yet there was no other I might don. The links were cold against me, even with my clothes as a barrier. And my chest and shield arm complained. There was no help for either. It was as I was throwing open the chest to grab an old Persian shield gifted me by the caliph that Buthayna and Rami, roused by the commotion, hurried in to see what was happening.

I told them that their master had been stolen by a wizard and that the Greek woman and I were going after him. Buthanya's brows furrowed as though she meant a tongue-lashing, then she said she would pack food and hurried off, her joints popping. I did not know when I would have the time to eat, but I looked forward to doing so.

Rami remained, his hair wild as a bird's nest. I passed the candle over to him and he used it to light two more kept upon a shelf. He then helped me with the shield, marveling at the lion embossed upon its surface, mouth open in a profile roar.

"Captain," he said hesitantly, "what happened to the lady Najya?"

I stared in shocked silence a moment, then blinked hard and offered a sad smile. Her fate would be long in explaining, so I simplified. "The wizards have her, too, Rami."

His eyes went wide, and he followed with the most natural question in the world. "Will you rescue her?"

I thought to tell him not all tales ended happily, or that some people were beyond saving. In the end, though, I tightened the shield strap on my aching arm and told him what I most wished. "I will," I said, "and when I marry her, I shall give you a place of honor at the feast, for being her friend when she had no others, and for bringing her into my life." I tousled his hair and he grinned up at me in confidence. He had no fear that I would fail, for he was young. "Find some gloves for the Greek woman," I suggested.

He said he would, and dashed away.

Buthayna hit me with useless advice as I passed through the kitchen into the courtyard, where Lydia already waited beside the carpet. I supposed she herself had borne it to its location, for she breathed heavily. Rami followed a moment later with gloves, and Lydia took them as if they were hers by right. Perhaps Lydia was only distracted, but I thought of Najya by contrast, who, no matter her high station and trials, had found the time to be kind to a stable boy.

"Do you have Jibril's book?" I asked her.

"Yes."

"And any other notes that were useful?"

"I know my business, Asim," she said. "I have not asked if your sword was sharp, have I?"

Now that question felt like the rake of a lion's claw. Often when danger loomed Dabir made that same jest, mocking something foolish Jaffar had once said. For all that it was grown tired, at that moment I would have given much to have him ask it of me. Lydia's arched brows drew together quizzically at my discomfiture, then she shrugged, apparently deciding it was not worth her time to inquire further.

It was only then, in the dim light of our lantern, that I finally got a good look at the carpet. I shook my head at the madness that it should carry us so far. It had once been very colorful, but its reds were washed out to a dirty brown and the greens to a dull gray. Faded flowers and leaves were worked all about its border. I could not really examine the black stallion rearing at its center, for Lydia sat down across it. I could not help thinking that our last two journeys had begun with the death of a friend; I prayed fervently that another was not shortly to follow.

Buthayna hurried out with a canvas bag that she passed on to Lydia, then stepped back, blinking, as the Greek took her seat on the fabric.

"What are you doing?" the cook demanded of me.

"Preparing to go," I said.

At any other time I might have relished her confusion. Perhaps she thought the Greek woman was at prayer; in any event, the old woman simply ignored our doings and wagged a finger at me, saying, "You bring him back, Captain. You shall never be forgiven if you fail, and the caliph himself will curse you."

She was surely right, and I nodded as I sank down onto the carpet behind Lydia. "Let us be off," I said.

While Buthayna and Rami looked on, Lydia put hands to the faded gold oval which circled the horse and we rose slowly into the air. Buthayna gasped and her eyes fairly bugged out of her head. I heard the boy cry out in pleased astonishment as we soared away.

"I shall take us high and toward the river," she said, "and we will see what there is to be seen."

"Fine, as long as we avoid the walls. Why did Erragal do this?"

She looked over her shoulder at me, meeting my eyes for a time. She did not reply, though, until she looked away. "He is curious about us, Asim. I think he fully meant to blast us into oblivion, but he did not find what he expected."

"What do you think he expected?"

"Someone else. A different story."

I mulled this over as we sailed out across the city rooftops and empty streets. The stars shimmered under a cloudless sky, and there was wind only because of our passage.

"What does he want with the weapons?"

"He fought once against the frost spirits. We can hope he means to do so once more. I'm wondering if that staff he carried was another one of the bones."

"I didn't see any figures on it," I said.

Her voice grew sharp. "Do you think he'd carve instructions on the side of his own staff?"

I thought that was a fair point, though I also wondered if she might be leaping to conclusions.

We passed well above the river wall, looking down over the silent docks, when I saw a blue flame soar up into the sky from deep in the vast ruins of Nineveh. I later learned that watchmen throughout the city noted it in alarm, and that the governor himself was wakened so that he might decide how best to deal with it.

Lydia guided us down to the snow-shrouded mound where the azure flames licked at the sky. Nothing fueled it. More wizardry. All about us were snow-banked broken walls and columns. Of Erragal there was no sign. Our destination, though, was clearly marked, for a perfectly square hole gaped beside the fire, the flickering of which revealed stone steps leading into the earth.

The moment that the carpet came to rest, I rose and peered down the gloomy stairwell. I had not thought to pack a lantern. Dabir would have anticipated this wrinkle and prepared for it, and once more I felt a pang.

"This fire gives no heat," Lydia said. She raised her hands to the flames, though her interest was not so great that she dared to touch them.

There was no point commenting. Sorcerous showmanship and secrets wearied me.

"We should take the carpet with us," Lydia suggested.

She meant to make me a packhorse, which did not suit me. "If I am to carry it, how will I defend us?"

She grumbled something in Greek. While she huffily rolled up the fabric under the eerie blue light, I drew my sword and took one step onto the old stairs. Instantly the fire behind us vanished, and a warm red light ignited below, although its source, at the bottom of the stairs, could not be seen.

It seemed we needed no lantern after all.

I led the way down, cloak over my battered armor, shield on one arm, sword in hand. Behind me Lydia walked slowly, the carpet hugged between her arms. It trailed on the ground beside her.

Deep we went, and though the stairs were old, they were hardly worn. While their edges crumbled, I thought age, not use, was the culprit.

We were forty steps down before we saw the torches flickering in the hands of crouching stone bird-men. The statues flanked immense doors fashioned all of bronze, shining with the wicked luster of reflected flame. I stared carefully at both sculpted abominations upon our arrival. Lydia, puffing, lowered the carpet to the flagstones before the doors. Neither statue seemed inclined to move, praise God. A rough recess was carved just past the bird-headed thing on the left. Within it a round bronze plate the size of a shield hung from two chains. I sheathed my sword and contemplated lifting the old hammer beside the bronze. Just then, the doors swung inward on silent hinges.

No one stood in the space beyond. I had the sense of a great void opening before us, but there was naught but blackness to be seen. And then a pair of torches lit, one on either side of us at head height. We stood not in a chamber, but at one end of a long square corridor some three spear lengths wide and perhaps as tall. A moment later, twenty paces on, another pair of torches lit, and after twenty more another, and on and on, for the length of Mosul's grand boulevard. I had never seen one so long, even in the palaces of Baghdad, and I contemplated it in stunned silence until Lydia dropped the carpet.

"I'm not carrying that thing any farther," she said.

"Leave it, then."

She scowled, but did as I bade.

I led the way forward, hand to hilt. Lydia followed after a last backward glance.

The floor was flat and even, and I saw after a few steps that it was formed of black marble, veined with other colors—streaks of white that resembled striations of clouds, and little flecks of red and gold. Polished to a high sheen, it mirrored both ourselves and the flare of the torches, and threw the sound of our footfalls back to us.

After we had advanced past the first six pairs of torches Lydia remarked that those behind us were extinguishing in pairs.

Eventually we arrived before another set of bronze doors, taller even than those that had opened onto this place, for the cavern had grown higher by degrees. These did not open, and this time no gong was present, nor alcove.

I glanced back. All but the torches just behind us had now died. A ringing thud reached us from far away. The first doors had shut.

"We're sealed in," Lydia said, though she did not sound terribly worried. In fact, a faint smile played over her features. She stood straighter and used her fingers to rake back her curling hair.

A moment later the double doors swung open. Another hall stretched before us, lit likewise with pair upon pair of torches, but whereas the corridor behind us had been of smooth stone, the walls ahead were set with intricate and colorful bas-relief. This hall stretched on two to three hundred paces, I think, and at its far end, in a throne of black marble, sat Erragal, grown triple his former size. His head reached halfway to the ceiling. At either side stood a giant man draped in black robes, features hidden by deep hoods. Both held gleaming spears in the hand farthest from the throne.

They moved not at all.

The images along the wall were all of fabulous beasts, armored hosts, and long-tressed women, painted with vibrant colors. Sometimes there were seascapes, and sometimes mountains, and once there was a sunset of glorious red and gold.

One thing else I noted—the hall grew subtly smaller as we advanced, though it retained the semblance of its dimensions.

By the time we had closed within twenty paces of Erragal, it was apparent that he was no more than man-sized, and that the ceiling was closer to our heads than it had been. The pictures to right and left of us were smaller than those that had opened the room.

The wizard frowned down at us. "Your arrival is timely. I have what I require from your leader; now I need only the woman. Warrior, you may go."

I'm not sure what I had expected, but it was not this. "I shall go nowhere without Dabir." I slid out in front of Lydia. "And you shall not have the woman—she is under my protection."

"Asim?" Lydia asked quietly from behind me. I think she meant some word of warning, but Erragal interrupted.

"Of course. You have been inconvenienced." The wizard clapped his hands. The robed figure on the left stepped forward, making an unsettling clacking noise as it moved. I peered close to see what sort of fingers clasped his spear, but the folds of his sleeve concealed how it gripped it. The other robed figure leaned his spear against the side of the throne and turned, bending. When he faced us once more, his sleeves had fallen back to show shriveled, skeletal fingers, wrapped about a small chest, its lid open. The thing advanced slowly to us, clicking the while. I watched, repulsed. It paused three paces from me, and I could look within the chest upon a riot of gold coins. Also there were rings, each crusted with diamonds, afire with rubies, glowing with emeralds and sapphires, and I saw part of a strand of what must have been a necklace of immense pearls.

If Erragal meant to impress me, he did not succeed, for I have looked on suchlike before. I turned to regard him. "Treasures worthy of a prince," I said.

"Or a king," Erragal countered. "But I shall give them to you, if you leave directly."

Was this recluse insane? "I shall not leave without Dabir," I repeated.

"Dabir and the woman are of use to me," Erragal explained. "I have no need of you. Take the treasure and go."

I was tired in general, and of wizards and magics in particular, and a foul mood wrapped me. "What manner of host are you, old one? You kidnap my friend. You try to bribe me to disregard my duty. You demand I abandon this woman. If you mean to fight me, then get to it, for I will not leave without my charges."

Erragal stood and looked down at me from the first of three stairs that led to his throne. For a long while our eyes locked, and then his hands thrust from his sleeves and on the instant a screen of blue fire flared before me, stretching the length of the room. I threw back one arm to shield Lydia and raised my blade with the other.

Three figures then walked from that fire, amber skeletons with horned skulls and low-slung jaws bristling with fangs. A sapphire flame floated in each of their rib cages where a heart should have been, and their bony hands gripped emerald-studded maces.

As the one on my left raised its mace I smashed my shield through its rib cage. The rim lit blue as it carried through to the creature's spine.

The skeleton fell into fragments, and its heart went out. I had no time to watch bones clatter on marble, for my next opponent was already swinging. I jumped back, parallel to the flame. My new adversary advanced; the other crept up on the side opposite the flickering wall.

Lydia stepped to my side and lifted her palm, fingers extended, to her mouth. She blew, and dark ash whirled up and into one of the warriors. The thing's bones were eaten away with dark blotches, and it caved in upon itself.

She turned to deal with the other, but I felt no sense of victory. I knew there was but one real chance. I leapt into the blue flames.

They burned me not at all; in fact, I landed unharmed beyond them on two feet and darted for the throne where Erragal stood, looking not so much surprised as reflective. He raised one hand and his robed guardian slipped suddenly between us, his weapon raised up like a staff.

I swept down at the guard's legs without breaking stride up the steps; the staff lashed out to block me, but I barreled on. I slammed into him with the shield and heard a crack. The thing clattered limply against the throne, a misshapen lump wrapped in cloth. I extended my sword to Erragal's neck. "Yield!" I said through gritted teeth. "And cease this game play!"

This time his gaze was frozen in surprise, and I thought for a moment that he dared not meet my eyes.

And then I heard the sound of a man clapping from some distance behind. The Erragal I threatened faded away to nothing. Snarling, I whirled to take in the altered scene around me.

The fire had vanished; the demon skeletons were gone, as was the one that had offered treasure. Lydia was unharmed, and advanced warily, surveying the room. Before me was a robe draped over protruding bones. Erragal, though, grinned up at me from the stair, a swords length below.

"I meant to test your mettle, warrior," he announced. "You have done well. Now you have but to pledge loyalty to me, as Dabir has done, and I shall reunite you."

I growled. "I shall pledge loyalty to no one until I know for what they stand. Man, wizard, djinn, or angel. You took my friend from me. Show me that he is safe, then we can talk of pacts and loyalties."

His teeth showed white in his beard. "The scholar spoke of your loyalty," he said, "and bravery, and also of your wisdom, which he said most overlooked."

"More games?" I demanded.

Erragal shook his head and addressed me gravely. "This was a test, not a game. Sheath your sword, Captain Asim, for you have passed it."

I glared down at the old wizard, conscious once again of the pains from the combat of the night before.

"Where is Dabir?" I roared, coming sideways down the stairs so that I might watch both the robed skeleton and the wizard.

"In the library," Erragal returned calmly, "learning the weaknesses of our enemies. Come. I will take you there."

I reached the bottom of the stairs. I did not yet sheathe my sword, but I did not point it at him.

Lydia advanced to stand near me. "How are we to judge you?"

"That is a fair question," he sighed after a time. "But I am not in a mood to humor you. Let me instead offer the hospitality of a true host. First, if you do not mind, I will raise my servant once more." One hand gestured negligently to the throne.

At the shuffling on those steps I turned my steel in that direction, for the skeletal thing climbed once more to its feet and lifted its weapon.

Erragal showed us a palm. "It will not fight you lest you attack me," he said.

It came slowly down past us and stepped ahead to the curtained area behind the throne. With one browned, bony hand, it lifted the fabric in front of us to reveal a small antechamber leading off into four man-sized hallways. The wizard strode for the one directly across from us.

"Dabir's plan is rather clever," Erragal said conversationally. "It destroys the bones, which I should probably have done ages ago, and uses their energy to good purpose. I am looking forward to seeing your notes, Lady Doukas, about the circle within the circle."

We started down the hall. These walls, too, were decorated with friezes, though here they were of folk setting stones and sighting down measuring sticks.

I could not help wondering if this was another trap.

Apparently Lydia still wondered the same, for she sounded skeptical. "What has Dabir told you?"

"How you plan to lure the spirits. Even with three working bones we may be hard-pressed to power so great a circle, but my own magics should supplement the effort. And I have contacted Enkidu, who is on his way to assist."

"Three?" she asked. "So the staff you have is one of them?"

"Oh, yes. Through it I felt one of the others activated from half a world away."

I grunted. It would be good to have allies, though I would remain unsure of him at least until I laid eyes upon Dabir. "Why do you want to help?"

His gaze shifted, and for a moment he was not the busy host, but a stern and powerful-looking man. "I am allowing you to help me," he said forcefully. "My brothers and sister shall not use my tools without permission. And those arrogant fools have opened the way through for the 'frost spirits,' as you call them. Again. My oldest and greatest friend died in the last battle against them. They shall *not* return."

"So you sensed us using the club—why did you care?" Lydia asked. "You obviously haven't cared about them for years. Why come looking for the tools now?"

"I am not so removed, young woman. Even in the south land I grew aware of the rising power of the snow spirits here. I had not troubled over them for generations," he added.

"Do you always lair here," I asked, "beneath these ruins?"

He flashed a half smile. "Not often, anymore. Once this city was mine. Or rather, I built it for King Senacherib. From time to time, I, too, have played at ordering the world of men."

I wondered what he meant by that.

He stopped at a door and gestured to me.

My eyes passed over the three square panels that adorned it, each depicting bearded scholars studying texts, and then I grasped the handle and pulled. It opened far more easily than you might have supposed, being as light to my hand as a slim block of wood, and I studied its edge. I had never seen a door so finely balanced.

On its other side was an immense chamber, large enough to fit most of a palace. It was filled with tables, neatly arranged in rows that were topped with model cities. Lamps burned on poles set every few feet.

"Where is Dabir?" I asked.

"We have not yet reached the library." Erragal sounded mildly irritated. "This is the chamber of cities."

Lydia remarked immediately that the intricate models were delightful. Mind, I was eager to set eyes upon Dabir and confirm his safety, so I did not let my attention wander. Yet I was not blind. So fine were the painted figures in the streets that you would have sworn real people had been shrunken and turned into tiny statues, though Erragal assured us this was no wizardry, and it had taken a very long while to mix the colors. There were all manner of cities, some built beside mountains with real flowing streams and others along coasts and others upon plains. Each was crafted with long straight roads, and Erragal pointed fondly to granaries, and aqueducts, and parks, as well as squares where folk might gather. As we passed on, he mentioned also that there was a way that lanterns might light each street at dusk, and a way that water would flow to each of a city's houses, and other such things.

"You should spread these ideas," Lydia said as we neared another door.

"Oh, I have," he assured us. "But men are too troubled with the smaller things, and tend not to think for the longer term. Those who can rarely come to power."

"You could come to power," Lydia suggested.

Erragal opened the door for us, his thick lips widening in a sad smile. "I did, my dear, we did, Koury, Anzu, and I. You should have seen Nineveh's aqueduct! And I built a great city named Harappa, with granaries just like those"—he pointed to his left—"and running water. Yet men destroyed her and her sister cities. Again and again we tried, once with a lovely dark-haired people of the islands south of Greece. They were my favorites." His voice grew tired. "But nature herself brought an end to our plans there. I have washed my hands of it."

We walked into another hallway, the lanterns flaring ahead of us. "Pressure pads, beneath the floor," he said in answer to my look, "are activated by our tread, and then the oil is released in the pipes within the walls, and ignited."

"You are a builder," Lydia observed. "I was told you were a destroyer."

Erragal's grin was mirthless. "To those who stood in the way. But I grew tired of creation, and destruction. Although, sometimes it takes greater strength to let things go." He said this last as if to himself.

While I puzzled over that, he spoke on. "I have seen the ebb and flow of men, women, children, entire tribes. Nations have climbed up, tottered to their feet, and strode mightily across the stage, only to stagger bloody through their final exit. So have your people come, so will they go. Only the language and stage dressing change." He stopped before another bronze door shining with the images of shelves and scrolls. He put fingers to the handle, then faced us. "That is not quite true. Always there are clever new ways to draw blood."

At that he opened the door.

Dabir sat on a low cushioned bench at a table, all three of the bone weapons propped in the corner. Next to him lay a set of rolled-up scrolls and a heap of food on shining golden plates. He smiled at the sight of me.

What I first thought a small room lit by a half-dozen wall torches, I soon saw was a balcony overlooking a vast hall full of shelves, so many that aisles were formed between them. And each shelf was weighted down with scrolls. Truly, it must have seemed like heaven to Dabir, and one within reach, for a stairway stretched down to that central floor just beyond the table where he studied.

"Have you found the texts instructive, scholar?" Erragal asked.

Dabir climbed to his feet and bowed his head slowly, in great respect. "I have. Your notes are thorough."

"I remain impressed that you can read them."

"He is real?" I asked Lydia. "And not another spell, like the skeletons we fought?"

"It is him," the Greek said simply.

"Skeletons?" Dabir asked me. His look of mingled concern and curiosity was so characteristic, I relinquished and finally sheathed my sword.

"A test," Erragal said breezily. "Now we four are here. Enkidu is en route to join us. We must get to work."

I could not help letting my attention stray to the platter of food.

Dabir pointed to the scroll he'd set aside. "So the others draw magic from different sources?"

"For the most part. Koury and Anzu work similar sorceries, as you see. But then, they came to immortality in the same way."

"How is that?" Lydia asked.

Erragal hesitated only a moment. "Flowers. They were ugly little things, growing only in the mouths of caves in the northern Zagros, in the spring. They're long gone, now, along with most of those who drank the draught brewed from them."

Lydia crept a little closer. "And what is Enkidu's secret?"

"And mine?" Erragal's head turned to consider her. "You do not wish to seem rude, but . . . well, you do not want to know mine. It would make you . . . uncomfortable and it is irrelevant as it cannot happen again. Enkidu is like Adapa was. He draws sustenance somehow from the world itself. And Lamashtu is more like Gazi, though she does not feast on hearts. I used to think her a monster," he added, "but she and Anzu are the only ones I ever speak with anymore."

"You said Enkidu is our ally," Dabir objected.

"He is my oldest living friend," Erragal agreed. "But his perspective is more akin to the beasts of the field. It is hard to find much to say to each other." He shifted smoothly to Lydia. "Now, Lady, let me see your banishing circle."

"I will be honored." Lydia said. However, she delayed and when she spoke again she sounded as though she were unloading a burden. "There's something that's bothered me for a while, and I was wondering if you could answer. Do you know what the other Sebitti want with the bones?" She paused, but before Erragal could answer she spoke on, and there was a rare nervous quaver in her voice. "I thought they were going to use them to control the frost spirits—as a threat to those who would not follow them—but I couldn't control the spirits when I tried it. Is there something I missed?"

"I cannot say what they are truly after," Erragal answered slowly, "though I now know why Anzu and Lamashtu both contacted me in recent years and spoke, in a roundabout way, of the old weapons."

"Do they have direct experience with them?" Dabir asked.

"Lamashtu does," Erragal answered. "She wielded mine, once, to aid me."

"So is she the one who told the others about them?" Lydia asked.

"Possibly they learned more from her, but Koury and Anzu studied with me for long years. I strove to teach them more than sorceries. History. Philosophy. Laws. Duties. They knew about the old ones, and their bones, and the brother and sister wizards who had preceded them. But I do not think anyone, even me, could use one of these things to compel those spirits to follow commands." His voice was tight. "I have tried contacting my sister and brothers, to ask, but they do not deign to answer. So. Whatever they are about," he concluded shortly, "they know that I would not approve. Now, Lady, while your company pleases me, we have work before us, and I am certain our time is limited."

I had only passing interest in the discussion that followed, for I cared solely about the result, and could hardly follow a talk about energy flows and linking symbols and other strangeness. I looked over our immediate surroundings while they examined Lydia's papers, then finally took off my shield, lifted some of the duck onto one of the ridiculous golden plates, drizzled the sauce over it, and ate. The meal did not wash away my worries exactly, although the flavors proved a delight. The throb of my injuries was dulled, and if the dark clouds had not precisely lifted, they had thinned a little.

Erragal listened attentively, making comments that Lydia hurried to scribble on the parchment. "We will have to conceal the circle," he said. "They'll hardly want to cross into the thing if they see it. Once we burn it into the ground, I'll cover it over with snow."

"Won't it be obvious that you've shifted snow?" I asked.

"I can manage it," he answered with a droll smile.

"What about . . . the woman that the frost spirit controls?" I asked.

The Sebitti nodded sagely. "Dabir has spoken to me about her. These are powerful sorceries we work. Anyone caught up within them is in danger. Much will depend upon her strength of will, and luck." He paused, looking off into space as though he had heard some important sound the rest of us had missed. I had seen that distracted, focused look before, and recently, and I realized I knew it from when Lydia's sentry had been attacked.

Erragal stood, and his brows drew together like storm clouds. "My home here is under attack."

Even as Dabir and I rose he raised a hand to us. "I will see to it," he said darkly.

Lydia spoke up eagerly. "Allow me to offer my aid."

His eyes raked her, then he took up the bone staff and strode for the door. "Very well. Come with me. You two stay here and keep to the work."

Lydia glanced back once, at Dabir, I think, as she left, and then it was we two, alone with the bones and the vast hall of books.

"That does not bode well," Dabir said.

"He seems more than capable," I offered, though I felt a stab of worry myself. "Why doesn't his staff have symbols on it like the others?"

"He crafted the others for ordinary men," Dabir said, "and left instructions on their sides so that their descendants, or friends, if they fell in battle, could wield them. He did not mean anyone else to use his, which is a little more powerful yet."

I glanced up at the door, to make absolutely sure I could not hear Erragal. Even still, I kept my voice low. "Did you tell him about Gazi?"

"That we fought and killed him? Aye."

"Well, what did he say?"

"Merely that Gazi's been mad for a very long time. Erragal wasn't upset so much as impressed."

"That," I said slowly, "is a better outcome than I had hoped for. Why did you say anything to him about it?"

"He warned me that he could see lies by looking at me. I am not sure that it's true, but I knew also that if we were to work together he had to trust me."

"It seems that he does. What's this he has you studying?"

Dabir's smile was a little sly. "The magics of our enemies."

Surely I had misheard him. "You do not mean to work them?"

"I am no wizard," Dabir said. "I'm learning their weaknesses, so I might counter their magics. As Jibril used to do, by breaking them. Erragal taught Anzu and Koury much of what they know. He has countless texts on magics and their working. And that is not all. My God, Asim, do you see that library?" He turned and regarded it, his eyes alight with desire. "I could spend a lifetime here. I wish," he finished, suddenly reflective, "that Jibril could have seen this." He fell silent and glanced over to the door, for he had heard, like me, footsteps in the hall, though they were strange.

I stood. "That may be one of Erragal's servants," I said, though the skeleton had walked in boots and did not clomp awkwardly.

"That sounds like wood on stone," Dabir said, rising.

We looked at each other with the same dire thought in mind, then both picked up our weapons. The footsteps drew closer and stopped in front of the door.

16

There was a metallic thump against the door as something hard was hammered into it, and then it swung sharply outward, revealing a peculiar figure: a bull with a crowned and bearded man's head reaching to the height of the generous doorway and filling it almost completely. It was carved all of wood, and was stained mostly black, save for large gray wings that were folded at its sides. Its unblinking eyes were bright green jewels, and its sharp metal teeth were coated red with blood still trickling down its curling beard.

I can assure you that sight was unique in all my long experience, before or since. Dabir grabbed up a bunch of the documents and shoved them under one arm. At my shout to move we raced down the stairs, but as we ran, two of the scrolls shook loose and bounced down the steps before us. Dabir let out a little cough of dismay and bent to chase one but I yelled for him to run on.

I risked a backward look. The monster was at the head of the stairs, where it glared down at us with those dead, unblinking eyes. By the time we reached the central floor it had begun to stomp its way down. One of its knee joints cracked loudly each time a leg bent.

Dabir ran between the lines of tall shelves, the spear swinging in one hand. The aisles were but a horse length wide, and the shelves, stuffed full mostly with scrolls wound tightly around wooden rods, stretched well above our heads toward the ceiling far beyond. Light flared in sconces set high on the wall, which meant the aisles were little more than dark alleys.

"That's got to be one of Koury's monsters!" I said. "The Sebitti have followed us here!"

"Aye—pray that blood is not Lydia's or Erragal's," Dabir said over his shoulder.

While that was fine sentiment, the way the monster gained on us it seemed important to pray that the thing would not shortly be decorated with our own blood. "Do you know where you're going?"

"Away from that thing!"

That also was fine sentiment, but I had a thought. "Go up! Dabir—climb the shelves!"

He skidded to a stop, glanced back at me in surprise, then, spear lengthwise in one hand, grabbed the shelf and pulled himself up. I heard him groan as a scroll crunched under one foot, but by planting boots carefully in cubbyholes he was soon grasping the bookcase height. The arched ceiling loomed a full story overhead.

The monster closed quickly, and was less than a full spear cast off now. There was no good way to climb while holding that club, so I handed it up to Dabir.

"Hurry!"

An unkillable monster with bloodstained metal teeth was but a leopard's spring away and closing fast, so I can assure you I started up with great haste. I did not care so much as Dabir that jamming my feet into cubbyholes destroyed ancient works. The next moment I was halfway over the lip of the bookcase, and the monster had skidded to a stop. The pointed crown carved at the top of its head was only a hand span below my dangling boot, and I thought at any moment to feel those teeth tearing off my toes. Yet it did not, or could not, leap vertically, and with Dabir hauling on my arm I was quickly standing atop what seemed a most sturdy board.

The monster could not look up very well. The best it could manage was to turn its head and tilt slightly, so that it could take us in with one eye.

"A design flaw," Dabir noted.

I grunted. "Go!"

He picked up his spear and took up running once more, this time atop the bookcase. It had not been a bad idea at all, for the case housed scrolls both from left and right, which meant its top was almost as wide as one of the aisles. There were two more sets of aisles and bookcases between us and the left wall, and three between us and the right.

The monster galloped along below, its head cocked at an angle that would have been uncomfortable to any living creature.

"Look for another door," Dabir called to me.

Even the finest plans have their challenges, and after a few paces more I discovered one when Dabir put on a burst of speed. By the time I realized what he was doing, it was too late to offer criticism.

There were periodic breaks in the lines of shelves, wider by several feet than the space between cases. Dabir had seen this and was preparing for a leap.

My warning cry died before I voiced it, for he was already airborne. He was ever agile, as I have mentioned, and landed crouched on two feet, as though he had spent many years working as an acrobat. I frowned a little, and raced at the gap myself. The monster paced me on the right, and it may be I spent a moment too long staring at the horrible thing, because I stumbled as I landed. If it had not been for Dabir's steadying arm I would have tumbled right over the edge.

He pointed across the aisles. "There is our way out."

This lane between the bookcases stretched to both walls. Set in the farthest was a large wooden door. "I hope it's unlocked."

"Let us run a little farther on this case, then leap aisle to aisle."

I immediately saw the merit to this plan—the monster would have farther to run, and would also lose sight of us. The flaw, of course, was that we had more leaping to do, and there would be less space to build speed. Yet what other choice did we have? I followed him twenty paces while the monster kept up with us. Then Dabir turned, quick as a rabbit, backstepped to the far edge of the case, and hurtled across the empty space. He landed almost as finely as he had on the longer jump, the spear held out in both hands before him.

I picked up my courage and followed. I landed more ably than the last time, though there was an ominous creak of timber as I hit.

"Good," Dabir said. "Let's keep moving!"

This we did, and we jumped between two more cases. I took Dabir's spear as he lowered himself to the floor. The moment his boots hit the tile we heard something that sounded rather like thunder, and the ground shook.

Surely that did not bode well.

I handed him the weapons and slipped down, then Dabir and I ran for the door.

Distantly I heard shouts; closer at hand came the swift approach of huge wooden hooves on tile. The damned thing could not only see, apparently it could hear, for it had followed, and now galloped between the cases toward us.

It was only twenty lengths behind when Dabir reached the door, which fortunately opened at his hand. The monster was at my heels as I darted to safety. Dabir slammed the door closed and pressed his back to it even as a mighty echoing thump rang against the wood.

Dabir was knocked several paces back by the force of the monster's strike against the door. I threw down the club and pressed with him against the barrier in time to feel it tremor mightily beneath my hands.

I glanced quickly to either side, and started at sight of what I first took to be men. We were surrounded by life-sized statues on stone plinths, each facing the narrow lane that led down the midst of the long rectangular room. There were dozens of them, and the twin pairs of lanterns flickering along the walls set their shadows moving in the gloom. I think I might have been even more troubled by the sight if there had not been a wooden monster with bloodstained teeth hammering on the door behind me.

"Can you hold it?" I asked Dabir.

"Hopefully," he said. "Find something to spike the door!" He grunted with effort as there came another bang. I dashed over and briefly considered the first statue, a severe-looking young woman in a long dress. I put hands to her thigh and discovered she was crafted from wood. It pained me to dull my blade, but I hacked off the statue's fingers and came running back.

While Dabir pressed himself to the door, I used my sword hilt to hammer the wooden digits into the narrow gap of the doorjamb. We stepped back cautiously, watching the door vibrate as the thing on the other side beat against it.

I allowed myself several deep breaths. Dabir, beside me, took in the same.

"That may hold it for a while," he said.

"Now what?" I asked.

"Erragal. We must find him."

We gathered up our gear and started down the aisle at the same moment the hammering started against a part of the wall behind us.

"It's trying to smash through stone?" I asked. It struck again, and we saw a rain of masonry flakes.

"Nay," Dabir said. "Much of the construction here is plaster designed to simulate stone. We may not have long."

"We could set it on fire," I pointed out as we hurried forward. It was my thought to douse it with flame from one of the lanterns as it emerged.

"Then a flaming monster with metal teeth would be trying to kill us," Dabir pointed out. "And it might set the library on fire."

A small hole had opened in the wall by the time we reached the door on the far side. Dabir suggested we just keep moving rather than spiking the next, and we stepped through into a narrow hallway, turned left, and almost ran into two of the snow women.

They did not face us, but were gliding up behind a short, broad-shouldered fellow in furs who wrestled one of Koury's animated wooden men.

Dabir and I slowed momentarily in astonishment, then lifted our weapons and charged the snow women. One had started to turn as my blow disintegrated it, but I did not see its face as it died, for which I was thankful. Dabir's spear thrust destroyed the other.

At that moment the wrestler looked over his shoulder at us. He had a dark rugged beard, matched in wildness by the tangled locks of his hair. His eyes were a soft green, almost like those of a blind man, sad somehow even as he strained to pin the arms of the wooden warrior. This construct Koury had not bothered robing, and we could clearly see the rounded elbow and ankle joints; it was decorated only by a sharp knife held in one mittenlike hand. One wooden leg was broken.

The stranger returned attention to the thing struggling in his arms. He set both hands to the arm with the weapon and bent it the wrong way so there came a gratifying crack.

Since this was no feeling creature, it did not pause in reaction, and immediately swung its other fist at the stranger's head. He ducked just in time.

And then came a loud smash from the direction of the room we'd just quitted, and the clatter of wooden hooves.

Dabir mouthed a curse I shall not repeat, then said, panting: "It is time again to move!"

"Come, man!" I told our new ally, and Dabir and I tore down the hall, our robes flapping behind. The wild man sprinted effortlessly ahead.

"Follow me," he said. So we did. Behind galloped the bearded bull with its grotesque, kingly head. The wooden man limped after.

"You are Enkidu," Dabir called to the man ahead of us.

"Yes." He halted at an unremarkable section of wall, with the monster no more than twenty paces back. At his touch a door-sized section opened silently inward. Enkidu passed through, and then Dabir and me. From this side, it looked like a solid wooden door. I grabbed the locking bar set in its back to push the door shut. Just before it closed on the jamb, the monster thrust in, sharp teeth in that wooden mouth clacking at me.

I had dueled with corpses and danced with great serpents, but the sight of that thing's dark, dead-eyed face, its metal-tipped teeth stained with blood, chilled me and set me near to panic. The head with its gnashing teeth was caught but a short distance from my face.

"One side!" Dabir called, and as I moved away I saw he'd picked up the club. A terrific blow smashed off some of the monster's decorative curling "hair" and sent it rattling to the floor. It pulled away and I pushed the door toward its frame, slamming down the bar.

"Hurry!" Enkidu called from up ahead. "The hall's defenses will go off any moment!"

"Come, Asim!" Dabir handed me the club.

I did not know what Enkidu meant, but I guessed that if he was worried, I should be. I raced after Dabir, who paused only to grab the spear.

This hall was narrower than the others through which we'd moved, barely wide enough for two of us to run side by side. Lanterns lit alternating walls. Some thirty paces ahead there was a stairwell up which Enkidu was running. Behind us came a series of heavy thuds, then a loud crash. Incredibly, the wooden monster had pushed itself in, smashing the door and much of the frame to the floor. It loped after us, building speed.

Suddenly there was a ringing clatter from the rear, and I risked a glance over my shoulder to see a rain of caltrops drop from the ceiling. A heartbeat later there came the distinctive twang of bowstrings and the rattle of dozens upon dozens of shafts against the corridor floor. The wooden monster was struck with ten or twenty of them. They stood out like quills, but neither caltrops nor arrows slowed it in the least.

"Hurry!" Enkidu shouted, and I then knew fear, for the urgency in his call made it seem as though worse things would follow.

Dabir and I sprinted for the stone stair ahead and my breath came now in such loud gasps I could not hear my friend. I risked no looks behind, but I heard the sound of liquid spraying from overhead and felt a few drops of something strike one shoulder. I smelled oil.

We had just set our foot upon the bottom step when we heard a roar of flame and felt heat against our backs. We pounded up, pausing only at the first landing to both turn and see curtains of fire rain into the hallway, completely obscuring our view.

"Bismallah!" Dabir managed.

The fire crackled loudly, but we could still hear the knocking steps of the creature ascending the stone, different now with the caltrops embedded in its feet. Further above, Enkidu was shouting that there wasn't much time.

"You mean," I gasped to Dabir, "it gets worse?"

We forced ourselves up the steps as fast as we could. I risked another look back and saw the monster emerge from the flames, wrapped in fire. The many arrows that stood out from its body were lit on their ends like candles.

I went on, gaining the final landing a moment before Dabir. I spun to aid him just as the stairs dropped completely away. One moment Dabir was there, the next moment some twenty steps broke into pieces and dropped. By pure reflex I reached out and snagged at Dabir, missing his arm but catching hold of the spear he still clutched. His weight unbalanced me and I staggered on what had become a ledge. The leaping monster and crumbling masonry fell away into a cavernous darkness, a pit lit only by the flaming monster itself, which was still opening and closing its shining teeth when I last caught sight of it careening off a rocky vertical surface.

I dug into the grainy stone wall on my left with fingernails. This steadied me, and I grabbed out for Dabir's sleeve. Then there came a ripping noise and I saw the whites of Dabir's eyes as he stared up in consternation.

But Enkidu joined me then, and the two of us hauled Dabir up over the rim. My friend stumbled along the stonework until he hit the wall across from me, where he leaned, spent and panting.

"That would have been a long fall," I said.

"Indeed," he said, gasping. "Thank you."

Enkidu waited a few paces on, leaning with hands upon his knees.

"Are all of Erragal's halls like that?" I asked him.

"Only the few to his personal chambers. I used a lever to activate his protections."

"Next time," I said, "you should wait a moment longer."

Enkidu let out a short, barking laugh.

"Do you know how far both groups of enemies have penetrated the palace?" Dabir asked.

Enkidu considered him with his sad eyes. This, I thought, was the strangest wizard I had ever met, for he looked like nothing so much as a gentle hermit. He smelled of wild places, and his clothes were fashioned all of dark, untanned leather and fur.

"I do not," he answered. "I had come up the river way to seek Erragal, but before I could find him, one of Koury's things found me."

"And the frost women are here," I said. "Again, both sides attack at once."

"Do you know where Erragal is?" Dabir asked.

"He should be beyond that door." Enkidu pointed to the rough stone against which Dabir leaned. "This is the safest of his rooms, the place to retreat when under attack."

I saw no door anywhere close to Dabir, though I looked now for seams. We stood in a rounded space no greater than ten paces across, walls on every side, the pit behind us. A single lantern flickered in one wall, at Dabir's right.

"He told us he was going to fight them," Dabir said.

"Then the way is still through here," Enkidu said after a moment of reflection. There was no other apparent choice that didn't involve leaping into a pit.

Enkidu touched a notched recess below a bracketed torch and another silent section of wall slid away. A short flight of stairs led down to a door of burnished bronze adorned this time with the image of a huge stone bridge arching over a river alive with fishes.

Enkidu descended without hesitation and pushed open the door.

Here at last we had come upon more living beings—a handful of older men and women clothed in simple robes. They were huddled together at one end of a long room furnished comfortably with rugs, pillows, and couches.

Apparently Erragal did not trust all his chores to skeletons.

The folk started at our entrance, though they calmed before the un-kempt wizard with us, whom they must have recognized.

"Have you seen your master?" Enkidu asked them.

The servants, or slaves—I was never sure which they were—told us that they had fled here when the attack begin. There followed a harrowing account of their fellows' deaths at the hands of strange wooden beings. They spoke Arabic, and I wondered if they had been recruited from Mosul.

Enkidu pressed for more details, and Dabir crowded in, listening closely.

They finished with the servants, who seemed much more content now that they'd told their story. Some even smiled. And, indeed, when the Sebitti turned to us, I, too, felt a flush of good fellowship.

"I think I know where Erragal is," Enkidu said. "Come with me."

We passed then through another door, to a landing where we could follow steps up or down. Enkidu went upward. From somewhere there came a rumble that shook the ground around us.

"I hope that's one for our side," I said.

We climbed behind Enkidu up those old stone stairs, much like the ones I'd descended with Lydia to enter this death trap warren, then emerged finally at a landing with another dead end. Enkidu pressed a faded red stone halfway up the wall, and we were met immediately with a blast of cold air as a door-sized swath of stone swung outward. We then looked upon a darkened field of snow-topped ruins. The wind whistled and little bursts of frost danced beyond the doorway, cleverly concealed in a substantial pillar fragment. We seemed to stand at the end of what had once been a wide avenue. Half-tumbled walls and blocks of stone lay to left and right, stretching ahead of us under the starlight.

Enkidu stepped through and halted a few paces in front of us, looking to both left and right. It was almost like watching a feral animal suddenly on the alert. We followed, weapons at the ready. I was about to ask Dabir if he thought we should activate their magics when Enkidu wheeled to look past us. We pivoted and found Lamashtu standing between us and the exit we'd just left.

She had been so swift when last we met that I'd forgotten how thick she was. Her appearance might almost have been described as matronly save that her eyes gleamed in the darkness like a cat's.

"Enkidu. What are you doing here? Shouldn't you be out chasing lions?"

"Erragal called for my help," he said.

"And so you came, like a good dog."

"You have gorged yourself, I see," Enkidu replied calmly. "But I do not mind, sister. We can still be friends."

I felt a wave of calm flood through me once more. It was good, I thought, to be near Enkidu.

Before us, Lamashtu smiled. "You know that has never worked upon me."

"I do not wish to hurt any old friends," he said. "You are outmatched. Withdraw."

At that she laughed. "Not me, but you," she said, and at that very moment something round as a barrel and black burst from behind the snowy ruins and hurtled at Enkidu. Our ally was lightning-swift, but even so the largest wooden serpent yet struck into his chest like a club. The attack would have killed a normal man, but he only let out a groan and staggered back.

Lamashtu advanced on us with a wicked smile.

"How did you know we would be here?" Dabir demanded.

"We watched all entrances," she said simply, "to see the rats flushed out. We had long since learned most of Erragal's defenses. He hasn't bothered changing them in centuries."

She looked as though she meant to say more, and with her distracted I did not think I would have a better opportunity. I drove at her, lifting back the club. She did not move, and I thought surely I would stave in her skull. There was the briefest moment of regret for killing a woman, and then she stopped my arm with a single, effortless lift of her own small hand. My strength and momentum meant nothing—the instant she caught me with her fingers, my swing stopped. She slid back a foot, but was otherwise unfazed.

She then stepped nimbly over the spear haft Dabir swung to trip her. She did not bother looking at him, but smiled into my eyes. "I will take your strength. If I feel merciful when I am done, perhaps I shall kill you. If you beg for it."

The might of that one hand was astonishing. I could not pull free. Dabir jabbed at her again with the blunt end of his spear. This seemed only to irritate her, for Lamashtu frowned a bit as she caught hold of the haft. Dabir immediately set to tugging on it, uselessly. I lashed out with my foot, but kicking her leg was like striking a tree trunk. I winced; she but looked annoyed and did not even rock backwards.

"Allah preserve us," Dabir whispered. I dared not look away, but I heard the crunch of footsteps in the snow behind and to right and left. I had the vague impression of lean figures ringing us.

From off to my left I heard terrific grunts and thunks and guessed that Enkidu battled still with the huge wooden serpent. Lamashtu's eyes still stared into my own, alien and dangerous, and I thought then of Najya's life ruined by these dark wizards, and Tarif and Jibril, and Abdul and the others, lost or frozen. All that we had endured of late passed swiftly before my memory, aye, even unto the death of brave Alexis, and an anger fired my very soul. It was not the devil of rage; it was a sense of righteous fury that so much evil had been done and that I had not the power to stop it. I wished that I'd had time to run through the form so that I might at least attempt to use the magic in the club as a weapon.

It was as I thought about the movement used to activate the club that its symbols lit with a white-gold brilliance. I had not noticed my weariness until it was lifted from me and astonishing vigor coursed through my muscles. I straightened, grinning. Lamashtu's expression widened in surprise as I yanked my arm free of her grasp and swung.

Lamashtu's inhuman speed kept her clear of my strike as she leapt back, but she still cried in pain, for a pulse of white light coursed out from the old weapon. She landed heavily on her side just in front of the open doorway. I had thought Lydia's farr black, until I saw that of Lamashtu's, which all but swallowed light.

"How—" Dabir began, but I was already turning to take in the rest of our foes.

Those who had closed upon us were dressed lightly, and possessed

Lamashtu's eerie eyes. Their whites gleamed in the glow put off by the club. For all that their clothes were nicely kept, the way that they stood, crouching with fingers held like talons, they seemed more like beasts. And with the sorcerous sight the club lent me, I saw they were cut from midnight cloth.

"You have but to *think* the form!" I called to Dabir. One of Lamashtu's fiends sprang, tigerlike, but my blow caved in his head, smashing through bone and tissue. There was a curious lack of blood. My swing carried me through into a second and I broke through shoulder bone. He dropped, screaming, at my booted foot.

Dabir then was at my side, his spear shining, and he drove it through the beast-man's chest. Our foe wailed, collapsed, and fell into dust.

"A fine strike!" I called to Dabir, who laughed.

The others charged as a mounted figure came round a snowcapped pillar. Even in the darkness a man could perceive the odd stiff gait of the beast and the strange way it held its head. Koury's stallion. And, from the darkly powerful glow of the rider's farr, Koury himself. Interestingly, he was not wrapped wholly in darkness.

"Back to back!" I called to Dabir.

So we stood thus as the creatures rushed us, and I fought with a fierce pride, wielding that great club as though it were a simple toy. On they came, and down they fell. The weapon smashed through bone like paper, and its light burned these men born of darkness. I left a field of broken bodies; Dabir, though, pierced their flesh, and those who did not go reeling back disintegrated, leaving only dust and empty garments that fluttered to the ground.

Koury did not leave his horse, but cast down two items from his satchel and wooden men sprang into being.

I saw a red flare of energy from the corner of my eye and risked a glance in time to see Lamashtu wielding a whip of fire. Dabir struck this with his spear. The flame blasted into a rain of sparks, and the sorceress screeched furiously.

Enkidu had triumphed at last over the snake and, holding its tail, lashed its long broken body at the sorceress. She stepped away, but two of her remaining minions were not as agile, and they went sprawling.

Enkidu jumped and landed hard on a nearby beast-man. He grinned at us. His farr was mostly blue and silver.

"Good!" he shouted, laughing. "We shall win this!"

On came the wooden warriors. Up rose the beast-men I had downed, no matter their horrifying wounds. They slunk to the sides, away from me, and I knew they waited until we were distracted. From far behind came a man's voice raised in a roar of fury and then a string of odd syllables. Two of the nearest beast-men disintegrated in a rain of ash. The others cried out and pulled away.

"Erragal!" Enkidu said with relief.

On my right I saw Lamashtu raise up another whip of flame. Enkidu tossed one of her lackeys at her.

Behind us, Erragal and Lydia had stepped forth from the doorway. His farr blazed with a riot of colors stronger than any others. Lydia unleased a trio of howling ghosts that came surging toward Lamashtu.

This apparently was enough for the death mother, who sneered something in disgust and winked out of existence. The handful of remaining well-dressed beast-men vaulted away over the tumbled walls.

This left only the wooden men Koury had sent forth, which were now returning to him. Lydia's spirit creatures soared after.

"What are you doing here?" Erragal asked us. We were but ten paces apart, and he had taken a step toward us when snow women flowed forth from the walls all around, dozens upon dozens of them. I started to brace myself for attack when I realized that they didn't mean any harm at all. They and the beautiful white animal spirits with them were friends.

I couldn't understand why Erragal and Lydia looked so upset as a giant wolf loped up to greet them, or why they lashed the spirit elephants with magical fire. They had not come to overwhelm, but to welcome.

"Fight, Asim!" Dabir urged.

I felt Enkidu's comforting hand on my shoulder. He stepped toward Dabir.

Erragal's robed skeleton, suddenly there beside its master, tossed down Lydia's carpet, which she kicked open. I did not know why Dabir looked so horrified when I smiled at him, nor why he lobbed the spear toward the retreating pair with both hands, as though he were tossing a log. I saw it fly, dreamlike, its glow fading. It passed through the snow women crowding toward Lydia and Erragal, leaving only fragments of drifting frost.

I watched as the elder Sebitti leaned from the rising carpet and caught the spear. The huge white wolf snapped playfully at the carpet as it flew up and out, the spear still dangling from Erragal's hands, and then all cares left me and I relaxed in the companionship of my most excellent friend Enkidu.

17

Enkidu himself took my club, and we marched obediently with him through the ruins as the black night gave way to dawn. On their eastern edge we came upon a force of Khazars, many of whom were busily erecting tents in the pale, chill air. The wind brought me the scent of horses and the bawling complaints of a variety of animals.

It was a camp for a small army of Khazars. We two followed Enkidu beyond their line of fur-clad sentries. The snow women had drifted away or wandered off—because of my own altered state I paid them no mind.

I don't remember feeling especially worried about the Khazars, even though the numbers impressed me. "There must be a thousand or more of them," I said to Dabir.

He did not respond.

I had heard that Khazar women sometimes rode to war at the side of their men, and as we passed deeper into the camp we saw some of these female warriors tending gear and standing about the fires. They considered us with fierce ice-blue eyes, and I sensed that they would kill us, joyously, on the instant if given the word.

Finally we came to a huge round tent fashioned of animal hides. I had seen smoke curling from the openings at the peaked roofs of other tents, but none rose from this one. Two huge warriors, hulking in their dark furred robes, stood before its entrance. They bowed their heads to Enkidu and held the tent flap open for us.

Inside was a gloomy space hung with colored curtains and floored with many rugs. I realized that other parts of the tent must be sectioned off by the curtains into separate chambers, for the tent was much larger than this single area. It was very cold within, and while there was a brazier, I had the sense it was more for light than warmth. It threw twisted shadows on the fabric walls.

And then my breath caught in my throat, and my heart raced like a rabbit's.

Beyond the brazier, in front of three kneeling Khazars, Najya sat upon a slim chair. Her hair was unbound and hung back in a cascade. She was garbed now in a brown dress with yellow diamonds, and it was of curious style, for while it was formfitting about her waist, it was flowing below, and had long sleeves that tightly sheathed her arms.

And her eyes were blue, a bright, piercing blue that glowed from within. At sight of that, the joy that had thoughtlessly leapt forward at sight of her fell suddenly, like a gazelle struck dead in midgallop.

Enkidu went down on one knee before her, and his influence fell away. I stood blinking as the reality of what had happened washed suddenly over me. I was aware then of great fatigue, and anger that Dabir and I both had been manipulated.

The Khazars sitting before Najya grew agitated and rose, pointing to us. I recognized one of them as the woman we'd encountered in the frozen village north of Harran.

Guards strode forward, hands to weapons.

"Down," Dabir said to me, and dropped to his knees. I was a moment too late, for the Khazar warriors arrived to point insistently at the ground in front of me, and one put a hand to my shoulder.

Almost I knocked his fingers away and drew, but I fought the impulse and did as I was ordered, even if I did not understand the words they spat.

After a short while Najya spoke to us. "You may rise." Her voice was commanding, calm, but with nothing of its usual warmth.

Enkidu stepped to our side and showed the club he had taken from me. "As you foretold, so has it come to pass."

At this Najya smiled coolly. She spoke to the trio nearest her. "I am done with all of you except Bersbek."

They rose and bowed, backing away from her. The Khazar woman smiled at me, short, thick, but clear-eyed, with a weathered complexion. Her male counterparts stared as they left us. They were garbed like all the Khazars—leather and fur, mostly—but were lean where the others were thick, and wore necklaces heavy with clanking symbols, bird claws, and what might have been mummified fingers. They were red-haired, a peculiarity of many in their race. A strange sweetness clung to them as they passed. I know it was not soaps, for they reeked of unwashed flesh.

"Where is the spear?" Najya asked Enkidu.

"This one," he gestured to Dabir, "passed it over to Erragal, who escaped. I am sorry, Daughter."

At the look on Najya's face it was easier to think of her as someone else, for her lip curled as she frowned. After a moment, though, her expression cleared, and she eased back. "We have dreamed that Asim will once more wield the club in a great battle, in our presence, when we seek the spear. We shall have both of them at that time."

"'We'?" Dabir asked. "Not 'I'? Are you one now, spirit and Najya?"

Enkidu and the round shaman woman, Bersbek, looked over at him, then at Najya, as if they expected to hear a reprimand, or an order to strike him for speaking out of turn.

But no such order came. "I cannot be rid of her," Najya's voice answered. "Her thoughts are useful to me, for she knows things that I do not." She turned her lovely face to the Sebitti. "Enkidu, take their swords, for these two are crafty."

"This will I do, Daughter. But, if you will forgive me, what further use will they serve?"

"They have used the bone weapons." Najya frowned slightly. "Do you know how to unlock their secrets?"

"No, Daughter," Enkidu admitted.

"I can master the secrets, O Daughter of the Frost," Bersbek declared, fervently bobbing her head. Her accent was thick, her voice harsh, though somehow compelling.

"So you claim." She calmly considered the shaman, who smiled almost stupidly in her eagerness. "You may study them here, with me. If you fail, I will learn the secrets from Dabir and Asim."

"I can command them to tell you the secrets now," Enkidu offered.

"No." Najya's voice was sharp.

"But they are foes," Enkidu said. "Let us take the information from them, and be done."

Najya scowled. "How is Asim later to wield the club if I slay him now?"

"Forgive me." Enkidu hesitated. "Is it possible that the mortal form you wear interferes with your judgment?"

"Do not question me! They must be kept alive. Take Dabir from me. Asim remains. Bersbek, take the club into the treasure chamber and study it."

I tensed, ready to battle. But I could offer no challenge, for Enkidu cowed us with such force that we allowed our swords to be removed without reaction. Dabir managed to look concerned as Enkidu guided him out.

Soon we were alone, Najya and I, save for two thickly built Khazar guards at either side of the threshold. Najya stood and then circled me slowly, as though she inspected me at the market.

I had thought over and again what I might say should I once more be in Najya's presence, yet now I found nothing clever upon my lips. "I know that Najya is still there—I want to talk to her."

"We are one." Her voice was cool as steel in the snow. She stopped in front of me and peered up with merciless eyes. "Do you like what you see?"

Oh, sweet agony. I found myself speaking the truth, at least in part. "Aye, my heart still speeds at sight of you, and my breath catches at the sound of your voice."

Her reply was a long time in coming. "This pleases me," she said at last, and drew nearer. Her speech was hesitant. "It is strange. When you speak to me, I listen with more than my ears. The whole of this body is focused upon your intent. It is interesting, and somehow pleasant, and occurs when none of these others talk." She paused. "I know all of these reactions come solely because the woman is drawn to you. But this form is useful to me; without it I could not command the allegiance of my followers. And the sensations this body provides interest me as well, and they do no harm."

"I see." A smile rose, unbidden, then faltered as I stared into eyes that should have been a rich brown and instead were ever-shifting shades of blue.

"I have a surprise for you. Come." She lifted a canvas flap and passed into another section of the tent. I followed to find a chamber set with cushions and fur pelts, and, at its far end, a grisly ornament.

"What do you think?" Najya asked, as though she had just returned from the market with an especially choice selection of cloths.

It was a great block of ice, and frozen in its center was Koury. He stood tall and straight, defiant, though his last expression had been one of shock.

I stared through the ice at the dead man not because of any real fascination, but because I was not at all sure what I would say.

"I know how much he angered you. He lied to me," she said with venom, "and he killed my husband. The woman's husband," she corrected quickly.

What do you say when your love has presented you with a cold corpse? "How long do you intend to leave him like this?" I asked.

"Forever, I think. He shall stand as warning and reminder to all who would oppose me. I thought you would be more pleased," she said, watching my reaction.

"I am very happy," I lied. Even I knew how badly I lied.

She stepped close. "The woman has wondered what it would be like, and I am curious. You will kiss me."

I do not think I would have hesitated so long, under normal circumstances. Her lips were cold, her manner stiff at first, but she relaxed after a moment and I felt her arms go up around my neck. My own slid down to clasp her waist.

After a time she pulled back. Over her shoulder dead Koury's eyes stared at me, lopsided and magnified through the ice.

"Oh," she breathed, "that was very nice."

It was then I noticed Najya's own eyes were warmer, not quite so bright. And her manner was somehow more animated. "Is something wrong?" She sounded, now, beyond merely curious, as though she actually cared about my reaction.

All sorts of things were wrong, of course, not the least of which was the frozen curio that faced me. But I was not so foolish that I failed to discern the difference in her eye color meant Najya's influence was waxing. I thought of what I might say or do to strengthen it further.

I took her hand, and she started in surprise. Her fingers were cold, cold as dead Koury's prison.

"You have your revenge," I said. "He wronged you, and he has died." I took up her other hand. I felt her flesh warming to my touch, and as her eyes searched mine I found more and more brown within their depths. "Now put these other things from you. Leave this place. Come away with me."

Her brows wrinkled in bewilderment as I dropped to one knee, so that I would not stand above her.

"Forgive me," I said, "for I do not know how it is done among Persians. But I will ask your hand of you, and of your family. Aye, I would journey to ask it of the old man in the mountain if that is what I must do to have you betrothed to me. I am but a soldier, but one who has risen far, so I do not think that they would be ashamed for you to be with me."

"They would not," she said softly. Her hands trembled in mine.

I forgot all around me. "I do not know if you need only the months and days prescribed by the Holy Koran, or if your people demand more time to properly mourn, but I shall wait however long so that I might have you always in my home, for you dwell already within my heart."

"Asim." My name fell from her lips as low as a word whispered in a dream, and I knew then that she loved me, and that I had her, safe.

"Leave this place," I said, "and this madness."

"Madness?" Her voice was suddenly sharp.

I climbed to my feet, and she seemed momentarily thunderstruck, as if I had dazed her. I thought, then, that she and the spirit warred. Her eyes glowed, then faded, and she shook her head.

"Najya, you're still there!" I squeezed her hands, desperate to retain my connection to her. "I see it in your face, no matter your unearthly eyes! You aren't a monster. You cannot want this—"

"I do what I please," she said, and as her own hands tightened I felt heat and life and strength failing me as if I had been dealt a hard blow. Her eyes blazed blue as I sank to my knees. She bent with me, still holding on, relinquishing me at last so that I knelt shivering at her feet. "You may return when you wish to apologize," she spat. "Go!"

She spoke to the Khazars, ordering them to guide me, but to spread word that I had her leave to walk free so long as I did not venture beyond the sentry lines. As I rose on shaking legs, one led me out into what had transformed into a double lane of tents, for the Khazars had worked swiftly. We walked only a bowshot away, to one with sentinels, and there my guard held conversation with the two on duty, pointing at me. He spoke to me in halting Arabic. "The daughter . . . gives you free walk . . . in camp. You. Not the man inside. Leave camp and die." Then one of them cast the tent flap aside and motioned me in.

I bowed my head to him—what else was I to do?—and I entered.

Dabir waited within, walking back and forth across richly brocaded carpets spread around a fire pit. He turned and exhaled at sight of me, looking relieved. He then asked if I was hungry, and swept a hand toward platters laid near the central fire. On it were bowls of cheeses and dried meats, but I had no hunger. I was thirsty, though, and I reached for a squat jug and lifted up a bowl.

"I'm not sure you'll want that," Dabir told me.

"What is it?"

"Mare's milk. Fermented."

I brought it up to my nose and discovered the scent profoundly sour.

"Allah! Do they mean to sicken us?"

"No, this is what they drink."

"Why?" I asked.

"To get drunk. I do not know why Allah could not have forbidden the drinking of *this*—perhaps God assumed we would have better sense. Now, what happened?"

I proceeded then to tell him all that had transpired. I grew more dejected as I spoke, and sank down finally beside the fire. "I almost had her, Dabir. I had her at the forefront. I could even see it in her eyes."

At this he grimaced sympathetically. He started to say something, then paused and looked over his shoulder at the entrance, for we heard the approach of men without.

Someone called "Easy!" and there were various grunts, as of men shifting some heavy burden. We both stood as the tent flap was held open and bright light beamed into the chamber, along with a blast of cold air. A single hairy face peered in at us, then got out of the way as turbanless men bore a glistening burden, carting the thing at their waists. So large was the object that it took some six straining Persians and Arabs, all tightly clustered about one another, to carry it into our tent. They took only a few small steps at a time, coaxed all the while by a short Khazar man with a huge nose, who provided helpful nuggets of advice like "Steady" and "Watch your step."

He flashed us an evil smile. "Set him here." He pointed to a spot beside Dabir, several paces from the fire in the tent's center.

The laborers slowly maneuvered toward Dabir, who stepped away, though he watched, fascinated.

"Upright, set it up," called the bulbous-nosed spokesman, but his charges were already tilting their burden, and it was then that I understood what they carried, for I had caught a glimpse of Koury's hair within the ice.

Dabir had not seen, though, and his eyes widened in disbelief as the laborers set down their strange burden with a final grunt.

"Go," their master said.

As they were turning I was startled to recognize one of them for our neighbor the jeweler. "Rashid!"

The heavyset merchant turned, his weary eyes widening as he noticed us for the first time. "Asim! What are you—"

"Silence!" shouted his master.

"Have they taken Mosul?" I asked. "Are they—"

"Silence!" Big Nose kicked at Rashid, who hurried after the other prisoners. He then bowed with a smirk and exited. Only then did the fellow who'd been holding the tent flap enter, and we found ourselves in the company of Enkidu. He frowned at us and crossed his arms.

"We have a visitor," I said to Dabir.

Dabir was clearly quite astonished to see dead Koury there in the ice, but turned from consideration of him to address the live Sebitti.

"Why have you come?" he asked.

"The Daughter of the Frost asked me to convey that since you did not like Koury in her tent, she has decided to keep all of her problem men in one place. It is to remind you what awaits you, should you displease her once more."

Enkidu frowned then at us.

Dabir glanced at me. "He is still wondering why we weren't killed."

"I have nothing against you personally." The Sebitti sounded almost apologetic. "But there is much at stake, and you two are dangerous and unpredictable. It would be safer to eliminate you."

"What is at stake, Enkidu?" Dabir asked, walking closer. "Why do you stand against the other Sebitti? Why did you betray your friend Erragal?"

The wizard raised his face to stare out the round opening in the roof through which the smoke of our fire curled. When he finally spoke, his voice was heavy. "Koury thought he could remake the world so that it is better for humans. Erragal, too, once thought this. But things have grown worse and worse with the rise of cities. The plains and rivers are thick with the stench of man and his works. Things were better when there were fewer."

"But you are a man," Dabir pointed out.

"I am," he agreed.

"Yet you would kill them all?"

"The Daughter of the Frost will level the great cities," he conceded.

"Then men will die out!"

"No. Frost cannot reach the warmer lands. When the ice comes, people will live again as once they did, closer to the earth and its creatures. We are not above them."

"So you will blast man into the ignorant past . . . and then lead them?" Dabir ventured.

"I have no wish to lead them. That was Koury. Nor do I wish to be worshiped, like Lamashtu or Gazi. Nor entertained, like Anzu."

Dabir paused for a moment, then watched shrewdly for Enkidu's reaction. "You are a man who hesitates to kill old friends, but will be the deaths of millions of strangers."

"It is for man's own good, and the good of the world, which they place themselves above. They are grown arrogant."

Dabir shook his head. "And you are not?"

"I have grown wise. You are but children. You cannot understand."

"And what do these Khazars want?" my friend asked.

"They think the daughter shall lead them to paradise, for they believe the world will end with her coming."

"You do not?" Dabir challenged.

He shook his head. "I have lost count of the temples I have seen rise up to gods. Did gods ever save the temples, or the people who worshiped there, when the end came for them? The world goes on without them."

"Only the righteous pass on to paradise," I pointed out, irritated.

"What is paradise, but a flowering field under a clear sky? Who needs more? Yet I see I waste my breath. To tell a man to seek happiness in this world, or that his god does not exist, is like telling him his sister is ugly. Even when it is true, he cannot abide it. Let the Khazars serve the daughter as they want. May it bring them happiness."

"And will you be happy, to have so much blood on your hands?"

"Blood can be washed off with clean water."

He started to turn away, but Dabir called his name once more, and he halted. "She does not trust you. Else she would have had you command us to speak the secrets before her. She does not want you to have that power, Enkidu."

"She craves to drink in that sorcery," he said, "and fears that it tempts me. I understand. She thinks I am like other men, and I am not."

"If she does not trust you, can you trust her?"

"I trust her to do as she wishes. That is all I need from her. You waste my time."

So saying, he ducked, pushed aside the tent flap, and left us.

"We tried," Dabir told me. "His path is set."

"Aye," I agreed. "And there is no one else to whom we might talk sense. It occurs to me that once again we have missed our prayers, and surely we are in need of them."

"Ah, my friend, God has provided for us anyway. We should give thanks, and pray a little later."

I thought him mad then, for he actually sounded amused. He was slowly circling Koury's block. "I don't suppose Koury ever expected this to happen to him."

"I don't imagine that he did. But what do you mean 'God has provided'?"

"Asim, mark you that pouch on Koury?"

I came to look where Dabir pointed into the ice. The layers deformed the man within, and his clothing. Following Dabir's fingers, I beheld the image of a good-sized bag with a flap that hung from Koury's belt. The clasp was distorted by a wave in the ice.

"I see it," I said.

"We're going to melt it free."

"Why?"

"Because unless I mistake myself, that is where he keeps his wooden figurines."

I brightened, then shook my head. "But they are in miniature. And how will we control—"

"Erragal taught him this skill, and I have studied how to counter it." He patted his robe and I heard a faint crinkle. "I managed to keep a few of the scrolls with me. It may be that I can control the beasts. Assuming Koury has any left. See, though, that his hand is reaching for the pouch. He must have had at least one more he meant to wield."

"It is something," I granted him. "But we must somehow obtain the club before we make this escape."

"Yes. And reunite with Erragal, and lure Najya after us."

This all seemed quite optimistic. "I do not think Moses asked for this many miracles."

"Do you have a better plan?"

I turned up my palms. "I have no plan."

"Then we will use mine. Help me tip Koury over."

First we rolled over a few of the extra logs, Dabir explaining as we did so that we'd need to prop him up. I did not ask why, though I soon understood. It was more challenging than you might suppose for the two of us to lower him without making loud noises or crushing our fingers. In moments Dabir set to work placing kindling beneath the ice at Koury's waist, then brought over a flame and set it alight. He stepped back. Steam rose immediately, and water began to drip from the underside of the block.

"Thus do the mighty fall," Dabir said, though he sounded more regretful than mocking.

"You do not think," I said, "that he but waits to be freed?"

"I cannot guarantee that," Dabir admitted. "But I doubt it. I think Koury has passed on to whatever awaits him. The immortal Sebitti are dwindling in number."

I had worried over a final confrontation with Koury for days owing to the power of his sorcery, and I found it rather unsettling that he had been so simply dispatched. It spoke volumes about the power of Usarshra, which set off a stab of anguish about Najya—I suppressed it only to worry once more about our friends. "Do you think Mosul is already fallen?"

243

"I would think not." Dabir stepped back to the fire and retrieved more fuel before returning to Koury's ice block. "Surely there would have been more commotion in the camp. Celebrations and laughter. Rashid may have been captured in a caravan entering or leaving the city. But time is running out. For all of us." He peered at Koury. "Do you suppose she'll freeze us like this, in the end?"

"Do not joke."

"I don't joke. I have been thinking of something, though. All this time I'd thought Najya kept from touching the bones because of sheer willpower. But recall the moment when she received the club in her tent—it seemed to me that the spirit is reluctant to touch them still. Else she would have snatched up the bone and drained it of magic immediately. Don't you think?"

"I suppose so."

"I think perhaps Usarshra couldn't touch the bones. They are warded against her. Maybe the same thing that keeps the power in the bones keeps her from getting that sorcery back. Do you remember how she was stricken when she first touched the spear?"

"How could I forget?"

"I am guessing the wards weakened her. She never touched one again."

This was all well and good, but brought me no solace. "What do you think she plans?"

Dabir stared at the deepening divots forming in the ice around the warm sticks. It was clearly going to take more effort to reach Koury's waist. "I'm not entirely sure, though I can surmise that she means to drain the bones as soon as Bersbek helps her through the wards, and that she means to use her spirits to drink up as much blood and life force as she can to increase her power. Which means Mosul is in great danger."

At this I nodded vigorously.

"This will take a while longer. You have the freedom of the camp. Go see what you can learn. Their numbers, their movements, anything."

I started to caution him to be careful, then to object that I shouldn't leave him unguarded, but neither comment seemed appropriate, for neither of us was safe, and both of us were going to be as careful as we could manage, given our circumstances.

"Good luck," I told him.

"And to you. Go with God." Dabir looked to me with a grave smile, but said nothing more.

I exited from between the two guards. They gave me no trouble, though their hairy brows were dark with suspicion as I passed. You would think folk who thought themselves close to paradise would be in a better mood.

The Khazars kept a fairly orderly camp. I realized after a little wandering that the tents must be arranged by tribes, for some sections were set up in circles, and others in straight lines, and there were slight differences in tent colors and even in the number of banners. Most seemed to display different numbers of oxtails, though rectangular wedges of fabric also waved at the height of some tent poles.

Only a few Khazars walked the tent city itself, and while there were many horses within the corrals, there were not so many as a horse-borne army would ride. By this I knew that the bulk of their force was at work somewhere beyond my view, and large plumes of black smoke billowing on the western horizon ominously indicated the troops had at least reached Mosul's suburbs.

But a little fire and a few dozen horsemen would be no good against Mosul's walls. I prayed that Usarshra had been too busy within the camp to wield icy sorceries.

These, I supposed, would come all too soon.

Eventually I returned to the central portion of the camp, and looked out from between two tents onto the great open space there. The sounds of wood chopping had echoed through the camp during my rounds, and I discovered several dozen slaves laboring to drag logs to a large pile of timber I could only assume would shortly transform into a bonfire. Glowering Khazar overseers were ready with whips and kicks, and so much effort was spent watching prisoners I wondered why the soldiers themselves simply did not make the preparations. Beyond that, prisoners finished the digging of long ditches in parallel lines, facing a small, broad hill that must have been intended for a stage. Their breath rose in vapor in the crisp air.

Misgiving filled me at this sight, even though I could not know with certainty what their efforts would accomplish. It felt as though death looked over my shoulder, which was why I started so violently at a sound behind me.

I whirled, my hand falling to my empty hilt.

One of the Khazar women had advanced into the narrow canvas alley between tents where I waited, and had come almost within striking distance, though she did not yet put hand to her pommel. Dark furs and leather wrapped her, and a few dark curls escaped from beneath her hat. Her face was smudged with dirt and she smelled of horses, even at this distance.

She stared up at me, then motioned me to follow, and backed away.

This I did, reluctantly. "The daughter," I said, in the hope that she understood Arabic, "gave me permission to walk the camp."

"It is me, dolt," she snapped, and I blinked, for this was Lydia. "Where is Dabir? Is he still alive?"

"Close by, under guard. How did you—"

She cut me off. "Are you truly free, or was that a lie?"

"Najya . . . Usarshra decreed it."

She eyed me suspiciously. "How did you manage that?"

"I don't truly know. I think Najya still has some influence. I almost got through to her—"

"We don't have time to waste on her. Where are the bones?"

"The club is in her tent." I suddenly remembered that Lydia was an uncertain ally. "What are you doing here?"

"I am looking for Dabir and the bones. I thought that would be obvious."

"Why doesn't Erragal just come for them?"

"He is too busy to come himself. What is Dabir doing?"

"Engineering our escape. Where's Erragal, and what is he doing?"

"He is already at work on our grand circle. We can't risk letting

Usarshra get stronger than she already has, Asim. We've got to find the bones before she drains them. She not only has the club, but a second staff Erragal said was formerly hidden farther north. That's probably why we didn't hear from her when we were in Mosul."

"You think she went farther north yesterday to get it? How could she get here so fast?"

"She can travel as swiftly as the wind can carry her, I think."

The image of Najya sailing through the skies on otherworldly powers made my stomach squirm. "Do you know what the Khazars are building out there? And why they're digging those trenches?"

"They're rounding up captives. For blood, most like. For magic. From their hygiene," Lydia went on, "you wouldn't think the Khazars were fussy. But they must plan to shovel dirt or snow over the corpses after the ceremony."

I ignored her callous disregard for the prisoners' fates. "What about Mosul? Does it stand?"

"The frost spirits surround it, and no one can come in or out. Two hawks sent from the walls with messages have been shot down."

Cut off. But help could not arrive in less than four days in any case. It was enough, for the moment at least, that the city stood. "Dabir thinks the people of Mosul will be used for blood magic, too."

"That is surely true. Shall we go find these bones, or do you have more questions?"

Once more I ignored her tone, and led the way forward.

Najya had said the shaman was to inspect the club in her tent, so we went there first. Lydia and I sized up the entrance from behind the cover of another tent. There was but a single guard in front.

"Maybe luck is with us," I offered.

Still we did not advance, for knots of riders trotted up and down what served as a main avenue of the camp. We waited for a long while, listening to the sounds of the wind whipping the oxtail standards, and the sawing and occasional shouting from the field beyond. Eventually there was a lull in traffic and we ventured over as though we had every right to approach the tent. We slipped around the back, then Lydia cut a slit in the canvas while I watched, and we sneaked through. We had breached what must be the treasure chamber, for open chests gleamed with gold coins and fine jewels: opals, emeralds, rubies, diamonds, fine necklaces and goblets. Such a collection might have excited even the caliph's treasury officers. Lydia let out a happy cry of surprise at the sight. Lovely as it was, I had no interest in anything but the club and the other weapon, but they were nowhere in evidence.

"The club's not here," I said, and turned to the interior opening. "Let's look in the other rooms."

Lydia did not follow, immediately, and there was no mistaking the jangling as she dug into the trove. When she joined me in the main chamber there was no obvious sign of her doings, lest you counted her satisfied smirk. I was about to remark that gold would not keep her warm when the earth became an iced-over wasteland, but the main tent flap suddenly opened and we found ourselves facing Usarshra/Najya and a gaggle of hard-eyed priests, as well as four burly soldiers.

Najya looked puzzled. I thought I might claim I had become lost and had this Khazar woman show me the way back to her tent.

"It is her," Najya said. "The woman who worked with Koury. Why is she here?"

Dabir later theorized that Lydia's sorcerous energies would have looked the same to the spirit regardless of what disguise the Greek wore. At that moment, though, I was bewildered, and could not guess how Lydia had been found out in a dim room while costumed so well. It was impossible to suggest that I had caught her and been leading her to Najya, for Lydia was quite clearly walking freely. It was equally bad to suggest that I had somehow failed to notice the Khazar woman near me was Lydia.

The Greek was a more practiced liar. "Erragal has sent me to speak with you."

At mention of that name, Usarshra drew back a step. Her guardians tensed. Yet she did not immediately respond. "You are the one who called me to the warmer lands. And for that I should thank you. Even if the woman loathes you. I have been thinking that I pay her too much heed." Usarshra glanced over at me. "But speak, then. You brought me, so why do you now work with my ancient enemy?"

Lydia's quick thinking impressed me. "Erragal does not want another protracted battle. He wonders what he can offer you so that you will return to your home."

"He fears me."

"You fear him."

This may have been the wrong thing to say, for Najya's nostrils flared, like a bull grown angry. Yet she waited a moment. "What," she asked tightly, "does he wish?"

"That depends upon what you desire. I am authorized to make several offers, contingent upon your intentions."

I understood then that Lydia was a most magnificent liar.

"At first," Usarshra said through Najya's lips, "I thought only to return home. But you had effectively anchored me to the woman's body. I have grown accustomed to it. And these people here obey me. So I shall give them what they wish, and I shall take from this place what I desire."

"But what do you desire most?" Lydia asked. "Erragal can return the final bone to you, if you will but return, and remain, in the frozen realms. This place cannot be comfortable to you. To the other spirit folk. And it shall not always be winter."

"Ah, but it can be. And you need not worry about my comfort. The woman's body shields me somewhat from the heat. No, if Erragal had wished me to return, he might have offered me the bones at the beginning. They belong to me. But he waited too long. I shall take back the power he stole from me! I shall use it to widen the gate to the frozen lands. When my folk come through, the greater cold shall come with them."

Lydia's eyes took in the Khazars at Najya's side. "Your human followers will all die."

"That is what they wish. Now. What can Erragal offer me? The remaining bone? He can give it to me, if he likes, but I shall take it from him regardless. More blood? That, too, shall I take."

Lydia addressed her with solemn dignity. "If you do not treat with him now, it will be too late. He has grown powerful in the long years since he battled you. He extends his hand now."

"And I would cut it off." She barked a swift word to her guards, who seized Lydia by the arms.

I started forward, then stopped myself. "What are you doing?" There was a panicked edge to my question, for I feared that they were taking her away to chop off her hands.

"Putting her with the other prisoners," Usarshra said. "Where I would place you, and your friend, were you not useful to me."

Lydia choked back a sob and her head fell, but she was acting, for she slammed her heel into the toes of one distracted guard. When his grip slipped she pulled an arm free of him and spun to jam her knee into the other fellow's groin. Freed, she darted through the exit.

My pleasure was short-lived, for Usarshra shouted and the other guards raced after Lydia, including the one still limping from her assault. I threw out my leg so that the nearest fell face-first onto the carpet.

Then I felt Najya's cold, cold hand upon my shoulder and for the second time that day I grew so numb that my knees shook.

"Whose side are you on?" she asked in my ear.

"It is wrong," I said with my shaking jaw. "You do not . . . kill . . . an envoy."

"I do what I please. And I think that you have deceived me. You shall remain in your tent, with your friend, until I have need of you, one way or the other. After the sorcery this morning my powers will be so great that I need not be troubled by the woman's thoughts ever again."

She released her hold on me, and I stood, shivering miserably, though more than the cold numbed me. She pointed at the fellow still bent forward holding his groin. "Take Asim to the tent. See that if he attempts escape, he is chained in place."

The Khazar nodded with as much dignity as he could manage. Usarshra strode away in the direction Lydia had fled.

My guardian took a comically long time to recover. I thought of running, but there really seemed no point, for I had no wish to be chained, and I needed to tell Dabir all that I had learned. So, almost sick with apprehension, I waited while the fellow's pain eased, then followed him back to my tent. He still walked with a hunch.

I had hoped to report that Lydia at least was free, but as we rounded the corner I saw her being led by no less than ten angry-looking Khazars. Her hat was missing and her hair wild. One of her guards had three bleeding scratches across his face. Behind them all was Usarshra, who looked at me through those ice-colored eyes and smiled with all the warmth of a winter sunrise.

18

Neither my guardian nor the two sentries bothered looking inside the tent, which was good, because Dabir's project would surely have aroused suspicion. The carpets were soggy and squished under my boots as I advanced into the darker space.

Koury still lay on his side, but a wedge of ice had been melted, exposing one waxy-looking hand and a good portion of his chest. Dabir sat near the fire pit, and once he saw it was me he did not ask about the success of my mission, or report to me about his own ventures.

"Help me get him back up," he said.

"Why?"

"So it will not be so obvious. We shall turn him so that the melted side faces away from the door."

I thought this a fine idea. Any wet bits of the carpet might then be explained away by the simple fact that the ice near a fire could be expected to melt. We might still be in danger if anyone were to look closely, but at least Dabir's work would not be immediately visible.

It had taken six men to carry that block, but Dabir and I managed to stand it up.

Dabir fussed with its angle a bit, then nodded as if to say that it was acceptable. Only then did he ask me what I had seen.

"We are out of time," I began, then told him all that I had learned—that a ritual for blood magic was being readied, and that many folk from the Mosul suburbs would likely meet their end when it happened. That Mosul itself would likely fall afterward when spirits were sent into its streets, and then its people would be harvested for further sorcery, and that Usarshra planned to widen the gate so more frost spirits could come through. That Lydia was to be sacrificed with all the others. It was not a report to inspire a great deal of confidence, but Dabir, while tense, did not look nearly as discouraged as I felt.

"Erragal is still free," he said. "We need only bring him the other bones, and Najya will surely follow. She has even foreseen that. A pity you could not ask for further details."

"You sound as though you expect this to be easy."

"Lydia's capture has complicated things." He fiddled with the back of his emerald ring. Dabir then stepped back to the dying fire and sank down near a blanket where I now perceived a handful of little wooden figurines. There were three wooden men, a snake, two horses, a dog, and three bulls, and each was no longer than a finger.

Dabir lifted up a piece of paper, then glanced back at the miniatures, as though he were eager to play with them after he finished reading. I stared at them in dull curiosity. Far away came the echo of deep-voiced drums. Also there were horn calls, high, plaintive, somehow sinister.

Dabir and I looked at one another.

"The ceremony must be starting!"

"Aye," Dabir said, and took a deep breath. He tossed his outer robe back on, closed his eyes, breathed out deeply, then bent to one of the small figures. A tiny bull.

The insistent cadence of the drummers grew in volume. "It sounds like the heartbeat of some giant," I said.

From far away, hundreds upon hundreds of deep voices rose in a threatening chant.

"Hurry," I said.

Dabir frowned at me, as if to say he perceived the need for urgency perfectly well, then sketched a curling symbol on the bull's head with his pointer finger, let out a multisyllabic sound rather like someone coughing, and pressed his thumb to its head.

On the instant I knew the familiar and unsettling sensation of magical workings, for the air was alive with a storm cloud's energy. My arm hairs stood on end. The bull grew under Dabir's hand, and my friend stood, still keeping flesh pressed to the thing. Up the creature came, dark and ominous, its painted red eyes blank. Its twin horns were capped with metal tips.

It stopped its growth when it achieved the size of a true bull.

I stared at it cautiously.

Dabir pointed to the left, and the thing stepped that way without moving its head. He grinned triumphantly at me, immensely pleased with himself.

"Is that all you have to do? Point?"

"I can feel its will, ready to obey my own, and vaguely sense what lies around it, though I cannot truly see. But it is instinctive to point." This he did, at the door flap, with a pained, resolute look on his face. Immediately the bull sprang forward, hitting the ground with its great legs so that the earth shook. Its passage tore open the flap. Outside there came a cry of surprise, and a masculine scream of fear. Following upon this came frantic shouting, and agonized scream. I hoped that the drums obscured the sound from those farther off.

I poked my head out of the tent. One of our guards lay groaning. The other moved not at all, and was so badly twisted he was surely dead. The bull stood still just beyond them, as if someone had decided the street was the ideal location to erect a statue. "Let's go." I looked over my shoulder only to find a black snake head the size of a melon, at my elbow. I am embarrassed to say I let out a shout.

"Sorry," Dabir said.

It was another of the wooden beasts, of course, and it stretched on another four good arm lengths beyond the two it was already raised into strike position. It was formed all of closely connected wooden discs. It was not as well polished as the bull man Koury had sent against us, though its mouth was full with the same sharp metal-tipped teeth.

"You should warn a man," I muttered.

A cruel wind jabbed at us as we emerged, the wooden snake sliding beside Dabir like a loyal dog, the bull trotting at my side. I knew he kept them active with us for protection, but I would much rather have had a sword.

Of the other guards I'd seen posted about there was no sign, and I wondered if they'd been ordered to attend the ceremony. The tent city was strangely quiet around us except for the deep, echoing drums and the sound of voices raised in song.

Only one sentinel waited in the shadows outside Najya's tent. He ordered me to halt as I ran up, then drew his sword, screeching when he saw the serpent. Dabir sent it at his legs and as he tried to fend it off the bull rushed him and knocked him clean through the canvas. We followed.

The Khazar was knocked senseless, so we left him sprawled on the carpet, the animals looming over him, and set to searching.

This time we did not bother with the treasure room. The other sections of the tent were compartmentalized into additional living space. In the sleeping area, near to the mattress and its fur coverlet, was my sheathed weapon. Dabir's lay with our knives on a nearby chest, which proved to hold only jeweled goblets. At no other time in my life would I have been annoyed to find riches rather than ancient bones.

Dabir was buckling on his sword. "Interesting, isn't it, that she set your sword near her bed? As if she wished something of yours near at hand."

I was not especially heartened by that observation. "Now what are we to do?"

"I'm afraid we will have to improvise. They must have taken the bones to the ceremony."

We left the unconscious guard in the outer room, hurried to a lane between tents at the edge of the field, and peered out.

Where before the ground had been mostly empty, there was now a great bonfire that roared up to the sky, and it was about this red blaze that hundreds of Khazars gathered. Closest to it were dozens of brawny, shirtless men pounding upon a mismatched assortment of wooden-sided drums, their flesh glistening with sweat. Most of the crowd swayed back and forth, chanting to the rhythm.

At the north end, some fifty prisoners knelt in front of the ditches, arms tied behind. And before them, upon that hill overlooking the Khazars, stood Najya, Enkidu, and Berzbek, the shaman woman, as well as a number of fur-clad warriors and male shamans. Berzbek rested the heavy end of the club upon the ground. In her right hand she grasped an ivory staff that stood taller than she. It was longer, thinner, and browner than the staff borne by Erragal.

"I gather she got them working," Dabir said with a frown.

"Perhaps she's smarter than both of us," I suggested.

He but grunted.

"How are we to find Lydia?"

"Look to the right of the shaman."

I found her then, still dressed in her Khazar garb, standing with crossed hands between two burly Khazar warriors.

We withdrew, then ran north along the row of tents just east of the crowd, drawing closer to the stage. Dabir's snake slithered alongside him in the trampled snow. Even though I knew it to be completely under my friend's control, sight of the thing was still alarming. The bull, at least, followed along behind us, so that while I felt the tramp of its passage I did not have to look at it.

We halted when we reached the end of the lanes of tents and peered round the corner. We had come to the east side of the hill being used as a stage, and could view those upon it in profile. At the bottom of this slope was one of the few places where men stood guard—four in all. I supposed no one wanted to risk having the Daughter of the Frost rushed out of devotion. Surely they weren't expecting anyone to attack.

We pulled back. "This is a bad plan," I said to Dabir.

"You don't even know what I'm going to say."

"I know it's going to be bad."

The drummers suddenly stopped as one. Dabir and I exchanged a look, and peered around the edge of the tent.

The shamaness called out to her people in a great, booming voice. I could not understand a word of it, of course, since she spoke Khazar to them. Whatever she was saying held them rapt.

Dabir dropped to one knee, fumbling with Koury's satchel. I kept watch. The Khazars roared approval as Najya walked to the edge. Even those warding the slope had their eyes upon her.

Najya motioned for silence, and the shouting fell away. For a moment all that could be heard was the wind and the crackle of the fire. A handful of prisoners moaned.

Najya then called to the crowd. She shouted in Arabic, but most of the words were whipped away by the wind. I could hear the bald shaman beside her perfectly well, but since he translated Usarshra's words into Khazar, this did me little good. The sound of hate, I learned, was universal. I despaired that the real woman remained within her.

Behind her I glimpsed the shamaness Berzbek working through a form with the staff.

I pulled back. "Dabir, we must hurry!"

Dabir motioned me down beside him and pointed to a wooden figurine that had fallen over in the snow. "You must control the horse. I will be too busy with these others. Do exactly as I say."

"I am to work magic?" I held up my hand in the sign against the evil eye.

He arched an eyebrow. "So it is fine for me to risk my soul to save the world, but not for you?"

"Ai-a—" I struggled for some kind of rejoinder, finally saying, gruffly, "Just be on with it."

"Put your finger to the animal's head. Just so. Now move your finger about the blaze carved into his forehead. To the left. Your left. Yes. Now press your thumb in, and repeat after me."

He enunciated a series of sounds very slowly, as though I were a simpleton. I repeated after him, and by Allah, the horse grew under my finger. At the same moment, I could also sense things in proximity to the wooden beast, including myself. It was most peculiar, for it felt as though I were in two places at once. I had not been so disoriented even when I had once suffered a head blow, and wondered if this was what being drunk was like. I clambered into the cushioned saddle of the life-sized wooden stallion with emerald eyes and carved mane. "Now what?"

"What you will it to do, it shall!"

The shamaness had handed over the glowing blue staff to Najya, who raised it high. The Khazars began to chant three syllables over and again.

Berzbek set to working through the steps to fire the magic of the club. I could only see her part of the time, as the form carried her forward and back, behind various people upon the platform, but well did I know those steps.

"By all that is holy, Dabir, hurry!"

Dabir was raising his wooden creatures to life, one by one. Another horse. One wooden man, a second, this one with a cracked torso and a notch in his back. Probably the same I'd fought in Mosul. A second bull, this one with longer and sharper-looking horns.

The staff was now almost incandescent with light in Usarshra's grip.

"Dabir!" I shouted.

"A moment! I'll get Lydia, you get the bones." He sent the bull galloping toward the slope. "Now!" Dabir cried, raising his arms as will a man shooing a horse.

My horse did nothing until I wished that it should do so, and then it sprang forward, and it is only my fine reflexes that enabled me to latch onto the handles carved into its mane.

The guards at the hillside saw us too late. The wooden bull plowed straight into one of them. Two others dived for safety. Only one was left to grab wide-eyed for his sword as I came galloping up. I slashed down and caught him hard in the shoulder. He dropped in a welter of blood, most of his screech drowned out by the unchanging chant of the crowd.

Then I was galloping up a snowy hill on the padded back of a wooden horse with jeweled eyes. The bull raced before me, and the snake came at my side. The Khazars cheered something I could not see, a thousand voices as one that might have shaken the throne of God, and surely struck fear in the nearer residents of Mosul. The noise covered our advance nicely.

As I mounted the hill I saw Najya cast down the crumbling staff and take the lit club of Herakles from the round shaman woman. Berzbek's face was wide in astonishment just before the bull slammed headlong into her and sent her tumbling downslope into the prisoners. Lydia's guards turned for their swords, and the wily Greek slipped away from them, almost tripping over the snake that sped for Enkidu.

I bore on toward Najya. The club glowing in one hand, she thrust her palm toward the bull and a blast of cold sprayed forth so quickly that the wooden creature was encased in ice, midgallop.

The chanting below had faltered, and there were cries of dismay as well, for as I slowed to grab the club of Herakles I glimpsed the rest of the wooden figures running wild through the crowd.

A wave of uncertainty struck me as I reached toward Najya. I could not recall why I should want the club at all, nor why I should be upon the stage struggling against my one true love. But Enkidu's confusion lifted at the same time there was a flash of eldritch fire off to my right, and I heard Erragal shouting wizardly commands.

From out of nowhere he had come to join us.

I could spare no attention, for a smiling Najya had touched her hand to my horse. White ice was born suddenly in the joints of its legs and spread upwards in sheets. It struggled mightily, but was swiftly overwhelmed, and began to wobble beneath me.

There was nothing for it. I jumped clear.

Now I had no intent of skewering Najya, or I might have slashed. I landed well, sliding only a little in the snow.

She glared at me, and the frigid air around her stung my face.

From every side I saw the snow women rising from the earth, rank upon rank of them. And then, over Najya's shoulder, there was a flash of blue flame speeding toward her from a figure on the far edge of the hill. Erragal. I reacted without thinking.

"Down!" I dropped the sword and tackled the woman into the snow. A terrific blast of flame passed over us both and what was left of the nearby frost women rained down across us. Najya lay half beneath me, looking a little dazed.

"Asim?" she said weakly. Her brown eyes locked with mine and I drank deep of their beauty.

And then she was gone from me, and I looked into the blue eyes of a snarling spirit. I pushed up, grabbing the club. Usarshra shouted in dismay as I pulled it free.

"Asim!" Dabir called for me from somewhere ahead. "Hurry!"

I took stock of my situation as I dashed forward, and discovered the promised chaos. The Khazars were rushing for the hill, though the wooden animals running circles through their ranks were a fine impediment. Nearer at hand the guards who'd kept the stage with Najya were down, crushed and gored by the second bull. A dozen snow women closed on Dabir and Lydia, she sitting back of him astride a wooden horse.

Enkidu was struggling to his feet as one of the wooden men hammered at him and the snake bit into one leg. White-robed Erragal lashed out with another blast of eldritch flame as a troop of Khazars charged the stage.

I sprinted for the remaining wooden bull a spear's cast away. Allah knows I never meant to sit astride a real one, much less one fashioned from lumber, but I saw no other way free. Erragal whipped around and sent a stream of blue fire coursing only a knife's breadth from my shoulder. Behind me Najya screamed in rage.

As I ran, I thought about the steps of the club's form, and the weapon lit in my hands. No longer was it bright with energy. My senses were still greater than normal, but stretched barely to the edges of the stage. The club was a vessel drained dry of all but a few last sips.

Between me and the bull two vaporous snow women rose up with outstretched arms. I gritted my teeth and charged through them. The club flared at the mere thought of combat and both burned in a flash before me. I vaulted onto the bull. Dabir sent the thing moving before I could find a place to take hold, and I wobbled precariously on the hard surface. Pure chance tipped me forward, and I snagged one carven ridge with my left hand while the right wrapped around the haft of the club.

Dabir's mount ran at my side as we charged across the height of the hill. Lydia clung to Dabir's shoulders while I cleared the way with swings of the club. The snow women were no longer as fragile to casual touch, possibly because the potency of their mistress had grown and not just because the club was diminished.

Erragal vanished, then instantly reappeared in a dozen places on either side of us, a small army of one wizard, each wielding eldritch fire toward Najya. "Go!" they shouted as one. "I shall follow!"

So we went, down the hill and away through more lanes of tents, our tireless wooden mounts galloping on and on. The rest of Koury's animals had not survived.

In mere minutes we were past a group of Khazar guards too astonished to give chase, and then we were riding on through the ruins.

"God is great!" I shouted in exultation. Once more we had defied the odds. "Where do we ride?" I called to Dabir.

"Straight to the conjuration circle," Lydia shouted. "West of Mosul!"

Allah, but I grew sore riding on that bull. Koury might have designed it to be capable of transport, but he had not intended that for its primary use, for there was no saddle. Riding that creature was akin to slamming repeatedly against a plank of timber.

I looked back time and again for signs of pursuit but saw nothing through the mounded ruins and broken walls. I wondered briefly how we might cross the Tigris until we came to it and discovered the river frozen solid. Though it was fortunate for us, it was also a disquieting reminder of the level of power employed by our enemies.

Dabir kept us well south of the smoking ruin of Mosul's outskirts. About the city walls a large force could be seen, only a few of which were men and horses. Countless snow women were there, but most disquieting were the tall transparent shapes in white. One looked like a great bear walking on its hind legs and reaching almost to the battlements. Another was a ghostly elephant, covered over in shaggy white fur. And one was an immense wolf, larger even than the beast Dabir and I had faced, and I swear that it turned its head toward us as we passed, though it did not leave its vigil to pursue.

I tried to imagine what the folk of Mosul must be doing. Frightened soldiers would be manning the walls, and women, children, and the elderly would crowd the mosques. The governor would be consulting his advisors and arming every able-bodied man and boy he could. Likely he would know there was no chance against these monsters, but perhaps they would reason that fire might be useful, and ready oil-soaked catapult missiles and barriers that could be set alight. I was glad that I was not trapped in there with them.

Soon Mosul, too, was behind us, yet on we galloped for another hour, slowing at last as we came in sight of a little valley. Apart from a few scrubby trees and bushes and a low hill near its center, it was entirely unremarkable.

"Straight up for that hill," Lydia told Dabir.

So on we rode, descending no more than two or three horse lengths to reach the lowland. A perfect circle inset with symbols was burned into the rock at a distance of ten feet from the bottom of the hill, and just on its other side a dark robed figure waited by a small fire. The bone spear lay near him, beside Erragal's staff, a length of ivory darker than the surrounding snow.

Dabir halted our animals and we swung down. I do not think I had ever been more bruised or stiff from a ride, not even after the first of my life.

"That is Erragal's servant," Lydia said, before I might ask.

"Nay," came the voice from within the hood. A hand cast back the cloth, and we looked then at the Sebitti known as Anzu.

19

Picture this, if you will. A woman and two men stand in a shallow valley under gray winter skies. The larger of the men is helmed and lightly armored. Snow lies a foot deep, stretching clean as far as the eye can see, disturbed only by a muddle of footprints and the straight line tracks of two hoofed creatures coming in from the east and two dark circles, perfectly round, one inside the other, that are burned through the snow, into the ground itself. A mix of letters and numbers—some Greek, some Arabic, but mostly some other strange tongue—fill the space between the circles. The woman, beside the leaner of the men, is small and beautiful, garbed like a Khazar warrior, complete with pants and boots, and her dark, curling hair is ruffled by frigid gusts. Nearer at hand are two life-sized sculptures in dark wood, one a powerful bull, the other a lean and noble stallion, each ornamented with scrollwork and occasional bits of jewelry and gold. They are motionless.

Just the other side of the rim stands a short, booted figure in a black robe near a campfire, and beside him is a strange spear, an ivory staff, and a small hump of blackish cloth from which old human bones protrude.

Behind the figure a small, steep hill rises some ten feet above the valley. On that hill is a stunted olive tree, barren of leaves and ornamented only by snow.

"I have not come to fight you," Anzu told us. "Erragal summoned me to aid him. But he is dead."

Howard Andrew Jones

"What do you mean?" I asked. My hands tightened upon the club.

He glanced quizzically at me.

"How do you expect us to trust anything you say?" Dabir demanded.

"It doesn't matter now." Anzu shrugged. "Erragal's dead. He teleported back, but most of him didn't make it." His eyes traveled to an off-white pile of robes I hadn't noticed a few paces to the right.

I watched Anzu as Dabir advanced to look, turning up the cloth. I caught the barest glimpse of Erragal's hair and a blood red mass below and then Dabir hastily drew the cloth back over. He looked horrified.

"How did it happen?" Lydia demanded.

"Someone or something must have pulled or grabbed at him as his transport spell went off," Anzu explained sadly. "Maybe the other part of him was frozen in place. I do not know."

"What are those bones from?" I asked, pointing at the pile beneath the black cloth.

"His servant collapsed in on itself the moment Erragal died."

"How do we know this isn't some trick of yours?" I asked.

He considered me wearily. "If I still wanted the staff and spear, I could have vanished with them. Erragal left them with me when he went after you."

"The servant was still standing," Lydia said after a moment, "when Erragal sent me to the spirit's camp. And he may well have called Anzu. He told me he was thinking about pulling in more aid."

This seemed unlikely, especially in light of the attack on Erragal's palace. "I thought you were trying to kill him," I said to Anzu.

"Kill Erragal?" He sounded as though I had suggested blasphemy. "No. I admired him too much." At our incredulous expressions, he continued. "Koury and Gazi are dead. Enkidu's allied with the doomsday cult. It didn't take much convincing when Erragal called upon me. And besides, I'm partly to blame for all this."

"Partly?" I would have said more, but his casual manner confounded me.

Dabir was uncharacteristically silent through this exchange and wore a troubled expression when I turned to him for reaction. He ran his fingers along his beard, then slowly faced Lydia. "So," Dabir said glumly to her, "we shall have to activate the circle ourselves. It is complete, is it not?"

"With what shall you power it?" Anzu interrupted.

Dabir pointed to the spear, and I indicated the club.

"But the club is nearly drained," Anzu pointed out. "Can't you see?"

"They aren't sorcerers," Lydia answered.

"It is true, though," I confirmed.

"Usarshra all but drank it dry," Lydia added.

"She didn't get hands on the spear, or Erragal's staff," I pointed out.

"Do you know how to use them?"

"The spear, yes," Dabir admitted.

Anzu shook his head. "It's not enough. Even if you knew how to use Erragal's staff, it's still not enough. Do you know how much magical energy it's going to take to power a banishing circle of the one Erragal hid, not to mention this circle here? And don't forget, you'll be under attack the entire time. You'll need even more power to defend yourself."

Dabir spoke to him at last, slowly. "What do you advise?"

Anzu met his eyes briefly, then looked away. I swear that he was shamed. "It is too late. You have Koury's animals. Take them and ride, as far as you can."

"You just said that you are partly to blame for this," Dabir said. "Will you not stay to fix it?"

Instead of answering he tried to excuse his actions. "We miscalculated."

"How many hundreds of thousands will die," Dabir asked tightly, "because of your 'miscalculation'?"

"There's nothing more I can do!"

"Good people are dead already," Dabir continued.

"I used every tool at my disposal to assist Erragal. It will take me decades to return to my full power. I am all but finished."

"What of Lamashtu?" Dabir asked him. "Will she help?"

Anzu let out a short bark of a laugh. "You're jesting. She won't care."

"Then why did she work with you in the first place?"

"I thought you understood. Koury is . . . was . . . a maker. He knew the words of power to shape life."

"Yes," Dabir said. "What more do you mean?"

He glanced over at Lydia. "It doesn't matter now. You should run. Climb on board the wooden animals and ride south, as far as you can go. The ice can't reach *everywhere*."

"No. It does matter." Dabir took a half step closer to him. I think, were he a fighting man, he would have grabbed the Sebitti by the scruff and shaken him. "What were you really planning? You wanted the spirit's power to grow, didn't you? By God, I think you even wanted this—a circle of power. You anticipated this."

"Almost all of it. We wanted the spirit to grow angry and call down its full power. But we needed Koury to live. It is no good now. You see, as the spirit's power grows, so does the tear it carries with it, the gate between the frozen realms and our own. When we assault her, she will surely summon more power through the tear. And when that gate opens, it rips a gap through our reality and briefly exposes the byways of the universe itself— the very wellspring of creation. A small gate, open for a little, would yield nothing. But if it were a great gate, like Usarshra would call forth to counter a powerful attack, a shaper mage with a great tool might use that access to recast anything in whatever form he wished."

Seeing the expressions upon Dabir's and Lydia's faces, I guessed that this was somehow more horrible than I understood. "What do you mean?" I asked.

"Suppose you do not like olives." Anzu glanced up at the bent little tree on the height of the slope. "A shaper might rename them all so that they transformed into oaks. Suppose," he said, steel shining now in his voice, "that you did not want hunger to trouble man. A skilled shaper might snip these threads from the tapestry of the world's making."

"And if you wanted a kingdom watered by running rivers, where crops flourished . . ." Dabir said, then let his voice trail off.

"You but glimpse a portion of what we would have given you. Not only a fertile kingdom. But a people blessed with health, and intellect. Beasts that would willingly give up their flesh. A sun that would warm, but never burn. Skies that would bring rain, but only just enough. There would have been an end to earthquakes, and famine, and disease. Earth would be a garden!"

"And would you have been its gods, or its serpents?" Dabir asked. "This is what Lamashtu wanted?"

He shrugged. "She had special requests, for her help."

"More sacrifices, for the cause?"

"I thought you, above all, might understand."

"I do. Such compassion you have," Dabir went on, "to take such risks for us. But it is we who have bled, and died, so that you might play at gods. You're worse than children, delighted with your cleverness. Blind to your cruelty." Dabir's voice shook with barely contained passion. "My friend, Jibril, whom you impaled upon your hook, actually admired your supposed wisdom!"

"We are not so different, Dabir," Anzu offered. "I, too, love knowledge. Moreso even than Erragal, who hid in his caves for a thousand years. I have never given up my search for it. We would have delivered a world where wisdom was no longer threatened by ignorance or prejudice. Where learned men and women would not perish before their time."

"If this is what you always intended," Lydia said slowly, "why didn't you stop after you'd found one of the weapons?"

"Many reasons, perhaps the most important of which was that there were four of us, and the spirit sensed three more weapons than we strictly required. Koury swore he would allow Lamashtu and I a hand in the shaping magic. Gazi didn't care. But more than that, Koury desired as many bones as possible on hand to command the sorcery, in case he drained them as he worked."

"And so great a sorcerer could not simply open this gate himself?" Dabir asked.

"Not and hold it open for any length of time. We needed sorcerous energy, and the spirit could find it for us. It seemed a perfect plan."

Dabir's frown deepened.

"There is no way to stop Usarshra at this point," Anzu went on. "The spirit's power has increased exponentially, not just because of the energy absorbed from the bones, but the life force consumed. You cannot cage her now, to send her back. Maybe if Erragal—"

"Go, then." Dabir interrupted. He sounded almost spiteful.

Anzu saw from my hard look there was no point in speaking to me, thus he directed his inquiry to Lydia. "And what of you?"

"I will stay," she said. Her chin rose, and she said, proudly, "This is partly my doing as well."

Anzu was silent for a long moment, then crouched down in the snow near the fire, and, with a gloved finger, sketched a jagged symbol in the snow. It glowed briefly green, then burned through the snow and left a smoking pattern in the ground. He rose to his feet. "Stay within fifty paces of this," he said, "and Enkidu will not be able to play with your mind. It will last you a day. So you will not be puppets when they kill you," Anzu added darkly. He turned his back to us and climbed up the hill, pulling his hood up as he did so. A most peculiar thing happened then, for he faded swiftly to nothing, as if he walked into a fog bank none of the rest of us could see.

Then there were but three of us, with the cloth-covered dead.

"You're planning something," Lydia said to Dabir. "I see it in your eyes."

He considered her shrewdly.

"You drove him away on purpose," she continued.

"I meant every word I said." Dabir turned to me. "Help me brush out an area. Six paces wide should do."

Lydia continued her harangue as I set to shoving snow aside with my boot. "Oh, you pretended well. But I have only seen you lose your temper once, even amongst all that we have done."

"You do not know me that well," Dabir said as he joined me.

"Do not play games. I have your measure." Her brow darkened. "Now you are readying a summoning circle. For Lamashtu?"

"Yes."

I stopped, my boot in front of a widening mound of snow. "She tried to kill us Dabir," I reminded him. "Jibril died, fighting her."

"Yes. But she knows how to wield Erragal's staff."

Lydia threw up her hands. "You don't know that! Erragal just said that she had used it once. He might have activated it and handed it off to her, like Asim did with me."

"That might be so."

We both carried on clearing snow.

"And should you really be activating a circle inside another one?"

Dabir looked blandly over to her. "The larger one isn't active yet, is it?"

"No," she admitted grudgingly.

"So there will be no problem."

Lydia threw up her hands. "No problem? You chased the most rational of the Sebitti off to contact the most deadly?"

Dabir returned to his work. We had exposed a circle of sparse grass pressed low by snow.

"Talk sense to him, Asim!"

Dabir shot me a look.

"It does seem a little desperate," I admitted.

"But we are desperate." Dabir sounded wearily playful. At some level, Lydia's worries amused him.

"Surely," I agreed.

"Desperate?" Lydia frowned at me. "Asim's too polite. He thinks you're as crazy as I do! Lamashtu doesn't work for free! What can you possibly offer her?"

"Now is not the time for debate," Dabir said.

"But what are you hoping for?"

"To work with people who ask fewer questions!" Dabir snapped, and whipped out his knife so suddenly that Lydia drew back. But Dabir crouched and cut into the ground, shaping the curve of a circle in the cold earth.

Lydia announced she would have no part of things, and stomped back to the fire.

Though I liked it not, I used my own knife to assist Dabir's work. He seemed pleased enough with the result, though it was more a lopsided oval than a circle. He then set to work creating a second, inside it. I aided with this, also, and fought back the urge to ask any questions. "Perhaps Lydia could help you speed this along when you start carving the symbols."

"That would be nice. We are not dealing with a surplus of time." He paused, looked up, then frowned as he realized he could not see around the hill. "We are crowding each other now anyway, Asim. I'm nearly done. Why don't you keep an eye on the horizon?"

I wiped dirt from my blade, sheathed it, and walked off to find Lydia beside the fire. Her jaw was set firmly.

"He plans something foolish," she said.

"Surely he does." I studied the skies to the east. The gray clouds sagged low over the white-blue blanket of snow shrouding the earth.

"Are you not worried?"

"Lydia," I answered patiently, "we are at the point where anything we do is foolish. I pray to Allah that Dabir chooses wisely, but then he is expert at that kind of thing. As for me, I am sworn to guard him, so that whatever step he takes, I take with him. His risk is mine, and if we fall, I shall fall first."

She stared up at me, searching my eyes, and she looked as though she meant to curse for a long time. I was not in the mood for an outburst, and so I looked off toward Mosul, but she wouldn't let the matter go.

"Look at you. He told you to scan the horizon, so you do. Brave and loyal to a fault. You don't know what he really plans, but you do not question."

"I trust him," I said.

"Yes"—she frowned sourly—"and he trusts you. I would that I had someone so loyal." She muttered this last almost inaudibly.

"You did," I pointed out. "Those soldiers gave up their lives for you."

"They but followed orders."

"Then you do not value enough what that means. With his last breath, Alexis made me pledge to safeguard you."

Her stare grew more fixed upon me. "He did?"

"Aye. He was most adamant."

"Is that why you rescued me?"

"In part," I said. "But you are our comrade."

"'Our comrade'?"

"Our friend," I explained.

She stared, as though she had suddenly heard that fish could speak, or that horses played shatranj. To hide her surprise, she turned her head. A long moment passed, and I scanned the horizon. It had not changed. There was only the vast white expanse, and the blowing wind.

"I didn't understand at first," Lydia said. Her voice was slow and quiet, but great passion roiled beneath. "I thought you were a thug."

"I would not have attacked your father if he had not held a knife to Jaffar," I said. That was not an apology, for I did not regret killing the man. I just wanted her to see the situation clearly.

"I know that," she said peevishly. "My father"—she paused to suck in a long breath—"wasn't a good man."

I grunted in surprise.

"You thought I didn't know that?"

"I assumed you hated me because I killed him."

"And for what I thought you were."

"A thug, you said."

"A thoughtless lackey. And I thought Dabir was little better; a clever servant. Unquestioning. Blindly obedient to the established order." She turned to look at him. Dabir's back blocked sight of his work, but we could hear the sound of his blade scratching into the soil. "Scheming and fawning and scrabbling for place like everyone else."

"Why would you say that?" I asked. "Dabir's no bootlicker."

"And it's a wonder he's risen so far." She laughed to herself, glanced at me. "A week ago, if someone had told me my feelings would be hurt because Dabir ibn Khalil did not trust me, I would have . . ."

"Cursed him?" I suggested.

"Likely."

"He does trust you," I said. "He has asked for your help."

She sighed at me. "Don't you see, he's planning something, but he will not tell us. You, because you would not approve, and me, because he thinks I might betray him."

"If you want him to trust you," I said, "you must trust him."

She studied me for a moment, and the wind tugged at her coat. She muttered something then in Greek, and extended her hand. "May I borrow your knife?"

I handed it to her hilt first.

"My thanks." She turned and walked over to Dabir.

She joined my friend and, working mostly in silence, they drew in the strange symbols that were almost familiar to me now. After a time Dabir sat back, and Lydia looked between the circle and his ring, which he rubbed absently as he contemplated the curling lines and wedges and triangles.

I joined them. "There is nothing coming, yet."

"Good. They will surely be here soon." He frowned at the circle.

"What is the trouble?" I asked.

"I believe I have spelled Lamashtu's name properly, but I cannot be certain about the lettering. Jibril's notes were a little unclear on this point, because once he finally had it working he did not record confirmed findings. By then," he said, "he was through with magics."

"With sorcery it is the intent, often, that matters more," Lydia offered.

"Then this will have to do. If she comes," Dabir added with a sharp look to us both, "I am to do the negotiating. Is that clear?"

We agreed that it was.

"Asim, you say there's a little more energy left in the club. Let's reserve the spear, and use your club to activate this circle."

"Now?"

Dabir let out a long breath and nodded. He was exhausted, of course. He climbed to his feet, extended his arms in a long stretch that also conjured a yawn, then gathered himself. He stepped over to retrieve the spear. "I will keep this on hand. In case Lamahstu proves less receptive."

"Allah forbid." I lifted the club, ran the form through my mind, and set the heavy end upon the circle. The club of Herakles did not light as brightly as previous, but still took up its brave glow. Apart from noticing that my own senses could not extend more than a few paces, the first thing I saw was that Lydia's farr was different. The blackness about her was not so pronounced, and the silvers were bolder. Dabir, too, had changed. All of his colors had a fuzzy edge, as though ebbing with his strength.

The paired ovals in the ground and the symbols between them flared with energy. Nothing else, though, happened at all.

"Where is she?" I asked.

"Behind you," purred a low feminine voice, and we turned as one to find a stocky woman in white dress, her face pale as the moon, her straight hair dark as the night.

Lamashtu. Her face was plain and expressionless, and her farr was a web of midnight darkness. "You have called; I have come. Though if you mean to fight me—"

Dabir was blunt. "Erragal is dead."

Lamashtu let out a short laugh, peered at us, then laughed again. "This is a strange bluff."

"No," Lydia told her. "Gazi is dead."

"And good riddance," she said.

"Koury is dead," Lydia continued.

"He was ever too arrogant. And what about his little helper, Anzu? Has he crept away?"

"More or less," Dabir answered.

"But what ploy of Erragal's can this be?" she asked. "He and I ceased playing games against each other centuries ago." She looked to right and left, as if she expected Erragal to step suddenly from hiding.

"He fell in freeing us," I said.

"In freeing you? Now I know you lie."

"He was after the weapons, really," Dabir said. "We just happened to be holding them."

"What's left of him lies yonder," I said.

She followed my gaze. She stared with those remorseless eyes for a long moment, then strode nimbly over, keeping us in her sight. Then she bent and cast back the robe to reveal the bloody hunk of man that had been a portion of the world's greatest wizard.

Realization spread slowly over Lamahtu's face, and then long unused muscles twitched along her jaw and brow. Grief came to her, as water comes sometimes to the deep desert, raging, destructive, and unfamiliar. Her teeth showed, and she struggled mightily to hold herself in check. Her farr rolled like a black thunderhead. "Have you called me to gloat?"

Dabir shook his head. "No. I called you to help finish what he began. His last work."

She cast the robe angrily over his remains and spun to face us full-on. "I have no need of his stupid works. His pointless plans for the ignorants who shall never perceive his worth!"

It was strange, to my thought, that she might hold all that the man did in contempt. Yet she had loved him, in her way.

"You and yours set the spirit free," Dabir said in a measured tone of voice. "Erragal died trying to ready the means to send her back." He tipped his spear, slowly, toward the horizon. "We stand in the midst of a great banishing circle that he has hidden in the snow. Usarshra is sure to come, before long, to retrieve the final weapons, and what is left of the power in the club. When she does, we will send her and her spirit army back to the cold hell from whence they came. We cannot do it," he finished, "without your help. We need to know how to unlock the magics of Erragal's staff."

"He did not tell you?"

"No."

"Perhaps I should take it, in memory of him."

"You could do that," Dabir said. "But I think if you had truly desired one of the bones, he would have gifted one to you centuries ago."

Her eyes narrowed, as though by doing so she might see Dabir better. "You are right," she admitted. "They are powerful, but their magic is . . . uncomfortable to me." She paused and considered Dabir with a crafty, covetous look I did not like. "I shall help you if you help me. We shall trade favors."

"What sort of favors?" Dabir asked.

"There is no need for a bargain," Lydia objected. "You need the world unfrozen as much as we do."

Dabir shot Lydia a warning glance before returning his attention to Lamashtu.

"Child," Lamashtu told Lydia, "I always profit from chaos, though some pleases me less than others." She stepped nearer Dabir. "Those are my terms. The favor is unspecified, as of yet, for I have not yet decided what it shall be. But you must swear a blood oath unto me, to bind it."

"We can swear no oath," Dabir said, "that breaks the commandants of Allah, or the teachings of Muhammad, may peace be upon him."

I nodded solemnly in agreement.

She bared her teeth. "You would make conditions?" Her face contorted in wrath and I think she readied to curse us, but then Lydia's voice rose up behind us.

"I pledge," she said, "without condition!"

"No!" Dabir cried, turning to her. Before me I saw Lamashtu's face shift into a smile and then she winked away, only to appear beside Lydia. The Greek woman had raised one hand, bleeding. Her other held a slim knife, dripping with her own blood. Lamashtu clasped the bleeding palm, then pressed her lips to it.

"No," Dabir said weakly.

Lamashtu stepped back, triumphant, and licked her bloody lips as she smiled at Dabir. "I meant not only to teach you the secret of the staff, but to loan you my own magics. Now you must but watch as she wields it. Great, though, must her services be, for now she owes for the three of you!" She turned to Lydia. "For one day I gift you a portion of my magic." Again the Sebitti pressed her lips to Lydia's hand, and drank deep. God help me, for because of the club I saw more than the shudder of the Greek as she cast back her head. I witnessed the energy flowing between the two, saw the darkness pass through from the ancient sorceress to Lydia. The woman stumbled, and would have fallen had not Dabir reached out to catch her.

Lamashtu cackled. "I shall return for you, my sweet Greek. Fare you well!" And with that she vanished, though her laughter hung in the air a moment after.

Lydia blinked. She turned her noticeably paler face to Dabir, who still held to her.

"You should not have done that," he told her.

"We had no choice."

I stared at her farr. It flowed in turmoil, but, you may not believe this, no matter the influx of darkness from Lamashtu, the silver strands in Lydia's energies burned more brightly than ever.

"I told you to let me bargain!" Dabir's voice rose, and his mouth twisted in torment.

"Stop speaking of what is done!" Lydia shouted, standing straight. "There was nothing else we might offer her!" She wiped something from her eyes. "I have the pattern of the staff now, in my mind. And the magics . . . I may just have saved us, Dabir." With that she turned back to the fire and walked stiffly for the staff.

Dabir did not move.

I let go of the club then so that whatever energy remained would not be wasted, and put a hand to my friend's shoulder.

"She did not have to do that," he whispered fiercely. "I cannot fix this!"

"She wants to help," I said.

Dabir sagged against the spear, head down, then slowly straightened his shoulders. "Come, Asim."

We joined Lydia at the fire, and she watched him through lowered lashes.

"So," Dabir said in a heavy tone. "There are two circles, created by Anzu and Erragal. The obvious one that will protect us. And the great outer one that Erragal concealed. You shall use the staff to defend us with the smaller circle, and the spear shall be used for the larger banishing."

"Will that be enough?" I asked. "Anzu said it would take a great sorcerer besides."

"I am a great sorcerer," Lydia asserted. "For today, at least." Lydia stared down at her hands, flexing fingers. I sensed, somehow, that she considered her own farr. She then studied the distance for a time. "There will probably be enough power to banish the lesser spirits. But what will we do if it doesn't bind Usarshra?"

"We will do almost exactly what the Sebitti planned. When Usarshra is threatened, she will widen the portal to call in more energy, more resources. I will then use the words of shaping to destroy the spirits."

Lydia stared at him. "How . . ."

"Erragal had me study Koury's magics, that I might counter them. Remember?"

A smile dawned slowly over Lydia's face. "But you did not say that to either Anzu or Lamashtu," she said.

"No. And I did not want either of you to reveal, through word or gesture, what I planned. I did not think . . ." His eyes sought Lydia's.

"Wait a moment," I said. "You know the words of creation?"

"I know the words of dissolution," he said, "to counter Koury's. And I have reasoned out a few more things."

Lydia laughed with joy. "You are a genius, Dabir!" She smiled at me, then took his hand. "You can remake everything as we wish! We can do what Anzu wanted, but to our ways. Why, we could reshape time itself!" She paused, her expression falling. "Why do you look like that?"

"Even if I knew enough to do such things, where would I stop?" Dabir asked. "Should I remake the day when Jibril died, or the moment when you pledged troth to the Sebitti? What about the day my wife perished with my newborn son? Might I undo *that* moment? It is a string of pearls, Lydia, and more, for if I reshape one thing, who is to say what others would happen."

She growled in frustration. "Don't you see what we might do?"

"First," Dabir said calmly, "I am not certain that I can even succeed. The only magic of Koury's or Erragal's I have worked was to get these beasts moving. I will be manipulating the very fabric of reality, and I have but a few words with which to guide me. Second, I shall only undo these otherworldly invaders. Nothing else shall I change. That is the work of God, and I am but a man."

"A foolish, stubborn man," she spat.

"Probably. And a very weary one at that."

This talk had grown pointless. "So," I said, "we await the spirits."

"Yes. Because the larger circle is hidden and not yet active, no wizard will detect the thing. It is a most excellent noose, if we but have the strength to pull the line."

I nodded in appreciation. "Do you recall how Najya said she'd foreseen herself advancing with an army of frost djinn and furred warriors toward a hill?"

"I do. I asked her about it at length."

I adjusted my fingers on the club. "Do you think that this is the place?"

"I have gambled upon it. Enkidu might be inclined to come alone, or to send only a few spirits after us. But we have angered them too many times, and then there is Najya's vision."

"God gives," I said.

"Look there," Lydia said, and we followed her pointing hand to the eastern horizon.

Storm clouds were rolling toward us at great speed, hugely gray and white.

"Unless I miss my guess," Dabir said, "they are on their way."

20

There are standard preparations before any battle, and these I saw to, though I wondered whether any of them would be of use. First I looked over weapons and gear, little of it though there was. Between us we had only the two knives and Dabir's sword, for I had cast mine down in the Khazar camp. I sharpened them anyway, and oiled Dabir's scabbard.

Next I saw that we were fed. I'd had the sense to bring as much of the Khazar meal as I could carry, and we sat around the fire with it, though both Dabir and Lydia claimed they had no appetite. I broke some branches off that poor tree on top of the hill and tossed them on the fire to keep it going. They were green, of course, so that set the fire smoking, but there wasn't anything else to use as fuel.

The horse shrank suddenly to its miniature size as we finished, then plopped over in the snow. All three of us stared, and Dabir rose slowly to recover it. He brought it back to the fire, weighing it in one hand. For a moment I thought he meant to throw it in.

"What happened to it?" I asked.

"The magic wears out eventually, depending on how much the creature is used." His eyes strayed to the bull. "I imagine Koury used the horses more. I don't know how to go about restoring it."

"What are you going to do with it?" I asked him

"It looks like a plaything." He smiled wistfully. "I thought I might send it on to Sabirah's child."

"It was created by a dark wizard," Lydia remonstrated, "likely with blood magics. I would give that to no child."

"It might fit in well upon our curio shelf when this all is over," I suggested.

At this he snorted. "You think that even one of us shall live?" He pocketed the horse nonetheless.

"It shall be as Allah wills," I said. "We should pray. The storm will reach us soon."

Lydia did not join us, saying she would rather rest a little longer.

Dabir and I washed in the snow for our ablutions, then threw down our prayer rugs and knelt.

Afterward we climbed to the hill's summit to see the creatures that moved within roiling, ashen clouds: towering figures of white and smaller, gliding figures that soon resolved themselves into rank upon rank of the snow women accompanied by monstrous wolves all the size of that we had battled, gigantic bears and cats, and all sorts of indistinct flitting things in white and blue. Behind all this were hundreds of dark riders.

"And all I have," I said, "is a club and a knife."

"And a magic bull." Dabir put a hand to the animal, which he had brought up top with us.

The club was a reassuring weight in my hand, and my fingers tightened around the haft. I wondered how many times Herakles must have adjusted it himself before striding into battle. His exploits had become legend, and his bravery immortal. He had been placed by loving hands within a tomb fashioned by the same people who had revered him. I was most likely to die forgotten, my bones covered only by frost.

I heard Lydia's feet crushing the snow behind us. "Why does she bring so many?"

"Usarshra knows we plan some kind of opposition," Dabir replied. "She surely has felt that we have brought the weapons here and await her."

I saw then a dark speck running ahead of the hordes, a large horned animal with a rider.

Lydia noticed my stare. "Enkidu's oryx," she explained.

I groaned only a little. "Is there anything else we will have to fight?"

"Nothing sorcerous will be able to cross the inner circle around our hill."

"And to think," I said, "I was wondering why Erragal crafted the outer circle so large. Now I'm wondering if they can all fit in."

"Where is Usarshra?" Lydia asked. "We will only have the one chance."

None of us could find her, and I could not be sure if I was pleased or saddened. I did not wish to see Najya die. And yet, I resolved to myself grimly, she might be dead already, her body animated only by the alien thing that had slain her soul. "She must be somewhere amongst that horde."

On the creatures came, the snow women gliding out in front, dozens upon dozens of them, their hair and garments flying out behind. Now we could clearly see Enkidu's oryx. This antelope was larger by half than any I had ever seen, and it was all white but for its black hooves and the mask-like pattern upon its long face. Enkidu clasped its straight, backward-pointing horns as he rode.

The frost women poured in behind him as Enkidu descended into the valley and crossed toward us. The space I had thought vast now seemed very small.

The great white snow spirits of wolf and bear were not too far behind the women.

"Are you ready?" Dabir asked of Lydia.

Once more Lydia brought out her necklace and brushed her lips to the pendant there. I have seen Christians kiss images of their saints before, when happy, or sad, and I remembered that Dabir said she wore an image of a saint. I had no chance to examine it, though, for she tucked the pendant away, closed her eyes for a short moment, then nodded. Her eyes narrowed in concentration as she hefted the staff, and then it took on its glow. She touched it to the circle. On the instant, circles and symbols sprang brilliantly alive with golden light.

I leaned closer to Dabir. "Can Khazars cross the barrier?"

"Well, yes. Unless they are *magic* Khazars."

I chuckled despite myself.

"It is a one-way barrier only to magic things—we can send things out, but they can send nothing in."

"What of Enkidu?"

Dabir mulled that over it. "I suppose he could cross, unless he's using magic at the time. His spells can't, though."

"And his oryx?"

"I do not know." Dabir's eyes narrowed into that contemplative look he adopted when his challenge was great. "It would depend upon whether the beast is purely supernatural, or an ordinary being endowed with magic."

"Huh. Well, Enkidu and a couple of hundred cavalry are more than enough to worry about."

"Usarshra's sorcerous troops are in the lead," Dabir pointed out.

They were only a bowshot out now from our position. They spread around us as they closed, slowly encircling our hill.

Enkidu guided his oryx to a trotted halt and stood staring up at us. Towering white man-shapes formed mostly of wind lumbered slowly around on our left flank. I now saw other, stranger creatures among those, large semitransparent serpents and huge billowing, shifting masses of cloud and frost that seemed sometimes to have shining crystalline eyes and sometimes maws with jagged teeth made all of icicles.

"You are sure I can channel the power of the spear to the outer circle from within ours?" Dabir asked Lydia.

"Erragal arranged for it to be done." She then said something to Dabir about directing energies through substrata and sympathetic resonances and linked glyphs, though she might well have been speaking her native tongue, for it was all Greek to me.

Once we were surrounded fully by eerie snow beings on every side, a dozen of the snow women tested the barrier they could sense before them, invisible until they drifted into it. They turned instantly to steam against the red screen of energy thrown suddenly in their path. More and more of them came on, and more and more of them melted.

After some three dozen had vanished they halted their assault.

Enkidu hopped down from his antelope, breath steaming, and grinned up at us. I would have given much for a javelin.

"This is your plan?" he asked, laughing. "To cower behind a sorcerous circle? When it falls, we will simply sweep over you all!"

We did not answer him.

"I wonder," he said, "will the barrier harm me?" And he reached up with his left hand and passed it through the circle just beyond the bottom of the hill. He laughed. "Come to me!"

He frowned a little, as we did not obey.

I allowed myself a smile. His mind magics had failed against us.

"Erragal left you a protective enchantment, did he? It will only delay things."

"You would be wise to let Asim be," Dabir called down. "Your messiah looks on him with special favor."

"She has grown weary of Asim, and bade me finish the matter. Thus am I here! Come, man, and end your days as a warrior!"

"Where is Najya?" Dabir demanded.

"That is not your worry!"

"It should be yours!" Dabir retorted. "Has she sent you here because she cannot bear to see our destruction, or because she fears she might change her mind?"

Enkidu strode toward the slope.

"I must fight him," I said softly.

Dabir looked over to me, and I almost saw his thoughts. For the first time, even though we were surrounded by an immense force of monsters, and an army of mounted Khazars still riding in with upraised weapons behind them, he looked frightened.

His concern touched me, and so I put a hand to his shoulder. I then called to Enkidu, halfway up the hill. "I will come and face you man to man!"

"Good!" Enkidu brandished his axe. His half-sketched bow was almost mocking, but he withdrew to level ground within our circle to await me.

"Asim, don't do this." Dabir's gaze pierced me. "A prophecy is little enough to pin your life upon."

"What prophecy?" Lydia demanded. "What nonsense is this? I'll just blast him with sorcery. Do not risk yourself!"

I shook my head, for I was certain in my course, and spoke to Dabir. "Najya said that she would see me wield the club, in battle near a hill."

Dabir started to protest but I cut him off.

"She has not been wrong yet. Here is the hill. Here is the club. There is my foe. But she is not here. And if you don't activate the circle soon, the Khazars will ride to the front rank and shower us with arrows, or simply charge the hill."

"What's going on?" Lydia insisted. "There's no need to face him one at a time! We only stand a chance if we coordinate."

"He's going to draw out the queen," Dabir said with cold certainty.

"She will come once the fight begins, and then you can work your magics," I continued.

I did not expect to survive a one-on-one battle with one of the Sebitti, and Dabir must have seen that in my face.

Lydia looked sharply between the two of us. I thought at first she would argue more but she beckoned me close. I bent to her, assuming she meant to confide some secret. Instead she brushed my cheek, just above my beard, with her lips. "Fight well."

I nodded.

"Go with God," I heard Dabir say, his voice strained.

I strode down as Enkidu crossed over the line and grinned, beckoning at me with his free hand.

Beyond Enkidu, beyond the circle, were rank after endless rank of cold and ghostly beings of frost. Hundreds of snow women, each with Najya's face, drifted above the surface of the snow, watching with glowing eyes. Beyond them loomed the larger monsters, so that I was ringed by the supernatural on all sides but from the hill where Dabir and Lydia watched.

Axes are most excellent weapons so long as you are on the offense, for they are devilishly hard to block. They are not, however, especially keen defensively. Thus I knew that the first move had best be mine. I feigned wary concern as I stepped out, then while Enkidu grinned, I cried out to Allah and swung the club.

It was a good blow, well delivered, but Enkidu had lived many more lifetimes than I. He avoided with a swift backwards step. I thought him off balance and pressed in with another swing, but the axe came down with terrific might. I sidestepped, and the speed of that blow set the air humming. With gritted teeth I pushed off and came in low, thinking to strike his arm, but Enkidu's hand snaked out and clasped tight around the club haft. I sought then to use the power within it, but he tossed down the axe and grabbed hold of the club in both hands. He lifted it up, laughing as I dangled, for he was taller than me and on higher ground. My concentration was momentarily shattered. I had forgotten his strength.

Still, he had not properly thought the move through, and my kick caught him hard in the abdomen. He let out a grunt and dropped me. A normal man would have been doubled over, but as I rolled he snatched up the axe. I slid on the frost, and crossed over the sorcerous barrier.

On the instant the temperature dropped. My heart, already racing, beat now in fear, but the ice women made room for me, for us, as Enkidu came charging and drove the blade at me—they were opening a lane at the end of which I glimpsed riders. I barely scrambled up and away. Again and again he swung that gleaming axe, and I backed farther and farther out. I wished that I might call on the club's power, but I did not, for there was so precious little of it left. Nowhere was there sign of Najya.

On Enkidu's fourth swing I slid on a patch of ice and hit the ground on my side. Enkidu laughed and slammed down his blade. I slid as I struggled up, and this is all that saved me from losing my hand, for he struck again with blinding speed.

"Slay him!" came a male voice upon the wind. "Set his blood flowing upon the snow!"

I became aware of the chanting of Khazars as they reined in a stone's throw off my left. Closer by, Enkidu's oryx snorted and beat its front hooves against the frost.

I was cold, and tired, and I knew that I was outmatched—and making a poor showing besides. Yet I thought, if I strove harder, I might well earn my friend a few minutes more so that Najya would appear, and the spell could be worked.

You would think Enkidu's tread would be heavy, but he was catlike as he advanced, whirling his axe without any sort of effort. "I have the gifts of the beasts of the field," he said. "The cunning of the fox, the speed of the gazelle. A bear's strength. What have you? I have no need of my magic to change your mood, though perhaps I should make you braver, so that you would fight better."

On he came, his axe held ready.

He might not need magics, but I surely did, and I called upon them then. The club glowed as I rose. If I might at least strike him, I thought I could venture to paradise with a smile, like Alexis.

I took a step for him and his axe came up. I feinted that my left foot was losing purchase and leaned as if regaining my balance. The axe swept sideways. And I pushed hard off my right leg, diving at him and swinging as one.

The back end of his swing caught my armored shoulder as I leapt, and I knew blazing pain, but I also knew victory, for the club of Herakles slammed into his arm. I heard a crack and a scream. I hit the ground gracelessly on my elbow and found more pain.

I rolled to my side, gasping for breath.

Enkidu's face was frozen in bestial rage, and spittle ran down through his beard. He switched his axe to his other hand as advanced toward me, and I had not the breath to rise.

It was then that something huge and black drove hard into Enkidu's back and sent him spinning to the ground. I saw with amazement that it was our black wooden bull, and I staggered to my feet, willing myself to move more quickly. Allah, but I ached.

The bull galloped through the transparent women, doing them little harm but collecting a sparkling frost coating. It circled back toward Enkidu. The Sebitti rose, shaking his head like a dog. He cast down his axe and crouched, waiting with his arms outspread, though he winced as he moved the one I'd injured. There were now seven paces between us, for the bull had knocked him far, and he was turned half away. Dabir had evened the field.

It was my thought to drive in at Enkidu when the bull next cast him down, but it was not to be, for Enkidu caught the creature's horns in his hands. He screamed with pain, but did not yield. For all that he was a madman, I admired his fortitude. The wooden bull's momentum set Enkidu sliding. His face strained from red to near purple, but he dug in his heels, lifted the creature by its horns, and cast the thing toward me.

I threw myself to the right, and the bull's horn passed only a hand span above my head as I landed in the snow. The club of Herakles rolled from my sweaty palms and kept on rolling until it lay a full man's length away. The earth shook as the bull struck the ground behind me.

I climbed, staggering toward the club, but a grinning Enkidu interposed himself.

The bull lay sideways upon the ground. One of its back legs was broken off entirely, and the other was twisted up to the right, poking up like an extra tail. It still pawed at the earth with its forelegs, but Enkidu's oryx plowed into the thing with its head and cast it sideways. The club of Herakles rolled a few feet farther away.

"Your friend should not have interfered," Enkidu said. "Now, mortal, make your peace, for I am coming to deliver your last blow."

So saying, Enkidu came for me, raising his axe.

"I am at peace with Allah," I said, only to myself.

He stopped before me and hefted up his weapon. "On your death, a new age begins."

With that, the axe rose once more, up over his off shoulder.

"Stop!"

Najya's voice echoed as through she had spoken from a thousand throats. Enkidu stood poised to deliver my deathblow, but looked from side to side, searching for her.

Dozens of the snow women shifted and flowed and converged one upon the other. Color came to them as they overlapped. Najya stepped forward as still more of the snow women flowed into her form. "Asim," the multiple voices said. And then, in the last three steps, she was suddenly there, in the flesh, her hand thrust up toward Enkidu, as if she meant physically to restrain the axe from falling.

Far above that hand, a transparent red dome of energy flickered into existence. A roar of anger, half curse, half wind, swept up from the thousands assembled there.

Najya spun to face Dabir and screamed worldlessly. I swear that icy winds rolled up as she did this. Enkidu backed away from her.

I pushed to my knees and threw myself for the club, grasped it, remembered those forms a final time. Its enhanced senses warned me of a looming power to my rear and I ducked as I turned. Enkidu's cut missed the top of my helm by only inches. He was just a little slower now, for all that I had injured him, and I managed to regain my feet.

Overhead I saw a tear within the sky itself all about Najya, widening at her gesture. A bright, deadly whiteness swept out, roaring, as though the old woman of the north had fully opened her sack of winds. Najya screamed also at her Khazars, who charged forward with their battle cries, lances leveled. The wind was too chaotic for accurate bow work.

Their beasts thundered around Enkidu and myself and they let us be, to battle alone to the death. I thought us well beyond the protective power of Anzu's magic, but it might be Enkidu was so taken with rage it had not even occurred to him to control me. Spittle flecked his beard and mustache like the froth of a mad dog. He pressed on, swing after tireless swing, driving me back and farther back through the ranks of snow women and up against a vast wall of some white cloud thing.

But it broke apart just as I approached it, and around me a strange, great horned beast fell suddenly into frosty fragments. It was as though a mighty hand was sweeping through the mass of spirits, and where it touched, all dissolved. Enkidu held off, staring in astonishment. Over his shoulder, I saw Dabir atop the hill. He had lifted up the spear and was laying waste, calling out in a clear, deep voice, the fingers of his free hand raised, clawlike. Where he swung that hand, swathes of the monsters fell before him.

Lydia stood beside him, just visible through a cloud of fire and smoke. She leaned still upon the staff, fixed to the circle, but in her other hand she wielded a string of fire like a whip, and where it touched it left empty saddles and seared, tumbling corpses.

The Khazars shouted and charged the slope, and I thought all was done until Dabir left off slaying spirits, his eyes glowing golden as the sun. I think he cast up the earth before their feet so that their horses plunged madly, and they fell or galloped clear.

Enkidu shouted, though I could not make out his words. And though I wearied, aye, almost unto death, a faint spark had lit once more within me, and it was hope. I backed from him, the club held down to my right. He came on again, and again, swinging madly, like an animal. From left. From right, from left, each time missing me by only hairs. Any single blow would have taken my head. He was swift, aye, but that one arm was slower on the recovery, and when he swung by once more on the left, I sprang.

The club blazed as brightly as it had that first time, light once more as the air itself. I came up from the lower right. Surprise warred briefly with rage in Enkidu's eyes as the club rose up and up, and he jerked back his chin, thinking he might avoid me. Yet he was too late. When I hit, a grisly crack echoed across that bitter landscape and he was lifted bodily into the air, his head half parted from his neck. Blood spewed fountainlike as he arced backward to land beside his axe with a thud. The blood flowed out for some time, dyeing the surrounding snow, but he had perished the moment I connected with him.

I stumbled after him, lost my balance, sank to one knee. The club was but dimly glowing now, its energies all but spent. Dimly could I perceive the sorcerous battle that went on around me. I thought at first the ground shook because my senses reeled, but at the last moment I turned my head to see Enkidu's oryx a few feet off, charging at full strength and snorting fire. I tell you, at that moment I knew I was done.

But a huge wall of earth reared up and swept the animal off its feet and away. I stared in wonder as the creature was shunted off, crying in distress, and the wall struck against a dozen Khazars beyond, charging the hill on foot. I looked up to find Dabir upon the height, sweeping that glowing spear from right to left. With each movement, landscape rose and fell. Beside him Lydia's whip stretched on for the length of a noble's courtyard. With a single blow she sent ten Khazars screaming from their saddles.

Najya, though, still shouted, and the spirits obeyed. Dozens at a time they tossed themselves against the barrier. They dissolved as they struck, impacting so often that the circle about the hill was a permanent wall of transparent scarlet energy. This one was far more powerful than that Jibril had once erected in his house, but there were hundreds of spirits set against it, and Najya herself conjured more from the rift every moment. Sooner or later that barrier was going to go down, just like Jibril's. Overhead, the red of the greater mystical dome—what I surmised to be the height of the banishment circle—flickered on and off. Anzu had been right. We did not have the power, probably because Dabir had to expend so much of it to fight the spirits.

I breathed in through battered ribs. Around me the spirits multiplied with astonishing speed, twelve appearing where but one had stood a moment before—women, clouds, vaporous monsters from ancient days—shunted in from the huge gap in the sky. The temperature plummeted further as they crowded into being, and the nearest stretched out to me with hands, tendrils, whatever they possessed, for I was life, and energy.

The club still flared, albeit dimly, and they recoiled. I knew that my protection could not possibly last much longer, and that they multiplied faster than Dabir could destroy them. I flung myself into a staggering charge. There was no longer any clear ground on which to walk, so thick were the frost spirits clustered, but they parted or disintegrated on contact with the club. My hands and face had left off stinging some time back and were now quite numb. Two Khazars and their mounts were toppled nearby, sheathed in frost and consumed by huddling spirits. I pressed on past a leering face formed of vapor, and an icy, skeletal bird thing. A few paces from Najya the club failed at last, crumbling apart in my hands as I passed through a final snow woman. Intent as I was, I knew a sense of remorse at the loss of the great weapon, which had served Herakles so well and never failed me.

And then I flung myself at the back of the woman I loved. Alerted by some sorcery, she spun in surprise just before I tackled her.

We hit the ground, hard, and the world spun. Starshot blackness blossomed across my vision. I shook my head. Najya, beside me, was already rising on her elbows. I rolled to face her, weakly raising one hand as she gritted teeth and brought one toward me, hate glittering in her sapphire eyes.

"Najya!" I gasped. "I know that you are there!"

"Weakness!" she screamed at me, and her cold hand dove at my neck.

The dome above us glowed gold, pink, red, blue. Najya's eyes widened and she withdrew her hand to stare at the sky. "No!"

I felt the greater circle's magic sweep over me like a strong current of water. Something pulled at my inner being, from far away, as though a hook had caught my soul. I pushed at thickened air with my hands, fighting it, willing myself to stay. Beside me, Najya convulsed. Her mouth worked, but no sound came.

"Asim!" Lydia shouted. "Get back to the inner circle!" Now, clearly, I heard Dabir chanting, and the spear in his hand glowed, brighter than ever, as though it burned its energy at an accelerated rate.

I looked down at Najya. I could not leave her there, like that. I supposed that if I had the strength to flee and if I bore her with me to safety, the spirit would be left within her. Better we should meet our end here, together.

The ice beings all about us raised voices in whistling agony, a song of death from a thousand throats. Najya screamed, too, a lone human voice among the monstrous things. She shuddered and shook, her eyes rolling in pain.

"I shall take her with me!" the spirit screamed.

Tightly I grasped those shaking, frigid hands. "Do not let her have you!"

"She is strong," she cried, and I did not know if it was spirit or woman who spoke.

The beings, all of them, blurred and stretched and twisted in upon themselves, and suddenly there was nothing there but thickened mist and droplets of water, cascading onto that cold ground as though a rainstorm had birthed only feet above the surface of the earth. I have never heard anything like the sound of those spatters before or since.

Najya dropped limp in my arm as if she were boneless.

"Asim!" I saw Dabir racing down the hillside toward me, frantic.

It was then the great wave of water rushed in from every side.

Instantly I was engulfed in a freezing wave and knocked from my feet sideways. I came up sputtering in the frigid, swirling water, clinging to Najya's arm. The current was too strong for me to stand. Though every use of my left arm brought agony, I stroked with it, and my hand struck something solid. It felt like wood, and I clung tightly to it.

It was the wooden bull, kicking its forelegs to propel itself. I knew then that Dabir must be controlling the thing still and praised Allah for my friend's cleverness. It ceased its kicking. I held Najya with a death grip, keeping her face above water. Dabir clung to the bull's other side with one of the handholds.

"Alhamdilillah!" he said. "You've made it!"

"Thanks to you." I said. "Help me with Najya!"

This proved a challenge, for the wooden bull was spinning in the wild, rocking current. Dabir managed to board and sweep Najya onto his lap, but he could not also leverage me. I had little idea whether Najya even lived still.

"Is she alive?"

"She breathes!" Dabir managed.

"Where is Lydia?"

"Safe on the hill," he said. "I think."

It is no easy matter to learn such things when spinning in a mad current holding on to the leg and tail of a wooden bull.

It seemed that we floated thus for a mad hour or four, but on later reflection I think only a few grains in an hourglass would have dropped. As we struggled we saw hundreds of Khazars floating lifelessly around us.

Also there were horses, some of which screamed and fought the water. But most of them, and their riders—men and women both—were dead.

Of a sudden my feet struck earth solidly. The bull lurched to a halt. The water had simply spread outward in a wave, and in a moment more it was but waist-deep, then barely to my ankles.

Of course I was thoroughly frozen, and shivering uncontrollably, yet that was nothing. I turned Najya's limp body to me and checked for her breath. I could find none.

"She does not breathe!" I cried. I thought for a moment Dabir had lied to me.

But he looked as horrified as me. "I could not always keep her above the water!" He hurried around to the side of the bull. His teeth were chattering, but he did not slow. Mine, too, were rattling. Around us was left a tide of washed-up, fur-clad warriors.

Dabir lay her over the motionless wooden beast and pressed against her back once, twice, a dozen times. I stood shivering, watching him, thinking this a lonely place to dig a grave and that this was a poor time to lose her, after she had come through so much.

But then Najya coughed. She vomited water and coughed once more and lay weakly against the bull's chest. I stepped to her side and touched her face with shaking fingers. She looked up at me and her eyes were brown.

"Asim," she whispered.

So great was my joy that tears slid from my eyes.

21

The hill where we'd made our stand was a fair distance off. Even with love to warm me it was a long, cold way to its height, and I was in some pain. Yet we three managed, shivering the while. Here and there lay the occasional Khazar corpse, or mount, or bits of their equipment. A few horses galloped away further off, shaking water from their manes.

The flood had not touched the hilltop. Lydia slumped at its height, her breathing shallow, her eyes rolling. But she had somehow fashioned a pit, with heated rocks, and with failing energy she set hands to our soaking garments and used her borrowed power to dry them.

Almost at the same moment the clouds rolled away, and the sun stood out in a clear sky. The wind died, and quiet, exhausted, we four sat crowded about the fire, feeling the sun on our backs. I ached thoroughly, throughout my body, but I did not care, for we had survived, and Najya was at my side. She did not mind that my good arm was about her; indeed, she was pressed tightly to my shoulder.

"Where did all that water come from," I asked Dabir, "at the end?"

He smiled sheepishly. "That wasn't on purpose. I was trying to break the hold the spirits had on any physical substance. I'd been shaping earth pretty effectively, and I'd broken smaller groups of them apart. When I tried it with the larger group . . . somehow I ended up transforming all of them to water. I warned you," he added, "I didn't really know much shaping magic."

"You knew enough."

Lydia had been listening attentively. She sat beside Dabir. Close, but not so close as Najya to me, who watched her with suspicion. "There at the end," she said, "were you actually using shaping magic to power the circle?"

"Yes." Dabir seemed strangely reluctant to speak of it, and hesitated for a moment. "I used the words of dissolution to break Usarshra's hold on the magics. Once it was no longer keyed to her, I 'grabbed' hold, and it worked. Though I could never have broken through her defenses if Asim hadn't distracted her."

Lydia's eyes were huge now, as though she meant to drink down every word. "What was that like?"

"To have that kind of power?" Dabir thought a long while before answering. "I only dared use it for a moment," he admitted finally. "It was frightening. I understood then the things I might do, if I but knew the proper words. And it was tempting to try them anyway. But then things went awry with the water, and I used all the spear's remaining power to seal the gate. Such deeds," he finished, sighing, "are not meant for one such as me."

"Well," I said, noticing that it hurt a little even to grin—I seemed to have pulled a neck muscle—"God be praised for your fine judgment and quick wit."

I then noticed Najya staring at Lydia. "Lydia helped us," I told her. "She worked hard to set things right." I thought then of her promise to Lamashtu, and frowned. "Dabir, what are we to do? The witch will come for her."

The Greek shifted in her seat. Her dark ringlets hung wild and un-kempt as she lifted up her open pendant and pressed it for a long time to her lips. Quietly she lowered it, then faced me. "You would stand no chance against her, Asim."

"But we cannot let her take you."

I looked to Dabir, who stared fixedly at the fire while furiously rub-bing the back of his ring, then back to the Greek.

She smiled, gently, as a man does when a young child says something foolish. Her careworn eyes roved over each of us. "Najya, I hope that . . . I hope that you will be well from here on out. I am glad you survived."

"Asim says that you helped them," Najya said guardedly. "I suppose I have that to thank you for."

"You owe me no thanks." Tired as she was, Lydia's accent was more pronounced than usual. "I am surprised you can offer anything but curses."

"I thought I would hate you," Najya replied. "But I cannot muster the will. Perhaps I am too relieved, or too tired."

"Do you feel any of the spirit still?" Lydia asked.

"Nay. I am wholly myself."

Lydia looked over to me. "Asim, I forgive you my father's death. He brought it upon himself."

She sounded very much like someone saying her good-byes, and I checked with Dabir to gauge his reaction.

One last time Lydia looked at the woman beside me. "Najya, he is all that he seems to be, and nothing more. If you love him as I think you must, treasure him for that. It is a rare thing."

"Lydia?" Dabir asked cautiously.

"Dabir." She smiled then, and no matter her fatigue, she lit with a shadow of her beauty.

She reached out and touched the side of his face with one hand. His hair hung loose about his face, owing to the loss of our turbans, and she ran her fingers through it.

He met her eyes tenderly, then bent forward and put his lips gently to her forehead, kissing her very softly. She closed her eyes at his touch.

When they pulled apart, she smiled again, sadly, and I saw that her eyes were wet with tears. "I could have loved you," she said, shuddering a little.

"Lydia?" Dabir asked.

"It will be hard for her to"—once more she shuddered, though it was for a longer time—"take me if I am already dead."

"*No—*" Dabir's words came out in a gasp, as though he had just been struck in the stomach.

"Do not be too sad . . ." She convulsed, and Dabir reached out for her.

"What have you done?" Dabir demanded, horrified.

"Poison. In my locket. A careful woman always keeps some on hand." I think she meant to laugh, but she sucked in a painful breath instead.

Tears glistened in my friend's eyes, and Lydia reached up to try and brush a drop from his face, but her hand was shaking. He took her in his arms.

She was a while dying, and it was hard to watch. Dabir murmured to her as she did so, and they spoke quietly together, but Najya and I did not listen, aye, and my love even cried a little, for she was of generous spirit.

Even after Lydia ceased movement, Dabir held her still, absently brushing her hair. It was only when he laid her down and closed her eyes that a vapor formed before us and Lamashtu appeared in its midst. She took longer to appear than she ever had before, perhaps because she was weakened.

I stood, shielding Najya with my body. I had no sword to draw, only a knife, so I put my good hand to it.

"You have come too late," Dabir said, rising. "She has died."

Lamashtu's eyes were bloodshot, her eyes white and staring. She strode forward and stared down at the Greek woman's body. "Who now will return my favor?"

"Do not look to her," Dabir said. His eyes shone with tears. "For she has surely passed on to paradise."

"You were her companions. You profited from her actions. The debt falls naturally to you."

"You made no bargain with us," Dabir said tiredly. "Your magic has no hold upon our blood."

Her mouth twisted in rage. "I should slay you for your insolence!"

"You bargained, and lost. But we have lost as well, for she was our friend."

She sneered. "I will remember you." She looked then to the still body, and extended a hand to it, and Lydia's corpse vanished in a burst of smoke. Najya gasped and Dabir's eyes widened in shock.

"I may yet have use for her," Lamashtu said with a mocking smile, and she disappeared as well.

There was no consoling Dabir then, and I sorrowed both for him and for Lydia. It was a bad end that had come to her, but a valiant one. I was to pray many times that she had escaped whatever Lamashtu planned.

We had no way to travel after that. Lydia's carpet had carried her to the Khazar camp and it likely remained there. The bull was destroyed, and the Khazar horses were long departed. No food was left us, and we had only the clothes upon our backs. Both spear and staff were drained of energy and dessicated, even had we known how to wield the latter. We would surely have starved and frozen if a caravan had not chanced upon us that evening. We did not try to explain ourselves, and I cannot be sure they would have given aid if Dabir and I had not shown our medallions.

By the time we reached Mosul a day later, the snow was melting. Spring came early that year, and before very long the trees leafed out and the birds sang in their branches. It was most welcome, and more wondrous than ever after the winter we'd suffered.

Upon our return, Najya was hosted by the governor. I healed well, and swiftly, for I was a strong man, and still relatively young. Even before my pains had subsided I was in fine enough shape to tell the governor all that had transpired on our journey, and so it was that I was there on hand to see Abdul and the rest of the men return to the city. He had been wounded by Anzu, but Kharouf had doubled back for him. They, too, had a tale to tell, of combat with a great dragon of snow. They had fashioned torches to fight the thing, and all but three had come through alive, though Ishaq had been frozen near to death in the monster's coiling tail. It gladdened my heart to see them, and the governor gifted them with many fine garments and other honors. It may be that you have heard the song Abdul's cousin wrote of the affair, for it is still popular in the north today.

The wooden horse was placed on the ledge above our curio shelf, as we both thought fitting. It sat there for long years as we accumulated other mementos. I have it with me now, as I write this in the tower. The bull, alas, had vanished in the flood, its magic spent, along with any fragments of the club of Herakles, which I would much rather have retained. We had thought also to bury Erragal's remains, but never found them.

The caliph shortly received word of the whole affair and commanded us to report to Baghdad so that he might hear all of the details in person. Being the just and noble ruler that he was, though, he gave us a deferral, that I might address important matters in Isfahan, which I shall now relate.

After a few days of rest I called upon Najya at the governor's residence. Things were much more formal and proper there at the palace with the crisis passed, with handmaidens waiting just beyond the curtains.

My first marriage had been arranged by my parents, which had been well and good, and my second through my second wife's mother, so I had never before directly broached marriage with the woman I hoped to wed. I had faced down all manner of horrors in the preceding days, yet I found I must summon a greater form of courage as I sat down beside her. She looked very lovely that day, dressed as she was in white and blue, her hair lustrous and well brushed. As she fixed those wondrous eyes upon me I lost most sense of what I had planned to say.

"I have been looking forward to riding with you in Isfahan," I managed finally, "and seeing these flowers you spoke of."

"That would be very nice," she replied, then watched expectantly.

I cleared my throat. "I was wondering if you would prefer to ride with me, as I am, or if you would rather I be a married man, first. To you, I mean."

Ah, she was merciless, and she insisted later that she found my discomfort charming. All innocently she blinked and said, "I am not sure I follow what you mean."

"I am asking," I said, "whether you would, ah, want to be married to me."

Still she waited, so that I struggled on to fill the silence. I did not want her thinking that I meant to go against the wisdom of the Holy Koran and form a secret agreement between us. "Naturally I will call upon your family in Isfahan, and speak with them. And . . ." I thought to assure her I would move her things to Mosul, then worried she wouldn't be happy to live so far from home, then remembered her family might not want her taken so far away. "But . . . if you say nay, I shall not trouble them," I finished lamely.

She waited only a moment more before finally taking pity upon me. "I shall say yes," she told me. "Yes, a hundred times would I say it." She raised her hand to my cheek and I swear that moment was like being kissed for the very first time. And great happiness did I know.

By the time Dabir and I and Najya—and her female chaperones (for this was a trip planned with all propriety, rather than expediency)—reached Isfahan, our fame had resided there awhile, though it bore only a strained resemblance to the truth. Some folk had already heard of our adventure in the Desert of Souls and the saving of Baghdad, and now their eyes goggled at the sight of us, for the tale of Dabir's monster slaying had reached them over the caravan trails. I, too, was not unknown, and Najya's brother and family met me warmly.

Spring was in full bloom by the time of our wedding feast, surely among the most splendid that I ever attended, and unquestionably the most lively, for there were storytellers and acrobats, and fine drummers and other such things, and all folk who were there, even those who came troubled, were seen to be smiling and laughing. The caliph gifted us with a tremendous chest of treasure, and Jaffar sent up a great bundle of beautiful cloths and a pair of very fine white horses. Seats of honor went to Dabir, of course, and also to Rami, who had never traveled farther than the fields of Mosul before. He beamed as though he had been appointed caliph for a day. Mosul's governor also was there, with many fine gifts, and Shabouh, and Abdul, and Ishaq and the other soldiers who'd escorted us to Harran and proudly guarded us on the journey to and from Mosul. And Buthayna came. She kept her distance from all the richly arrayed folk, though she found time to bake a heavenly selection of sweet cakes.

The celebration went on for three days, and I handed out nearly as many fine presents as those given to my wife and me. Dabir presented a copy of the *Iliad* to me, one illuminated as grandly as a fine Koran. When I reminded him he had lost the bet, he only laughed and said that he hoped I would read it anyway. I did, eventually, and discovered that the story had many splendid moments, even if its end was abrupt.

But among all the presents was one most puzzling, for a long caravan arrived as we were dining on the second day and there was some confusion, for everyone thought it a grand gift for my bride and me. Instead it proved to be an allotment of scrolls and stone tablets that the caravan master delivered to Dabir, along with a single short letter initialed only with an A:

> I have removed most of the contents of Erragal's library, for it is
> no longer secure, but I thought you might enjoy these selections.
> Perhaps you will accept them as some small token of apology.

I thought Dabir would be better pleased to have such a gift, yet he frowned. "If Anzu means to make a project of me, he shall be disappointed." He ended up turning the entire collection over to his favorite institution of the north, the library of Iskander, in Mosul, though you should not think he kept from reading the texts. He also sent most of his own half of the treasures bestowed upon him by the governor and the caliph—a great deal of which had been recovered from the Khazar camp—on to the family of Jibril, whose body the governor went to great pains to recover and inter with honors.

But let me speak again now of Najya, who became so natural a part of my life that it swiftly grew difficult to recall how I had managed without her. Long were we together, and almost always did we find happiness in each other's arms, for we were better matched than most couples. While she never again demonstrated any sign of Usarshra's presence, I never doubted that a strong spark of something mystical remained within her. But then all wise men know their women are touched with magic.

These were not the end of my adventures with Dabir, of course. I am sorely tempted to speak on about our summons to Baghdad, and the curious sword gifted to me there by Jaffar, and the whole black plot that swept up Sabirah's husband upon our arrival, but I shall save that for another time, for this tale is done.

Afterword

Many times I've said that my chief source of inspiration rises from the adventure stories that have thrilled me since I first began reading, most especially the tales of Harold Lamb, Robert E. Howard, and Leigh Brackett, although my wife will tell you it was Roger Zelazny I was trying hardest to imitate for many years. I loved his splendid imagination and plot twists and his flawed, opinionated narrators, particularly Corwin of Amber. I probably read Zelazny's first Amber series more times than any other books in my youth, with the possible exception of Harold Lamb's *The Curved Saber* and Fritz Leiber's *Swords Against Death,* which was the first sword-and-sorcery collection I ever laid hands on, and by sheer luck contains the most solid run of the adventures of the great rogues, Fafhrd and the Gray Mouser. *Swords Against Death* did not, however, print the map I saw in another book of the pair's adventures. On that map, among all the glorious place names that dripped storytelling promise was a worn-down mountain range far to the north named the Bones of the Old Ones. I don't recall Fafhrd or the Mouser ever spending much time there, and I always wanted to know more about the region. The bones in this book ended up being very different from Leiber's mountains, but they would not have existed at all if I had not spent long moments savoring that map.

That the stories of Herakles were leftovers from Stone Age legends is no theory of mine, but of the undeservedly neglected speculative fiction writer Manly Wade Wellman. Wellman is better known today for his stories of John—sometimes referred to as Silver John—who wanders the Appalachians with his silver-stringed guitar fighting creatures man was not meant to know, but Wellman based an early cycle of pulp stories around a neolithic hero, Hok, whom he intended as the man whose exploits had been misremembered as the adventures of the Greek hero. The tomb found by Dabir and Asim is not meant to be Hok's, but the prehistoric Herakles in this book was inspired by Wellman's musings. The look of the tomb itself is loosely based on the prehistoric hilltop ruins in southern Anatolia known as Göbekli Tepe, which form the oldest known religious structure in the history of mankind.

The Herakles stories were not the only myth cycle I plundered for this tale. Legends with groups of seven are to be found all over the ancient Middle East. There were indeed stories of a group known as the Sebetti, though so far as I have been able to learn they were more like an anthropomorphic depiction of destructive forces of nature than individuals. There were also legends of seven sages, led by Adapa, who refused an elixir of immortality. I saw no reason not to combine these and other bits of ancient mythology, including the names of some gods, heroes, and monsters, to ground incidents more firmly in the setting, although I freely invented other pieces and sewed it all together into what hopefully feels like one cloth. As to pure fantasy, the Khazars did *not* have a doomsday cult that welcomed the world's end in ice. In the eighth century, the Khazars were a large nomadic group, and both men and women were known for their ferocity in battle. Shortly after the time period of this book, all the Khazar tribes are said to have converted to Judaism, and that conversion may well have been under way among some of the tribes in the late eight century, although historical details are scarce.

Any real historical figures were far offstage in this particular book, but Jaffar and the caliph Harun al-Rashid were quite real. Jaffar was not yet vizier, but would soon replace his father in that post. Most of the scholars and reference books mentioned or consulted by Dabir and Jibril really did exist, once, but are now only known because of mentions in other texts or fragments of texts. Sometimes only the reputation of said authors remains. Poor Ocnus might have been brilliant; we have little to go on now but the opinion of one or two other writers who did not care for him, which may be a worse fate for an author even than to be completely forgotten.

Speaking of authors, if Mosul and some of the other locations of this book have been brought to life, it is thanks in no small part to the travelogue of Ibn Jubayr, who described most of the cities I depicted. He was writing some two centuries after the time of Harun al-Rashid, but we can assume that most of the important places looked quite similar in both eras, for technology had changed little. Ancient Mosul was pretty much leveled by the Mongols, which means that any details aside from major landmarks mentioned by Ibn Jubayr are my own invention, although many of the more curious items were real—the number of universities along the river, for instance. Harran, heat-blasted though it was, really had long been famed for its school and scholars, and Ibn Jubayr describes its roofed marketplace.

I strove to portray the tension on the border of the caliphate exactly as it was in these years, and there truly was a long series of forts between the Byzantine Greeks and the Abbasid caliphate, who were intermittently at war; there would be peace for a few months or a year, and then more attacks. When you imagine this warfare, though, you should not think of modern fighting, or even ancient campaigns of conquest like those of Alexander or even Belisarius. These conflicts seem to have been more like extended raids to acquire loot and slaves rather than territory, although some cities did change hands multiple times.

A few words should be spared to the drinking of alcohol in the eighth century. Islamic tradition relays that the Koran was revealed to Muhammad by the Archangel Gabriel over many years, and earlier revelations concerning alcohol discouraged but did not forbid its consumption. The later revelations seem fairly clear on the matter, but those who wished to drink had many excuses, including mentions of it in older passages of the Koran, and in the eighth century wine was widely available and widely consumed. Some explained away the drinking of alcohol with legalese (taught that not one drop should be consumed, drinkers would spill one drop, then drink—and no, that doesn't quite make sense to me, either, but let he who is without sin throw the first grape). Some would drink, then ask forgiveness, or try to reinterpret the Koran's injunctions to mean something other than complete abstention. One way around, of course, was by imbibing sorts of alcohol not expressly forbidden—alcohol made from something other than grapes or dates. Later religious writers would point out that the revelations should be interpreted to mean *any* sort of intoxicant is off limits, but those writings didn't seem to have come along at this time even if some imams are almost certain to have been speaking of the matter to their congregations.

A word should also be spared for shatranj, which readers will have probably inferred is a forerunner to chess, with similar pieces. One of the biggest differences between the games is that there is no queen in shatranj, and the corresponding vizier is not nearly as powerful. Late in the book, when Dabir mentions drawing out the queen, he is making an analogy to drawing out the king in shatranj, but uses a female title because the person they're drawing out is, of course, a woman. In final editing I realized those in the know about shatranj might think I was confused about the pieces, and those who didn't might assume the game had a queen. Rather than contorting the surrounding prose to explain shatranj pieces and show Asim deducing Dabir's meaning, I decided to leave the text as it was, and explain matters here.

In the writing of *The Bones of the Old Ones* I strove to simulate the people and period, but it must be remembered that this is a story of fiction, with fantastic elements, and there is much invention here, and in homage to the ancient tales of *The Arabian Nights* glitter is emphasized a little more than grit. Some names and concepts are simplified (for instance, the Greeks in this story would have thought of themselves as Romans, and the folk of the caliphate likely would have referred to them as Roumi). Some of the reference texts Dabir is reading probably weren't available yet, and it is unlikely, though not completely impossible, that *The Iliad* had been translated and accessible, for it was scientific works that Arab translators found of greatest interest. It is improbable that the ancient languages Dabir and Jibril can read were still understood at the time, though not completely beyond the realms of possibility.

Those seeking a more realistic description of life in these times can find a number of suggestions in the afterword to *The Desert of Souls*. Most of those same books were as useful in the writing of this book as that one, although this time I leaned even more heavily on the aforementioned Ibn Jubayr. I used three other sources, new to me, and will continue to use them moving forward. The first is a primary resource (translated by John Alden Williams) entitled *The Early Abbasi Empire*, by Al-Tabari, who, among other things, wrote an account of the important events and people of the Abbasid caliphate, setting down the events of the reign of Harun al-Rashid only a few generations after the caliph's death. I found Amira K. Bennison's *The Great Caliphs* highly engaging and full of interesting insight and anecdotes that brought the eighth century and its ruling set to life. Hugh Kennedy's *When Baghdad Ruled the Muslim World* was enlightening as well, and I recommend both books to readers interested in an entertaining and authoritative overview of the Abbasid caliphate.